The Hinterland

Audrey Faletic

Welcome to my world. Make yourself at home.
-   AF

Chapter 1

This story begins–as most good ones do–on an uncharted path.

Cottages with quaint, thatched roofs and brightly painted doors lined either side of the road, but the candles in their windows had gone out long ago. No one was awake to see the two tall figures walking down the center of the path.

The figures swept down the road. The hoods of their floor-length cloaks shadowed their faces, pulled tight to fight against the biting wind, and hiding all but a few strands of their long, white hair.

Their expressions were nearly as cold as the frosty air, their strides long and purposeful. The one walking to the left had a slight limp, but he was still a couple steps ahead of the other, as though determined that the injury would not slow him.

The other figure glanced at his partner before lowering his voice to speak. "Should we bring it out, Argon?"

"Patience, Aurum," hissed the second, still walking ahead. He scanned the street, nodded at its barren state, reached into the inside pocket of his cloak, and withdrew a small object: a stone. It was about the size and make of a good skipping stone: one that might bounce four times before sinking. Small cracks were scrawled over its black surface like veins, glowing bright orange. He cupped it in his palm to hide the light. "We're close."

The figures reached a fork in the road where a sign stood between the two paths, words impossible to read under the shroud of night.

Argon looked in both directions before starting left, still refusing to let his limp slow his lead on Aurum. They walked for only a minute before the light coming off the stone dimmed ever so slightly. Argon whipped around and walked back to the fork in the road, Aurum close behind. This time, they went right.

As they walked, the orange glow of the rock intensified so that its veins shone like thin streams of volcanic magma.

Out of the corner of his eye, Aurum watched the stone in Argon's hand. He opened his mouth as if to speak, then hesitated and shut it again.

The stone flared—bright and vivid, like it was breathing in and coming alive. Light was now streaming from its veins with such brightness that, from a distance, a stranger might have thought Argon was holding a small star.

It was as though the faces of the two figures were streaked with sunlight as they peered at the small symbol that had appeared at the stone's center: a spiral marred by a slashing, diagonal line.

"Here," said Argon, "it must be here." Together, they looked away from the stone and up at their surroundings.

The closest house sat, unassuming, to their left. The curtains of its two windows were pulled shut, like closed eyelids.

Argon shifted to face it.

Aurum swallowed and did the same. "Are you ready?"

But the second figure was already walking toward the house. If he had heard the question, it seemed he didn't care to reply.

They walked up the simple stone walkway to the house's front door, which Aurum knelt in front of, pulling a long, thin metal instrument from his boot. He inserted the slim tool into the door's keyhole, turning it a few times with precise, purposeful motions. After only a moment he pulled it out, leaned forward, and turned the handle. Silently, like a fleeing shadow, the door swung open.

They crept into the house, their boots making no noise on the wood floor. If anything, it seemed to become quieter when they entered.

The house was cramped, with only one room. The kitchen, nothing more than a table and washbasin, was to the left, and a bed was jammed to the right. It loomed over a small cot on the floor.

The intruders slipped toward the bed where two snoring adults lay: a man and a woman. The cot below them was occupied by a sleeping girl. She could be no more than fourteen years old.

Argon walked toward the bed so that he stood right beside it. Carefully, he held the stone out over the adults. The shine was still bright, illuminating the sleeper's faces and Argon's unnaturally pointed ears.

Argon frowned, moving the stone closer to the man and then the woman. The glow remained the same, not shrinking or growing. His brow creased. "It's not responding."

Aurum's brow knit, then at the same time, both elves' eyes widened. They turned to look at the sleeping child, her black hair spread around her face, her breathing deep and steady.

Aurum opened his mouth to speak, but without hesitation Argon walked to the foot of the bed, crouched down, and held the stone over the sleeping child on the cot.

The stone ignited. A blinding light came from the symbol in the center, so bright that he quickly slipped it into his cloak pocket.

"It's the child," said Aurum, throat suddenly dry.

"Yes," agreed Argon. "It's the child."

"We can't–," Aurum whipped around to face Argon. "We can't– not a youngling!"

"Would you disobey the commands of the Empress?" asked Argon, turning his gaze to the other elf. His stare was as sharp as a knife, and Aurum flinched as though cut by it.

"Of course not," his gaze flicked away from Argon's.

Argon turned back to the child, eyes closed and hands extended toward her. From the center of his palms came a dull white light. It spread quickly outward until his hands were completely lit in a dim glow. After just a few seconds he opened his eyes, and the light went out like an extinguished candle. The girl rolled over on her cot, breathing still deep and unbothered.

"The spell should hold for a few hours. She won't wake over the journey," said Argon.

Aurum nodded, looking at the child at his feet. He took in her scrawny arms and wisps of black hair, spraying out from where they were tucked behind her ears.

"What are you doing?" asked Argon, his voice becoming a ferocious hiss. "Grab her."

Aurum shook his head, but even as he did so, he walked slowly toward the girl. Kneeling quietly next to her, he slipped his arms beneath her neck and legs and picked her up, cradling her in his arms. She was small and light, wearing only a thin tunic and pair of breeches. He couldn't help but think about how peaceful she seemed, and he looked quickly upward away from her sleeping face.

He glanced around the room, gaze falling on the two adults in the bed. Soon they would wake up and see that their child was missing.

The elf closed his eyes and shook his head, as though to push away his thoughts. Then his eyelids opened, and he turned away from the bed and back toward the door.

Argon was already waiting in the street when Aurum exited the house. "What took so long?"

Aurum said nothing.

Argon's eyes narrowed. "You should be proud to do the Empresses' bidding."

"I know." The words came out in something close to a snarl as Aurum's jaw tightened. "I am. I just pity the youngling."

"Pity is just an excuse for weakness."

The elves glared at each other, neither of them blinking until Aurum gritted his teeth and looked away from the other elf. "Call the griffins."

"Already on their way," Argon looked to the sky. "I sent up a flare while you were inside."

High above, they could just see the outline of two large, winged creatures.

Moments later, the griffins landed on the street in front of the elves, talons scratching the stone. Lean and muscular, they had the tawny, tan bodies of lions, but their heads were beaked and paired with the sharp, intelligent eyes of eagles.

Aurum gently passed the girl off to Argon while he climbed onto his griffin, before Argon lifted her up for Aurum to hold again.

"We should have brought a blanket," Aurum said, positioning her small body carefully. "She's going to freeze."

"She'll be fine," said Argon, scowling as he mounted his griffin. "She'll be asleep the whole time." He clicked his tongue, and wings burst from the animal's sides. With a yank of the reins, it and its rider were airborne.

In only a few seconds Aurum was in the air too, the girl propped in front of him so that his arms were on either side of her body, stopping her from falling and allowing him to grip the reins that dangled from the griffin's beak.

The griffins rose above the small, sleeping town, their powerful wings causing torrents of wind that made the elves' hoods blow off and their white hair stream behind them.

They flew in silence.

The Hinterland

The sun was just coming up when the griffins came into view of their destination: a huge gray mass far beneath them. They circled downward, and the mass revealed itself to be a castle, perched on a cliff overlooking a wide, rushing river.

The castle was large, and turrets rose from its craggy sides. It was surrounded by a high, mossy wall, all except for the side that sat right on the edge of the cliff with a perfect view of the river beneath. Below in the mist, the elves could just make out soldiers moving around on the castle wall like termites swarming about a colony.

The griffins dove downward, screaming toward the fortress. Aurum held on tightly to the reins with one hand and just as tightly to the child with the other. Moments later, the griffins had landed on a balcony jutting from the highest turret, riders jolting with the impact.

Argon leapt gracefully from his ride. He landed silently on his feet, although his face tightened as his limping leg made impact. Aurum took a little longer, sliding slowly off his beast so as not to jostle the girl in his arms.

Once the elves were standing on their feet, the griffins rose into the sky before plummeting downward toward the castle entrance.

Now the elves and girl were alone on the balcony—or so it seemed—until a voice came from the dark balcony entrance.

"So, you have returned."

A woman stepped out from the shadows: lithe and tall, dressed in a floor length blue gown. Despite stepping away from the darkness, it seemed to follow her, clinging to her edges and bordering her in black.

"Empress," Argon's and Aurum's voices came in unison as they bowed their heads.

"I see the mission was successful." She stepped closer to Aurum, and the girl clasped in his arms. Her cold eyes roved over the angelic face and delicate features, examining the girl as you would study a rare specimen never seen before. After a few moments of silent speculation, she looked up. "Argon, mission report?"

"We found the house easily," began the elf, voice cold and unfeeling. "The youngling was asleep. We cast a spell to keep her that way. Aurum hesitated to take her–"

Aurum interrupted. "There was no hesitation, my liege–"

She held up her hand, and he fell silent. "Continue, Argon."

Argon nodded. "We carried her here on the griffins as planned. We encountered no trouble on the way."

"Good," nodded the woman. She turned to Aurum, the smallest hint of a frown curving her perfect lips. "But you were hesitant?"

"No, there was no hesitation," Aurum replied, shaking his head so quickly his white hair whipped around his face.

"Then you are calling my chief commander a liar?" the woman asked, gesturing to Argon and cocking her head like a cat watching a mouse.

"No–I mean–" Aurum faltered, licking his lips.

She took a small step closer to him, her feet light, dainty even, on the hard balcony floor. "So, you admit to being disloyal?"

Aurum shifted backward, still holding the girl against his chest. "I wasn't being disloyal." His eyes darted to Argon with a silent plea, but the second elf was watching with a clinical, detached expression. "I just felt bad for the youngling, that's all."

"You were hesitant to fulfill my orders. That is disloyalty," said the woman, voice smooth. "Disloyalty cannot go unanswered." Aurum took a sharp breath as the woman's large brown eyes darkened. "Get down."

"My liege–"

"*Get down.*" There were icicles warmer than her gaze.

Silently, Aurum turned and transferred the child to Argon's arms before turning back to the woman. He sank down slowly onto one knee before her, head bowed and eyes on the floor. The woman took a step toward him, leisurely rolling up the long sleeves of her dress and watching the elf intently, as though fully aware that every second of time felt like an eternity to him.

Slowly, she extended her right hand, palm down, toward the elf, her fingertips a breath away from his white locks. Her lips curled, and in a swift, brutal motion, her fingers flexed.

Aurum gasped as though hit by an invisible force. Instantly, he sagged forward, one hand clutching at his chest, fisting the front of his tunic. He shuddered, something like blue smoke curling from his body toward the woman's hand. It spiraled around her fingertips like tendrils of azure fire.

Aurum clenched his teeth, eyes shut, face even paler than before.

But the woman only frowned, eyes narrowing into slits and fingers going taut as she stiffened them.

The elf let out a cry, dropping to both knees. Now his hand was desperately clawing at his chest, as though there was something buried under his rib cage that he needed to rip out of himself. A wave of the smoke burst from him like the tide, seeking the woman's hand to join her blue blaze. The elf let out a moan and collapsed at her feet.

The woman withdrew her hand, face turned to the sky, and a sigh escaped her lips as the blue mist soaked into her skin. When the mist was gone entirely, she turned her gaze back to the elf. "This is your final warning. I cannot have commanders who are disloyal to me."

She crouched downward toward the gasping elf, skirts whispering against stone as she sank. Her voice was barely audible as she leaned forward, placed a hand on his cheek, and gently turned his face to hers. She stroked it with her thumb, soft and kind against his skin, and cocked her head. "Aurum, the next time you hesitate will be your last."

Then she straightened, turned, and walked into the castle with Argon on her heels.

Only Aurum remained: alone on the highest turret, panting on the cold balcony floor.

Chapter 2

Once upon a time. That right there is a sentence fragment. But despite coming short of a full and proper sentence, the phrase "once upon a time" is a magical one. Don't you feel it? When you hear that phrase, you know that you're about to hear a story. Something great is about to happen. You don't know what the great thing is, but you trust the fragment. Goes to show that small things can make a difference, doesn't it?

Scarlet held the book in her two small hands. She ran a tiny finger over the words on the page. It was a picture book. Her friends loved picture books. They liked looking at the colorful drawings of the princesses, dragons, and knights in their bright, shining armor.

She never opened a book for the pictures. She did it for the words. It was the flow of the writing, the way it could paint a picture in her mind and create worlds that existed only in her imagination that called to her.

"Once upon a time," she whispered, letting the warmth of the phrase envelope her as she ran her finger over it. She knew this book by heart, had listened to her father read it over and over again, had flipped through the pages enough to wear the edges, but that first sentence never ceased to excite her.

"You feel it," said her father, winking down at her. "You're feeling that fairytale magic." They sat on the bed, reading in the shine from a single candle. It was past her bedtime, but she had begged him for just one story, and

he couldn't ever tell her no when she stuck out her bottom lip and pleaded with her big, brown eyes.

She nodded, three times and fast, looking up into his gentle face. The top of her head barely reached the bottom of his prickly chin.

"Once upon a time," read her father, "there was a princess." He pulled her against him and put his arm around her shoulder, tracing the words with the pointer finger of his right hand so she could follow them as he read. "She was a kind and clever princess, and she lived in a magical kingdom."

As he read, Scarlet fought the beckon of sleep, rubbing her eyes to stay awake until the end, eyelids drooping further with each turned page.

"The princess was trapped. She was afraid that she would never escape. The darkness crept in and tried to grab her."

Her eyelids sagged as she surrendered. And as she fell asleep, the real Scarlet, the Scarlet of flesh and bone instead of memory and thought, floated out of the dream and into the sudden sharpness of reality.

Scarlet opened her eyes.

She blinked a couple of times, brushed her black hair out of her face, sat up and stretched, and, for a few moments, remained blissfully oblivious to her surroundings. Then she realized that she was not where she was supposed to be.

Scarlet was sitting in the center of a small cell.

There was a solid stone wall behind her, but on her left she shared bars with another cell, and on her right with a third, both of them empty. In front of her was another row of thick iron bars, and beyond them, a narrow hallway. Scarlet took this in–and she tried to wake up.

She closed her eyes and opened them, closed and opened, and tried to come up and out of the dream that she was certain she was stuck in. It wasn't until she had done this for a few moments that panic rushed in like the tide.

"Help!" She jumped to her feet. "Hello? Anyone? Help! Where am I?" She ran to the bars at the front of her cell, hands fisting around the metal as she shook them, trying to push her face into the space between. In the light of a couple low-burning torches, she made out a figure standing against the wall in the hallway beyond.

The figure, who seemed to be just a little taller than Scarlet, was dressed from head to toe in armor, face entirely covered by a helmet except for two eyeholes. The armor was too big, hanging off the person's skinny form.

"Hello?" she called. "Where am I?"

The armored guard stood still as a statue.

"Please! Where am I?"

No answer.

The guard made no movement to indicate having even heard her.

"Please–I–please answer." Nothing. Scarlet opened her mouth again, this time voice coming out in a cracked whisper. "Please?"

Silence.

Scarlet backed into the depths of the cell like a wounded creature retreating into shadow. Her back hit the wall, and she sank to the ground, huddling against the stone and sniffing as tears began to fill her eyes. Soon they overflowed, trickling down her cheeks. "Dad? Mom?" This time it wasn't loud. This time, she wasn't expecting a reply.

In the darkness, she remembered the words from her dream. They whispered around and around the nooks and crannies of her mind.

The darkness crept in and tried to grab her.

She hugged herself, pulling her knees up to her face and blocking her view of the dank dungeon.

A sound came from outside the cell and Scarlet jumped to her feet, swiping at the tears on her face.

A door had opened at the end of the hallway, and two figures were approaching, backed in light from the doorway.

They made their way down the passage, the guard stepping quickly out of their path. The first figure's steps were uneven as he limped. The second figure trailed behind. They stopped in front of Scarlet's cell, still one in front of the other, and she took a step back from the bars.

For the first time, she got a good look at their pale faces. The one in the back had long hair that he'd pulled into a ponytail. The second had left his hair loose, streaming down to his shoulders with not a stray strand to be found. On his shoulder was perched a large, black bird. Scarlet recognized it almost immediately as a crow. Its feathers and sharp beak were pitch black, but its eyes were even darker, like glimmering chunks of obsidian.

The second thing Scarlet noticed was their ears–sharp and pointed–sticking up through their hair. She took another step back, breath catching in her throat and lungs tightening in her chest.

She'd heard stories about ears like those.

Scarlet had always known elves were real, but she'd never seen one–had figured she never would. Not in her remote village, so far from any hint of magical activity. Now two were staring her in the face.

"Aurum, these torches are not enough," said the front elf. His voice was cold, and his eyes did not leave Scarlet's face. "Summon more light."

Aurum held his hand in front of himself and focused on it. A light spread out from the center of his palm.

For a moment, Scarlet forgot her fear and the stories she'd heard about elves, mesmerized by the white light creeping toward his fingertips. The elf grunted, and his fingers sparked, like one would expect if flint and steel were struck against one another.

His eyes narrowed as he stared at the light and his fingers sparked once more, but this time, when the spark disappeared, the light coming from his hand began to recede back into his palm until it dissipated altogether. "I can't yet, Argon," his voice was tense, and he didn't look at the other elf, instead focusing with determination on the floor in front of Scarlet's cell.

Argon didn't reply, casting Aurum a sharp sideways look before holding out his own hand and flexing his fingers. In less than a second, light blazed from his palm.

Scarlet yelped, jumping back into her cell so that her shoulders banged painfully against the stone wall.

The elf held up his hand so that the light shone across his face and Scarlet's. The other elf was left in shadow.

"Let me introduce myself," he said, his words far too smooth and far too cold. "I am Argon, and this is my bird, Silander."

"Where am I?" Scarlet asked. "Why am I here? Where are my parents? Please let me out!"

"Youngling, I'll be asking the questions today," said Argon. "Firstly, I need your name."

"I just want to know where I am," Scarlet said, voice pleading. "Can you just tell me where I am?"

"If I were you, I would cooperate and answer the question." Argon's voice slid into her, freezing her blood. She felt like the air had been knocked out of her lungs.

"Scarlet," she answered, a bit breathless. "My name is Scarlet Mount."

"How old are you?"

"Fourteen."

The elf in shadow crossed his arms and continued to look at the floor. Argon raised his eyebrows. Scarlet felt as though even his crow was staring her down. Its round, unblinking eyes made her feel itchy. It seemed unnatural for the bird to be so quiet. Argon continued onward. "Do you know why you're here?"

"No! I just asked you that."

Argon ignored her. "Have you been contacted recently by anyone... out of the ordinary?"

"Why would I be contacted by anyone out of the ordinary?"

Argon looked at her sharply. It seemed, under his intense stare, that he grew even taller. Or maybe she was shrinking.

"Answer the question."

"No. Well... define out of the ordinary." Scarlet was certain that she hadn't been contacted by anyone the elf might be referring to, but if he wasn't going to give her information, she would have to find other ways to get it.

"Anyone with magical abilities, perhaps?" said Argon.

"You mean another elf?"

"Could be," said Argon, eyes narrowing.

"What, specifically, do you think they would be contacting me about?"

Argon's nostrils flared, and he glared at her. "I thought I made it clear who was asking the questions here. Do not try to play games with me, human." He shifted, and with a sudden jolt in her stomach, Scarlet caught sight of the knife at his hip. She got the distinct feeling he had meant for her to see it.

She swallowed, mind and body going still. "No. No one has tried to contact me."

"Good." Argon studied her for a few more seconds. His eyes looked her up and down, scrutinizing her face. "And, most importantly... what is so special about you, youngling?"

The way he said it, quiet and tense, she wasn't sure whether she was supposed to answer or whether he was just thinking aloud. She decided it didn't matter. Clenching her fists, she looked him in the eyes. "You tell me." Her throat was as dry as desert sand, but she forced her voice forward. "There has to be a reason I'm here, and I think you know it."

He nodded. "An astute observation. However, you are only partially correct. I know why you are here, and at the same time I don't know why *you* are here. But time will tell." He clenched his blazing hand and the fire illuminating the hallway went out so that only the dim light of the torches remained. "In the meantime, I wish you luck in the dungeon, Scarlet Mount."

Listening to him say her name was like having an icicle slowly lodged into her ribs. It was a shiver that started from somewhere deep inside her.

She watched the elves' backs as they turned and walked away, down the hall, and out the door. Now the dungeon was silent again, except for a steady drip coming from somewhere in the darkness. But even in the elves' absence, their presence had stayed behind, Argon's voice echoing around her head.

What is so special about you?

She didn't know, but if he didn't either, who did? And what would they do to her if she wasn't who they thought she was?

She sat down on the floor of her cell and leaned against the bars, her back to the hallway. Again, for the second time that day, tears spilled down her cheeks. But these were only partially the tears of fear from earlier. Mostly, this was frustration and confusion leaking from her. She swiped impatiently at the tears with her sleeves.

She flinched as a sound came from behind her, and something white appeared through the bars of her cell. She'd forgotten that she wasn't alone.

Scarlet twisted and found that the white thing being offered was a dingy handkerchief, extended in the gloved hand of the guard. Cautiously, she accepted it. She couldn't see a face behind the helmet, but she could see a pair of soft brown eyes through the eyeholes.

"Thanks." She scrubbed the tears off her cheeks and held it back out to the guard.

"Keep it." The voice was clearly male, and he didn't sound much older than her.

She opened her mouth to argue, but he was already returning to his straight up and down position against the wall.

She took a deep, shaky breath and held the handkerchief in her fist.

Once, during a nighttime reading session, her father had taught her about symbolism in stories. He had taught her how normal things could be made special with a hidden meaning. Sometimes, she would make a game of it, finding things within her life and trying to decide what they symbolized in her personal fairytale.

She looked down at the handkerchief in her fist and decided all hope was not lost.

Chapter 3

Curiosity killed the cat.

This is a saying that you may be familiar with. It was one that Scarlet knew especially well.

Sitting in her cell, she could picture her mother saying it, standing over Scarlet with arms crossed, lips pursed, dark hair pulled back into its usual bun.

Scarlet had never been one for keeping quiet. She liked asking questions about things. Everything. Questions about things that didn't matter. Questions about things no one had the answers to. Questions about questions no one had the answers to.

As she sat in her cell, fighting the urge to address the guard in the hallway and ask him what was going on, she heard her mother's voice in her ear. "You know, Scarlet, curiosity killed the cat."

But in her other ear, she could hear her dad's gentle voice with his usual reply. "That's what the good Lord gave the cat nine lives for."

Scarlet smiled at the thought before the warm feeling in her chest was cut short, as she remembered that her parents were not with her now, and she had no idea when she would see them again.

She stood up and began to pace back and forth in her cell. Finally, she stopped and looked up at the guard, who was standing straight against the hallway wall. "Listen," she paused for a second, giving him a chance to indicate that he was listening, but continuing onward when no such indication was offered. "I get it. You obviously don't want to talk to me. But I'm going to lose my mind in here if I can't talk to anyone, so I'm going to talk to you whether you reply or not." She paused again. "Alright?"

No response.

"Alright." She started pacing again.

"I've never been a prisoner before. I've read about it in books. Of course, the prisoners in the books I've read are usually more interesting than me. I read one about a queen one time. She escaped because her friends snuck her a key inside a loaf of bread." She waited for a reaction.

There was none.

The guard was still standing against the wall, although Scarlet thought maybe he was watching her. Between the dimness of the lights and the distance between the two of them, it was hard to see his eyes through the eyeholes of his helmet.

"I'm Scarlet, by the way," she said. "Scarlet Mount. Although I guess you know that since you were here when the elves came. Since I don't know your name, I'm going to make a guess, because I'll feel weird if I don't have anything to call you."

Still silence from the armored figure.

"When I was five, I had a little stuffed bear named Fluffles. How about that?" She nodded, "I think I'll go with that."

"My name's Tobin."

Scarlet almost jumped in surprise at the guard's voice.

Tobin.

She grinned, pure relief rushing through her at hearing another voice that wasn't coming from a cold elf. It was a cool gust of wind in a burning desert. "Nice to meet you, Tobin."

"Listen," he said, looking toward the door before addressing her. "If I talk to you, you're not going to tell anyone, will you?"

She shook her head. "No. I won't tell."

"Alright," he sounded relieved. "Because I'm not really supposed to have any communication with prisoners."

"You don't sound very old," said Scarlet, brow creasing. "Are you sixteen?"

He shook his head.

"Seventeen?"

He shook his head again.

"Fifteen?" she asked. She felt sure he couldn't be older than seventeen.

This time, the guard nodded.

"I'm fourteen," she said. The dungeon fell silent for a moment as she tried to decide what to say next. "Isn't fifteen pretty young to be a guard?"

"I dunno," he let out a small laugh. "Isn't fourteen pretty young to be a prisoner?" The laughter stopped almost instantly as he seemed to realize what he'd said. "Sorry, that was a bad joke. I didn't mean that." He reached up as though to run a hand through his hair before realizing he was wearing a helmet and dropping it back to his side.

Scarlet smiled. She didn't really care what he said as long as he was talking.

Tobin cleared his throat. "Just so you know, I didn't help kidnap you or anything. I didn't even know I was going to be guarding you. They just assigned me to this hallway."

She blinked, taken aback by the sincerity in his voice. "Okay."

"I just wanted you to know I wasn't part of it." He looked at the floor, as though trying to avoid eye contact, although his helmet made it hard to see his eyes anyway. "I would never kidnap someone. Well, probably never. I mean, I guess it would depend on why they were being kidnapped, or maybe–," he stopped, sounding flustered. "I just wanted to say that I'm really sorry about all this."

"Do you know why I'm here?" She watched him intently, hoping he had the answer to the question that had been running circles in her mind.

He shook his head. "No. I'm not in an important position in the castle. They don't really tell us guards anything that matters unless you're ranked really high. Like an officer or troop commander."

Scarlet nodded, and then her eyebrows shot upward. "Wait–did you say castle? We're in a castle?"

Her eyebrows rose as Tobin cursed and scuffed the floor with his boot. "Probably shouldn't have said that."

"Doesn't really change anything," said Scarlet quickly, worried he might stop talking. "Must be an interesting job. Being a castle guard."

Tobin gave a humorless laugh. "You'd think."

"So... it's not, then?"

He shook his head. "It's not a job, really."

"What do you mean?"

"Well, it's like this," said Tobin. "The queen of the castle has this whole army, and they took control of my village. It was either start working for her, or–you know."

"What?" asked Scarlet, brow furrowing.

Tobin drew a pair of gloved fingers across his throat.

"Oh!" Scarlet's cheeks went red as she realized. "Oh... so, how many guards are forced to work here?"

"Most of us," said Tobin. "Mine wasn't the first village she took control of. Won't be the last either."

"If there are that many of you, just fight back," said Scarlet. "What's she going to do if all of you turn against her?"

"That might work well against a normal queen," said Tobin, "but she's not exactly normal."

"In what way?"

Tobin, as though by instinct, glanced toward the dungeon door before replying. "She's magical–and a really dangerous type of magical." His voice dropped. "I've heard stories. Stories saying she can suck the magic out of people. It's called draining."

"Well humans don't have any magic," said Scarlet, crossing her arms. "So you wouldn't have to worry about her sucking it away."

"Not if the stories are true," said Tobin, voice still quiet. "They say draining can be lethal for a human–and painful too. Someone told me it feels like your ribs are splintering."

Scarlet felt a chill go through her like a cold, wet finger sliding down her spine. "What about if she takes magic from a magical person like an elf?"

"Don't really know how it works," said Tobin slowly, "but they've got extra magic. You know, to use for spells and stuff. So, she can take that first without killing them, I think. Like I said though, it's painful. Really painful."

Scarlet bit her lip as she processed. She felt like there was a little person in her head stirring her thoughts around with a spoon so that it was impossible to separate just one and think it through.

"So–" started Scarlet, before something on the floor caught her eye. She yelped and jumped backward. A rat sat outside her cell, beady eyes staring at her down a long, quivering snout.

At her yell, Tobin started. "What?"

She pointed. Back at home she'd always had her dad to scare the occasional rodent off. But he wasn't here now. Her chest tightened as she wondered where he was. She knew for certain that there were no castles near her village. Exactly how far from home was she?

"I've got it," said Tobin. He hesitated, then stepped off his post against the wall and kicked at the rat with his boot. It scampered into darkness.

"Thanks," breathed Scarlet, watching its tail disappear into the black.

"No problem," Tobin shrugged. "I'm used to them. They're all around the castle."

"So, you've been a guard for a while then?" Scarlet asked.

"A month or so," Tobin replied. "Only before I helped with the horses, not in the dungeons."

"Is it boring?" asked Scarlet, lying down on the cell floor and staring up at the gray ceiling.

"Yeah," said Tobin, nodding. "But sometimes I make up stories to help pass the time."

"What kind of stories?"

"Oh, you know," he cleared his throat, "fairytale sort of stories. I mean–not fairytale, just–well, hero stories. Stories with some brave hero who comes in and saves the day when no one else can." He scraped his boot across the floor. "I know it sounds dumb, but–"

"It doesn't sound dumb at all," said Scarlet, perking up. "I love those sorts of stories. Could you tell me one?"

Tobin shifted against the wall. "I've never really told them to anyone before." He brought a hand up and scratched the back of his neck. "They're probably really bad."

Scarlet laughed. "Well, it's not like I have anything better to do with my time."

"True," said Tobin. He gave a light laugh. "And if it's really bad, I guess there's no one for you to tell anyway." He winced. "Sorry, that was another bad joke. I've never guarded a prisoner before, I don't really know what to say. I should've asked for a dos and don'ts manual." He gave another weak laugh.

Scarlet closed her eyes and put her arms behind her head. "Just start the story, Tobin."

So, Tobin started the story, and it wasn't bad, it was actually kind of good. It had a dragon, and a tower, and a hero, and it started with once upon a time, which is about everything a story needs. And while she listened, Scarlet found herself in a different world. A world where she wasn't lying on the cold, hard floor of a rusty dungeon with the chill of doom creeping in over her.

And that made it one of the best stories she'd ever heard.

Now, while they're telling stories in the castle dungeon, we will give them some privacy and catch up with them later. There are other things for you to see.

If you were a ghost in Scarlet's cell, nothing but drifting memory and thought, you would be able to fly straight through the cell bars and into the dingy hallway beyond. From there you could float right through the wall and out into the big, wide world.

If you were to continue onward for miles and miles, over forests with trees like cotton balls below you and a river spread beneath you like a long, satin ribbon meandering across the ground, you would eventually come to the Hinterland.

I won't tell you about the Hinterland now.

I don't want to scare you.

Not yet.

Only a handful of miles into the Hinterland you would find a mountain. A thick, craggy mountain. If you didn't know where the entrance was you would have no chance of finding your way inside. Except you're a ghost, so you do what you want.

Through the grim, gray mountain, through dirt and granite you would pass, and if you flew through the right place, you would find yourself in a cozy room.

The Hinterland

The room was small and warm, containing a flickering fireplace, a table in the corner, and a whispered conversation between two elves, which tends to make a room more interesting.

One of the elves sat at the table. His hands were clasped on its surface, like he might be about to say something wise and profound, and his cloak fell down around his shoulders like a long purple waterfall, its edges pooling around his feet on the floor.

"The Council wants to send you off in the morning." His words were brisk, and he wore an expression that suggested he was at a funeral. "You know the plan: you and four from your unit."

The second elf looked ready for war. She was wearing a sleek set of armor that fit her slim form perfectly, a loop built in to hold the curved blade at her waist. Her brown hair was pulled into a tight braid so that not a single strand fell in her eyes, which were a striking color of bite-me-blue.

"Why only five of us?" she asked. "This mission could decide the fate of the war. My entire unit is ready to fight, why not send us all?"

"For the same reason we're not sending dwarves, Elowen. This is a stealth mission that will require the utmost discretion. It's going to be hard to sneak five of you into the fortress, much less two dozen of you."

Elowen nodded.

"And keep in mind," continued the elf at the table, "this mission is extremely important. If it fails we alert the enemy that we know they have the girl. That would risk her relocation, or at the very least, increase her protection. Worst of all, it could compromise our spy."

"I understand." Elowen's eyes had hardened like ice.

The other elf nodded. "Then all that's left is for you to choose the four who join you."

For the first time Elowen's face changed, a flicker of something other than determination sparking in her eyes like a rare strike of lightning. Something like dread. But if it was dread, it didn't show in her voice. "I'll put a team together tonight."

The male elf watched for a moment, face solemn, as though he understood the weight of putting a team together. But after another second he nodded. "Then that is all."

Elowen nodded back and turned, making for the door.

"Oh, and Elowen–" she turned to face the other elf. He inclined his head slightly and put a fist to his heart. "May your tomorrow soon be your yesterday."

If the battle blessing surprised her, she didn't show it. She simply nodded her head again, opened the door, and stepped out. It closed behind her with a final thud.

And now I think you've seen enough. You have the gist of it. I think it's time to zoom out of the mountain, and the Hinterland, back over the river and forest, and into Scarlet's small cell.

Chapter 4

"Well, this is interesting."

Scarlet opened her eyes on the edge of a cliff. The wind was racing past her: through her hair, across the skin on the back of her neck, and between her fingers, numbing her fingertips. The edge of the cliff was behind her, and when she turned, she could see water stretching out ahead of her. It went on and on and on, like a seething, blue eternity.

The waves thrashed at the cliff. The ocean, it seemed, was furious.

"You're very small, aren't you? Not what anyone would expect."

Where was that voice coming from? Scarlet turned circles, trying to find the person it belonged to.

"I hear your name is Scarlet."

The voice was calm, blanketed in a layer of friendliness that couldn't fully cover the menace underneath. It seemed to be coming from all directions, twisting around the cliff's edge. The darkness tightened. Mist soaked into the night air to circle Scarlet.

"Where am I?" she asked.

"You're asleep."

Scarlet whipped around, finally finding the source of the words as a woman appeared from the mist. Her smile cold and forced, she was still undeniably beautiful: the kind of stunning beauty that makes people stop and stare. Her long, white dress was almost as pale as her flawless skin.

Tendrils of black hair fell across her forehead, framing brown, almost black, eyes.

Scarlet shook her head, trying to calm her nerves. She felt like someone was scribbling in her chest—a toddler maybe, who didn't know how to color in the lines. "This is a dream. It isn't real." She murmured, even as she felt the wind bite at her, felt the spray of the sea, smelled the salt in the air. "I'm dreaming."

"You are dreaming. But I'm still real—same as you," said the woman, still standing in front of her.

"*This* isn't *real*," Scarlet repeated.

The woman ignored this comment and circled Scarlet lazily. "It's intriguing, the ones who are chosen. Always fascinating. But really, it doesn't matter who you are, as long as you're mine."

"I'm not yours," said Scarlet. She crossed her arms, hugging herself tight. "You're just a woman in my dream."

"Well, I thought I should visit," said the woman with a shrug that sent soft rustles down the skirt of her white gown. "After all, you are going to be a piece in the game that is beginning. A pawn in the grand scheme of things."

"If I'm a pawn, what are you?" said Scarlet, her fingernails digging into her arms as she gripped herself.

The woman turned to look at her, facing Scarlet again with eyes that were as dark and deep as graves. She laughed, and the laugh echoed around the circle of mist, over the roar of the waves and wind. "I'm queen of the castle."

And then she was gone.

Scarlet woke up panting. Sweat was dripping down her face. She found that she was curled on the dungeon floor, her arms around herself.

She looked around. The dungeon was silent except for a constant drip from somewhere in the darkness. The torchlight cast shadows across the corridor. Tobin was standing, but slumped against the wall. Faint snores were coming from beneath his helmet.

The only thing left of the dream were the marks on Scarlet's arms where her fingernails had bit into her skin.

Could the dream have been real? Had the queen of the castle just visited her in her sleep? Scarlet shivered–and not from the cold. Tobin *had* said the queen was powerful. Scarlet looked up at the ceiling and wondered if she was somewhere above, wandering through dark hallways like a crowned shadow.

Suddenly Tobin moved. He stretched and his armor scraped against the wall he'd been leaning against. A yawn came from beneath the mask.

"Hey, Tobin," he jumped before realizing it was Scarlet speaking. "Hey."

"You fell asleep standing up. I didn't know that was possible." She smiled, trying to break the tension within herself.

"It's one of my many skills," he said with an air of exaggerated bravado. "I have lots. I can also trip over air and zone out in the middle of conversations without even trying."

Scarlet laughed. "Trip over air? I think that's just another way of saying you're clumsy."

No response.

"Tobin?"

"Oh, sorry," he replied, "zoned out for a second there."

She grinned. She could only assume he was grinning back. "I wish I could see your face."

"Sorry," he said, "I can't take the helmet off. If I get caught not wearing it, I'll be in major trouble."

She frowned. "It just makes it harder to tell when you're being sarcastic or joking. Plus, you know what I look like. It's weird not knowing what you look like too."

"Well, truth be told," said Tobin, resting his back against the wall, "I'm smoking hot–like drop-dead gorgeous under here. Real handsome, just take my word for it." He paused. "See, *that's* me being sarcastic."

Scarlet snorted.

A creak filled the space as the door down the hallway opened. Like lightning Tobin pushed off the wall to stand straight up and down. Scarlet peered down the hallway, squinting to see who was coming. The torches did almost nothing for visibility.

In a couple moments a fat guard shuffled into view. He was holding two trays. On the first tray was a bowl of chunky brown stew that looked like it had been chewed and spit back out. Next to it was a small wooden cup. The other tray also held a bowl, along with a bruised apple, a chunk of bread, and another cup. The guard handed this one to Tobin, then turned to Scarlet.

"Go to the back of the cell," barked the guard, stopping in front of the door.

Scarlet backed against the wall.

The guard pulled a key from a pouch at his waist and stuck it in the keyhole. He opened the door and set the tray on the floor.

Scarlet's eyes followed the silver key as it went back inside his pouch. He turned and left the cell, door automatically locking behind him with a closing click. The guard scuffled out of the dungeon without another word.

Scarlet examined the tray. The cup contained a few sips of dirty water. Specks floated on its surface.

"I wouldn't drink or eat that stuff," said Tobin when the dungeon door had slammed shut. "I'm not even sure where the meat in that stew comes from, and sometimes guards in the kitchens spit in the prisoners' water."

Scarlet suppressed a gag as she looked at the spotty liquid. "I doubt I'm going to get anything else though."

"Here." Tobin took the bread off his plate. He ripped off a chunk and handed it through the bars along with the apple. "And you can have a couple drinks of my water."

"Thanks," said Scarlet, sitting down and digging into her meal. They ate in silence for a moment. When she finished, she wiped her mouth with the back of her hand and looked to Tobin. He had lifted the visor of his helmet enough to eat, but she couldn't really see his face, especially with the dungeon's dim lighting. "Tobin, why are you being so nice to me?"

It was a question that had been bothering her, like an itch in her mind.

He shrugged.

"First you gave me your handkerchief when I was crying, then you talked to me–even though you're not supposed to, and now you're sharing your food with me. Why?"

He sighed and set the empty bowl on the floor. "I don't know. I guess you kind of remind me of someone."

Scarlet cocked her head. "Who?"

"One of my sisters," Tobin replied, "or maybe a couple of them."

"How many sisters do you have?"

"Four," he answered. "Willow, Paula, Anne, and Lilly. No brothers."

"Whoa," Scarlet's eyes widened. "That's a lot of siblings."

Tobin laughed. "That's what everyone says, but I don't mind it. There's someone to hang out with for any mood, you know? Like Willow and Paula? They're twins, but they're complete opposites. Willow is thoughtful and smart as a fox. She's reading all the time. Then Paula is this crazy ball of energy, always in a tree or floating leaves across the river. Anne's different too. She's quiet most of the time, but boy, can she hold a tune when she doesn't think anyone can hear her. She's got this voice that makes God listen when she sings. And then there's Lilly."

Scarlet smiled as Tobin described his siblings. She couldn't see his face, but the way he said their names told her everything. He would fight dragons for them.

"Lilly likes to mess around with how things work. She's always taking stuff apart. The only problem is, she never knows how to put it back together."

Scarlet laughed before asking, "Who's the oldest?"

"I am," said Tobin. "I guess you would call me the man of the house." Scarlet wondered if she was detecting a hint of boyish pride in his voice.

"Technically," said Scarlet, a teasing grin lighting her lips, "your dad would be the man of the house."

Tobin shook his head. "Dad died a while back. It's just me and Ma and the kids. Ma's got a bad arm though, so I do most of the work around the farm. Well–I did." He stopped. "Before all this." He gestured around at the dungeon. "So they'll have to figure it out for themselves this year." This time Scarlet was certain that she detected worry in Tobin's tone.

Scarlet looked down at the floor. "I'm worried about my family too, and whether or not they've been alright since I disappeared. Not that my parents need me to take care of them or anything, but I'm their only kid and I don't know…" she trailed off.

"Sorry," said Tobin after a moment.

"Me too," said Scarlet. She pressed her lips together, tapping her fingers against her leg as both of them sat in the wake of the apologies.

"Have you made up any more stories?" asked Scarlet, breaking the silence.

"Lots."

"Care to share?"

"Whatcha in the mood for, wicked giants or witches plotting evil schemes in swamps?"

"Definitely witches."

As Tobin started the story, she closed her eyes and tried to let his voice transport her away from the dungeon, but it didn't work as it had before. No matter how much she tried to focus, her mind kept taking her back to the cliff edge from her dreams. She could hear the waves crashing against the rock and imagine how it would feel for those waves to swallow her, sending her into the black depths of the frothing sea.

The wheels on the cart rattled as Elowen led her horse toward the castle gate. She walked beside it, holding its reins as it carried the load. As she neared the gate, she sized up the guards. There were two of them, one standing on either side of the gleaming bronze portcullis. It glinted under the setting sun.

One guard leaned against the wall with obvious boredom. She couldn't see his face because of his helmet, but it was clear from the way he was reclining. He was holding an apple in his hand and every now and then he would toss it into the air so that it rose up like a little red sun before he snatched it back again.

The second guard was large and stumpy. He stood straight up and down, arms at his sides. He was standing so still it was like he was frozen there.

Elowen stopped the horse in front of the portcullis, the roll of the cart coming to an end behind it. She tried very hard not to look like an elf. The hood of her cloak was nestled carefully around her head, and her hair had been pinned and stuck into place to doubly conceal her pointed ears. There should be no way for either of the guards to tell what she was by looking at her, but she still felt as obvious as a dragon in a herd of unicorns.

"Halt! State your business!" It was the large guard. Elowen stepped aside from the horse to stand next to the cart as he came toward her.

"Hay," she said, "for the horses." As she looked at him she feigned a look that she hoped was completely innocent and naive: head cocked, lips parted slightly, and a couple of well-timed blinks. Ironic, really, how much thought went into looking clueless.

"We're not supposed to get a shipment of hay right now," he said, grunting and pulling a scroll out from where it had been tucked in his armor.

"My employer told me I was supposed to bring it today." Cue biting the lip, a little frown. This would be easier if they could penetrate the wall without any fights.

"I'm afraid I can't let you in," said the guard, rolling up his scroll and tucking it back into the space between his metal armor and big belly.

"Hold up, Bernie." The other guard had decided to get involved. He sauntered over and leaned against the cart. Stray pieces of hay drifted down from the top of the stack as he raked his eyes up and down her slim form. She tried to breathe calmly even though she felt as though she was suffocating under his gaze.

He took off his helmet to reveal sweeping brown hair and a blinding white smile. "Hey, sweet cheeks." Words paired with a wink. They didn't go well together.

Somehow, Elowen managed to turn her gag into a giggle.

"How about I give you a tour?" asked the guard, continuing to lean against the cart. A wisp of hay floated down to land on his head.

She giggled again. In her experience, Elowen had found that humans preferred to communicate with laughter rather than actual words.

"Elsden!" Bernie glared at the second guard. "She doesn't have the proper authorization!"

"Ah, don't be like that, Bern," said Elsden. "It'll be fine. Besides," he gave her a sideways look and a menacing grin that he must have thought charming, "what's the worst she could do?"

This time she almost laughed for real.

She was not offended. This was a triumph. Let him underestimate her. Let him make that mistake.

33

When Bernie didn't reply, Elsden spun the crank to the portcullis, and it rose upward like a retreating wave.

"Thanks!" said Elowen, taking hold of the horse's reins and leading the cart through it.

"How about that tour?" Elsden asked, following her through.

"How about later?" she said, voice teasing, then she quickly walked away without waiting for an answer. She could hear Bernie laughing at Elsden behind her.

Elowen spotted the horse barn to the left and veered toward it. The entire fortress, minus the side facing the cliff's edge, was circled with a guarded wall. The only entrance was through the portcullis she had just walked through. Just inside the wall was a massive courtyard. Looking around, Elown could see that the courtyard housed more than just horse barns. She spotted blacksmith workshops, medics, and even some training arenas. In one she could see a couple of soldiers sparring, the clashes of their metal painfully loud throughout the courtyard. Dead center was the fortress itself, looming above everything else. She had to tilt her head back to see the speared top of its tallest tower.

Elowen pushed the cart straight through the horse barn's open door, receiving a faceful of dust and a dim view. Five stalls lined either side of the stable, only a few currently occupied. She stopped the cart in the center of the barn, walked quickly to the entrance, checked both ways, and closed the door. The barn was completely silent except for the whinnying of the horses. If it weren't for a few, flickering lanterns it would have been pitch black.

The elf turned a circle, slowly breathing in the musk of the barn, observing the wooden beams, the wisps of hay that lay in golden mounds, and the dust that sifted through the air like powdered sugar, quietly covering the interior of the barn.

The horse, still attached to the cart, gave a low snuffle that echoed through the silent space.

Elowen took one last sweeping glance and nodded. "The premises are secure."

Immediately, the hay exploded.

Four elves sprang from the cart, landing gracefully on their feet like cats as the hay whirled around them. Four armored soldiers amid a golden tornado.

The first elf was female, white hair in a pixie cut with spiky orange edges. Another female elf stood next to her, braid down her back and crossbow in her arms. The other two were males, both long-haired, both with matching stony expressions.

Elowen wasted no time. "Get out the disguises." The elves turned to the cart and began digging through the remaining hay. One by one they pulled out musty breeches, dresses, and cloaks. Elowen nodded in approval. "Now–" A sound filled the barn as someone started opening the door. The elves went stiff, all but Elowen who looked to her band urgently. "Get down!"

The elves dropped like stones, nestling against the side of the cart out of the door's view. They sat, shoulder-to-shoulder, breathing slow, shallow breaths.

Light flooded across the floor as the door swung open and the sound of footsteps bounced off the walls.

The elves sat with rigid anticipation.

For a moment the footsteps stopped.

Then Elsden rounded the corner.

He stilled, mouth falling open as he stared at the elves pressed against the cart's side.

Elowen didn't give him time to turn his shock into a cry for help– didn't give him time to even consider it before her knife was in her hand and her hand was at his throat.

This is what happens when you underestimate me.

Chapter 5

Scarlet lay on the floor of her cell staring at the ceiling. The minutes trickled past her like small, pocket-sized eternities. She counted the seconds. She counted the drips from the black of the dungeon. She counted Tobin's snores.

She noted a small fracture on the ceiling that looked like a pig.

Scarlet closed her eyes and tried to fall asleep, but her mind was restless. She felt like a mini version of herself was inside her own head, pacing and muttering, too loud to let her slumber.

So, she went back to counting drips.

One.

Two.

Three–

And then a new sound penetrated her cell, a sound she hadn't heard before.

Her eyes came open, scanning the dungeon's darkness.

It was a scratching sound. Scarlet went still, listening. It made her think of fingernails scraping against a hard surface.

Slowly, she sat up.

She could swear the sound was coming from right outside the dungeon door.

"That doesn't sound like a mouse," she muttered aloud. It wasn't random or abrupt like the skitter of a rodent. Each scratch was long and purposeful–*there*–gone–*back again*.

"No, definitely not."

Scarlet jumped. She hadn't realized Tobin had woken up.

But the scratching was loud, and getting louder, stretching toward them across the dungeon darkness.

Tobin shifted, pushing quietly away from the wall he'd been sleeping against. "I guess I have to go see what that is." He said it almost like a question, like he was hoping Scarlet would tell him to ignore it and go back to sleep.

"Well, I can't check." She stood up, going to stand right behind the cell bars. The sound was definitely coming from the dungeon entrance, although she couldn't quite see the door from her angle.

"Right," said Tobin. He inched toward the door. "I guess–I guess I'll just do that then." He grabbed the hilt of the sword in his belt. One step toward the door. Two. Three. He stopped in front of it and glanced back at Scarlet, who gave him an encouraging thumbs-up. Slowly, he leaned forward. "Hello? Is someone there?"

The scratching paused. Scarlet held her breath. Then it started up again, just like before.

Tobin hesitated for a moment before reaching forward to grab ahold of the door handle. Scarlet pushed herself against the bars, trying to see him, but she could still only see half of his body before the rest was cut out of her view.

She heard the door come open.

Clang!

There was a bang, a crash, and Tobin fell to the floor.

"Tobin!" Red-hot fear washed through Scarlet as she stared at him on the ground, helmeted head unmoving.

Then someone walked into view.

The someone was wearing a simple, brown peasant's dress. A gray cloak hugged her shoulders, the hood cradling her face. A few strands of loose brown hair crept from under the cloth. She was pale against the dark, dirty walls of the dungeon. Despite her run-down outfit she looked too perfect—too elegant even—to be in such a grimy, dismal place. But behind her dainty features Scarlet could see a raw fire in her face. She looked sharp in every way: her expression, her eyes, her scowl, and her dagger, which she held firmly in her hand.

Suddenly, with the speed of lightning, four more figures darted into view behind her: two men, two women, all dressed to match. Snapping out of her initial shock, Scarlet backed farther into the cell.

"Who are you?" Her voice came out small. She felt like a bar of iron was resting on her chest.

The first woman took a step forward, studying Scarlet with ice-blue eyes.

Scarlet scrambled backward, slipping and falling. Her palms smarted as they hit the stone, but she didn't even notice the pain, forcing out words through gasping breaths. "Please don't hurt us."

The woman paused and gave her a single, sweeping look before stepping forward. "We're not here to hurt you. We're here to save you. Get off the floor, you're coming with us."

Behind them Tobin groaned and Scarlet felt a rush of relief. He shook his head and pushed himself to his feet, reaching for the sword in his sheath. Quick as a snake the nearest man, green-eyed and tall, turned and knocked it from his hand, swiftly pinning him against the dungeon wall. The blade clattered to the floor.

Green-Eyes flipped up Tobin's visor, putting a gloved hand over his mouth. Tobin writhed against the stone, trying to free himself, but it was useless.

"Stop!" yelled Scarlet. "Stop!"

"If I were you, I'd be quieter," said Elowen, stepping toward the bars. "I realize you're afraid, youngling, but there are guards wandering the halls above us. If you want to be freed, I suggest you stop yelling and listen carefully."

Scarlet went quiet.

"We're trying to save you," continued Elowen. "I understand that in your current situation you have no reason to trust us, but we're your only chance to get out of here." She glanced over her shoulder toward the dungeon door. "We need to do it quickly, though."

Scarlet hesitated. Her thoughts were swirling in her head like soup, but one word rose to the top: *freedom*. And really, what did she have to lose?

She dug her fingernails into her palms, words coming out in a whisper. "I'll come."

"Good," said Elowen, turning to the cell door. "Because we have to go." She turned to the woman behind her whose face was shrouded by orange-tipped hair. "Get the cell open."

Orange-Tips stepped forward, taking a small knife from her belt. It was glowing red. Strange symbols were carved into the blade, but Scarlet didn't get a good look at them before the woman slipped it into the keyhole of the cell door. There was a sizzle, and smoke issued from the lock. A pop echoed through the dungeon, and she pulled out the blade, yanking the door open.

Scarlet slowly stepped out, eyeing the figures.

"What about the male?" asked Green-Eyes, still pinning a flailing Tobin to the wall.

"He's an enemy guard," said Elowen, voice dismissive. "Kill him."

The blood in Scarlet's fingertips froze ice cold—Tobin yelled—the man lifted a dagger to his neck—the blade flashed in the light—

"Stop!" All heads turned to Scarlet.

The blade quivered against Tobin's throat. The man holding it looked to Elowen.

"Who are you taking orders from?" Elowen barked, "me or the human youngling? I told you to kill him."

The blade touched Tobin's skin.

"Stop or I die!"

Everyone froze.

Now it wasn't just Tobin's throat with a knife pressed against it. Scarlet had grabbed Tobin's sword from the floor, holding it firmly against her own neck. "If you kill him, you kill me."

Elowen growled–an actual growl of frustration from deep in her throat, but she waved her hand and the dagger was lowered from Tobin's neck.

"Now let him go," said Scarlet, still holding Tobin's blade against her own skin.

Elowen scowled. "Fine, but listen to me, guard," she stepped toward Tobin, teeth bared in a way that made her flawless features sharp and frightening to look at. "If you yell, we will kill you. If you run for help, we will kill you. If you even think about alerting other guards of our presence, I will drive my knife into your back and I will not stop until I see silver on the other side."

Through the helmet's eyeholes Tobin's eyes were as wide as two round buttons. He had stopped struggling.

"Understood?" asked Elowen.

Tobin attempted a nod.

"He understands," Scarlet said.

Elowen waved her hand and Green-Eyes released Tobin. He fell to his knees, breathing short, ragged breaths.

"He's coming with us," said Scarlet. Her mind, which earlier had been slow and groggy, was now going a mile a minute.

Elowen's eyes sparked. She opened her mouth to speak before one of the others grabbed her arm.

"We don't have time Elowen, we need to go now."

"Fine!" said Elowen. "He comes. Let's go."

As the band of jail-breakers started toward the dungeon door, Scarlet finally lowered the sword from her throat and ran to help Tobin to his feet. He was panting, and the fear had still not left his eyes. A bead of blood dribbled from the small scrape on his throat. Scarlet swallowed, thinking of how much more blood there could have been.

He was slow to get to his feet, even though Scarlet was using her free, sword-less hand, to help him. "I can't go," he murmured. "If they find out I left with you–"

"If you stay here and they find out that I got away, they'll kill you," said Scarlet. "And I'm not letting that happen."

"But–"

"No buts! We need to go, c'mon!" And she pulled him out the door to where Elowen was waiting.

They had only taken a few steps down the hallway when Elowen froze. Her band of followers stopped behind her.

"What?" asked Scarlet, almost running into one of them.

"Someone's coming," hissed the woman with the long, brown braid.

Scarlet strained her ears, trying to hear what they were hearing. Complete silence. She glanced at Elowen with scrunched eyebrows. Were they really picking up on something? All she heard was the drip she had come to despise.

Elowen motioned to her crew, and in sync they all flattened themselves against the wall, Orange-Tips pulling Scarlet and the second woman grabbing Tobin, long brown braid swinging behind her.

Now Scarlet could hear a sound–faint footsteps. As she listened, the sound came closer, and closer, and–the door banged open as a guard stormed in.

Brown-Braid detached herself from the wall and launched toward the guard like a deadly shadow. There was a flash of silver and he fell to the floor, killed in two silent seconds.

Scarlet gasped, eyes seizing on the body and the fresh spurt of blood on the floor tiles.

"What?" asked Elowen, looking at Scarlet and scowling. "We don't have to take them all with us, do we?"

Scarlet felt frozen, staring at the red on the gray. She had never seen anyone die. And definitely never like this–murdered without hesitation or remorse. She wondered who was under that helmet? Whose blood was soaking across the floor? Whose son or daughter lay dead at her feet?

Then with a sudden yank Tobin tugged her through the dungeon door. The two of them ran after the others who were already sprinting down a stone hallway. Elowen stopped at the bottom of a flight of stairs, allowing Scarlet and Tobin to catch up.

"Listen closely," whispered Elowen to Scarlet. "We tried to leave as little mess as possible sneaking in, but they're bound to figure out we're here soon. It's almost guaranteed that we're going to have some trouble getting out." She looked to Tobin. "Take your armor off. It'll be too loud and heavy."

Tobin began to quickly detach parts of his uniform, taking off all his armor except for his helmet, which he kept on. "This won't be loud," he said. Then to Scarlet: "and a little extra protection won't hurt."

They mounted the steps.

Scarlet panted, Tobin's sword swinging in her hand as she tried to keep pace with Elowen. The stairs twisted around like a snake so that they could no longer see the dungeon behind them.

"When one of us gets killed just stay behind the others," said Elowen to Scarlet. "You're the one we need to get out of here."

Scarlet swallowed, noting that Elowen had said "*when* one of us gets killed" not "*if* one of us gets killed." Her heart pounded against her chest like it was trying to get out before the trouble started. She wondered why they wanted to save her so badly.

But there was no time to think on it, they were pelting up the stairs now. Then, as Brown-Braid reached the door at the top, it flew open. Scarlet winced as unfamiliar white light met her eyes. *Sunlight*. The first she'd seen in days.

If she'd had any hesitancy of leaving, it disappeared as the light hit her face, flooding the stairway and reminding her what it meant to be warm.

Brown-Braid collided with a guard.

Everyone watched as the two struggled, then with a swift, brutal motion, Brown-Braid and the guard switched places so that she was standing on the landing and the guard was in front. She kicked him down the steps and Scarlet scrambled to the side to avoid being hit as his huge, meaty body flew downward. She winced at each crash of his metal armor. It sounded like a drum solo.

"Let's go!" yelled Elowen. Any pretense of stealth had died with the guard's tumble.

They whipped up the remaining steps, out onto the landing, and straight into an ambush.

They came to an abrupt stop, surrounded by guards on all sides.

"Go back down!" Elowen yelled to Scarlet, whipping daggers free from her belt. "Back down the stairs!"

Scarlet didn't need to be told again. She and Tobin backed quickly down a couple of steps so that she couldn't see anything but Elowen's back in the doorway.

The Hinterland

Shouting filled the air. Scarlet cowered in the dark stairway listening to the crashes from above. Tobin crouched next to her. He was so close she could hear his breathing.

An arrow whizzed down the steps, so near to Scarlet's face she felt a shift in the air. She gasped and pressed herself back into the wall.

A helmet clanged down the stairs past her. It crashed downward toward the dark dungeon. She could still hear it long after it was out of sight.

One of the men stumbled down the stairs, fighting off a castle guard that was bearing down on him. He slashed his daggers forward, but the guard hit them aside with his plated arm. The man fell back, and then before Scarlet had time to process what was happening, a sword was in his stomach.

Scarlet and the speared man screamed, a sickening duet echoing off the walls and around the stairway and in and out of Scarlet's mind. Her vision smeared as his body went rigid, then still. Beside her she was dimly aware of Tobin yelling in shock.

The guard turned to face them, holding the red tipped sword. Behind him the man lay on the floor like a crumpled piece of paper.

With shaking hands Scarlet lifted Tobin's sword to point at the guard. It was a toothpick in comparison to his weapon. The guard advanced on them, shadow falling across Scarlet's face.

"*No!*" Brown-Braid flew from the top of the stairs like a pouncing tiger, tackling the guard backward and away down the steps. They two tumbled down into darkness and around the corner.

"We're gonna die," said Scarlet numbly, listening to the yells coming from the doorway above and the dungeon below. They were sandwiched between two battles.

Tobin crawled to the man on the floor, reaching for his wrist and feeling for a pulse. "He's dead."

The man's cloak had come loose and his hood had fallen off. With a jolt Scarlet saw what the hood had been hiding. Ears pointed enough to cut. "Tobin," she whispered. "That's an elf."

Tobin saw the ears and flinched. He scooted back as though the body was suddenly a threat. "Do you think they all are?"

"Probably."

They both stared at the corpse. At home Scarlet had heard the village elders tell tales of elves. None of them had been encouraging. Neither had her last experience with one. From the look on Tobin's face, she assumed he was thinking the same.

They sat watching the dead elf for a second. Scarlet felt like they were inside of a small, separate bubble, with battle raging around it.

Suddenly there was a final clang from the stair landing and the steps went quiet. There was no sound from above or below. The deafening silence pressed in on the bubble.

"C'mon, time to go!" Elowen's face appeared in the doorway.

Scarlet and Tobin crept up the stairs to the wreckage of a battleground. Shields, helmets, swords, and bodies lay on the floor. Most of the bodies belonged to soldiers, but one elf lay among the mess, bleeding heavily from a gash in his stomach. It was Green-Eyes.

Tobin stepped to him, kneeling down and feeling for a pulse.

There were only two elves standing now, Elowen and the orange-haired one. One was dead on the stairs, Brown-Braid had tackled a guard into the dungeon, and Green-Eyes was bleeding out on the floor.

"Let's go," said Elowen. She was holding a long dagger in her hand, but it wasn't half as sharp as her expression. She no longer wore her cloak. It was crumpled on the floor, soaked in dark blood. She now wore just a suit of armor. It was sleek, fitting against her perfectly, and made of silver plates that looked slim but sturdy. Scarlet figured it must have been concealed under her dress. Orange-Tips was dressed the same, her previous cover also balled on the floor.

"He's still alive!" said Tobin, dropping Green-Eyes' wrist.

Elowen's sharp expression didn't change. "We need to go."

"But someone tackled a guard down the stairs," said Scarlet. "Maybe she's alive too!"

"We don't have time to check," said Elowen.

"We can't leave them!" Scarlet protested, shaking her head with vigor.

"They knew the risks." Elowen looked down the open hallway. "It's time to leave!"

Scarlet opened her mouth to reply, but it was too late as Orange-Tips grabbed her arm and yanked her down the hallway. In a moment they had turned a corner and the dying elf was gone.

The new hall was longer, the left wall lined with tapestries and the right all windows running from floor to ceiling. The only break in the windows was an archway leading out to a balcony, lined by a low railing. Through the glass Scarlet could see a view of trees, river, and brilliant blue sky. Had she not been afraid for her life, she would have stopped to stare.

As it was, she didn't even slow down.

Orange-Tips was still gripping Scarlet's wrist, Tobin was sprinting behind them. About twenty feet away the passage turned out of sight again.

Simultaneously both elves stopped in the center of the hallway. Scarlet tried to stop in time but failed, smacking into Orange-Tips. The elf didn't even seem to notice, she was firm as stone.

"Get to the side!" Elowen yelled.

"Wh–" started Scarlet before Orange-Tips grabbed the front of her shirt and pulled her through the archway onto the balcony. Elowen followed, pulling Tobin with her.

An arrow thudded into the side of the arched balcony entrance. It happened so fast Scarlet saw little more than a blur.

Through the window Scarlet could see armored guards spilling into the hallway like red ants, surfacing to face the enemy disturbing their colony. Scarlet kept expecting the flow to stop, but the mass at the end of the hallway continued to grow like an out-of-control tumor. Yelling, stampeding down the hall, waving weapons: the soldiers gathered at the entrance of the balcony, but didn't move onto it. Instead, they watched like wolves sizing up prey.

They waited.

Someone was pushing his way through the crowd. He stepped to the front of the swarm. Tall, thick, and blunt in every way, the soldier's face had a flat quality to it. He held up one fat, stubby hand and the crowd fell silent.

"Elves are not welcome here." His voice sent a shiver through the air that scampered straight down Scarlet's spine.

"Good thing we were just leaving," replied Orange-Tips, stepping toward the soldier. She was nothing compared to the army, and yet when she came forward the mass seemed to shift back an inch. "Where's your leader? Or is she too cowardly to face us?"

Elowen grabbed Scarlet and backed her even farther toward the balcony's edge. Scarlet grabbed Tobin's sleeve and pulled him with her.

"She's off on business." The guard smiled, taking a step forward as though well aware they had nowhere to run. "But I'm sure she'll be happy to visit you in the dungeons when she gets back." He turned his face toward the seething horde behind him. "Soldiers, take them!"

The horde surged in.

Orange-Tips stepped forward. "Go!"

And that was the last Scarlet and Tobin saw, because that was when Elowen tackled them off the balcony.

Chapter 6

Scarlet gagged. Wrenching open her eyes she sat up and coughed, squinting as she pushed a handful of stringy, wet hair out of her face.

She was sitting on the muddy shore of a river. The water rushed by with violent speed. She sat in numb silence, listening to the constant sound of the river running its path. Then, with the suddenness of a crash of thunder, she remembered everything that had happened prior to waking up on the shore. The escape. Flying off the balcony. Tobin. Elowen. *Where were they?* She looked back and forth, trying to spot them, or anything that might hint at where they'd gone.

Pawing through her thoughts she found that she couldn't remember climbing to the bank. In fact, she couldn't remember anything after the jump, except for immense fear, and then the jarring impact as her body hit the water. Someone must have pulled her to the surface and dragged her to shore.

"Tobin?" She stood up. Sand showered from her clothes and hair. She spit out a gritty glob of saliva, nostrils burning where water had gone up her nose.

She wished the river wasn't so fast, or she might have waded in to wash the mud off of her skin and the twigs out of her hair.

Cautiously, she began to examine the surrounding area.

"Elowen?" Her voice bounced off the landscape: rushing river in front of her, forest behind, and dirty, damp riverbank stretching to her left and right. "Hello! Anyone there?"

A hand clamped over Scarlet's mouth. She screamed into it, eyes widening, clawing at the fingers before a familiar voice spoke low in her ear: *"Stop yelling, or I'll throw you back in the river."*

Scarlet stilled, and the hand released her. "Where were you?" she asked, rounding on Elowen. "Why did you grab me like that?"

"I was scouting," replied Elowen, crossing her arms and scowling. Despite fighting through a dungeon, jumping off of a balcony, and diving into a river, she still looked immaculate in her sturdy set of armor, braid still neat and pulled out of her eyes. "Trying to get a look at where our enemies are located. They're still hunting us." Her dagger gleamed from her belt, shiny as ever. "And you yelling makes their job a lot easier. We need to move."

Scarlet nodded. She bit her lip, about to ask how close their enemies were exactly, when something else struck her. "Tobin! Where's Tobin?"

"Your boy's fine," said the elf. "He's unconscious. Both of you were when I pulled you out of the river. But he'll recover, same as you."

Scarlet crossed her arms and frowned, "He's not *my* boy."

The elf smirked, something that caught Scarlet off guard. It was a small action, but it seemed strangely human. Somehow it was reassuring.

"Where is he?" Scarlet asked, looking around.

"He's already in the boat," said the elf. "He washed up right next to it so I hauled him in before I left. Speaking of which, that's where we need to be, too." Without another word she turned and started down the shore, her shoes making slapping sounds against the wet sand and mud.

The elf stepped behind a bush and, like a magic trick, reemerged pulling a small boat behind her. "We had this ready for our escape," Elowen explained, seeing Scarlet's surprise. With a pang of guilt Scarlet noticed that the boat had seats for six. Images of the wounded elf on the castle floor flashed across her mind. He had been alive, and they had left him to die. In an instant her thoughts were filled with blood. The blood of the guard, killed in the dungeon. The blood on the wounded elf's clothes. The blood of the elf gutted on the stairway.

Now it was blood on Scarlet's hands.

It was because of me. The thought came to her unbidden and unexpected. But she believed it.

A wave of nausea gut punched her.

"Hey–*hey,* you listening?"

"What?" Scarlet's eyes refocused on the elf and her mind returned to the riverbank.

"I said get in the boat."

"Oh–sorry," Scarlet clambered in. Elowen shoved the boat off the shore and into the river before leaping onto it herself, landing gracefully on her feet even as it rocked.

The elf began to direct the vessel into the current, but Scarlet's focus had turned elsewhere.

She was staring at Tobin. He lay on the boat's floor, eyes closed and body completely soaked. Now, with his armor off and time to look at him, she could see that he may be skinny, but his arms were muscular–the side effect of farm life.

But something else grabbed her attention–he was no longer wearing his helmet.

She had never seen him without his helmet.

Sliding onto the floor next to him she studied his sleeping face. He was tan with a dusting of small freckles across his nose, hair brown and curly, and, though she couldn't see them now, she knew from her past few days in the dungeon that his eyes were a soft brown. His features weren't traditionally handsome, but he had an impish, mischievous look about him that sent a dash of warmth through Scarlet's chest. She had to fight the sudden urge to touch one of his perfectly round freckles.

She felt a sudden urge of protectiveness over him as he lay, sopping wet and limp, on the boat floor. She hadn't been lying when she'd told Elowen he wasn't her boy. He wasn't. But she also had nothing else but him in this boat, in this river, or in this strange world she had woken up to a week ago.

He was all she knew.

The boat flew down the river like a rider on a wild mare. The river galloped, free and alive as Scarlet watched the castle slowly move farther and farther away, but she felt like it was the one watching her, staring her down as they made their escape. She looked away from it, but she could still feel its cold gaze on her back.

Zinggg.

Scarlet got a face full of river as something punched through the water's surface.

"Down!" And then Elowen's hand was on her head and in an instant her face was against wood, her cheek pressed against the boat's rough floor.

Zinggg.

Shouting filled the air.

Scarlet twisted to see Elowen, standing at the boat's center. Elowen's toe slipped under one of the boats' oars, and she flicked it into the air, catching it as it rose to eye level.

And then it rained arrows.

Scarlet yelled, covering her face with her arms, crawling next to Tobin. She searched in vain for something to shield them. Her efforts were unnecessary. The arrows rained, but Elowen was their umbrella. She wielded her oar like a flyswatter, smacking arrows out of the sky and into the river below. Her speed was incredible. Scarlet felt like she was watching a living, breathing tornado of flesh and bone and blood: a force of nature trapped inside a body.

Whiz–thunk–whiz–whiz–thunk–thunk–

The arrows were like lightning, but Elowen and her oar were thunder, always coming after the strike.

Scarlet stayed pressed to the boat floor, breaths coming too heavy. Her hair stuck to her sweaty face. She grasped for her courage, but it slipped through her fingers. She was powerless.

Finally, abandoning reason, she popped her head over the edge of the boat and peeked at the river bank beyond. Elowen kicked her down again.

"Stay down!" she yelled, using her oar to swat left and right with an intensity that suggested she was exacting revenge on each and every arrow she hit.

Scarlet was only too happy to stay on the boat floor. She had only wanted to get a view of what was happening, and now she wished she hadn't.

Now she suddenly wished she could forget the dozens of soldiers clamoring down the riverbank toward their boat, but their yells wouldn't let her.

Her head pounded. Someone was playing drums in her mind. Her thoughts slurred to the beat. She couldn't think.

She crouched low, trying to stay calm, looking for anything she could use to help–

With a gasp Tobin came to life beside her. His eyes darted to Scarlet shaking beside him, the elf brandishing her oar above him, and then to the wooden benches and rocking sides of the boat. In less than a second his look of confusion turned to one of immense fear. "What the–"

"Boat, arrows, oars," said Scarlet, gesturing weakly at Elowen and then the shore.

Tobin spluttered, but Scarlet had stopped paying attention to him. The yelling from the shore was getting farther away. They must be getting ahead.

Again she risked a look over the edge and found that they had, indeed, gained some on the soldiers. In fact, the soldiers seemed to be slowing down. *Were they giving up?* They were still firing, occupying Elowen, but some were even stopping, watching the boat careen down the river. Scarlet felt like cheering, but something stopped her. A nagging suspicion that it had been too easy. She looked ahead, and the realization hit her like a hammer.

"Waterfall!"

Tobin looked. "Oh, you've got to be kidding me."

"Elowen," Scarlet waved her arms. "Waterfall!"

Elowen didn't hear, completely focused on the task at hand.

Whiz–thunk!

Scarlet slapped at her leg. "Waterfall!"

The elf registered the warning and her head snapped to the right as she looked.

*Whiz–*Scarlet waited for the thunk– "Agh!"

The elf let go of her oar, clutching her arm. Tobin yelled as the oar fell toward him. Scarlet watched the edge of the waterfall get closer.

And then–as Elowen yelled, and Tobin yelled, and the distant soldiers yelled–the world went weightless and Scarlet was yelling too.

For a second they flew. For one righteous moment that seemed to slur into ten, the boat seemed to freeze in midair as it was propelled from sea to sky. Gravity unbuckled itself from them–then swiftly slammed them back toward the ground.

Scarlet just had time to think, *not again*, before she was catapulted into the river for the second time that day.

The Hinterland

The water swallowed her. Everywhere was brown. Everywhere was black. Everywhere was nowhere and was up down or was down up? She flailed. She saw light. She surged forward.

Scarlet resurfaced gasping for breath. The world was blurry. The water churned around her. She felt something grab her arm and shook it off before she realized it was Tobin, coming up for air beside her.

"Where's the elf?" he asked, water streaming down his face.

Scarlet scanned the river. The boat had smashed into a rock, wreckage drifting away. Panic rose in Scarlet's throat as she pictured what it would mean if Elowen had been in the boat when it crashed. Her breaths started coming faster, her kicks becoming more frantic.

"She's there." Tobin pointed. Scarlet let out a slow breath, the tightness in her chest loosening as she spotted Elowen.

The elf was crawling onto shore. She looked up, scanning the water, and Scarlet realized she was probably looking for them. She raised her hand and Elowen spotted it, instantly wading into the water toward them.

"It's okay, we'll come to you!" Scarlet shouted, she and Tobin beginning to swim. The current was strong, but by swimming at an angle they were able to reach the river's edge.

Tobin hauled himself out of the water. He put his hands on his knees and coughed. "Well, this is not how I saw this day going."

Scarlet twisted the bottom of her tunic, wringing out the hem, but it was pointless. She was completely drenched. Tobin pulled off his shoes and shook out two streams of sand, sticking them in the river water and washing them out in the flow.

Elowen was waiting for them, cleaning her arm with a strip of cloth she'd pulled from somewhere under her armor.

"Are you alright?" asked Scarlet, laying down on the shore and closing her eyes. Her arms ached from the swim and her chest hurt. She felt like she'd been kicked by a horse. "I thought you got hit with an arrow."

"It grazed me, but I'll be fine," said Elowen, standing up. "It was blunt anyway, they couldn't risk one hitting and killing you. Besides, it's not important. We have to be at the checkpoint before nightfall to meet someone."

"Wait," said Scarlet, "before we go, I have some questions, and I think I deserve some answers."

"You deserve some answers?" replied Elowen, raising her eyebrows. "You're very demanding for someone just rescued from a prison cell."

"Well, as someone who just got chased through a castle, tackled over a balcony, and launched off a waterfall, I'd really like to know what's going on," Scarlet answered. Facing Elowen, she didn't know where she was getting the courage, arguing with an elven warrior who could kill her in an instant, but she'd already been certain she was going to die so many times that day that some of her fear had been ripped away.

"I second that," said Tobin, straightening up.

Elowen turned and walked away toward where the woods met the shore. Scarlet started to protest, thinking she was avoiding the conversation, when Elowen stopped and leaned against a tree, beginning to wrap her wound with the same strip she'd used to clean it–which Scarlet was sure couldn't be very hygienic. "You have a minute. Be fast."

"You're an elf, right?" asked Scarlet. She was already certain, but she wanted to hear it just to be sure.

Elowen nodded. "I'm a Crescent Elf."

Scarlet cocked her head.

Elowen's eyes flickered with annoyance. "That would be a moon elf to you."

"Okay," said Scarlet slowly. "Next question. Why did you save me and Tobin?"

"Firstly, we never intended to bring the male," said Elowen, brushing a smattering of dirt off of her armor. "But if we can't kill him, I suppose it was imperative that we bring him."

"Why?"

"He knows too much," she said, continuing to wipe at smudges on her gleaming suit.

"Like what?"

"Like you."

"Yeah..." said Scarlet, getting to her biggest query. "I've been meaning to ask you about that. Why am I so important?"

Elowen pressed her lips together, seeming to consider the question for a moment. "You're a piece of something far larger than you realize, Scarlet."

Scarlet's brow creased. "What's that mean?"

The elf used her thumb to eradicate a final smear of brown on her chestplate. "I'm not at liberty to say."

Scarlet felt like something inside her was bursting. "You–you won't tell me?"

Elowen shook her head. "I'll leave that to my superiors. You have one more question."

Scarlet continued to stare at Elowen, mouth moving in silent indignation as she formed invisible words.

"Where are you taking us?" This question came not from Scarlet, but Tobin. He was sitting on the shore, letting the water lap at his feet as he stared at the elf intently.

Elowen was silent for a moment, then she shook her head. "Another question I don't know if I'm at liberty to answer. But I can assure you that it's safe." She paused, the corners of her pink lips turning down as she considered. "Actually, I can assure you no such thing. I can assure you that it's better than the dungeon you were hosted in previously."

This time Scarlet found her voice. "This isn't fair! You said you were going to save me, but this feels more like a kidnapping. I just want some answers and you shouldn't withhold information from me—not after everything I've had to go through today!"

A faint voice in the back of her mind warned her that she sounded like a child, but she *was* a child, wasn't she? She was fourteen. She was tired. She was wet. She had been launched off both a balcony and a waterfall in the last hour. She had watched multiple people die. Faced with this logic she clenched her fists, the voice in her head fading.

Elowen pushed away from the tree and approached Scarlet, who fought the urge to flinch. She felt like an ant Elowen was about to step on. In just a few long, purposeful strides, Elowen stood in front of Scarlet, so close she could see the crest on the elf's armor in full detail: a small depiction of a slashed-through spiral.

"Maybe it isn't fair, youngling," she said, voice smooth as silk and hard as iron. "But neither is anything else in the world. For example, it's not fair that four elves lost their lives on this mission today, but it happened anyway. And it's also not fair that I will have to visit their families and explain why they're not coming home, but I will anyway. The least you could do is not act as though their sacrifice is an inconvenience to you, because I can assure you that being here is far better than where you were before."

Scarlet lowered her eyes. In her mind she could see the elf, bleeding on the floor. The blur tackling her attacker down the stairs. The elf, stabbed through the stomach. "I'm sorry." Her voice was small. "I didn't mean to make it sound like I wasn't grateful for what they—for what all of you did. I just want to know where we're going."

Elowen's voice softened, if only slightly. "I can't tell you exactly where we are going, but I'll tell you the general vicinity. We're going into the Hinterland."

Scarlet swallowed. Behind her Tobin cursed. The word was one Scarlet's mother would definitely not have approved of.

The Hinterland. I suppose now is as good a time as any to explain to you what the Hinterland is.

Have you ever been afraid of monsters under the bed? I'm sure you have at some point. Children fear monsters under the bed, because when lying in the dark at night they can't see beneath the mattress. Their imaginations run wild. They gouge eyes into the black, rip mouths into the darkness, stick them full of teeth, and feed them hunger. The Hinterland is like the dark space beneath the bed: miles upon miles of twisted, uncharted territory, too dangerous to be mapped or explored. The biggest difference between the darkness under the bed and the darkness of the Hinterland? The monsters under the bed are make-believe: figments of the imagination, harmless scraps of creativity gone wrong.

The monsters in the Hinterland are real.

So, you can understand Scarlet's and Tobin's fear. They had both heard the stories of the Hinterland. It was little more than a breeding ground, so overrun with dangerous creatures no one had ever explored it and come out again. On maps it was depicted as only a large, black splotch.

"That's–that's–," Scarlet couldn't seem to find the words to explain just how bad a plan she thought this was.

"That's crazy!" Tobin found the words for her. "I'm all for an adventure, but I'm also pro-not-getting-killed. We go into the Hinterland and we're deader than a mouse in a cat house. That's basically common knowledge like–like don't let the barn cat in the house, or don't go swimming right after eating. You just don't."

"Swimming after eating is fine," said Elowen, "that's just something humans made up."

Tobin put his hands up to his head, running them through his hair. "Can we focus on the actual problem? We can't go into the Hinterland."

"Why not?" asked Elowen. She seemed to be almost entertained by Tobin's concern.

"Oh, I don't know," he replied, scratching his chin with an over-exaggerated face of contemplation. "Maybe because no one ever comes back out!"

"I did."

Tobin stopped talking. His eyes went wide.

"You mean you're from the Hinterland?" Scarlet asked, tone hushed, although she wasn't sure why.

"Every mission member you met today came from the Hinterland. It's where the fortress is. It's the safest place, because no one goes in."

Tobin made a noise of disbelief that suggested the irony of the sentence was not lost on him.

"But–" Scarlet couldn't believe that she was standing in front of someone who had walked into the Hinterland and walked back out alive. "But what about the monsters?"

Elowen sighed. "There are monsters everywhere, Scarlet. Inside of The Hinterland, outside of The Hinterland, in every town, in every place, in every time. There will always be monsters. We can't control the existence of monsters, only which ones we fight. Besides, I think the beasts of the Hinterland are the least of our worries. In the long run I think it's the monster we just escaped from that we should be most concerned about." She went quiet, looking deep in thought. Then, with a sudden, swift motion she pushed off the tree. "Time's up. Let's go."

She turned and walked into the forest, Scarlet and Tobin hurrying after. They walked side by side, a little ways behind Elowen.

For a few moments they ambled along in silence. After their last hour of terror it seemed almost funny to Scarlet to be here, ambling through the forest as though on a peaceful afternoon stroll. She grinned at Tobin. "Can you believe this? I mean we did it–we're out. We actually made it."

The Hinterland

She beamed at him, expecting the same reaction, but he was still wearing the expression he'd acquired at Elowen's announcement that they'd be entering the Hinterland: fear. Now it was streaked with defeat.

"Are you okay?" She asked, stopping.

"Yes. No." He cursed, another word Scarlet's mother wouldn't have allowed inside her home, and kicked a tree. "No." He wrung his hands out like he was trying to fling off the anxiety.

"We're going to be fine," said Scarlet. "I trust Elowen."

"It's not that."

And Scarlet understood. The realization hit her like a blow. His family. Of course, this was about his family. Hadn't he told her that they would be in danger if he didn't follow orders and keep her guarded? She hadn't even thought about it. She hadn't even considered what it would mean, telling the elves he was coming with them. She'd only been thinking of the knife at his throat. But now she realized she'd just redirected the knife's target.

Tentatively she put her hand on his shoulder. He tensed, but didn't pull away.

"Tobin, I'm sure they'll be fine."

He said nothing.

"Elowen tackled you over the balcony, I bet the guards will think you were taken hostage or something."

He continued to look at the ground. His hands were in his pockets but she could still see that they were balled into fists.

"We'll figure something out," she whispered.

He took a deep breath and when he looked up his jaw was clenched. Scarlet desperately tried to think of something else to say, but her mind was an empty pocket. She dug around in it, reaching for the words she needed, but found nothing.

Luckily she was saved from saying anything else by Elowen. "We're at the checkpoint." Elowen had gotten a good twenty feet ahead of them during their talk and was entering a clearing.

Scarlet and Tobin nodded, quickening their pace.

As she walked Scarlet added them up in her head. One, for the elf down the stairs, two, for the elf on the stairs, three, for the elf at the top of the stairs, four, for the elf on the balcony. *These are the people who have died for me. These are the people who have died* because *of me.* And Tobin's family might be five, six, seven, eight, and nine.

She clenched her fists just as Tobin had done only a minute before.

Letting out a long breath through her nose, she tried to regain composure, bringing the surrounding forest back into focus as she stepped into the clearing—and the air left her lungs.

The Hinterland

Chapter 7

They were lions. They were eagles. They were—"Those are griffins," said Tobin, mouth falling open. He seemed to have temporarily forgotten his prior fear in the face of the creatures.

Scarlet's eyes went wide as she looked at them. They were just like the ones she'd read about in stories or seen in illustrations. But these were not drawn on paper, penned in ink, or printed into a children's book. These beaks and feathers and whipping tails were real: six griffins in total, moseying around the clearing.

"Elowen! I've been waiting." A head appeared from behind a griffin. Scarlet wasn't surprised to see that it was another elf. He looked noticeably younger than Elowen, maybe eighteen or nineteen.

"Avenbeck?" Elowen's eyebrows raised. "I didn't expect you. I thought they'd send another member from my unit."

"At some point you'll have to give in and start calling me Beck like everyone else," he replied, "And yeah, they were going to, but my dad volunteered me, and you know he has some sway. Said this'll look good when I try to qualify for the court."

Elowen's eyes darkened and she looked like she'd tasted something sour. "Not if you get killed out here."

Beck shrugged, a broad grin spreading across his face. "C'mon, gimme some gold. You know I'm the best we've got. Other than you, of course." He put his hands up as though in mock surrender, before dropping them and adding, "but seriously, don't worry. I'm not in an elite unit for my charm." The way he spoke was so smooth he might have been giving a speech.

He was tall, with tufts of neat, black hair shadowing summer-leaf green eyes. His smile was slightly crooked: a perfect imperfection that made his grin instantly endearing. He wore a set of armor similar to Elowen's: sleek and fitted, nothing like the chunky armor of the guards in the fortress they'd just left. He stood straight up and down like a soldier, and though he looked young, he held himself with a kind of confidence Scarlet hadn't even seen from her village elders back home. She bit her lip as she wondered when she would see them again.

"Where are the others?" Beck asked, peering through the trees behind them. "And is that the one they've been talking about nonstop all week?" He pointed to Scarlet.

"That's her. That's Scarlet." said Elowen, "And the others aren't coming. We're the only ones left. They didn't make it."

Beck paled. He ran a hand through his hair once–then twice. Elowen was silent, letting him process. In ten seconds he seemed to flick through multiple emotions at double speed. First a small shake of the head, like he couldn't believe what she had said. Next sadness joined the green in his eyes. Then anger: brief, but strong. Last of all, acceptance. He took a deep breath and when he met Elowen's gaze again, it was as though he hadn't heard what she'd said at all. "Who's that?" He'd spotted Tobin.

"He was her guard," said Elowen, grimacing.

Beck's face tightened, eyes narrowing. "Why's he here?" His hand went automatically to the hilt of a sword at his belt.

"Scarlet insisted," said Elowen, stepping to the elf. "She seems to have become... emotionally attached."

Scarlet blushed, heat dashing across her cheeks. "He's my friend. And he's a good person. He didn't deserve to be killed or left behind."

Elowen exchanged looks with the new elf. "She's very adamant. It seems he has to come."

Beck's eyebrows inched upward. "Well, that's a plot twist." He inspected Scarlet, standing with her arms crossed, ready to defend Tobin. His hand left the handle of his blade.

"This is Avenbeck," said Elowen, turning to Scarlet and Tobin and introducing the new elf officially. "He's been waiting for us here with the griffins."

"Beck," he said, stepping forward and extending his hand to Scarlet. "My friends call me Beck." He cocked his head toward Elowen. "Except for her. She's always worried about professionalism and other pixie dust."

Scarlet shook his hand. His grasp was warm and sure, like he'd practiced it a hundred times.

As he let go and took a step back she had a feeling he was sizing her up. She suddenly felt hyper-aware of her skinny arms and muddy face–the way dirt was caked to her skin and her hair hung around her head like limp strands of seaweed. She didn't know what he was looking for, but she had a sneaking suspicion the wet, exhausted, mess of a person in front of him, was not it.

"We should go." Elowen, in a hurry as always, was looking up at the sky. The sun was beginning to look tired and heavy, sagging toward the tree line. It wouldn't be long until it slid down the sky and out of sight.

Scarlet knew Elowen was right, but she groaned inwardly. She wouldn't mind just taking in the forest for a minute. The clearing was peaceful and hushed. The surrounding trees seemed to bow inward slightly, like they were protecting the space. She could smell pine. She could hear the chattering of birds. She could taste freedom and it was delicious. Part of her just wanted to rest and enjoy its flavor a little longer.

"Scarlet, you're riding that black one." Elowen interrupted her thoughts. "Tobin, take the gray. The one on the left."

Scarlet came to attention. "I'm riding a griffin? On my own?"

Elowen nodded.

Scarlet watched as Beck stepped to his griffin and gracefully vaulted onto its back like he'd been doing it his whole life.

She approached her own. Its feathers were jet black, a shocking contrast to its sleek golden body. Where the gold and black merged, there was a soft layer of gray down. Scarlet crept around the griffin's side and, throwing caution to the wind, attempted to mimic Beck. She set her hands on the griffin's side and jumped.

In a couple seconds she was on the ground, having leapt sideways onto the griffin's back and rolled off the other side. She stood up and dusted herself off as Tobin laughed.

"Are you okay?" he asked, shoulders shaking.

She glared at him.

"Sorry," he apologized, snorting in an effort to stop his laughter. "It's just you–" he snickered.

"Well, why don't you try," said Scarlet, crossing her arms.

Tobin walked to his griffin, braced his hands against it, and leapt onto its back.

Scarlet's mouth fell open. "How did you–how?"

"I grew up on a farm," said Tobin, shrugging. "I know how to ride horses. This is just like getting on Betty."

Scarlet had never ridden a horse. Back home everything had been within walking distance. She hadn't had a particularly extravagant upbringing, but she'd spent most days at school while her parents had worked at the shop down the street. She had never needed to learn how to ride like the kids in the country who spent all day working the farms, loading hay and harvesting potatoes.

She blew a strand of hair off her face and turned back to her griffin, determined to mount.

But in a few moments, she found herself back on the ground again. She sat there for a second, panting.

Beck whistled. "Struggling there?" He dismounted. "Let me help."

"No, I got it," said Tobin quickly, sliding off his griffin.

Beck nodded, remounting.

Tobin extended his hand and helped Scarlet to her feet. "Look, your hands need to go here, and when you jump move your legs like this." he demonstrated, mounting her griffin before sliding back to the ground.

Carefully running over the steps in her head, she placed her hands on the griffin's warm side, and jumped, focusing on swinging her legs around like Tobin had instructed. She landed comfortably on the animal's back.

"I did it!" She grinned broadly at Tobin and he returned it.

"Let's go," Elowen said, sitting atop her griffin. She shook her head. "Humans have no sense of urgency."

Tobin hurried to remount his griffin. When he was perched on its back Elowen yelled "UP!"

The griffins' wings thrust outward, and with a mighty rush they rose into the air.

Scarlet gulped. She wasn't afraid of heights, but she realized she did have a fear of falling from the sky off of winged beasts.

"This is safe right?" she looked to Elowen, who was ascending on her right.

Elowen was smiling as her griffin rose. It was a real smile like Scarlet hadn't seen from her before. On the griffin's back she looked like she was in her element, like maybe she belonged in the air. Stray pieces of hair had come loose from her braid and the strands were waving back and forth like snakes swimming through wind.

"A little late for that question, isn't it?" answered Beck, rising up beside her.

The color left Scarlet's face.

Elowen shook her head, giving Beck a disapproving look. She looked like she might be fighting the urge to roll her eyes. "Yes, it's very safe. Griffins are extremely reliable. They know how to keep their riders mounted. And if you fall they're trained to catch you. Not to mention all the extras who are also ready if you slip." She nodded to the griffins without riders, who were flying under them.

Scarlet swallowed. She felt only slightly reassured.

And then the griffins shot upward.

Scarlet screamed and clutched at the down of the griffin's neck, but to her surprise she stayed snugly nestled between the creature's wings. She heard Tobin yell beneath her as his griffin also burst forward.

"Why didn't we use these sooner?" Scarlet yelled, her hair streaming out behind her. "Why did we use the boat when we could have used these all along?"

"Too obvious," Elowen shouted. "They've got patrols watching the skies just for things like this. We should be far enough away now though."

"Exactly who are 'they'?" Scarlet asked. Her voice had to fight over the rushing wind.

"The army of the Wraith," replied Elowen. She didn't elaborate. Instead, she turned her gaze to the setting sun.

Scarlet closed her eyes and let the warm air soak into her skin. It didn't make sense, but the higher they got the braver she felt—like it was her problems she was flying away from, not the earth. She was afraid of what was coming, but there, on the griffin, she felt happy. And she wasn't going to waste the moment. Slowly, she loosened her grip on the griffin, and lifted her arms out at her sides, feeling the breeze tickle her as the last rays of sun warmed her skin like a kiss goodbye.

This was what it felt like to be alive.

The Hinterland

They soared. Scarlet, Tobin, Elowen, and Beck flew together, the griffins without riders flocked around them. As they flew, the sun began to sink faster. Night was on their heels. It would catch them soon.

"Hold tight," called Elowen, "we're about to land."

Scarlet startled. She hadn't realized how far they'd gone or how long they'd been riding.

She peered over the griffin's side to look at the ground. "Why?" She couldn't see anything beneath them that might be worthy of landing for. Directly below them stretched a forest. In the distance Scarlet could see where the forest stopped and led into plains, and even farther she could see a mountain, ascending into clouds.

"We're about to enter the Hinterland." Elowen replied. She cut an impressive figure, sitting regal atop her mount, armor glinting in the setting sun, brown hair contrasting her striking blue eyes. In comparison, Scarlet knew that she must look a mess. Her tunic was rumpled from days of sleeping on a dungeon floor, her hair was grimy, and her face was red with sweat. She was in desperate need of a bath, she was starving, she was tired, and she was confused. Tobin looked equally uncomfortable. In fact, he looked worse than uncomfortable. He looked like he was about to be sick. His face was alarmingly pale.

"Wouldn't it be safer to enter the Hinterland in the air?" Scarlet asked. "From what she'd heard about the Hinterland, going in on foot was a good way to get killed.

Elowen shook her head and said something–but it was lost to the wind.

"What?" hollered Scarlet.

"Dragons," came the reply.

Scarlet swallowed. "Dragons?"

"Can you clarify on that a little bit?" said Tobin, who was sagging on his griffin. "When you say dragons, do you mean like *dragons*, dragons? Or is that a code word or something?"

Elowen gave him a look that answered the question.

"The Hinterland is infested with flying raptors!" yelled Beck. "Small dragons that fly in swarms. Like the piranhas of the sky. There are probably bigger dragons in there too, but not so close to the cuff."

Tobin nodded. "Well, I've never liked piranhas much even without wings, so I agree with the landing plan."

Scarlet nodded–and then her stomach dropped as her griffin twisted in the air and dove downward.

She squeaked, holding onto its mane and leaning into the griffin's fur. She tried to keep her eyes open, but the wind bludgeoned at them, and she resigned, closing them tight.

Tobin yelled and she could only guess that his griffin was diving beside hers.

They plummeted toward earth. As she hurtled toward the ground, Scarlet could feel gravity's fingers retract from her, letting her go. She had to twist her fingers into the griffin's fur to stay anchored to it. She couldn't remember ever being more afraid, but she also couldn't remember ever feeling more free.

The joy was excruciating.

Then the griffin slowed. It began to circle above the treeline, gently drifting to the forest floor like a loose feather.

They landed.

Tobin jumped off his ride and threw up on the forest floor. "That's–that's enough of that," he choked, panting.

Scarlet slid off of her griffin and stroked its beak. "That was the most amazing thing I've ever done!" She turned to Tobin who was sitting against a tree. "Are you okay?"

"I think I prefer horses," he replied.

"You alright there?" Beck asked Tobin, dismounting smoothly off his ride. "Cause you aren't looking like the top dragon right now."

"Fine," wheezed Tobin. "I just think I might be allergic to riding griffins."

Beck laughed. "Don't worry. This happens to everyone their first time. Well, except her." He pointed to Scarlet. "You're a natural."

Scarlet felt a beam of pride light in her chest like sunlight.

"Now we enter the Hinterland," said Elowen, bringing an end to the conversation.

Scarlet looked around. They were surrounded by foliage. The trees covered them, but light filtered through the leaves, dancing over bunches of flowers, patches of clover, and thick clumps of fern. Nothing looked like the entrance to the highly dangerous territory she'd grown up hearing about in legends and songs. "How close are we?"

Elowen pointed. "You see the symbol on that tree over there?"

Scarlet looked. Emblazoned like a tattoo on the oak's rough brown skin was a skull.

"Yup," she nodded, "I see it." The skull was slashed into the tree with two gouge marks for eyes. Still, with the day's final rays of sunshine flitting over it, Scarlet wasn't impressed. Maybe the Hinterland wasn't as bad as it was made out to be?

"That's where The Hinterland begins."

"It doesn't seem too bad," said Scarlet.

Beck laughed. It seemed like a thing he did a lot. "The most dangerous things never do. That's what makes them dangerous." Even with the laughter there was a note of sincerity in his voice.

"You're wise all of the sudden," said Elowen. She was so straight-faced that it took Scarlet a second to realize she was teasing Beck. His grin indicated that he had caught on right away and left Scarlet wondering how long they'd known each other.

"Let's go," said Elowen, focused again. She stepped forward and passed the marked tree, Beck right beside her.

Scarlet came after them, but stopped before she crossed over the invisible line that separated forest from Hinterland.

Tobin heaved himself up from his tree and joined her. He, too, gazed at the other side of the line that wasn't really there. "You ready?" he asked.

Scarlet took a deep breath. She had a feeling that if she took another step, there was no going back, but her mind was made up. "Put it down in the books," she said. "Scarlet Mount is no coward."

And she stepped into the Hinterland.

Chapter 8

"This isn't bad so far," Scarlet whispered to Tobin as they walked through the forest. It was calm, and everything was a shade of green. The peacefulness almost scared Scarlet, she felt like the forest was trying to trick her.

"That's because we're only on The Cusp," Elowen replied, "we need to be cautious, but we shouldn't encounter anything large yet."

"The Cusp?" asked Scarlet.

"Or, as us High Elves say, The Cuff," commented Beck.

Elowen nodded. "Different groups call it by various names, but simply put, it's the edge of the Hinterland."

"Which is what the dwarves call it," added Beck, snorting.

Elowen ignored him and continued. "The farther in you get, the more dangerous it becomes, and the more dangerous the monsters get. We've traveled through a couple of times and we've never faced anything too powerful here on The Cusp."

Scarlet nodded. That seemed like a good thing, but she still felt on high alert. She didn't like how relaxed the elves seemed. The Hinterland seemed like a place that killed relaxed people.

Elowen saw her skepticism. "Look, the Hinterland is like a whirlpool. The edge of a whirlpool has some tug, but it's not till you get closer to the center that you're in trouble. We're just on the edge of the whirlpool."

Scarlet bit her lip. She wondered how far into the Hinterland they were going. "What's at the center?"

"What do you mean?"

"If it gets worse as it goes, what's at the center of the Hinterland?"

"Well, the Hinterland is unmapped," said Elowen. "We have an idea of what The Cusp looks like, but large parts of the territory are unexplored, especially farther in, and we've never ventured too deep. So, it's hard to say exactly what's at the center."

"We do have some theories, though," said Beck.

Elowen pursed her lips.

"*I* have some theories," corrected Beck.

Scarlet's attention was snared. Behind her Tobin also perked up, listening intently.

"According to the legends of old," Beck began dramatically, "The Spire sits at the Hinterland's center. The legends say that The Spire is a mountain that reaches the clouds. Some say it holds up the moon." He paused for effect. It seemed he was thoroughly enjoying his job as storyteller.

Elowen scoffed, but Scarlet could see a hint of a smile turning up the edges of the elf's mouth.

She turned her attention back to Beck. She could see it in her mind: a mountain so tall its tip was frosted with snow and sky, scraping the moon's bottom. It sounded like the type of story her dad would have told her. The thought of her dad hit her like a swift punch to the gut. She wondered whether she was walking in the direction of her home, or farther away, and momentarily slowed before giving her head a quick shake and pushing forward.

"As the story goes," continued Beck, kicking a stick out of his path, "a monster lives in The Spire: a king of dragons, stronger than any who came before, or any who will come after. But its strength comes with a weakness. It sleeps in the mountain until awoken by a master to serve."

"A youngling legend," said Elowen, shaking her head.

"Legends can have truth in them," replied Beck. "In lots of human villages elves are little more than legend and you seem plenty real to me." He poked her arm.

She swatted at him and he dodged, crooked smile reappearing.

"Wouldn't you know if there was a giant mountain in the center of the Hinterland?" asked Scarlet. "I mean, wouldn't you be able to see it?"

"Actually, probably not," Beck replied. "The mountain range in the Hinterland is easy to see around the edges, but it gets really misty farther in. It's impossible to see the whole territory through the mist. It's not unthinkable that there could be a hidden mountain at the center."

Scarlet processed the information as the elves moved ahead.

Without the conversation she realized that the woods seemed unusually quiet. She couldn't remember whether it had been this silent the whole time, or if the silence was new. "Tobin, wasn't it louder before?"

He didn't answer.

"Tobin?" She turned to look at him. But he wasn't there.

Tobin was gone

Scarlet stopped. "Where's Tobin?"

Elowen and Beck paused too, turning to look.

"He was behind us a moment ago," said Scarlet. She turned a slow circle. "Tobin? Tobin!"

There was no reply.

A feeling of panic hit Scarlet like a wave, flooding the crevices and crannies of her mind with fear. "Something got him. We shouldn't have come here–something got him!" Her voice was loud, echoing off the trees, but she didn't care.

"Calm down," said Elowen, pulling out a blade from her belt. She was already on her toes, preparing for a fight.

There was no movement around them.

Elowen scowled. "We don't have time for this. He must have run away."

"No, he wouldn't have done that," said Scarlet. Her breaths came fast and hard, painful as she forced them out of her chest. "This was a bad idea, I shouldn't have trusted you. We shouldn't have come here!"

"Pull over the pony," said Beck, coming up behind her. He put a hand on her back. The pressure was oddly comforting. "I'm assuming Elowen's accurate. He was a guard at the castle. Honestly, we should have anticipated the maneuver."

From what little she knew of Beck, Scarlet wouldn't have expected the words "accurate", "anticipated", or "maneuver", to come out of his mouth, but she had also never seen him look so serious.

She was too distraught to think about it much.

"Tobin!" She turned a circle, scanning the area. Her palms were sweating. "Tob-"

"Yeah?" Someone popped his head out from behind a tree. Someone with freckles and brown curls. "Sorry, are you calling for me?"

"Tobin!" Scarlet ran forward. "Where were you? You scared me!"

"Sorry," he apologized. "I saw something and went to investigate. I didn't hear you calling."

"How could you not hear me calling?" said Scarlet. "I was pretty loud–"

"I said I was sorry," said Tobin, cutting her off. "I got curious and went to look at something, but I'm back now."

Scarlet's brow creased. "What did you go to look at?"

Tobin waved his hand. "Just some flowers."

Scarlet frowned. "Okay. I didn't know you were into flowers."

Tobin shrugged.

"Though this reunion has been lovely," said Elowen, "I think it's time we move on. It's going to be pitch black in half an hour. We should get as far as we can before night falls and nocturnal creatures start coming out."

The group moved onward, trekking through the forest. The strange silence still sat over them, and even the trees seemed tense, like they were holding their breaths.

Scarlet wondered if Elowen felt it too. Her eyes were uneasy, flicking from left to right. Even Beck, though he continued to walk with an easy gait, kept his hand close to the hilt of the sword at his belt.

Soon, all Scarlet could see of the ground was a sheet of black. With every inch forward she felt sure she was going to step on something.

"How do you know where you're walking?" she asked the dark figure of Elowen beside her.

Elowen stopped. "That's right. You're human. You can't see."

"You can?"

"Elven vision is far superior to human vision," said Elowen. "We're able to see very well, even in the dark."

Scarlet briefly re-experienced the feeling of amazement she kept getting every time she remembered that these were actual elves, just as powerful and extraordinary as the ones she'd heard about in the stories.

Elowen lifted a shadowy hand and called, "Beck, the younglings can't see, could you–"

"Got it." Beck grunted, and suddenly there was a flash of light and a bright, glowing orb came to life above his head.

With the golden orb drifting above, Scarlet could now see at least ten feet in every direction.

Ahead, something on the ground glimmered in the orb's glow. A few steps closer and Scarlet realized that the glimmer was water. She walked toward the water's edge and looked out. They were standing on the shore of an expanse of murky wetness. It was as if the forest had flooded from Scarlet's feet out.

"It's a lagoon," she said.

"A swamp," corrected Elowen.

"How will we get through?" asked Scarlet.

Elowen smirked. "We walk," and she stepped into the water. With a squelch the swamp swallowed Elowen's foot, coming up to her shin. "It's shallow."

Scarlet eyed the swamp. "There aren't any snakes in there, are there?" she asked.

"Course there are snakes in here," said Beck, stepping in. He shot her a backward glance. "Don't worry, I won't let them swallow you."

"They won't come near the light," reassured Elowen.

"Besides, I'm sure you could take out a snake. How old are you two?" asked Beck.

"Fourteen," said Scarlet.

"Fourteen," mirrored Tobin.

Scarlet felt a prickle in her consciousness, like a maggot squirming in her mind. "I thought you were fifteen?"

"No," he shook his head, curls bouncing around his ears. "Fourteen. You must remember wrong." Scarlet frowned. Was she remembering wrong? But hadn't he told her? Hadn't he told her that second day in the dungeon–

Elowen waved her arm. "Let's keep going."

They were a strange band. The two tall figures and the two short ones, wrapped in a sheet of golden shine as they wove through the shadowy trunks and half submerged roots of the flooded forest. Silence wrapped around their container of light, and cold seeped in through the trees, stealing over the glassy surface of the water and bringing the musky, midnight smell of inevitable adventure with it.

After they'd walked for another half hour Beck said, "Let's stop here."

"Here?" asked Scarlet, staring at Beck incredulously. "We're standing in water." She gestured emphatically at the sheet of icy liquid pooled at their feet, voice echoing around the swamp. The only other sounds were the watery murmurs of their footsteps.

Beck looked at her. Even after trekking through the woods his hair was still neat: not a single strand out of place. "Sprites, you must think I'm dull as a dwarf's hammer. I meant there." He gestured to a point in the darkness.

"Where?"

Elowen and Beck sighed simultaneously. "Humans."

Scarlet scowled.

"Look," said Beck, and with a flick of his hand the orb zoomed ahead of them to illuminate a small island, about the size of a few kitchen tables pushed together.

Scarlet quickly moved toward the shifted light, hating the feeling of the darkness closing in around her, clogging her senses.

She dragged her feet out of the water and onto shore. Now, with the sweet temptation of sleep so near, she suddenly felt the weariness of the day fall over her like a thick, wool blanket.

"I'll grab some firewood," said Beck, looking around the swamp. There were small patches of dry land here and there. Scarlet hoped they would be able to find enough tinder to get a blaze going.

"Couldn't you use your magic to light a fire?" asked Scarlet.

Beck shook his head. "I would prefer not to. I'm running low. Orbs like that aren't super easy to keep up."

Scarlet blinked at him. "Your magic runs out?"

Beck's eyebrows went up. "Of course it does, I'm not a magic wand."

"I just didn't realize it worked like that," she said. "Maybe Elowen can make a fire then?"

"I can't," said Elowen, shaking her head and eyes flicking down to her hands.

"Because you're running low too?" Scarlet asked.

"I can't use magic. I was born without the ability."

Scarlet's eyes widened. "But you're an elf!"

Elowen smiled, but the smile was tainted around the edges with a hint of sadness. "It happens sometimes. I'm what's called *hollow*. It's a rare condition."

"Her work with a sword is practically magical though," butted in Beck, and Elowen's smile turned a little more genuine. She looked up at Scarlet.

"Is there a way you can get magic? Even if you weren't born with it?" Scarlet asked.

Elowen shook her head. "That's not how magic works, youngling. You're either born with it or without it. If you have it, you can practice with it, learning techniques and training your accuracy, but you can't develop a wick if you were born without one."

"A wick?" Scarlet asked, eyebrows raising.

Beck shook his head. "I keep forgetting you don't know anything about this yet. When you can use magic, you have a wick. At least, that's the branch of magic us elves have. Basically, a wick dictates how long you can use your magic for. Once you go through your wick, you have to wait for it to recover before you can do magic again."

"So, a human can never be born with a wick?"

"No," Elowen shook her head. "Humans are never born with magical abilities, nor can they ever get them."

"Except–" Beck began.

"Avenbeck." Elowen turned threatening eyes to him.

He put his hands in the air in mock surrender. "Sorry, sorry. My tongue is tied."

Scarlet opened her mouth to ask another question, but Tobin interrupted. "Firewood?"

Scarlet looked at him, surprised he'd stop such an interesting conversation. He didn't return her look.

"Right," said Beck, turning to the swamp.

"You guys are in all that armor," said Tobin. "Let Scarlet and I do it."

Elowen and Beck exchanged uneasy glances before Elowen opened her mouth. "I think it would be more logical for the two of you to stay here. Just because we haven't come across trouble yet doesn't mean it's not out there."

"We won't go far," said Tobin. He sounded almost pleading. "We'll stay where we can see the orb and we can yell to you if something happens."

Elowen shook her head, "I'm afraid that wouldn't be safe."

"If something were going to attack us it would have already," said Tobin. He looked to Scarlet, asking for help with his eyes.

She bit her lip. "We won't go far."

Elowen's face softened. "Well, we've never been attacked here on past journeys." She seemed to be talking to herself. "I'll let you go for two minutes, but stay where you can see the orb, and come back when we call for you."

Tobin nodded. "Let's go."

Scarlet followed him off the island and into the water, eyes combing the small patches of dry land for sticks or anything that could be used as kindling. Tobin walked in front of her, his footsteps like squelchy moans.

"Aren't we getting a little far?" Scarlet asked after a minute. She paused in her tracks.

"We can still see the orb," Tobin replied.

True, thought Scarlet, but it was small and the conversation the elves were having was faint.

"Besides," Tobin continued. "Beck and Ellow can come help us if we need."

Scarlet frowned. "Ellow? Do you mean Elowen?"

"Yeah," he said, shaking his head. "My bad. This swamp is psyching me out. I guess it's making me nervous."

But he didn't look nervous. She couldn't see him very well in the dark, but he looked completely relaxed as he led them deeper into the swamp's maw. His arms swung loosely at his sides.

Scarlet stopped walking.

Tobin heard her footsteps stop and turned to her. "What?"

"You know, I was just thinking about the day we met," said Scarlet carefully. "Remember? When you almost ran into me in the market?"

"Oh yeah," laughed Tobin, and his laughter sent spiders down her spine.

"You're not Tobin," she whispered.

"What?" he asked, taking a small step closer to her. "What did you say?"

She stood as tall and straight as she could, almost his height. She could see his eyes. There was a cold glimmer in them that had never been there before. "I want to go back."

He eyed her and her palms began to sweat. Then he took another step forward, closing the distance between them. They stood face to face.

"How did you figure it out?" And now the voice was not Tobin's. It was crackly, rough, raw–like breaking glass.

"I didn't meet Tobin in the market," said Scarlet, then she turned and ran.

A scaly hand grabbed her arm and yanked her backward, hurling her into the swamp. She landed on her back, shallow water surging in around her, but she kept her head up.

She flipped over, opening her mouth to yell, and then her head was forced into the swamp.

Scarlet choked, inhaling water through her mouth and nose. She bucked into the air. The thing that was not Tobin pulled her upward from the back of her shirt.

Again, she tried to scream, but its hand clamped over her mouth and the shriek lost its breath and died.

"Scarlet? Tobin?" Elowen's voice came from the distance. "Are you alright?"

Scarlet struggled to speak against her captor's grip, but when her voice answered it did not come from her mouth.

"We're fine! I just fell down."

Where had her voice come from?

She tried to twist around, but she couldn't. Not-Tobin was too strong.

"Head back this way," came Beck's voice. "I can't see you through the trees, and this swamp gives me the shivers."

This was her salvation. They would come find her when she didn't return. She went limp in Not-Tobin's arms.

Then something moved in the trees. She squinted before her eyes went wide. The movement was *her*. Her–skipping through the trees toward the light. She could actually see her own black hair bouncing around her shoulders, her own feet running across the swamp. Behind Not-Scarlet trailed another Not-Tobin.

Scarlet just had time to think *how many of them are there?* Before something hit the back of her head and she blinked out like an extinguished candle.

Chapter 9

"Scarlet?"

Scarlet floated in nothing. She was drifting. She was spinning. She was wheeling through space.

"Scarlet!"

She wrenched her eyes open. The world she came alive to was almost as dark as the one she had woken up from. Everything was pitch black. She tried to rub her eyes but found she couldn't. Her arms were bound to her sides and her back was against something hard. What was going on? She felt fuzzy. Her mind was blank.

"Scarlet, are you awake? It's me."

And with Tobin's voice Scarlet remembered. "Stay away from me!" She tried to pull away from his voice but realized more than her hands were tied down. A rope was wrapped around her stomach, attaching her to the hard surface she was sitting against. It seemed she might be bound to some sort of pole. "I know you're not the real Tobin!"

"Scarlet, it's actually me now."

She couldn't see anything, but it sounded like he was behind her.

"I'm tied up too," he said. "On the other side of the post."

"I don't trust you."

"Why would I be tied up if I was one of the monsters?"

"As a trick?"

"Scarlet, they don't need to trick you. I hate to break it to you, but I think you're caught."

It did seem like Tobin, but Scarlet couldn't see him to tell if he really was tied up. Sure, it seemed the monsters would have no reason to trick her, but she could still feel the terror of realizing Tobin wasn't Tobin. She needed proof. "Tell me something only Tobin would know."

"Um..." he fell silent. Scarlet assumed he was thinking. "The first time I saw you was in the dungeon. You were crying, so I gave you my handkerchief. Then the elves came in and started questioning you, and you looked the one in charge straight in the eyes like you weren't even afraid, and I thought you might be the bravest person I'd ever met."

Scarlet blushed. She was suddenly very glad they couldn't see each other.

"Is that enough for you?"

"Yeah," she replied. "It's you. What do we do? What even were those things that got us?" Although she was relieved that Tobin was really Tobin this time, she was still panicked. She felt like she had an ocean in her stomach. The waves and whirlpools were making her sick and shaky.

"I've decided on calling them Mimic Monsters," said Tobin. "A pair of them snatched me in the forest while Beck was talking about The Spire. Then they sent a mimic of me to sabotage you guys: split you up so they could grab one person at a time. I heard them talking about it. They were trying to lure you away first, then they were going to try to separate Beck and Elowen before attacking them. I don't know if they actually got them though."

"Do you know where we are?"

"Some sort of camp. We're in a tent right now. I think we left The Cusp because we were in plains when I woke up. I was unconscious for a little while though."

Scarlet frowned. "We can't be too far from where we were before then, because when I was on the griffin I saw the plains right after the forest."

"Maybe Elowen and Beck will come save us?" said Tobin hopefully.

"Think again, human." A piece of the darkness peeled away from the tent wall as two shadowed figures entered. Shadowed figures that were far too tall and lanky. Scarlet shrunk away from them.

Then the flap closed, and the darkness returned, leaving Scarlet and Tobin blind with the monsters.

"We've apprehended your elven friends." The monster's voice came from somewhere in the blackness. It was rough and smooth all at once. "They were only too happy to rush straight into an ambush when you and Tobin ran off together into the woods."

Scarlet wanted to close her eyes and curl into a ball. To whimper and hide. But she couldn't. She straightened her shoulders and tried to steel herself. *I am not afraid,* she told herself, gritting her teeth. *I might be the bravest person Tobin has ever met.*

She stared the dark in the eyes. She couldn't tell where the monster was, but she could hear it breathing. "Let us go!"

The darkness laughed and then it grabbed her face. The scaly hand gripped her cheeks, forcing her chin up. "You're a feisty one. But there is a thin line between feisty and foolish. Be sure not to step over."

Tobin let out a strangled sound and Scarlet could only guess the second monster had grabbed him too.

The voice next to Scarlet spoke. She could feel its breath on her, but still couldn't see it. "This one is frail." Her head was thrust left, then right, and she let out a wordless cry of indignation. "But she has a pretty face." It seemed as though the monster must be able to see her. Maybe it had eyes like the elves. "And this black hair," the hand stroked her head, sifting through her black locks with its fingers. "Rare to find hair quite this dark. We can get some good furs for this one I bet."

"Can't say the same for the male," grunted the second monster. "He's strong, but skinny. I doubt we'll get anything more than a couple rabbit skins for him."

"We'll pawn him to the orcs," said the one before Scarlet. "They're not picky. It doesn't need to look pretty if you're going to eat it."

Both monsters laughed as though a joke had been made. The laughter was metal forks scraping against glass plates. Scarlet wished she could cover her ears.

"You're going to... sell us?" she asked as the hand let her go.

"We're going to try," said the monster closest to her. "Welcome to the Hinterland, human."

And then there was the sound of footsteps, and before Scarlet even got to see the monsters' faces, the tent flap opened and closed. They were gone.

Scarlet and Tobin sat in silence for a few moments.

Finally, Tobin spoke. "I'm worth more than a few rabbit furs."

"Is that seriously what you're worried about right now?" said Scarlet. Before the monsters had come in, the ocean in her stomach had made her feel queasy, now it was surging up into her chest. Soon it would rush through her throat and explode out of her, and she would drown in it.

"No," Tobin sniped back. "I'm most worried about getting eaten, but I didn't want to be discouraging!"

There was a flash of light and the flap opened and closed so fast Scarlet didn't even see who'd come through.

There was silence and Scarlet and Tobin waited for the new arrival to introduce themselves. When they didn't, Scarlet gathered her courage and opened her mouth. "Hello?" She desperately hoped it wasn't one of the monsters, returning to reexamine her or Tobin.

There was a rustle in the darkness.

"Hello?" Scarlet asked again, a little louder than before.

She peered into the black. "Hel–"

And then she froze as she felt something cold and sharp against her throat. Scarlet sucked in her breath, trying to pull away but trapped by the solid surface at her back.

"Quiet," whispered a voice in her ear, so low she almost didn't hear it. It was an unrecognizable voice: female, and sounding older than Scarlet.

"What's going on?" Tobin said. "Who's there?"

Scarlet tried to reply but surrendered to the pressure at her neck, swallowing her words.

"Scarlet are you alright?" He sounded like he was starting to panic.

Then the voice spoke again. "You're going to get me caught." The voice was still quiet, but loud enough this time for Tobin to hear. He fell silent.

So this wasn't a friend of the monsters? Did that make her a friend of Scarlet's, or just another enemy to add to the list?

"I am going to remove my knife," said the voice slowly. "And if you make a noise, you'll regret it."

And just like that, the cold point was gone and Scarlet took a deep, relieved breath.

She bit her lip. She could hear the person moving around in the darkness. "Can you help us?" she whispered.

Tobin groaned.

"What did I just say?" The words were sharper than the knife had been. "If I get caught because of you I will kill you before they do."

"I'm sorry," whispered Scarlet. "But we need help."

"Not my problem," replied the voice.

There was some shuffling, then something in the dark opened. It sounded like a chest of some sort. There were rummaging sounds, and then it closed. Scarlet heard footsteps go past her, getting closer to the tent exit.

"So, you're really going to leave us here?" said Scarlet. It was her last chance. "Two kids, being held prisoner in a camp of monsters? They're going to sell Tobin to the orcs!"

The footsteps stopped. The voice cursed quietly, then suddenly Scarlet heard movement and there was a yank on Scarlet's stomach. The rope fell away so suddenly Scarlet wondered if it had been slashed through.

"Thank you," she said, starting to stand up, but the tent flap was closing and the voice and its owner were gone.

Something touched her arm, and she jumped.

"It's just me," said Tobin. "She got me out too. Are you ready to make a run for it?"

"One thing first," said Scarlet. "We need a code word." It was a concept she'd been thinking on since she'd first realized what the monsters were capable of. "That way, if we get separated out there, they can't play the same trick and mimic us. We'll use the code word to identify each other."

"Got it," said Tobin. "What's the code word then?"

"It can't be something they could guess."

"Spoon?"

Scarlet frowned. "That's the first word that came to mind?"

"I'm hungry."

She grinned and shook her head. "I was thinking pumpernickel."

"Like that one kind of bread?"

She nodded, then remembered that Tobin wouldn't be able to see her nod in the dark and amended with, "Yeah."

"You're hungry too then?"

She stifled a laugh with the back of her hand.

"Alright," said Tobin. "If we're split up and reunited one of us will ask for the code word and one of us will answer with it, and then we'll know that we're, you know, us."

Scarlet took a deep breath. "I'm scared." They stood in the blanket of darkness, and who knew what lay beyond the black? Who knew what they faced outside the tent? Mimic Monsters for certain, but after that, miles and miles of Hinterland, with no Beck or Elowen to protect them.

She could hear Tobin shifting in front of her. "We'll be okay, we just have to stand straight and go for it. It's like I tell my sisters, sometimes you have to face the dragon to find the treasure."

Scarlet frowned, trying to see how the saying fit their situation, "What's the treasure in this scenario?"

He was silent for a couple moments. "Not dying?"

"That's good enough for me," she conceded, appreciating his attempt at encouraging her even though her fingertips were still tingling with nervous energy.

They were quiet for a few seconds, as though both stalling their exit. Then he cleared his throat and said, "Ready?"

"Yup," she stepped toward the spot where she thought the entrance, or her exit, was located. "I found the flap."

She pushed it and stepped out onto grass. They were in the center of a camp, tents scattered around them in seemingly random places. The sky was pitch black, but a flickering light was coming through a pair of tents. She could see shadows playing across their canvas sides.

Creeping to peer between them she saw that the Mimic Monsters were around a large fire in the center of their camp, laughing and feasting on what seemed to be the corpse of a horse. Their backs were to Scarlet and Tobin.

"Let's go," said Scarlet, and she tugged Tobin around their tent. It was on the edge of the camp, and when they rounded the other side they faced open Hinterland. It was laid out before them: a long plain, stretching as far as they could see. To their left, not more than a mile and a half away, were the mountains Scarlet had seen from the griffins earlier. They loomed over the camp, sending shivers down Scarlet's spine. The closest one looked odd, jutting out in places Scarlet wouldn't have expected, but in the darkness she couldn't see any details.

Tobin looked back at the camp and then took a step into the plains. "Wait," said Scarlet. "We should check these other tents on the edge. If they really did get Beck or Elowen, then maybe they're near here."

He looked hesitant, glancing out to the Hinterland, then back to the camp, then toward the Hinterland again. "Yeah, you're right." He and Scarlet crouched behind the tent.

"I'll check the tents on the left," whispered Scarlet. "You check the ones on the right."

Tobin nodded. "Make sure to stay to the edge. Don't try to check any farther in, or we'll get caught for sure. Meet back here. And code word when we get back."

Scarlet nodded, then she turned and carefully tiptoed to the edge of the tent. She glanced toward the direction of the fire. She couldn't see it, but she also didn't see any movement, so she quickly darted from her cover to the shelter of the next canvas frame.

She wasn't sure how to check for Beck and Elowen. If she went inside the tent, she risked the chance of running into a monster, but she also didn't want to miss the elves if they were here. She settled for pressing her ear against the canvas. She didn't hear anything, so she moved on, darting behind the next tent.

Nothing.

And to the next one–nothing.

And to the next one–nothing.

And to the next one–"Holy sprites, seriously, could they have made these any tighter?"

Scarlet smiled, a rush of relief flooding through her, diffusing her sparking nerves.

"We need to get out and find Scarlet." Scarlet recognized Elowen's voice.

"Agreed," now it was Beck again. "If we don't make it back to the fortress soon, we'll miss breakfast."

"Can you be serious for two seconds?"

"Thaw off, I'm working on the ropes, and keeping optimistic isn't making me any slower."

"It's not making you any faster, either."

"You know, has anyone ever told you how mean you get in near-death situations?"

"Focus."

"I am focused–"

They both froze as the flap came open. Elowen's mouth parted. "Scarlet, is that you?"

Scarlet nodded, almost crying in relief at seeing their faces. She stood in the tent entrance, looking in on them. They were tied to the tent's central post, just as she and Tobin had been, but they had been mummy-wrapped in rope. It seemed that with elves, the monsters weren't taking any risks. "It's me, promise. You're Elowen, and that's Beck, and we just escaped from a dungeon not too long ago with a whole bunch of other elves, but they didn't make it, and–"

"That's enough," Elowen nodded. "It's really you."

Scarlet nodded again, studying the rope holding them down. "You couldn't use magic to escape?"

Beck shook his head. "They slapped some magic-resistant cuffs on me. Elowen too, they didn't realize she's hollow. We won't be able to get these off till we get back to the fortress. You escaped?"

"Well," Scarlet hesitated. "Sort of."

He grinned. "Legendary. Alright, come in here."

"But if I come in the tent flap will close and it'll be too dark to see."

"But we can still see," reminded Elowen. "Hurry."

Scarlet stepped into the tent, letting the flap fall and darkness descend on her.

"In my shoe is a knife," said Beck. "I need you to get it."

Scarlet felt around in the dark.

"No–no Scarlet, that's my knee. Farther down. To the left a little."

She shifted.

"More left. There you go."

She felt his shoe.

"Just against the side." She slipped her hand into his shoe. It smelled like swamp and she pulled a disgusted face.

"I can see that, you know."

Scarlet stopped making the face. Her fingers hit something, and she pulled out what felt like a folded pocketknife.

"You're going to have to open it." He sounded serious this time. "Be careful. Don't cut yourself."

Carefully, she felt along the grooves and slowly opened it.

"Good, cut me free."

Scarlet knelt down and felt for the rope. She began to saw through it. Her hands were sweaty and the knife slipped. There was a sharp intake of breath from Beck.

"Are you okay?" Scarlet asked, eyes widening. "Did I cut you?"

"It's fine," he said. "Keep going."

She sawed at the rope and suddenly the knife went through it and Beck pulled free. She heard him stand up, then he took the knife from her hands.

A couple seconds later she heard Elowen say, "Thanks."

Light flooded into the tent and Scarlet gasped, thinking they were caught, but it was only Beck opening the flap. He nodded toward the exit, slipping out with Elowen and Scarlet behind him.

"This way," whispered Scarlet, and she led them behind the tent, around the edge, and to where Tobin was waiting.

A look of relief flashed over Tobin's face the second he saw them, but Scarlet didn't let her guard down. "Code word?"

Tobin smiled. "Pumpernickel."

"Huh?" asked Beck.

Scarlet opened her mouth to explain when a yell went up from the camp.

"They realized we're gone," said Elowen.

"Find them!" someone bellowed from the forest of tents.

"That's our cue to go," said Beck.

In an instant the entire camp was in uproar, the yells bludgeoning Scarlet's ears.

"Wait, look." Elowen pointed. Down the row of tents, still to the edge of the camp, a pair of horses were tied to posts.

Beck, Scarlet, and Tobin nodded, understanding right away. Scarlet glanced toward the noise just once before sprinting for the horses. It took the group only a few seconds to reach them. Beck and Elowen began to free the mares, untying the ropes keeping them in place.

A sudden cry went up from the camp. "I got someone!"

Scarlet and Tobin froze. They looked at each other, understanding flashing between them.

"We can't leave her–" started Scarlet.

"Scarlet, we can't go in there," said Tobin, looking at her with the desperation of a person who already knows they're losing the argument.

"She saved us," said Scarlet. "We can't let her get caught because of us!"

"What are you talking about?" asked Elowen, registering their argument for the first time. She was holding the horse's reins in one hand.

"Someone helped us get out," said Tobin. "A girl. We don't even know what she looks like, it was too dark to see."

Beck glanced toward the camp. "We don't have much time."

"Scarlet wants to go back for her," said Tobin.

"She let us go!" repeated Scarlet. "And now they've found her because of our escape." She had to shout to be heard over the yells in the camp. "I'm going back for her."

"I'm sorry, I can't allow it," said Elowen. "Let's ride." She mounted her horse, facing the open Hinterland. Beck mounted next to her. Scarlet turned toward the camp.

"Don't do it–" started Tobin.

And Scarlet was running.

She had no plan. She had no idea what she was doing. She was no longer sure she even had an ounce of sanity remaining in her head. All she knew was that someone who had saved her was in trouble for it, and she wasn't going to leave her like she'd left that elf to bleed on the castle floor. She wouldn't do it again.

"Scarlet, stop!" Beck's voice was behind her. She was sure he would have caught her by now if not for the delay of getting off his horse.

She burst between tents. An explosion of sound erupted to her left, and she veered toward it, flying through an opening–and another–and stopping so suddenly she almost fell flat on her face.

She had come to the center of the camp where she'd seen the campfire only ten minutes before. The monsters were ringing the space, howling, waving weapons, gnashing their teeth–it was the first time she'd seen them undisguised, and she wished she hadn't.

They were rubbery, pale white, and bald. Their eyes were black and lined with scales, and they had small fangs protruding from thick lips. They looked like they could take Scarlet out just by looking at her wrong, so it was lucky that they were completely distracted.

They were in chaos, and the cause of it, in the center of them all, was a blur of vivid red. Monsters threw themselves at it, and it cut them down like lightning. Scarlet caught sight of a dagger before it was in and out of a monster's chest.

It had to be the girl from the tent, but she no longer seemed like a girl at all. She was a demon contained in a body. A force to be reckoned with. A sharp-edged storm.

She was death come alive.

The monsters jabbed at her with spears and she dodged the stabs, leaping over blades, ducking under punches, moving so fast it seemed like magic. It looked like she was going double speed and the monsters were in slow motion.

Scarlet was so entranced it took her a moment to realize Elowen, Beck, and Tobin were behind her, also hypnotized by the massacre.

Tobin's mouth hung open slightly.

Elowen looked stunned.

Beck looked speechless, something that Scarlet was sure didn't happen often.

A monster yelled and Scarlet jumped backward as it fell to the ground in front of her.

The monsters crumpled around the girl like blades of grass she was slicing and throwing to the wind. In less than a minute she stood alone, the bodies of her enemies strewn around her, lying bloody in the clovers.

For the first time Scarlet got a good look at her. She was tall and lithe with wine-red hair streaming down her back. She wore a leather jacket with fitted, brown pants and a belt with loops for the two daggers in her fists. Her eyes were deep brown, almost purple, and she couldn't be more than eighteen. She was beautiful in an intense, dangerous way, a sentiment that perfectly matched the expression she was wearing.

"I don't know whether to be impressed or afraid," whispered Tobin.

"Both," Beck and Scarlet whispered back simultaneously.

And then Scarlet's eyes went wide. "Behind you!"

The Hinterland

A wounded monster had gotten to its feet, sprinting toward the girl, who whipped around and slammed both her daggers deep into its chest. It grunted, a look of shock frozen on its face, and fell into the grass.

The girl cursed. The monster had cut her arm, slicing through her leather sleeve. She slid the daggers into her belt, ripped a piece of cloth off the shirt she was wearing under the jacket, and, so fast Scarlet wondered how many times she'd done it before, tied it around her sleeve, not even bothering to take off the jacket first.

It was only then that she realized she had an audience.

Her daggers were back in her hands so fast it was like they'd teleported there.

"Wait!" Scarlet, put her hands up. "Remember me? You saved me and my friend from the tent. We were prisoners."

A flash of realization crossed the girl's face. It had been too dark in the tent to see, but Scarlet assumed the girl recognized her voice. Even so, the daggers did not lower.

"I thought you would have gotten out of here by now," said the girl, eyes wary.

"We had to save our friends first," said Scarlet, gesturing toward the elves. "And then we thought you were in trouble, so we came back to help."

The girl shook her fiery hair out of her face and scowled. "That's the kind of thing that'll get you killed out here."

"Oh–um–" Scarlet didn't know how to reply to that statement. She turned to the elves, hoping they might know what to say, but found them deep in whispered conversation.

"That's the kind of person we need–" Beck was saying when he realized Scarlet was watching him.

He turned to face the girl, who was finally sliding her blades back into her belt. "Hey, I'm Beck," he stepped toward her, crossing the distance between them and holding out his hand. "Nice to meet you."

The girl's hands flashed away from his so quickly it was like they'd been stung. "I don't shake hands." Her face was tight as she looked him up and down. She was sizing him up, and she wasn't trying to hide it.

"Okay," he said, sticking one hand in his pocket and ruffling his own hair with the other. "That's alright, I'm not big into handshakes either. You never know where people's hands have been. Anyway, that was pretty impressive." He gestured around at the corpses littering the clearing.

The girl raised a single eyebrow.

"What's your name?" he asked.

She eyed him for a moment. "You don't need my name."

He blinked, but continued without argument. "Alright. You alone out here?"

"None of your business." She began to turn away from him and he reached out to grab her arm.

She whipped around to face him, dagger suddenly in her fist. The blade stopped an inch from his throat and Scarlet's stomach dropped. "Don't touch me."

"Sorry," he backed up a step. "I only wanted to say that you could come with us if you're out here alone. We're going somewhere safe."

Scarlet, who had been watching the interaction, turned to Elowen. "Aren't you in charge? Why don't you try to talk to her?"

"Beck's better with people than I am," Elowen replied. "He has a better chance at this than I do."

"I don't think going anywhere with strangers is safe," replied the red-head, mouth a flat line. "Especially not in the Hinterland."

"We're with a group," he replied. "You probably haven't heard of us, but I'm sure you'll have heard about who we're fighting–the Wraith and her army?"

The red-head shook her head.

Beck's eyebrows rose in surprise. "You haven't heard anything at all? How long have you been out here?" A corner of his lips quirked upward, the tease evident on his face.

"Five years." She looked at him, her mouth taut, arms crossed.

Beck did a double-take and Elowen's eyes went wider than usual.

"No one can survive in The Hinterland alone for five years," said Beck.

"I can," the red-head replied. "And not by joining strange groups." She walked to the edge of the clearing and grabbed a small bag from the ground. "I have what I need. Have a good evening." And she walked between a pair of tents and out of sight.

Elowen and Beck looked stunned.

Scarlet and Tobin glanced at each other.

"What's that?" asked Tobin, focusing on a spot behind Scarlet's shoulder. She turned. Through the tents, out on the plains, she could see a cloud of dust.

Scarlet squinted at it. "Beck, Elowen, look."

They turned and peered at the cloud.

Elowen's face sharpened. "We've got to go."

Beck went pale. "Those are orcs."

They turned and ran for the horses. Beck swung onto his ride and Tobin mounted behind him. Elowen pulled Scarlet up in front of her.

With a jerk of the reins and a kick the horses were flying, speeding away from the Mimic Monster camp. With the powerful beast moving under her, Scarlet felt capable of conquering the world, but the feeling was diminishing as the cloud behind them came closer. In the light from the horizon, where the sun was just beginning to rise, she could almost make out figures.

From where she was sitting Scarlet could see a flash of red move on the plains. "The girl! They're going to get the girl."

"I'll get her, you take Scarlet," Beck called to Elowen.

Elowen nodded, face set. The horse charged onward as Beck's mare peeled off in an opposite direction.

"Do you think she'll come?" asked Scarlet.

"Maybe," answered Elowen.

"Why do you two want her so bad?" asked Scarlet.

"After seeing her capabilities? Of course, we want her on our side. She eliminated an entire encampment of monsters."

Scarlet glanced back. "They're getting closer!" She could now see hulking figures riding on howling, loping creatures–creatures that seemed to be faster than horses.

Elowen leaned forward. "We're close."

The mountain was rising up in front of them. The base of it couldn't be more than a mile away. Now she could see what had made it look so strange before. Towers, balconies, and flags were rising out of the stone from random places. It looked like a castle had been plucked from the earth, rolled into a ball, and smeared against the mountain.

"That's the fortress?"

"I'm going to need some quiet," Elowen snapped.

Scarlet fell silent. The wind was whipping past her. The sky was streaked pink.

And then all at once she could hear the orcs behind them and the snarling of the beasts they were riding.

Where were Beck and Tobin? Had the orcs gotten them? Bile rose up in Scarlet's throat. *Not when we're this close. Please, not when we're this close.*

She could see the beasts in clarity now. They were black and sinewy, with whipping tails and snapping jaws. The orcs on top of them were huge with broad shoulders and dark eyes. They were only a stone's throw away.

Now a smaller stone's throw–

Now a really small stone's throw.

We're going to get caught. Right here. Right in front of the fortress. She closed her eyes.

And then something collided with the side of the horse. Scarlet screamed as one of mounted beasts charged into them—and then again as a second slammed into the horse's other side. The orc atop the first creature pulled back its arm, spear in hand. It prepared to let loose—before both the spear and the orc's head fell to the ground.

Elowen pulled back her blade and lashed out at the orc on the other side. She cut it down, but the beasts were still clawing at the horse's sides, and more orcs were flooding in to fill the spots of the fallen.

Zinnng.

Scarlet ducked, hiding her head under her arms. That was a sound she recognized.

"Stay down," called Elowen. "They're shooting!"

"The orcs are shooting?" Scarlet yelled, voice muffled.

"No, our side is shooting," shouted Elowen. "They're trying to help."

Zinnng. Zinnng. Zinnng.

The orcs were falling away. The beasts were shrinking back. The horse was breaking free, charging forward.

It sped on, less than half a mile away from the start of the mountain's incline. There was an explosion of color from the rocky base and people began flooding from it like a roaring wave.

Now the orcs were in full retreat, but the crowd kept coming. They were shouting, but these were not the bloodthirsty shouts of the orcs, or the terrified shouts of the Mimic Monsters as they'd died. These were happy shouts. Victorious shouts.

The horse galloped toward the crowd—the crowd ran toward the horse—and then the two collided.

Suddenly Scarlet was in a sea of voices, a sea of faces, a sea of hands that were reaching for her. She felt like her ears had gone numb. Her eyes blurred over the people, seeing only patches of color.

Elowen turned to her. She smiled–one of her rare, genuine smiles. "Welcome to the fortress, Scarlet."

Chapter 10

The crowd was an ocean, surging around Scarlet, and the horse was her island, keeping her from going under.

"Back up!" called Elowen, but the ocean was not obedient. The waves grabbed at Scarlet. Hands were on her, people were yelling, she didn't know which way to look.

Elowen leapt from her horse, waving her knife above her head. "Back away!"

This time the crowd backed up. They still circled around Scarlet, but they remained a few feet from her horse, staring at her as though she was the main attraction at a circus.

Elowen began to walk, leading the horse behind her. The crowd parted to make a path for them. At the base of the mountain was a large archway, which Elowen led the horse through.

Looking up Scarlet could see that a portcullis had been raised and the archway must usually be blocked off.

On the other side was a long hallway with a high ceiling. The walls were of cobbled stone and lit with torches.

"Get off here," said Elowen.

Scarlet slid off the horse.

Elowen turned to face the crowd, who was following a few feet behind them. "Friends," she paused to let the talking hush. "I understand that you are anxious to meet the newcomer. We have waited a long time for this moment. However, you must be patient for a while longer. It has been a long journey, and we must get her settled. Please, return to your daily duties."

Protests rose from the crowd: protests from everywhere and everyone, and just as Scarlet thought the noise might drown her, Elowen grabbed her arm and yanked her through a hallway door Scarlet hadn't even realized was there. Elowen locked the door behind them. They were now in another hallway, this one smaller than the one before, but otherwise exactly the same.

Scarlet could hear clamoring on the other side of the door, and the doorknob rattled.

"Follow me," Elowen said, walking down the hallway. "You have to meet the Council, but I'll take you to get a clean set of clothes first."

Scarlet looked down at her outfit. It was unrecognizable as the outfit she'd been wearing that last night at her house. It was caked in dirt and sand, stained with grass stains, and damp with sweat. Not to mention the stench, which was nothing like Scarlet had ever smelled. She was wearing a completely brand-new odor: Scent of the Hinterland. The thought almost made her laugh. A new outfit wasn't a bad idea.

But Scarlet had other things to worry about.

"What about Tobin, Beck, and that girl?" asked Scarlet. "Are they alright? I didn't see them."

"I saw them," said Elowen, and Scarlet let out an internal sigh of relief. "I'll get you a pair of clothes, then I'll figure out where they went while you get dressed."

Scarlet nodded as Elowen continued to lead her down the passage. "You said I have to meet the Council, what's the Council?"

"The Council is the head of this whole operation. It's made up of a representative for each population living here. There's a representative for the Sun Elves, Crescent Elves, High Elves, Forest Elves, nymphs, dwarves, and humans. They hold authority over all decisions made in relation to the fortress and the war with the Wraith."

They started up a set of stairs.

"Who's the Wraith?" asked Scarlet. She'd heard Elowen say the name multiple times.

"That's for the Council to explain. I have explicit instructions to let them tell you about the cause."

Scarlet nodded, biting her lip as she realized that she was about to meet elves, a dwarf, a nymph, and a human representative all at once.

"Here we are." Elowen opened a door in the hallway. She rummaged inside for a couple moments, then she pulled out a clean tunic and trousers. "These look your size."

"Where are these from?" Scarlet asked, taking them from Elowen.

She gave a small, apologetic smile. "Lost and found. Don't worry though, we'll get you a new wardrobe. We couldn't prepare anything before because we didn't know enough about you."

Scarlet nodded.

"You can change in there," said Elowen, pointing to a door. "When you're finished just wait here; I'll come get you after I check on what's happening with the others."

Scarlet stepped into the room. It was a bathroom with a washbasin in the corner, a chamber pot to the side, and a mirror on the wall. She pulled on the tunic, which was baggy on her, and the trousers, which happened to be just her size. She felt out of place wearing other people's clothes. She felt out of place standing in a fortress full of elves, nymphs, and dwarves. She felt out of place being welcomed by a crowd like she was a hero when really, she was just a fourteen-year-old girl with no idea what was going on.

She looked at herself in the mirror. Her hair was a mess. She tried to straighten it with her fingers. When she was done, it looked a little better, but not much.

Scarlet stepped back out into the hallway and paced up and down while she waited for Elowen. Soon the elf rounded the corner.

"Let's go see the Council."

"Are the others okay?" Scarlet asked, rushing to her side and following her down the hallway and up a flight of stairs.

"Beck is in the infirmary–" started Elowen.

Scarlet's eyes widened. "Is he alright? Did the orcs hurt him?"

"He's fine," said Elowen. "Just a cut on his arm. Probably from the escape in the tent."

Scarlet had almost forgotten the knife slipping from her grasp while she was cutting Beck free. She felt the weight of guilt drop in her stomach like a rock. She hadn't even noticed the cut in their escape.

"Don't worry," said Elowen, who must have read the feelings on her face. "Knowing Beck he's most likely just annoyed that he's not in on the action. He'll be fine. The red-head is with him too. They dragged her there when they saw the cut the monster gave her."

Scarlet felt the weight in her stomach lessen, but only slightly. "What about Tobin?"

Elowen opened her mouth, closed it, opened it again and said, "I'll tell you later."

"Why?" asked Scarlet, instantly worried.

"He's fine," said Elowen, "but we're about to enter the Council Room." She gestured to a door in the wall.

"This little hallway is the entrance to the Council Room?" Scarlet asked. It felt too unimportant for a fortress that seemed so grand and expansive.

"It's a side entrance. We can't take the main hallway, it's full right now with people trying to see you."

Scarlet didn't think she would ever get used to the feeling of being important.

The Hinterland

"Here we go," said Elowen, and before Scarlet could stop her to ask for one more minute, two more minutes, another hour or the entire day to catch her breath and prepare herself, Elowen swung the door open.

She stepped in, and Scarlet followed behind.

The room was large. In fact, it was massive. Directly above her head hung a chandelier draped in jewels, so far above that the precious stones were nothing more than glinting dots. To the back of the room was a tall, semi-circle stand. There were seven seats atop it and a podium before each, all facing huge double doors. Scarlet could hear noise behind the doors and had a feeling they were the main entrance. Each seat was occupied, but all seven figures stood as Scarlet and Elowen entered.

Elowen led Scarlet to the center of the floor, directly in front of the half-circle stand.

She cleared her throat. "May I introduce Scarlet Mount."

There was silence. Then all at once the standing spectators began to clap, the sound echoing around the room. Scarlet blushed looking from smiling face to smiling face.

"Nice to meet you, Scarlet," came a voice from the seat on the far left of the stand. The person speaking was a pale female with blonde hair falling down her shoulders. "I am Nylla, Forest Elf Representative." She spoke with a calm, clear, almost musical lilt to her voice.

"Nice to meet you," said Scarlet.

"Just listen," whispered Elowen. "Let them introduce themselves, you don't need to reply."

"Greetings, youngling," came the second voice. The next in line on the table was a male elf with long black hair, his ears particularly sharp. "I am Raynon, Sun Elf Representative."

Scarlet nodded to him.

"Welcome, Scarlet," said the next elf. He wore a long purple cape. "I am Eldritch, Crescent Elf Representative." He smiled at her warmly and Scarlet found herself smiling back. He had shoulder-length gray hair and wrinkles around his eyes. "Congratulations on a successful mission," Eldritch added, looking to Elowen.

Elowen nodded curtly. She was standing slightly behind Scarlet with her hands behind her back.

"Scarlet, good to meet you at last." The next elf was speaking. His spot was at the center of the stand. Looking at him it took Scarlet's breath away just how similar he appeared to Beck. He had the same hair, though his was gray at the roots, the same disarming smile, and even the same green eyes, though his might have been a shade darker than Beck's.

"I am Deimos, the High Elf Representative." His words even had the same smooth delivery as Beck's did.

"Are you Beck's dad?" She remembered only after she asked that she was supposed to be keeping quiet.

The High Elf nodded. "That I am."

"Isn't Beck in the infirmary?" asked the Crescent Elf Representative–Eldritch she remembered. "If you wish to go to him, feel free. We can welcome Scarlet without you."

Deimos shook his head, "It's quite alright, Eldritch, as a member of this Council and the current head of the Lotus Line, I feel that it is my duty to help greet Scarlet."

The Lotus Line? Scarlet looked to Elowen, hoping for clarification. The elf shook her head slightly in a way that told Scarlet now was not the time.

"Hello Scarlet, I'm Wren," now the person to Deimos' left was speaking: a woman with short brown hair and wrinkles. She was smiling at Scarlet with what might have been pride in her eyes. "I'm the Human Representative. I'm more than overjoyed to meet you."

"I'm Burk," came the next voice. The next representative was over a foot smaller than everyone else at the table, but thicker than them all. He extended his arms and raised his eyebrows, making a face that suggested he knew the clarification was unnecessary: "Dwarf." His voice was gruff, but not unkind.

"And I'm Thayla," said the last person at the table. "The queen of the nymphs. Welcome." Thayla had hair just as dark black as Scarlet's, but thicker and flowing down her back. The tips were blue. She held herself like she was someone who had always been in charge and expected she always would be.

Scarlet nodded to her.

The Council members sat down, all except for Deimos, who remained standing. "I'm sure you have a lot of questions, Scarlet, but we would like to begin by first explaining who we are and what our mission is."

Scarlet nodded. Finally, answers.

"We call ourselves The Alliance. We are a war movement, assembled to ensure the defeat of the enemy whom you just recently escaped from. We are of many races, but we are united under one common goal in order to defeat one common threat."

Scarlet raised her hand.

Eldritch smiled from his seat and said, "This isn't a class, Scarlet, you may ask what you wish when you wish."

Scarlet reddened and lowered her hand. "Who is the enemy exactly?"

Thayla stood. Deimos sat.

"The enemy is a unique one," said the nymph. "We've never seen anything else like it... well, not yet, anyway. She's a leech."

"A leech?" The words made Scarlet shiver. "What do you mean by that?" The woman Scarlet had seen in her dreams had definitely not been a blood-sucking water creature.

"A person who can steal the magic out of others in a painful process we call draining."

Scarlet nodded, understanding. She remembered Tobin telling her about this back in the dungeon. "So, she's unique because no one else is a leech?"

"Actually, no. There are others," said the nymph. "In fact, Deimos here has the power. It's rare, but not unheard of among magical persons, and often hereditary."

Scarlet glanced at Deimos. His eyes had a hint of cold pride in them. "So, what makes her unique then?"

"Because it should be impossible. She is not of a magical race."

Scarlet opened then closed her mouth. What the nymph was implying hit her like a powerful gust of wind right to the mind, toppling over all her other thoughts. "She's–she's human?"

The nymph nodded, brushing a black and blue strand of hair over her shoulder. "She is. Never have we seen a human with any magic at all, and not only is she a leech, but from the tales we've heard, she is extremely skilled. So, you begin to see why she is a threat to all magic users, elves, nymphs, and dwarves, alike."

"But can humans be harmed by a leech?" asked Scarlet. She was certain Tobin had said something about it.

"A good question," said the nymph. "Yes. Life has an energy that can be drained. However, a leech gains nothing from draining a human unless they drain them completely, killing them and taking their life energy. Because humans have no excess magic, they have no other magical energy to offer."

Scarlet swallowed. "When a leech drains magic, what happens to it?"

"Another good question," replied the nymph. "A leech is strengthened by it for a temporary amount of time until the stolen magic wears off. In the same way the victim is low on magic for some time until it replenishes."

"So, this human, can she use magic when she steals it?"

"We believe so."

Scarlet dug her nails into her palms. The situation was looking worse with everything the nymph said. "What does this have to do with me?" she asked. "What's important about me?"

Eldritch stood. Thayla sat.

"We–" he hesitated. "We don't know."

Scarlet felt like she was going to combust. "You don't know?"

"No," said Eldritch, shaking his head. "We don't know."

Scarlet didn't have a reply to that. She felt like she was spinning. Why was she here? What was going on?

"Let me explain," said Eldritch, and Scarlet was too overwhelmed to tell him that he'd better. "A few years ago a prophecy was spoken deep in the halls of the High Elf palace in the hidden realm. News of the prophecy spread quickly among the elves, though none but those present knew what it had said. The contents of the prophecy were largely kept a secret but eventually parts were leaked. The prophecy spoke of an eminent war, and a group of chosen ones who would determine who came out victorious. With the Wraith amassing her army it became clear to us that the time the prophecy spoke of was upon us, and you, Scarlet Mount, are Chosen."

Scarlet shook her head. "I'm... Chosen? What does that mean exactly? How do you know?"

"When prophecies are issued we use Fate Stones, extremely powerful magical artifacts, to track down the ones spoken about in the prophecy. The first Fate Stone to activate found you."

"How many Chosen are there?" Scarlet asked.

Eldritch heaved a sigh. "We don't know."

This time Scarlet laughed: a laugh born from the feeling of insanity rising in her stomach. "How do you not know?"

"The prophecy doesn't specify."

"Well how many Fate Stones are there?"

"There are five Fate Stones in total, but that doesn't mean they will all activate for this prophecy. There may not be five Chosen. Then again, there might be. We'll just have to wait and see how many Fate Stones awaken over time."

"When do they activate?"

"We don't–"

"You don't know?" asked Scarlet. Somehow this was getting funnier and funnier in a way that made her brain want to explode in a very not-funny way.

"The Fate Stones have minds of their own," said Eldritch. "They activate when they feel like it, and not a moment before. We have no way of knowing when they will activate, how many will activate, or for whom they will activate."

"So we just watch these five rocks and wait for something to happen?"

"Actually, we are only in possession of two."

"Where are the others?" asked Scarlet. She held up her hand. "Wait, let me guess–you don't know?"

"Actually, we do know," said the elf, ignoring her tone of sarcasm that would've had her mother scowling. "The other three are in the Wraith's possession."

That answer was far worse than the "I don't know" Scarlet had been expecting. She wet her lips. "So if I go home, then that means that..."

Eldritch nodded. "The Wraith will only find you again."

Scarlet said nothing for a moment, feeling as though the floor might be tilting a bit where she stood. For as long as the Wraith and her army persevered, she was stuck here. It seemed a war stood between Scarlet and her home.

She cleared her throat. Once. Twice. Inhaled deeply through her nose before continuing her conversation with Eldritch. "How did the Wraith get the stones?"

"The Fate Stones were lost for decades. When the prophecy was made a search mission was immediately initiated to track them down. One of those sent on the mission was a traitor who managed to flee with three of the recovered Fate Stones, taking them to the Wraith."

"So, when they activate she's going to be able to find those Chosen right away?" asked Scarlet.

"It has already happened once," replied Eldritch. "With you."

Scarlet's eyes widened as she understood. "You don't have my Fate Stone, she does?"

Eldritch nodded.

"Then how did you know I was in the dungeon? How did you know where to find me?"

"We have spies within the Wraith's army," answered Eldritch. "They alerted us of your arrival to the Wraith's castle. They couldn't give us specifics, except that you were younger than we'd expected and were being kept in solitary confinement apart from other prisoners. With that information we launched a recovery mission—a successful recovery mission."

"You had no idea who I was before you got into the dungeon?" Scarlet asked, looking to Elowen for confirmation.

Elowen nodded.

The nod crushed her. Of course, they hadn't been looking for her specifically. They were probably disappointed that she was the person they were stuck with.

She swallowed, feeling like she might be shrinking. "You have no idea what actually makes me an important part of this war?"

"We do have a theory," said Eldritch. He glanced to the Council and a few of the others nodded. He looked back to Scarlet. "The Wraith is a human, but she's also a leech. This is completely unheard of. In fact, it's never happened before. We wonder if... if you might be a leech as well."

Scarlet's jaw dropped. "You think I might be magical?"

"Now that we know you're human, it is plausible that you are meant to counter the Wraith's powers. It's possible that you have abilities to match hers–powers that would be extremely instrumental in defeating her."

"How–" Scarlet stopped, then started again. She felt out of breath all of the sudden, like she'd been hit in the stomach. "I've never used magic before. How will we know if I have the power?"

"There are some tests we would like to run," replied Eldritch. "But we will allow you to get settled in before we do. We'd like to perform them in a couple of days."

Scarlet felt like she needed to sit down, as if it was the effort of standing up that was stopping her from fully comprehending everything she'd just heard in the last few minutes.

"Where's Tobin?" she asked, turning to Elowen, momentarily forgetting that she had an audience. She needed someone to talk to who would understand the shock she was feeling, and he was the only person who would do.

Elowen hesitated. She looked to the Council. Deimos stood up and Scarlet turned to him. He had an attention-grabbing effect to him. It might be something about his height, or the way he held himself, or maybe it was the way his green eyes dissected you piece by piece like you were an experiment. "Tobin has been placed in confinement."

"Wait–" Scarlet paused as she translated his meaning. "You mean Tobin is a *prisoner?*"

"We know that you have a special connection with your former guard," answered Deimos. "But he was previously serving the Wraith–"

"But he didn't want to!" interrupted Scarlet.

"Scarlet–" started Elowen, putting her hand on Scarlet's shoulder.

"No!" said Scarlet, wrenching away. "You can't do this, he hasn't done anything wrong!"

"We can't trust him yet," answered Deimos. "We will question him and begin the process of clearing him, but it will take a couple of weeks at least. We do apologize."

Scarlet didn't think he sounded very sorry.

"We'll make sure you have clearance to visit him," said Eldritch. "But for now, I think Elowen should take you to your new room. I'm sure you're tired after your long journey."

Scarlet opened her mouth to argue, but before she could do so Elowen grabbed her arm, pulling her across the room, and out of the door they'd come in through.

When they'd gotten through the door, she let go of Scarlet's arm.

"Did you know?" Scarlet asked, stepping away from her. "Did you know they would put him in prison?"

"Scarlet, it's not the same as the dungeon you were at, it's different."

"So you did know?" Scarlet asked, crossing her arms tightly across her chest and glaring at the floor.

"I knew that they would likely take certain safety protocols, yes," said Elowen, sighing, "but if you stood in their shoes, I think you would see why they did. Still, I'll make sure he's comfortable and that you can go see him."

Slowly, Scarlet unraveled her arms. She continued to scowl, but she allowed Elowen to lead her down the hallway.

They traveled up stairways and through torch-lit passages. The fortress, from what Scarlet could see, was massive and maze-like. It was a tangle of hallways, stairs, balconies, doors, small rooms, big rooms, and huge rooms, all thrown together like a messy knot that would never come undone. Scarlet was sure that without Elowen she could've gotten lost in it for years.

"Here we are," said Elowen, stopping. They were standing in a circular room. Four doors led off from the space, all of them closed. "This is the West Tower," said Elowen. "And this," she opened the door on the far left, "is your new room."

Scarlet stepped inside, mouth falling open. "This is all mine?" The room could have fit her whole house inside. A massive bed sat against the back wall. It was wide with curtains draped around the sides like the bed a queen might sleep on in a fairytale. Against one wall was a wardrobe and hung mirror. On the other side of the room were windows and a set of double doors, which were open and led to a balcony overlooking the Hinterland.

"All yours," Elowen replied. She stepped over to the wardrobe and opened it. "They put a few outfits in here already during your meeting with the Council, but don't worry, there's more coming."

Scarlet barely heard her. Her attention had been snared by a shelf on the wall. It was full of books–more books than Scarlet had ever seen in her life. Thick books. Books with hard covers and decorated spines.

Elowen watched her for a moment looking slightly amused by Scarlet's awe. "I'm sure you're exhausted," she said after a minute. "I'll leave you on your own for a bit," then she turned and left, the door clicking shut behind her.

Alone in the room Scarlet turned in a slow circle. This day couldn't have been more unbelievable. She was in the Hinterland, she was in a prophecy, and most of all, she might have magic.

She turned to the bed and instantly felt her knees weaken. The temptation of sleep was irresistible. But first–she crossed the room to where a fat, cushioned chair sat in the corner. Bracing her arms against it, she began to push, grunting as it scraped across the floor. In less than a minute it was in front of the door.

She studied it as she backed to the bed and climbed in. It would do. No one could get in without having to fight the chair's weight, and by then she'd have heard their attempt.

The Hinterland

She lay down and closed her eyes, feeling that she had done her best to ensure she would be in the same place when she opened them.

Chapter 11

"I said no." Tasha glared at the approaching nurse.

Tasha was standing in the infirmary: a long, clean room with a row of beds. After escaping the orcs, they'd arrived in the fortress where she and the black-haired elf, Beck, had been instantly forced to the infirmary as soon as the cuts on their arms had been spotted. Tasha's cut was still under the sleeve of her jacket, which she'd wrapped with a strip of cloth in the monster camp. "I told you," Tasha repeated, "I'm fine. I'll take care of it myself later."

"Please, just let me take a look at it," said the nurse. She was a sweet-faced elf wearing a white dress, hair pulled back into a tight bun.

"No, thank you."

"Come on, Miss-One-Man-Army," said Beck. "Just let her check it out." He was sitting on one of the infirmary beds. His feet were planted on the floor, shoulders slightly hunched as a second nurse, a thick, rosy-cheeked woman, examined his muddy arm. His cut was long, but not deep. He sucked in a breath as the nurse dragged a wet cloth across it.

"Miss-One-Man-Army?" Tasha asked, scowling.

"Yeah, you know," he said, looking up at her scowl and ignoring it, "taking on a whole camp of monsters by yourself? That kind of earns you the title."

"I would like to decline the title." Her voice was stiff.

"That nickname doesn't win the tournament?" he asked. "That's fine, I'll come up with another one."

She gritted her teeth. "Tasha. My name is Tasha. But I wouldn't get too attached if I were you." She picked up her bag, which she'd left lying on the bed. It contained nothing except what she'd been stealing from the monsters' camp when all this had started–food and equipment to maintain her daggers. She slung the bag over her shoulder, strands of her red hair getting caught under the strap. She pulled them out and tucked them behind her ear. "I'm leaving."

"What–*now?*" asked Beck, eyes widening.

Tasha nodded. She looked around the infirmary, located the door, and started toward it.

"Wait," Beck jumped to his feet. The nurse let out an indignant sound as the bandage she'd been wrapping around his arm fell to the floor. "Sorry, May," he apologized before turning his attention back to Tasha. "You can't go now. The orcs are still in the area. And you're hurt." He gestured to her arm.

"This is nothing," she replied, looking at it with a critical eye. Though, she thought, he did have a point about the orcs. Walking into the plains with a tribe of orcs nearby would be a stupid decision. And she hadn't survived on her own for so long by making stupid decisions. She turned back toward Beck. "I'll stay. Just for a few days until the orcs move on."

Beck nodded and sat back down on the bed. The nurse hmphed and began to re-bandage his cut.

Tasha leaned against the wall, unsure of what to do. She wasn't going to let them work on her arm, so there was no point in staying in the infirmary, but she also had no idea where she was or where she could go.

"When I'm done here, I'll take you to the living quarters, they'll have a spare room," said Beck, almost as though he could read her mind. She wondered if her confusion had played across her face. She hoped not.

The nurse finished Beck's arm and backed away. "Thanks, May," he said, standing up. "You're the best. And tell Tye good luck on his unit entry test for me."

"Will do, dear," she answered with a smile.

Beck walked to the door, waved Tasha over, and led her out of the infirmary into the torch-lit hallway beyond.

Almost immediately there was a yell and something came barreling toward them. Instinctively, Tasha reached for her daggers, then saw that Beck was smiling and the yelling figure was a dwarf about their age. He tackled Beck, making him stagger backward.

"Prince Charming!" cried the dwarf. "They weren't letting me in, said I had to wait for you to come out." The dwarf stepped back. He was a little over four feet tall with dark skin and long, brown dreadlocks. "Man," he said, rubbing his chin, "I thought you were dead for sure when those orcs came down."

"Pixie dust," said Beck, waving his hand and shrugging with exaggerated cockiness. "Have some faith in me. You know I can't be killed. I'm invincible." He was grinning from ear to ear.

"Invincible, huh?" asked the dwarf, grabbing his arm and taking a look at the bandage. "You get an ouchie boo boo?"

"Aw, you worried about me?"

"Nah, course not," said the dwarf, dropping his arm. "Wasn't worried at all."

"That's why you were waiting here for me to come out of the infirmary? Because you weren't worried at all?" Beck teased.

The dwarf rubbed his nose.

Beck smiled. "Yeah, I got cut, nothing serious though. May bandaged it up for me."

"May?" asked the dwarf. "The cute one?"

Beck swatted at him. "The married one. The one who's like ten years older than both of us."

"Why do the cute ones always gotta be taken?" said the dwarf, kicking the floor. "Anyway," he looked up, snapping out of his slump almost instantly. "I was thinkin', now that I know you're not dying and all, wanna come over to Buckle's tonight? He's having a party to celebrate you guys getting the prophecy girl. It's gunna be starting soon."

"Can't tonight," answered Beck.

"C'mon, your dad's gunna be busy all night with this Chosen business," said the dwarf, shaking his head so that his dreads whizzed around his ears. "He ain't gunna know. It's gunna be dragon fire."

"It's not that this time," said Beck, "I've got some work to do for the Council tonight. And I've got to show Tasha to her room." He pointed to Tasha.

Tasha had been watching the conversation from against the wall, silent and unnoticed, but now the dwarf turned all his attention to her. He whistled and took a step closer. "Nice to meet you. You into short guys?"

Beck groaned. "Tasha, this is my friend Lug."

Lug held out his hand. "Nice to meet you."

"She doesn't shake hands," said Beck, speaking before Tasha even had to open her mouth.

"No problem," said Lug, retracting his handshake.

"I've got to take her down to the living quarters," said Beck.

"Alright, fine," answered Lug. "But just remember, Buckle's place if you get bored tonight." He started down the hallway.

"And you remember that we have training tomorrow, so don't do anything stupid," Beck called after him.

"You sound like me mom," he called back, then he turned a corner and was gone.

"Are all your friends like that?" asked Tasha, eyebrows rising.

"Only the good ones," Beck replied with a laugh, then he turned and started down the hallway in the opposite direction as the dwarf. "Let's go."

They walked through what seemed to be an endless series of passages. Every now and then they would pass someone else and Beck would wave and call them by name, usually getting an enthusiastic greeting in return.

Finally, Beck stopped in a hallway lined with doors. He stepped to the fourth door on the left. "This one should be free." He turned the handle and pushed it open. It was indeed empty.

"You can sleep here," said Beck, "and breakfast is right down the hall in the mornings."

Tasha nodded.

"Is there anything else you need?" he asked.

Tasha shook her head. She was sure she could figure everything else out on her own. She always did.

"Alright," he nodded. "I'll see you around then." He turned away.

"Thank you." The words sounded foreign in her mouth–chunky on her tongue. When was the last time she had said those words? But she did mean them, not just for showing her to her room, but for earlier in the Hinterland, when he'd arrived just in time to help her escape the orcs. Without him she was pretty sure she would be dead... or would have been forced to drastic measures.

"No problem," he said, then he was gone: down the hallway with long, purposeful strides as though he was off to do something important.

Tasha entered her new room. It was small with a bed crammed in the corner, a tiny mirror on the wall, a carpet on the floor, and a dead fireplace. Simple and unextraordinary, but it had been years since Tasha had even slept in a real bed.

She stared at it: wooden legs, clean white sheets tucked in at the sides, a cream blanket on the top. And as she stared, she was transported back to another time, another place, another bed.
She gritted her teeth, trying to stop the memories from coming, but they were unwelcome visitors in her mind, entering without knocking.

And it was like she was ten again.

The Hinterland

Tasha woke up quickly, eyes wide. She jumped out of her small bed and pulled off the blanket. It was dark–too dark to see, but she could smell it. The burnt smell. She felt the blanket, combing it up and down with her fingertips. Soon she found the holes, still smoldering and hot.

She clutched the wool blanket against herself and looked around the room to see if anyone else was awake. The other girls were still sleeping soundly.

Carefully she tiptoed across the dorm and to the large door at the end. As quietly as she could, she opened the door and slipped out like an anxious shadow.

She crept down the following hallway and proceeding stairs, turning into the Matron's office and opening the drawer to the left of her cabinet. She felt in the corner and found the needle and thread.

It was too dark to see her surroundings, or even the object in hand, but she had made this journey many times in the last few weeks. She'd memorized the steps.

She slipped out of the office, slid through a few more hallways, in and out of a few more doors, and entered the kitchen where a single candle was always left burning.

She pulled up a chair. Laying the brown blanket across her legs she began cinching the sides of the holes together and started to sloppily sew them shut. It would be messy, but maybe it would make them less noticeable. She couldn't be caught with holes in her blankets again. The matron thought she was playing with matches–something she'd made clear was not tolerated at Ms. Pinchin's Orphanage before slapping Tasha's palm with a ruler.

But Tasha wasn't playing with matches. She would simply fall asleep and wake up with hot fingertips and holes burnt into her blankets. It was something she couldn't seem to stop, control, or even understand. But it had to end or, as Ms. Pinchin had warned her, she would be sent to the "school for bad girls." She'd heard too many stories to let that happen.

So, she sat in her chair, small and skinny, and with bags under her eyes, sewing holes shut and wondering what was wrong with her.

Now a much older Tasha stared at the small, white bed. She watched it for a moment, as though it might attack her, then she turned, closed the bedroom door, sat down against the wall, and closed her eyes.

She had gone without a bed for five years. Another day wouldn't hurt her.

Chapter 12

Scarlet woke up with a small gasp. She'd been dreaming about being back in the dungeon: behind bars, cold, hungry, and alone except for–"Tobin!"

In an instant she was pulled back to the present.

She had to find him.

She sat up quickly. She was in her new bed. Yesterday it had felt like a nest, soft and warm. Now it felt a bit like a trap, the mattress sinking under her hands as she tried to escape.

Finally she heaved herself off, taking a moment to look around the bedroom and remember that it was all hers. It didn't seem real, but when she ran her fingers over the bed post it was solid, and smooth, and very, very there.

She shook her head trying to clear it of distractions. She needed to go find Tobin and make sure he was safe. Elowen had promised to make sure he was comfortable, but Scarlet kept picturing him trapped and all alone.

Scarlet walked across the room, pushed her chair to the side with a grunt, and reached to open the door just as a knock sounded from its other side.

"Scarlet?"

Relief like a ray of sun ripped through Scarlet as she recognized the voice, opening the door.

Elowen stood in the hallway. She was dressed in the same set of armor she'd been wearing during their trek through the Hinterland, but it gleamed as though it had recently been washed. Elowen too looked fresher. Her brown hair was intricately braided back out of her face, not a single stray hair to be seen.

"I wanted to give you a bit of a tour if you're up to it," said Elowen. "I have half an hour off before I need to be in the Council Room."

"Do you have a job on the Council?" asked Scarlet.

"I'm a Right Hand," answered Elowen. Scarlet's brow creased and Elowen elaborated. "Every representative has a Right Hand, or sometimes multiple. Our job is to..." she paused, as though trying to find the right words. "We do anything our representative needs from us. Usually, things they don't trust anyone else to do. Jobs they want to ensure are done right."

Scarlet nodded. "You're Eldritch's Right Hand?"

She nodded. "I'm his only Right Hand." Scarlet was sure she wasn't imagining a hint of pride in Elowen's voice.

"Is Beck a Right Hand?"

Elowen nodded. "Deimos' only." She tapped her foot against the stone floor and nodded down the passage. "Now, do you want to go look at a few places or not?"

"Could we go see Tobin?"

Elowen nodded. "But breakfast first."

Elowen waited outside the door while Scarlet hurried to change into a new set of clothes. Her wardrobe was already stocked with a few outfits, all her size. Scarlet pulled on a green tunic and a pair of comfortable brown trousers. She hastily pulled her hair back and washed her face. She didn't look quite as put together as Elowen, but still better than she'd appeared in days.

Exiting the room, Scarlet joined Elowen, and they began to walk down the passage.

As they walked Scarlet looked more closely at the stone walls of the hallway than she had the night before. Many of them were intricately carved with depictions of dragons, towers, or in some cases, orcs like the ones she'd seen yesterday.

Elowen noticed her interest. "We managed to stumble upon this fortress when we first entered the Hinterland. We'd been planning to set up camp in the plains, figuring no one would want to search for us here. Now, with what we've discovered, we know we would have been killed if we had tried to settle out in the open like that. Luckily, we discovered this abandoned fortress almost immediately. We've theorized that it could have been created by dwarves, but we can't be sure. The dwarves among us now know nothing of it." They turned a corner.

"If dwarves built it, why did they abandon it?" asked Scarlet.

"We don't know," said Elowen as they started down a short set of stairs.

Scarlet felt unease slip through her.

"Here we are," said Elowen. They had reached the bottom of a set of steps. A set of doors was in front of them. "Through these doors is the Dining Hall," said Elowen. "Be prepared, people may be excited to see you."

Scarlet nodded. A couple days ago she would have thought Elowen was kidding, but after her entrance into the fortress she couldn't help but feel anxious as she stared at the closed door.

Elowen swung the door open, and they stepped into the Dining Hall. It was large and filled with rectangular tables. One side had no wall, just a few columns and a set of steps leading down to a courtyard that was open to the sky. From it, she could hear the sounds of clashing metal.

A few dozen people were sitting at tables in the Dining Hall: elves, dwarves, nymphs, and humans, each group separate from the others.

"This Dining Hall is open every morning and every evening," said Elowen. "Everyone is allowed two meals every day. You can get food over there." She pointed to the counter on the left side of the room. Behind it Scarlet could see a nymph woman serving a line of people waiting in front of the counter.

Before Scarlet could start toward the food, there was the scraping of chairs and at least fourteen people began to walk in her direction.

She had been spotted.

Others in the Dining Hall noticed the movement and in a moment there were no chairs left occupied.

A roar of noise filled the room as everyone recognized the Chosen. The first person to reach her was a squat, female dwarf who grabbed her hand and shook it. "So yer a Chosen, are you?" she asked, eyes crinkling as she smiled. "Nice to meet you, dear."

"Nice to meet you, too." Scarlet said, voice small.

"We've been waiting for you," said an elf. He was tall and brown-eyed.

"So this is her!" A woman, this time human, pushed her way through the crowd. She had a cheery, red face. "And look, a human to boot. That'll show all you magic users who think you're better than us." She let out a cackling laugh. "She's the first Chosen and she ain't no elf, or nymph, or nothin', she's human!"

There was some cheering from the crowd. Scarlet guessed the ones cheering were also humans.

"You represent us," said the woman, nodding to Scarlet. "Yer our champion." She grinned.

Scarlet hadn't realized she represented anyone, and the thought made her feel a bit dizzy.

The crowd continued to clamor toward Scarlet.

"What's your name?" someone cried.

"Scarlet–Scarlet Mount," Scarlet answered, trying to find the person who had asked among the shifting mass of faces.

"Do you know who the other Chosen are?" came a new voice.

"I–no–um–" Scarlet glanced to Elowen, but Elowen was deep in quiet conversation with another elf. They were talking low and rapid and the new elf's hands were moving at an alarming rate as he gestured.

"Scarlet, I'm sorry, I have to step away for a moment," said Elowen, catching Scarlet's eye. "I'll be right back."

And she was gone.

Scarlet swallowed. Despite being surrounded by dozens of people, she suddenly felt very alone.

She bit her lip and faced her audience again. People were shouting things at her, and she figured it would be very rude to cover her ears, no matter how badly she wanted to.

"Is it true you brought your guard from the Wraith's castle?"

Scarlet nodded numbly. The crowd began to murmur.

"Why–"

"So, this is our hero," came a cool voice, and it seemed to cut through the rest of the hubbub like a butcher's knife through butter. A figure stepped through the crowd. The figure was tall and white-haired. Behind him came two others, one male and one female. Glancing at their ears, Scarlet guessed they were all elves.

"All that waiting," said the newcomer, and the crowd seemed to back away, leaving Scarlet alone with the elf and his small group. "And this is what we get." He looked Scarlet up and down and her palms began to sweat. "Tsk, tsk, they just don't make heroes like they used to." He smiled at her as though he was making a joke, but his eyes didn't match.

Scarlet took a step back. She wasn't sure how to reply to that, but it didn't matter. The elf wasn't finished.

"Look at you," said the elf. "A child, and human, of course." He turned to the crowd. "Rejoice! We're saved!" His voice became a low growl as he looked back to Scarlet. "Scarlet will save us. Won't you Scarlet Mount?"

Scarlet rubbed her palms against her tunic. The elf's two friends watched her discomfort with amusement.

The elf's smile disappeared. He leaned in close to Scarlet. "Tell them," said the elf quietly. "How will you save them? How will you protect them?" he gestured toward the crowd. "Tell them exactly how you're going to save their lives when the enemy breaks down the fortress door."

"I–" Scarlet stopped, looking around desperately for Elowen.

"You see that woman there?" asked the elf, his voice elevating to a roar, his face two inches from Scarlet's as he pointed to a woman in the crowd. "How will you keep her children safe when the enemy comes? How will you–"

"That's enough." A new voice entered the conversation. Scarlet and the elf both turned to see who had spoken.

"You should go." Tasha stood a few feet from the elf, just within the circle the crowd had created. Her face was set and there was a spark in her eyes.

"I'm sorry, I was having a discussion with the new hero," said the elf, saying the word "hero" like it was a curse.

"Discussion over," said Tasha. She didn't seem the least bit intimidated by the elf, and watching her, Scarlet wished she could be half as brave.

"Are you looking for a fight?" asked the elf, stepping toward Tasha and closing the space between them so that they were less than a foot apart.

Tasha's eyes narrowed. "Did I find one?" Deftly she shifted her jacket, revealing the hilts of the daggers in her belt.

"That's the monster massacre girl," said someone from the crowd, loud enough for everyone to hear. It seemed Tasha already had a reputation for her actions in the Hinterland.

Recognition shot through the elf's eyes. He licked his lips, eyes darting to the crowd encircling him, and then to his two friends, standing to the side. They too looked uneasy.

He glared at Tasha.

She glared back.

Finally, after a few moments he put his hands up, as though in mock surrender, his cold smile spreading across his face again as he stepped away from Tasha. He and his cronies disappeared into the crowd.

"Thank you," said Scarlet, looking to Tasha–but she was already gone, walking away through the mass of people, wine-red hair bouncing on her back.

"Don't mind them," said the human woman, stepping forward with a scowl on her face. She glared at the backs of the retreating elves. "The High Elves are nasty pieces of work. Don't like none of the elves myself, but 'specially not them ones."

Scarlet nodded, but her knees felt weak. She'd never considered that anyone here would dislike her, not after hearing about the prophecy. But it seemed she had been mistaken to think she would be so easily accepted.

After a few more minutes the crowd around Scarlet finally began to dissipate, leaving Scarlet standing alone, the elf's words still playing through her head.

Suddenly a voice was in Scarlet's ear. "Tour is over, Scarlet." Scarlet whipped around. Elowen had appeared behind her.

"Why?" asked Scarlet, unable to stop herself from feeling a flicker of annoyance toward the elf for abandoning her to fend for herself, like a kitten in a den of wolves.

"Because a Fate Stone just activated," Elowen replied. Her face was lit up with excitement like Scarlet had never seen her wear before. "And we think the next Chosen is somewhere in this fortress."

Tasha spun, flashing the first dagger in and out of her opponent's chest.

She followed up with the second, slashing across the training dummy's fabric skin. The tear mended instantly on the enchanted material. She did the sequence again and again, drilling it into her mind. It was a maneuver she'd tried at the monster camp. It had worked, but she'd executed with less precision than she would have liked, and she wanted to make it exact.

Finally, Tasha stepped away from the training dummy and into the shade of the wall. She leaned against it, letting the breeze cool the sweat on the back of her neck and on her forehead.

She was standing in the fortress courtyard. It was one of the first places she'd stumbled across after venturing from her room. The courtyard was massive and square, with tall walls and no ceiling. She could see the blue sky above her, and every now and then a bird would fly past.

Against one wall the courtyard was lined with training dummies, spread apart from each other to allow everyone room to train. The other side was lined with arenas. They were round, with shin-high, wooden walls and floors of dirt, unlike the stone floor of the rest of the courtyard. There were three arenas in total. At the very center of the courtyard was a square of mulch hosting a large tree with sprawling branches and broad leaves.

The courtyard was fairly busy. There was a group of young elves under the shade of the tree, a pair of dwarves sparred in one of the arenas, and almost every training dummy was being used. Still, many of the people entering the courtyard did not stay to train, they seemed to be using it as a kind of shortcut, entering from one of the four sides, and exiting out another. Most of them made a beeline for the Dining Hall.

Tasha stretched. Her muscles were burning. She'd been training in the courtyard for over an hour, taking only one break to step into the Dining Hall–which hadn't been especially relaxing.

Still, the exhaustion was a small price to pay for what she got in return.

When she fought or trained she became focused, driven like a hammered nail. She became nothing more than a pair of daggers—and daggers don't feel. Which meant that, when she used her daggers, she wasn't dangerous. Well... that wasn't necessarily true. She was certainly dangerous, but only in the most predictable way.

She closed her eyes and let herself relax, sliding her blades into their places in her belt.

As her mind wandered, she thought back to the conflict in the Dining Hall. She frowned. She shouldn't have gotten involved. It was best to stay as separate from everyone else here as possible. Not to mention that it wasn't her problem, and she had enough problems of her own without picking up more.

She palmed her daggers and attacked the training dummy again, this time with more vigor than before. She struck fast, her feet flying, barely touching the ground at all.

"Tasha."

She ignored the voice, mid-swing.

"Tasha, I need a word."

Tasha slowed, giving the dummy one last jab. She sunk her blade deep into its stuffed stomach.

She looked up and found that the elf from the Hinterland was watching her. The one with the braid. *Elowen—that was her name.*

"What?" She pulled her knife from the dummy before slipping both into her belt again.

Elowen took a step toward her and Tasha watched with narrowed eyes. "You've been summoned to the Council Room."

"Why?" Tasha asked, crossing her arms.

Elowen pursed her lips. It seemed people didn't often question summons to the Council Room. "Something has happened. I can't discuss it out here, but I have a hunch that you have something to do with it."

"I didn't do anything," Tasha said, scowling. This was one of the few times she'd said that phrase and been telling the truth.

"I didn't mean it that way. Just come with me."

Tasha frowned. She gave the training dummy one last look before following Elowen.

Ten minutes later Tasha and Elowen reached the Council Room's double doors. Two guards stood on either side, but when they saw Elowen they swung the doors open. The two of them walked in. Side by side their heights were almost perfectly matched.

They stopped in front of the semi-circle stand.

The Council members were seated at their places, alert as though they'd been waiting.

"This is her; she's the one we found in The Hinterland," said Elowen. "I have a feeling this is the one we're looking for."

"A human?" asked the center elf, looking her up and down. While he sized her up, she did the same. She didn't try to hide it. He was Beck exactly, except older, a little grayer, and with a sharper stare. She didn't need to ask whether he was Beck's father; it was obvious.

"Yes, I'm human," replied Tasha before Elowen could speak. They would have no reason to believe any differently.

"She fights very well," added Elowen.

A few of the Council members murmured to each other.

"Bring out the stone," said Eldritch, "If Elowen is confident this is the one we're looking for, I am too."

The nymph sitting on the far-left side of the table stood up, a box in her hands. She set it down on the table and palmed something inside before stepping down the stairs at the side of the elevated table and crossing the floor to stand in front of Tasha.

"Hold out your hand," she said.

"Why?" Tasha asked, eying the nymph's fist.

"Just do it," prompted Elowen.

Giving in, Tasha held out her hand. The nymph dropped something onto it.

As the object hit her palm, Tasha felt something rush through her. It was like ice-cold water burning through her body, enveloping her senses. It was an exhilarating, terrifying feeling. Almost instantly her hands, not just the one holding the object, seared.

She dropped the object, a flash of panic slashing across her mind, which only made the heat in her hands intensify. She shoved them in her pockets, clenching them into fists and forcing her mind blank–forcing the feeling out of her.

"Never doubt the hunch of a Crescent Elf," said Eldritch, looking at the floor.

Sitting on the ground was a small stone. A symbol was scratched on its surface, though Tasha couldn't make out what it was. Most shocking of all, the stone was glowing like it might explode, deep, currant red from both the symbol and cracks spider-webbing around its sides.

The Council members were silent, all of them looking at the stone on the floor. All except for Beck's father, who was watching Tasha, eyes on the clenched fists in her pockets. They narrowed, and Tasha quickly pulled her hands out. The heat was still there, but it was subsiding.

"You're the next Chosen," said Elowen, looking to Tasha, then the nymph, then back to Tasha. "I knew it. As soon as I saw that the stone was activated, I told them it would be you."

Tasha looked at her, nonplussed. "I don't know what that means."

"We have a lot to talk about," said the nymph.

Chapter 13

"Take the stairs..." Scarlet mumbled to herself, as she did, indeed, take the stairs in front of her. "And turn left... was it right... no, it was left."

Elowen had escorted Scarlet up to her room and rushed off again, instructing her to stay there and out of trouble. In the commotion she seemed to have forgotten that Scarlet hadn't eaten. And that Scarlet wasn't good at staying put.

Scarlet had paced the room for only a few minutes before she'd grabbed a bag from the wardrobe, filled it with a couple items she thought she might need, and left the room. She had navigated her way back to the Dining Hall, managing to snag a piece of toast just before breakfast had closed.

She didn't like being left out of the action, but she hadn't forgotten Tobin. She had to find him and make sure he was alright. It was with this determination that she had asked for directions to the dungeons and started on her way.

"It was left," Scarlet decided out loud, and turned. Her footsteps echoed down the hallway as she passed mermaid sculptures, carvings of tusked beasts, and massive tapestries, before she came to a doorway. The sign on it read: Holding Cells. She had been expecting something scarier, maybe some steps leading down into darkness, or axe-wielding guards, but the door was plain and wooden. She opened it and stepped in.

"Stop there." She was met with an order as soon as she entered. A guard sat at a desk a few feet before her. They were in a long room which was lined with more doors down either wall. "Please state your business," said the guard, rifling through papers on the desk. He was wearing a full suit of armor and holding a monocle to his eye. The combination would have made Scarlet laugh, if not for her tingling nerves.

"I'm here to see Tobin..." she realized she didn't know his last name.

The guard looked up at her for the first time. "Scarlet Mount?"

Her eyebrows went up. "I–yeah, how did you know?"

"Elowen warned me last night that you might be coming down to see the boy in cell fourteen. She said you should be granted access." He stood up and stepped around the desk to shake her hand. His ears revealed that he was elven, and it seemed that he wasn't that old, perhaps in his early twenties.

"I'm Lindle," he said. "It's nice to meet you."

"Nice to meet you, too," said Scarlet. This was sweet relief after her run-in with the elves in the Dining Hall.

"Right this way," said Lindle, gesturing for her to follow. Scarlet followed the elf down the room to one of the doors at the end of the left wall. The number fourteen was emblazoned on its front.

"Elowen said you wouldn't need supervision," started Lindle, pulling a ring of keys from his pocket and unlocking the door. "So, I'll–" but Scarlet didn't hear the rest of the sentence because she'd already yanked the door open and whipped inside.

It was nothing like she'd been expecting. Torches left the room brightly lit and a small bed was in the corner. There was a tiny table pulled up to the bed, and on it was a deck of cards.

Tobin was seated on the mattress. He'd pulled the table up to where he was sitting and he was stacking the cards to make a card castle, but when he saw Scarlet he leapt to his feet so quickly he bumped the table and the cards flew in every direction. "Code word?" he asked, grinning.

"Pumpernickel," she replied, running across the room to hug him. He froze for a moment, caught by surprise, then hugged her back. "I'm sorry I couldn't come sooner," she said, pulling away. "I wanted to, but a lot of stuff happened. Are you all right? I was worried."

He laughed. "I'm fine," he noticed her skeptical look, "no, really, I am. This cell isn't much of a cell at all really, it's comfortable. This isn't even the real dungeon."

"It's not?"

"Nope," he shook his head. "Apparently, they've got a big, heavy-duty one called The Keep for important criminals, but they said they usually just use these cells for younger people, lesser crimes, or temporary holding."

Scarlet grinned. "That's great! Maybe you can get out soon."

"Elowen said she'll try to speed up the process. She came down last night."

Scarlet nodded.

"And," Tobin added, face lighting up, "I made a friend."

"What?" Scarlet glanced around the room as though expecting to see someone else, even though she knew it was just the two of them.

"Watch," he wiggled his eyebrows at her and stepped to the wall. He lifted up a fist and knocked on the stone–*dum*–then two quick raps–*du-dum*–then another slow one–*dum*.

He watched Scarlet, a big, goofy smile on his face. She scrunched her eyebrows, nonplussed. Then, from the other side of the wall came an answer: *dum-du-dum-dum*.

Dum-du-dum-du-dum-du-dum, Tobin replied.

And again, the person on the other side answered with the same rhythm.

"You made friends with the criminal in room thirteen?" Scarlet asked, laughing.

Tobin shrugged. "Yup. I'm just a friendly person like that."

"Do you have any idea who's over there?"

"Nope," said Tobin, still looking extremely pleased with himself.

"What if it's a really bad person?"

"Can't be too bad or they would be in The Keep," said Tobin.

"I guess that's true. Oh–" she said, remembering something. "I almost forgot, I brought this for you."

From her bag she pulled out a few sheets of paper and a pencil that she had found on her bedroom's bedside table. "Here, you can write down your stories."

"Oh, thanks," he said. He reached out his hands and slowly accepted the gifts, looking at them like he wasn't quite sure what they were for.

"I thought in case you get bored."

"Yeah." He looked them over before setting them down on the table. "Maybe. So, anything happened to you while I've been down here?"

She nodded. "A lot. I've been busy." She sat down on the cot and began to tell him everything that had occurred, leaving out the part about the elf she'd met in the Dining Hall.

"That's crazy," said Tobin, fifteen minutes later when she finished. He lay back on the cot. "If you're magical that would be incredible."

Scarlet nodded. She felt light now every time someone said the word "magic". She looked over at Tobin, sprawled out next to her.

"Someone got you new clothes," she noticed, saying the thought aloud.

He now wore a pair of trousers and a clean blue tunic that made his brown eyes seem deeper in contrast. He'd clearly been allowed to wash off too, because the mud and grime that had collected on him during their trip over the Hinterland was gone, and she could see every one of the freckles across the bridge of his nose.

"Yeah, Elowen took care of that," he said.

Scarlet felt a rush of gratitude for Elowen. The elf had said she would make sure that Tobin was comfortable, and it seemed she had kept her promise. For someone who was a prisoner, Tobin seemed happy.

"What's that?" asked Scarlet, pointing at his arm.

He sat up so quickly it was as if someone had pulled a string attached to the top of his head. "What's what?"

"That bracelet," said Scarlet. The bracelet was small and red. It looked like it had been crafted from multiple strands of crimson thread braided together.

"That?" he asked, relaxing back onto the cot. "I was wearing that back in the dungeon, but I guess you couldn't see it because of my armor."

"Oh," she nodded. She wondered where he'd gotten it from. Had someone given it to him? Maybe a girl back in his village? She frowned.

He noticed that she was still looking. "My sisters made it," he said sheepishly, fidgeting with it. "They each have one, and they made one for me. They wanted me to wear it and I couldn't say no after they'd worked so hard on making us all matching ones." His face reddened.

"I think that's cute," said Scarlet, grinning.

He shrugged, looking down at it with the shadow of a smile.

Scarlet leaned back against the wall behind the cot. They were silent for a few moments before Scarlet spoke up. "You know the first thing I'm going to do if I'm magic?"

"What?"

"Learn how to make flames with just my hands."

He cocked his eyebrows, "How... sweet."

"And then," she said, looking him in his brown eyes. "I'd set the Wraith's castle on fire."

He laughed like it was a joke.

But looking at the bracelet on Tobin's arm, and picturing his family at the hands of someone like the Wraith, she meant it.

Every. Word.

Tasha stood in the middle of the Council Room, arms crossed, and brow creased. The Council Members watched her. Some of them fidgeted. Thayla and Deimos looked completely relaxed. They'd just finished explaining the prophecy to her, and that she had been chosen by a magical stone, and that she was going to help decide who won a war.

And now they were staring at her. All of them watching and waiting in complete silence.

Tasha let them sweat for a few seconds, then slowly she asked, "You want me to stay here and help you defeat an army?"

Deimos gave her a smile, like Beck's but lacking the slight crookedness. "You are a deciding factor in the result of the oncoming war. We don't yet know how, but without you we cannot win. So yes, you will stay here as one of the Chosen." He didn't say it as a question or a suggestion, more like a statement.

"No, thanks."

The smile disappeared. The kindness in Deimos' eyes evaporated so quickly Tasha wondered if it had ever really been there. "No?"

"There seems to be a miscommunication here," said Tasha. The sharpness of his gaze could not cut her. Her skin was too thick for that. "You want me to stay, but I don't have to. Don't act as though I don't have a choice, I do. And I choose no–I will not be a part of your war movement. In fact, I'm leaving tomorrow."

"I'm afraid that you don't understand," said Deimos, grinding the words out between his teeth. "You need–"

"No, I'm afraid it is you who doesn't understand," replied Tasha. "I don't *need* to do anything."

Deimos leaned back in his chair. Tasha thought he was trying to seem relaxed, but his clenched jaw gave him away. "Leaving would be very unwise," he said slowly.

Tasha narrowed her eyes. His every word was spoken like a weapon. "My leaving may not be in your best interest, but that does not make it unwise," she answered. "And I would strongly suggest you don't try to stop me. I would prefer to leave without a fight."

"You seem very confident in your abilities," said Deimos.

"I am," Tasha answered. She and Deimos glared at each other.

"Stop, stop," said Thayla, standing up. "No one is fighting anyone." Deimos looked like he disagreed. "Tasha, we know this is a lot to take in. All we ask is that you would consider staying as an option. This fortress is much safer than roaming the Hinterland. Not to mention, once it's leaked that you're the next Chosen it will only be so long before the Wraith finds out. If you leave this fortress, she *will* find you."

Tasha ground her teeth. "What would be expected of me, as a Chosen?"

Thayla frowned. "We don't know why you were Chosen and what your role is in the inevitable war. For all we know you'll make a difference by simply being in the right place at the right time. But for now we would place you in a unit. You must understand that you would also be a beacon of hope for those in the fortress. It is a possibility we would want you to give the occasional speech to rally morale."

Tasha shook her head. "I don't give speeches."

"We could negotiate that point if you stayed."

Tasha tightened her already crossed arms. She ran through the options in her head and decided on the answer that would get her out of the Council room quickest. "I'll consider it."

Thayla nodded, "Thank you." She sat down.

When no one said anything else, Tasha took a step backward. "I'm going now."

She looked back to Deimos one last time before turning and leaving the room. She could feel his eyes burning holes in her back.

It seemed she had made an enemy.

Tasha marched out of the room, through hallways, down some stairs, through the Dining Hall, and into the courtyard. This was not going according to plan. She had wanted this visit to be easy, but it seemed this prophecy had other plans.

She wasn't sure what to think about everything she'd just learned, but she knew three things to be true. If she stayed, she would be thrown into battle. There was a chance she would get hurt–or worse. If she went back into the Hinterland, the Wraith might find her, again meaning she could be hurt–or worse. And lastly, if she didn't get away from the people in this fortress, they might end up hurt. Or worse.

There were no good options.

As her mind became overwhelmed, her fingertips began to warm. It was a tingling feeling, like the feeling of one's legs falling asleep.

She took a stabilizing breath, focusing on the night sky above and blocking out all whispers of fear or anger in her mind. She stared at the star-studded blackness until she felt nothing. The tingling went away.

Chapter 14

Scarlet woke up early the next morning to sunlight streaming in through the windows. She got out of bed and proceeded to get ready for the day: brushing her hair, picking out a new outfit, and making her bed. When she was ready she removed the chair from its usual spot in front of the bedroom door, walked into the hallway beyond, and made her way down to the Dining Hall.

Scarlet went through the breakfast line. There was a wide selection of foods, some Scarlet didn't even recognize. She helped herself to a steaming bowl of porridge and a chunk of bread. When she emerged at the end of the line, she looked out across the Dining Hall, searching for familiar faces. She saw none. In fact, the Dining Hall was fairly empty, it seemed she had missed the breakfast crowd.

She took her tray to an empty table and sat down, facing the side open to the courtyard. She could see a group of people training. Deimos seemed to be leading it. He was yelling at a figure who looked like he wanted to disappear into the ground. Scarlet watched Deimos grab the figure's sword and throw it to the stone floor.

Peering at the group Scarlet thought she might see Beck among them.

She was taking her first bite of porridge when she saw a blur of red out of the corner of her eye. She swiveled in her chair to see that Tasha was walking across The Dining Hall. Scarlet watched her as she went through the line, got her food, and looked for a seat.

Scarlet waved. Tasha noticed and nodded to her, then went to sit at an empty table on the other side of the room.

Scarlet frowned, suddenly feeling very lonely. She wished Tobin weren't stuck in a holding cell. He would have had breakfast with her.

She began to dig into her food. She tapped her foot against the floor and glanced at the empty seats to her left and right. Suddenly making up her mind, she picked up her tray and crossed the Dining Hall to Tasha's table.

"Hey," she said.

Tasha looked at her but didn't reply.

Scarlet decided to treat the stare as an invitation and sat down across from her. "I'm Scarlet," she said. "I met you in the Hinterland, but I never got to introduce myself."

Tasha nodded, watching her as though wondering how long she planned on talking.

"I wanted to thank you for helping me and Tobin escape from the tent," said Scarlet, shifting in her chair as though it was the seat that was making her uncomfortable and not the girl staring her down. "You saved us."

"I almost didn't," said Tasha. She didn't say it with remorse or pride or anything in between–just stated it like a fact.

Scarlet tapped her spoon against the side of her bowl. *Taptaptaptaptap*–"Well, you did, that's all that matters."

Tasha's eyes were burning holes in her. Scarlet was beginning to regret her decision to come over.

"So," she cleared her throat. "Why were you out in the Hinterland?"

Tasha looked down at her tray and ripped a chunk from her piece of bread. "To get away from people."

Scarlet swallowed. Under the table her leg bounced up and down. "How's your arm?" she asked, gesturing to the arm the monster had cut the day before. She couldn't see the wound, still under Tasha's jacket sleeve, but there was a bulge beneath the fabric and Scarlet assumed it was wrapped.

"It's fine," Tasha said, swallowing the chunk of bread and beginning to down her porridge.

"You were amazing out there," said Scarlet. "I mean, really amazing. Some of those moves you made–like that one where you jumped over someone's sword and ducked and then hit that one monster's knife away with your foot–it was incredible." The words came out fast like they were racing each other.

Tasha shrugged.

"Do you think maybe you could teach me some of that sometime?" Scarlet asked. "I bet you could show me some really cool things. Who knows, maybe we could be friends?"

Tasha stood up. It was so abrupt, Scarlet jumped in her seat. "I don't think so."

Scarlet wasn't sure whether she was replying to the question about teaching Scarlet or being friends–or both. Tasha shoved the last piece of bread into her mouth and her tray was empty. Scarlet had never seen anyone eat a meal so fast.

"That's alright," said Scarlet, "I'm sure you're busy." But Tasha was already walking away to return her tray.

Scarlet kicked the floor. Tasha was the most interesting person she'd ever met, it was a shame she was also the most unfriendly.

"Scar, what's in the envelope?"

"Huh?"

Scarlet turned to see Beck walking across The Dining Hall toward her. He was coming from the courtyard, fully dressed in his set of armor.

Though it was early and there was sweat on his brow, he looked as perky as ever, green eyes alive and his step energetic.

"What's in the envelope?" he replied. "I'm asking what's going on with you."

"Oh," said Scarlet. "I'm good. I hadn't heard that phrase before. Is it elven?"

"Nope," he said. He pulled a chair from the table and turned it backward before sitting down on it so that he was facing Scarlet. "I just made it up. But be sure to use it sometime today, we'll make it a thing before long."

"I understand the mission." said Scarlet, grinning and giving him a fake and greatly exaggerated salute.

"You need to come with me to the Council Room," he said. "They want to talk to you."

"What about? Are they ready for my magic test?" Scarlet asked, excitement sparking in her stomach.

"Not yet," he replied. "It's about something else. You're too young to be in a unit or fight in battles, but they want you to be prepared to defend yourself if you need to, so they've found you a trainer."

Scarlet stood up. "They're training me to fight?" *Just like in the stories* the voice in her head added.

He nodded. "It's important that you can protect yourself." He stood up and twisted the chair back around. "You ready to go?"

She nodded. She ran to return her tray, then she and Beck started out of the Dining Hall. "What are the units?" she asked as they walked.

"There are lots," replied Beck. "The top dragons are in the elite units. There are three: one for ranged weapons, one for melee, and one for magic fighting. Elowen leads a melee unit, my father leads the magic, and Thayla runs the ranged."

"Aren't you in an elite unit?"

He nodded. "My father's."

They turned a corner and mounted some stairs. "What are the other units?" Scarlet asked.

"There are the secondary units right below the elite," said Beck, "and they're second best. Usually, the people in those are right on the brink of making elite but aren't quite good enough. Then there are the Marching Units. The Marching Units are everyone else. Some of the marching units are solely elves, or dwarves, or humans, and so on."

"Why's that?"

"Some jobs are better fitted to an elf's skills than a dwarf's, in that case, we'd send an elven unit. And flip side of course."

They turned another corner and passed a statue of a dwarf kneeling next to a wounded tiger.

"So that's everything?" Scarlet asked.

"There are also Lone Wolves," said Beck.

"What's that?"

"Solo fighters. They get sent on missions alone. Usually assassinations or espionage sorts of stuff. I've always thought it would be cool to be a Lone Wolf."

"Aren't you really good?" Scarlet asked, looking at him.

"Well, not to light my own torch, but yeah, I'm good."

"Then why can't you be a Lone Wolf?"

He shrugged, "My father says being in an elite unit looks better for getting on the Elven Court."

"You mean the Council?" asked Scarlet, cocking her head.

Beck shook his. "No, the Elven Court is separate from The Alliance. It's similar to the Council here sort of–it has a High, Wood, Crescent, and Sun Elf Representative, but it's been around for centuries."

Scarlet nodded. "What's it do?"

"Mandates trade, handles inter-realm policies, addresses issues that threaten the elves–that kind of stuff."

147

Scarlet nodded. "So why isn't the Elven Court representatives here?" The Wraith definitely seemed like an issue that would threaten the elves.

"They are," said Beck. "You already know them. The representatives for the Elven Court were also the ones chosen to represent for the Council."

"Oh–" Scarlet's mouth came open as she understood. "–Is that how the others work too? Like the nymphs and dwarves?"

Beck didn't answer for a moment, pausing to wave to a nymph walking across the hallway before returning to the conversation. "No. The nymphs have a queen. That's Thayla. The dwarves have a king. He's not here. He refused to join our cause and bring his clans. The only dwarves here are from separate tribes, or deserters from the dwarven kingdom. It's only the elves who have a court."

"And you want to be next on it for the High Elves?"

Beck's answer was automatic. "The Lotus Line has represented the High Elves in the Elven Court for years."

That was the second time she'd heard the Lotus Line mentioned in the last two days, but before she could ask about it, he stopped. "We're here."

Scarlet halted in front of the big Council Room doors.

"Are you coming in with me?" she asked.

He shook his head. "Can't, I've got agility training in five minutes. Actually, I'm probably going to be late. Gotta crack the cobblestone, see you later." Then he took off down the hallway.

Scarlet turned to the Council Room doors. The guard in front began to push them open, and she stepped inside.

"Scarlet," Deimos' voice met her. "Thank you for joining us."

He'd cleaned up fast. She'd seen him only ten minutes before in the courtyard. Now he looked immaculate in long resplendent robes of deep green.

She stepped into the wide space in front of the tall stands.

"As I'm sure Avenbeck informed you," said Deimos, "we have summoned you here today to introduce you to your new trainer. We feel it is crucial for you to begin preparing yourself if ever you must defend your life."

"That's great! I mean–" she cleared her throat and tried to stand up straight, glancing down the row of representatives. "I would be willing to accept your proposal."

Eldritch smiled at her.

"Would you like to meet your trainer?" Deimos asked.

Scarlet nodded.

A side door opened, and an elf walked in.

"This is Enyalios," said Deimos. "He is one of my own kind, a High Elf, and of an impressive line. He will teach you well."

Scarlet barely heard what he said, she was too busy staring at the High Elf. He looked familiar.

"It will be my pleasure to train you, Scarlet," said Enyalios in a clipped, starched tone, gaze turning to her. Instantly she recognized him. Her stomach dropped. He was from the Dining Hall–not the elf who had yelled at her, but one of his friends.

He looked at her with the lazy look of a cat surveying a mouse. He was pale and sallow with stringy black hair so oily-looking Scarlet thought she would have to wash her hands if she were to touch it. A long white scar marred his pasty neck.

Scarlet looked up at the Council, then back at him. She swallowed, throat dry. Should she say something? She hadn't told anyone about what had happened in the Dining Hall, but should she?

Enyalios looked at her, one of his eyebrows rising slightly, like maybe he was curious about what she was going to do. Like maybe he expected her to turn to the Council for help just like the weak human his friend thought she was.

Her foot began to tap against the ground. "I look forward to it."

Enyalios gave a thin-lipped smile as Scarlet's hands fisted at her sides. "Good, because we start tomorrow."

Tasha left the Dining Hall as quickly as she could. People here were way too friendly. She'd lived in the Hinterland for five years to avoid people, and now Scarlet was asking her if they could be friends.

There was no doubt about it, she couldn't stay here.

She stalked into the courtyard and started surveying her surroundings. Most of the training dummies were being used. One was being hacked at by a dwarf with an axe, another by a nymph with a long blade. Yet another was being punched by a human, and farther away she could see an elf attacking his stuffed enemy with bolts of light from his hands.

She crossed her arms, unsure of where to go–back to her room seemed the best option.

She turned and startled back as someone darted in front of her, causing her fingertips to instantly warm. She clenched her fists as her fingers cooled. "Watch where you're going," she snapped at the figure: a human girl with two braids on either side of her head.

"Sorry!" The girl shouted the apology over her shoulder as she scampered away, running toward a group of friends clustered in the corner of the yard. As she neared them one of the little boys looked up and said, "Lily, we're playing Rat Catcher."

Rat Catcher. The words hit her like a blow. Almost instantly she felt her mind slipping back to the past.

She shook her head, trying to clear it. But the memory surfaced like a dead fish floating to the top of a pond.

And she was eleven again.

Tasha had learned to be careful. She was smarter now.

She'd stopped sleeping with a blanket altogether. She would throw it under her bed as soon as the matron left their room for the night and the lights went out. It was colder that way, but it was safer, too.

After she'd woken up to find a spot on her bed mattress burned black, she'd begun wrapping her hands with cloth before bed. She would wake up to find the cloth black and hot, but there were worse alternatives. She stole the cloth every day from the cabinet in the sewing room, throwing the burnt leftovers in the trash can out back.

It was a strange process, but it kept her out of trouble and out of the "bad girl school", which had become her greatest fear.

She'd learned to be careful during the day, too. She couldn't tell what was causing her hands to heat, so she stuck to the safe side. She avoided touching people and things as much as she could.

She realized that her hands were less likely to heat up when she was tired, so she began to stay up late, wake up early, and do push-ups in the mornings while the other girls slept, trying to exhaust herself. The effect never lasted more than twenty minutes, but it was worth it.

All in all, she was confident that her problem could remain hidden. She was sure she could control it.

She just didn't realize it was getting worse.

"Tasha? Are you paying attention?"

Tasha became suddenly aware of her surroundings again, having zoned out.

"Sorry, I'm paying attention." She pushed her wine-red ponytail over her shoulder.

"Good, okay, everyone remember the rules?" The speaker was a pigtailed girl who was a year older than everyone else, which naturally put her in charge.

It was supposed to be their study time, but the matron had fallen asleep in her office and the girls were feeling rebellious. So, instead of taking meticulous notes over subjects they cared nothing for, they were sitting in a circle organizing a game of Rat Catcher.

"*Yup,*" *spoke up a red-cheeked girl.* "*Everyone runs and hides, and the rat catcher has to find everyone, and if they find you, then you become a rat catcher too.*"

The ring of girls nodded.

"*Okay,*" *said the pig-tailed leader.* "*I'll be rat catcher first. I'll count to thirty while you all hide. And remember, the office is off-limits, because we'll be in trouble if we wake Ms. Pinchin.*"

The girls, giggling with excitement over the game and their own daring, rushed off as Pig-Tails began to count.

Tasha scrambled out of the room, down the hallway, up the stairs, and into the dorm room. Frantic, she looked for somewhere to go from there. The counting must be almost done. In desperation she slipped behind the open door, pressing between it and the wall.

She stood there for a full minute with that kind of excited-fear that you only get when you are small and playing a game when you shouldn't be. Her hands began to tingle, but she clenched and unclenched them, which she found sometimes worked to stop the process. She heard footsteps coming up the stairs and tried to silence her breathing.

It seemed the quieter she tried to breathe the louder her breaths became. Someone entered the room, and she stopped breathing altogether, going completely still.

There was a silence in which Tasha assumed the girl was scanning the room.

"*Doesn't seem to be anyone here,*" *came a murmur from the doorway. Tasha grinned.* "*Unless....*"

A girl whipped around the door. "*Found you!*"

Tasha, caught by surprise, let out a shriek and fell back into the wall. Her hands seared. It was sudden–intense–fiercer than it had ever been before.

And then they caught on fire.

"Tasha, are you alright?" Tasha refocused so suddenly it was like having her head shoved under cold water.

Beck stood in front of her. He waved a hand in front of her face. "Looked like you went to fairyland for a second."

"Get your hand out of my face."

He dropped it. "Sorry, I was just checking. You seemed–" he ruffled his hair. "Sorry, I'll leave you alone. I've got to go, anyway. I'm going to be late. But I was thinking maybe we could have a friendly duel sometime? I think we could teach each other some things."

"Maybe," she said, hoping that the answer would satisfy him enough to get him to leave.

"Alright, sounds great," he said, then he turned and jogged across the courtyard and out a side entrance.

Tasha started toward the training dummy the dwarf had been attacking. He had left while she'd been zoned out. She faced it and pulled out her daggers. She needed to fight–needed to release the constant effort it took to control her own abilities.

She stayed there, waging war on her stuffed foe, until the sun left the sky and day turned to night.

Chapter 15

The next morning Scarlet woke with a bubbly feeling in her chest. Her first training session would take place that afternoon. She couldn't tell whether she might fly or throw up.

Only ten minutes after waking, she started down from the West Tower and entered the Dining Hall.

Beck was already there and seated at a table, Tasha across from him. She had her arms crossed and Scarlet didn't think she looked especially happy to be there.

Beck saw Scarlet right away and waved her over. She gestured for him to give her a minute, then hurried to get her food before taking a seat at the table as far from Tasha as she could. As interesting as Tasha was, she was also intimidating. Even sitting in the sunny Dining Hall, she looked dangerous. Her hair was like a veil of fire. She wore her usual leather jacket and her daggers hung at her hips. They were plain with wooden, well-worn handles. Scarlet hadn't ever seen her without them.

"Hey Scar," said Beck, smiling. "I was just trying to convince Tasha here to duel me."

Scarlet couldn't think of any reason anyone would want to duel Tasha, not after what she'd seen in the Hinterland. But Beck didn't look the least bit afraid. He was relaxed in his chair, a steaming bowl of porridge in front of him. "Do duels happen here a lot?" Scarlet asked.

"Fairly often," replied Beck. "Sometimes friendly. Sometimes not. They also use duels to evaluate newcomers. That's how they'll test you, Tasha, to choose which unit to put you in. If you stay, that is."

Tasha gave no indication that she cared.

"Beck," said Scarlet hopefully. "You know everything that goes on here. Do you know when they're going to have my magic test?"

"Probably in a couple of days," said Beck. "They were going to do it sooner, but they've been distracted with other things."

"Like what?"

Beck lowered his voice. "Like Tasha being the next Chosen."

"You're the next Chosen?" said Scarlet, jaw dropping as she looked to Tasha.

Tasha shrugged.

"Don't spread it around," warned Beck. "We're trying to keep it in the back streets to avoid any spies hearing about it and reporting to the Wraith. The Council said you should probably know, though. We have no idea how either of you will affect the war and you might need to know about each other to do it."

Scarlet opened her mouth to ask another question, but was interrupted as a gruff, jovial voice cut into the conversation. "How's it going?" A dwarf plopped down in the seat next to Beck and threw his tray down onto the table.

"Scarlet, this is Lug," said Beck, taking a bite of bread.

"Nice to meet you," said Scarlet.

Lug nodded. "You too. It's good to meet the Chosen person everyone's talking about." He began to dig into the meal piled onto his tray: multiple loaves of bread, two bowls of porridge, an apple, and some strips of red meat.

"And you already met Tasha," added Beck.

"Monster massacre girl!" said Lug. "Everyone's talking about what you did in the Hinterland."

"How do people know about that?" asked Scarlet.

"Things spread around here fast," Lug answered. "People couldn't keep things to themselves if their mouths were tied shut."

Beck grinned, leaning back in his chair. "You're just mad everyone found out about you and Dina in the Astronomy Tower."

Lug mumbled something unintelligible and jammed an entire loaf of bread into his mouth. When he finished chewing and swallowing, which only took him a few, loud seconds, he looked back to Tasha.

"You're getting wild famous around here," said Lug. "They all saying you might be as good as Prince Charming here."

"Prince Charming?" Scarlet asked.

Lug elbowed Beck. "It's my nickname for him." Beck made a face. "Why?"

"Do you only speak in questions?" said Lug, wiping his mouth with the back of his hand. "I call him that because he's charming. Don't try to deny it. And he's basically High Elf royalty."

"I didn't think High Elves had royalty," said Scarlet.

"We don't," said Beck. "But we have family lines. I'm a member of the Lotus Line."

"And they do this whole family honor thing," said Lug.

Beck snorted. "Yeah, well the 'whole family honor thing', as Lug so eloquently put it, is pretty important in High Elf culture."

"All them High Elves think they're better than the rest of us," said Lug, "just 'cause their family lines are named after flowers–"

"That's not even true," said Beck shaking his head. "They're not all named after flowers."

"Beck's one of the only ones who doesn't make me want to stab my eyes out," said Lug, ignoring him.

Beck put a hand to his heart, "You're too kind."

Lug belched. "Well this was fun, but I've got to go." He stood up and stretched, "Training. See you later, Prince Charming," he nodded to

Beck. "Monster Massacre Girl," he nodded to Tasha. "And girl with a lot of questions," he nodded to Scarlet. Then he turned and left the Dining Hall.

Scarlet watched him go, then turned her attention back to Beck. "I've never heard of High Elf lines before. Do the other types of elves do things the same way?"

Beck shook his head. "Just the High Elves. But it's a serious part of our culture. Any High Elf in this room right now could probably tell you the family line of every other High Elf in this room. And some lines are more... admired than others."

"Like yours?"

He nodded.

"Do the other elves know about the High Elf lines?"

"They know they exist; they don't really pay attention to them though," said Beck, finishing off his last bite of food and standing up. "I'll see you two later. I've got training with my unit. Tasha, we on for a duel later today?"

She shook her head. "I'm busy."

"No you're not," he replied. "Yesterday you practiced with your daggers for three hours straight. I know because when I left for training you were there, and when I passed through later that day you were still there. That's not busy, that's bored."

"Well then I'm too busy being bored for the rest of the day," she said, crossing her arms.

"Alright," he nodded, not looking the least bit discouraged as he turned and said over his shoulder, "Some other time then." And just like that he was gone.

"He's persistent," grumbled Tasha, more to herself than Scarlet.

"Yup," Scarlet replied anyway.

"I've got to go," said Tasha, standing up.

"You have to get busy being bored?" asked Scarlet, smiling.

Tasha looked at her with no hint of an answering smile. "Yes."

She walked away. Scarlet watched her go. Her red hair waved as she walked and her daggers swung at her hips. For a fleeting moment Scarlet wanted nothing more than to be her: powerful, confident, and dangerous.

She finished her meal and stood up, returning her tray.

Again, just like after breakfast the day before, she was on her own. She felt the loneliness yawn in her stomach like a physical pain. Everyone else here had a purpose. Everyone else here was part of the machine, a puzzle piece, a thread in a seemingly complete tapestry. Everyone but her. Apparently, she was supposed to impact the war, but she didn't know when, or how. So far, she'd been pretty unhelpful.

But, she reminded herself, her magic test would be soon. And when it came, she had a feeling she would find her purpose. She would have magic, and it would make her special. Special enough to be here, with all these fighters, magic-users, and Council members.

She puffed up her chest, acting on her self-pep-talk, and decided that she would look around the fortress. She'd never gotten the tour Elowen had meant to take her on.

Scarlet walked into the Courtyard. She noticed a sign on the wall reading: *Main Courtyard.* Did that mean there were multiple?

Scarlet had only seen the room from within the Dining Hall, but it seemed bigger from the inside. She scanned the training dummies, arenas, and the massive tree at the courtyard's center. There were four entrances to the Main Courtyard. One was through the Dining Hall, and the others were archways, one on either wall.

She took it in for a minute before moving on, walking to the archway across from the Dining Hall.

She walked through the arch and up a wide set of stairs. At the top Scarlet found herself in yet another courtyard–so there were multiple. This one had targets around the walls. There were various people milling around. Some were throwing axes or daggers. Others were shooting arrows. A sign on the wall read: *Ranged Courtyard.*

Scarlet could have stayed there forever, watching the action unfold around her, except with every room her curiosity of the next one grew.

She walked through another archway and up another set of stairs. As soon she reached the top Scarlet was hit with a new wave of sound, movement, and color.

This room was the size and rectangular shape of the other courtyards, but held no fighting dwarves or training nymphs. Just stalls and stalls and stalls of stuff. There were three rows of these stalls, one against the left wall, one against the right, and one down the middle. They were simple, with small canvas roofs and tables covered in colorful cloth.

The tables were laden with all sorts of objects. Scarlet saw swords, food, jewelry, scrolls, crystals, feathers, clothes, artwork, and even a stall that seemed to be inking tattoos. And then there were the people: elves arguing with a vendor, a gaggle of dwarven boys ogling over the swords, a human man contemplating whether to get a tattoo, a nymph mother chasing her small daughter, a little boy buying a monkey, and many, many more. They milled around the stalls, groups migrating from place to place like flocks of birds.

Scarlet just stared for a moment, shocked by the sudden colors and scents. It was like her senses were trying to catch up to what she'd just walked into.

Carefully, she moved into the crowd. The noise of dozens of conversations fought for her attention as she slipped through the market like a shadow. She paused to look at a cage of bright lizards, then hurried to stare at a table selling iced buns that smelled good enough to set Scarlet's mouth watering. She rushed down the path between the rows, eyes widening more with every new, strange thing she saw.

Her wonder was cut short as her foot hit something and she tripped, sprawling to the ground and smacking her chin against the stone.

She bit back a yell at the sudden slash of pain and twisted her head to see what she'd tripped over. It was a small, woven basket, sitting in front of a stall.

Scarlet set her palms on the ground to push herself up. Her hair fell over her face, obscuring her view.

"Hey, you better be paying for that!"

Scarlet jumped to her feet, hair still in her eyes. "What?"

A man was coming out from behind the table. He was a broad human with a red face and thick hands. "You damaged my property, you better pay for it." He gestured to the basket.

"Sorry, I didn't mean to," said Scarlet. "But it's not damaged. It looks fine." The basket sat innocent and uninjured on the stone floor.

"It looks fine?" The man asked, crossing his arms. "Are you blind as well as clumsy? You need to pay for that."

"I'm not blind," said Scarlet, scowling. "That's how I know it's fine. And it was in the path, so it's not my fault."

"Are you suggesting that it's my fault you–"

"Leave her alone," came a voice at Scarlet's side.

Scarlet looked to the left and found a girl, about her height, standing with her hands on her hips. She had blonde, curly hair–the coils going every which way. "Are you alright?" she asked Scarlet. "I saw you fall."

Scarlet nodded, "I'm okay."

"Young lady, this does not concern you," said the man, facing the newcomer. His eyebrows descended down his forehead to crest his eyes like furry clouds.

"Your basket was out in the path," said the girl. "And you're just in a bad mood because it's been there for two weeks since no one wants it."

"Mera Bonningham, show me some respect," said the man, face reddening. "Don't speak to me like that or I will tell your mother."

"Go right ahead," she replied, blue eyes narrowing. "And I'll tell your wife what you said about her the other night when you were dead drunk in The Dining Hall."

The man blinked.

Then, to Scarlet's surprise, the girl took Scarlet's hand and led her away from the stall.

The girl, Mera the man had called her, pulled Scarlet farther down the path until they'd put a few stalls between them and the red-faced vendor.

"Are you alright?" asked Mera, pulling out a handkerchief. "You hit your chin pretty hard." As she handed the handkerchief over to Scarlet, Scarlet saw a flash of recognition go through her eyes.

"I'm alright," said Scarlet, wiping at her chin with the handkerchief. It came away tainted pink. "Is my chin bad?"

"Just a scrape," said Mera, shaking her head.

"Thanks for saving me," said Scarlet. "I didn't mean to trip over that. I didn't see it."

"Don't worry about it," said Mera. "It wasn't a big deal, but Mr. Spurn is always mad."

Out of sheer curiosity Scarlet couldn't help but ask, "What did he say about his wife in the Dining Hall?"

Mera snorted. "Probably nothing, but he doesn't remember what he did say, so he won't remember what he didn't."

Scarlet laughed.

"You're Scarlet Mount, aren't you?" Mera asked, blue eyes turning inquisitive.

Scarlet nodded. "Yeah. That's me."

"What're you doing here?"

Scarlet shrugged. "Trying to get a look around the fortress."

"Would you like me to give you a tour?"

"Really?" asked Scarlet, eyes widening. "That would be great!"

"Alright, just give me one second." Mera turned to look at the booth they were standing next to. Scarlet hadn't really looked at it before, but now that she did she saw that it was laden with a collection of seemingly random items. There were stones, flowers, a cage of butterflies, feathers, and spices in little jars.

"Mama!" said Mera, yelling over the noise.

A head, alive with golden curls even more ecstatic than Mera's, popped up from behind the stall. "Mera, have you seen the tree frogs?"

"Mama, did you lose them again?" Mera asked, putting her hands on her hips.

"No," the woman waved her hand, "I misplaced them."

"That's the same thing as losing them."

Mera's mother shook her head, "No it's not, that's why it's a different word. Anyway, what did you need, sugar?"

"I'm taking a break," said Mera. "I'm showing someone around the fortress."

"Alright," said the woman. "But as your mother I have to tell you not to die, injure yourself, or start any fights. And if you do start a fight, make sure you win. And if you don't win, blame it on the weather."

Scarlet looked up at the clear, sunny sky above.

"Got it, Mama," said Mera. "Let's go," then she led Scarlet down the row of stands.

"Your family runs the stand?" asked Scarlet.

Mera nodded. "Yup. Well, my mom does. My dad isn't here. This way," she led Scarlet out of the market. "What have you already seen?"

"Just the Dining Hall, the Main Courtyard, the Courtyard with all the targets, and obviously the Marketplace."

"So nothing interesting yet."

Scarlet disagreed, she didn't think she'd ever been anywhere more interesting in her life.

"I'll show you the really cool places," said Mera. "Just down this way." They started down a set of stairs and a handful of hallways.

They walked for just a minute before Mera stopped. "Here we are. This is the Alleyway."

The Alleyway didn't look very impressive. It was like all the other hallways: stone, lit with torches in sconces on the walls, and lined with wooden doors.

Scarlet frowned.

"Hold on," said Mera, seeing her expression. "Just give it a chance. This is where everyone heads for fun. It shouldn't be very busy right now, but it will be later in the afternoon when the market shuts down and training stops."

"Everyone comes to this hallway?"

"To the rooms in this hallway," said Mera, stepping to the side and setting her fingers on a door handle. "I don't know if you'll like this one. It'll depend."

"On what?"

Mera swung the door open. "If you like to read."

Scarlet stepped in and this time she felt like her mind was exploding.

The room was round and tall, stretching high above their heads. Scarlet figured she could throw a stone upward as hard as she could and it still wouldn't hit the ceiling. The sides of the room were lined with shelves fitted into the circular wall. The shelves extended all the way up to the walls' top, and they were jammed with books. Big and small, colorful and drab, tucked neatly onto the shelf or thrown on top of a row–they were everywhere.

Every seven or so feet up there was a balcony going around the circumference of the room. There were four balconies in total. The first was accessible by a ladder against the wall, the second by a ladder on the first balcony, the third by a ladder on the second balcony, and so on. The

The Hinterland

center of the room was empty of shelves, but jam-packed with large, squashy red chairs and short-legged tables. All of it was lit by a massive chandelier, glowing like a miniature sun above their heads.

"This is–" Scarlet felt breathless. "This is–"

"Amazing?" asked Mera.

Scarlet nodded wordlessly.

"I think so too," Mera said, "but this is the most unpopular room in the Alleyway. With everything going on around here, reading isn't everyone's biggest priority."

"I could stay here forever," said Scarlet, stepping to the center of the room and turning a slow circle. She had the sudden urge to climb up every single one of those ladders, all the way to the balcony at the top, find a good book, and curl up to get lost in it.

"Me too, but I'm not done with my tour," said Mera. "Come with me," she stepped out of the room.

Scarlet took one last, long look around the library, then followed her.

"This one is also interesting," said Mera. She opened the door next to the library one, and she and Scarlet stepped in. They entered a small space with a second door in front of them. Scarlet stepped forward to open the second door, but Mera grabbed her arm, stopping her.

"We have to close the first door all the way first," she pulled the first door closed tight. "Go ahead."

Scarlet walked in. She was expecting something that would amaze her just as much as the library had, but instead–there was nothing. The room was bare. "What's this supposed to be?" asked Scarlet, turning to Mera.

Mera only smiled. "Look up."

Scarlet looked up and her knees went weak. "Those are dragons."

Mera nodded, "Good eyesight you have there."

Above their heads were logs, suspended in the air from chains. There were four or five of them in total, so thick Scarlet figured if she wrapped her arms around one her fingers still wouldn't touch. Crawling under and over the beams were over a dozen dragons. Some of them were pocket-sized; Scarlet could have easily held them in her palm. Others were larger, like small dogs. They were bright red with small barbs lining their backs.

"Are they dangerous?"

"No, their claws are clipped and their fire glands have been removed. They've also had their teeth blunted," said Mera. "They keep them here because shavings from their spines and scales are used medicinally."

As Scarlet watched, one of the dragons hissed and dove into a hole at the log's side. It seemed the wood was hollow. Now that Scarlet was looking for it, she saw that the other logs bore holes as well.

"Here they're tame," continued Mera. "But in the wild they're as vicious as Fire Benders."

Scarlet watched them climb above her. "What's a Fire Bender?"

"You know, super dangerous, out-of-control, incredibly rare fire people. They're mostly in legends, I doubt anyone here has ever met a real one."

"I've never heard of them."

"That's alright, I didn't know anything about the magical world before I got here a month ago. I was living in a human village."

"Why'd you leave?" asked Scarlet, looking at her.

"The Wraith got to it." Mera didn't elaborate, instead she watched the dragons with increased focus. "Here, there's something you should try," she turned to the wall where there was a small box attached to the stone. She opened the top of the box and pulled out a strip of blue cloth, handing it to Scarlet. "Hold this up."

"Why?"

"Trust me, just do it."

Scarlet took the cloth and held it up above her head. Almost immediately a red flash zipped down from the ceiling, seized the strip and sped back up to the beams. Scarlet watched the red tail and tip of blue cloth disappear into a hole.

"What's he doing with it?" Scarlet asked, watching the spot where it had disappeared.

"They have nests inside the logs. In the wild they pad their nests with leaves and brush, but we find cloth makes less of a mess." Scarlet imagined the inside of the log, layered with soft strips of colorful fabric, like a dragon-made quilt they could snuggle up in. She smiled without meaning to.

"Pretty cute, aren't they?" asked Mera.

"Yeah," agreed Scarlet, although "pretty cute" didn't even begin to describe it.

"There's some more cool rooms," said Mera. They stepped out of the dragon room, letting the first door close behind them before opening the second. This kept the dragons from making a "jailbreak" Mera explained.

"This door over here," said Mera, stepping across the hallway to the door next to the pool, "is the pub. Technically we're not supposed to go in there because we can't drink, but Cerulean says that they stop monitoring who comes in at around ten o'clock."

"Is it open right now?" Scarlet asked, looking at the door. She didn't want a drink, but she did want to know what a pub looked like when it was hosting dwarves, nymphs, elves, and humans all together.

Mera shook her head. "It won't open until the end of the day when everyone stops working and training."

Training–the word jogged Scarlet's memory, and she felt a sudden jolt in her stomach. "Oh no, I have training! I have to go!"

"Alright," Mera paused, "Will I be seeing you around?"

Scarlet was already beginning to turn down the hallway, but at Mera's words she looked back. "Absolutely." She didn't wait for Mera to respond before breaking into a run, but even with her stomach doing flips, she couldn't help but grin. Maybe this would be the end of her loneliness.

Chapter 16

Scarlet ran through the fortress, excitement and fear going off inside her like fireworks. She entered the Dining Hall, eyes on the Main Courtyard where she knew Enyalios would be waiting.

She stepped into the courtyard. It only took her a moment to locate Enyalios, standing in the farthest training arena. She hurried to it, arriving red-faced and sweaty, and leaning forward slightly as she tried to catch her breath. She resisted the urge to put her hands on her knees.

"Sorry I'm late," she said, breathing hard.

"No matter," said the elf, surveying her sagging figure. "It's to be expected. After all, humans are known for having little respect for the time of elves."

Scarlet straightened up and stepped over the knee-high wooden wall lining the arena's perimeter. "No, it wasn't disrespect for your time, it was that I met someone in the–"

He waved his hand, cutting her off. "Let's get started. You have already cut into our appointment with your untimeliness, we cannot delay any further." He went to the edge of the arena and picked up a sword from the ground. He tossed it through the air and she caught it by the blade. Luckily it was made completely of wood.

"I would suggest not holding a real blade like that," said Enyalios, casting her a scathing look.

She quickly adjusted her grip. The sword felt heavy and awkward in her hand. "What are we going to do?"

"We're going to duel."

"I'm dueling you?" Scarlet asked, eyes widening.

He nodded, bending over to pick up a second wooden sword from the ground.

"But I've never even held a sword before," protested Scarlet. "I don't know how to duel."

"Interesting," said Enyalios, scrutinizing her in a way that suggested he found her to be a walking insult. "High Elves learn sword play the moment they can walk."

"I'm not a High Elf."

"I know," said Enyalios pointedly.

Scarlet clenched the sword handle so hard her knuckles turned white.

"But they say experience is the best teacher," continued Enyalios. "This will get you some experience."

"I–"

Enyalios batted her sword out of her hands, hitting her knuckles as well as the wooden blade.

"Ouch!" She wrung out her hand.

"If you can't handle such a trivial blow, you will never hold your own in a real duel," said Enyalios, the corner of his mouth curled up in what might be disgust. "Get your sword."

Scarlet ignored her stinging knuckles and bent to pick up her sword. She straightened and held it in front of her.

"Go ahead," said Enyalios. "Try an offensive attack."

Tentatively, she stepped forward, swinging her sword at him. Again, he hit the sword away, and again his wooden blade rapped against her knuckles. This time she managed to keep a hold on her sword, but it threw her off balance.

"This is disappointing," he said, lowering his weapon. "For someone so anticipated, I was expecting you to have natural talent. It seems I was wrong."

How will you save them? How will you protect them? The words from the elf in the Dining Hall drifted through her mind like a cold voice whispering in her ear.

"I'm a quick learner," she said, brushing black hair out of her eyes and scowling at him.

"You're human. No amount of learning can fix that."

Scarlet's eyes widened. She hadn't expected anything quite so directly hostile. It made her chest hot with anger like there was a burning ember resting where her heart should be. "And what's wrong with being human?"

"Let's try again," said the High Elf, ignoring her question.

She hefted the blade.

He lunged, so fast she couldn't even see the sword before it smacked her side. She doubled over, holding the spot where the wood had slammed against her ribs.

"If you're not even going to try to stop me, we might as well continue this session tomorrow," said Enyalios, watching her as she massaged her side with her hand.

"I was try–" but the High Elf was already walking away.

Scarlet's first training session had lasted no more than five minutes.

As he left Scarlet remembered Lug's words from the Dining Hall. He had said that High Elves thought they were better than everyone else. She couldn't help thinking he was right. So far she hadn't had good experiences with any of the High Elves she'd run into. Well, except for Beck. But there had been the High Elf in the Dining Hall, now Enyalios, and thinking back to her meeting with the Council, Beck's father had seemed prideful as well. He hadn't said anything cruel, but was that just because the Council was there? Could he hate her too? Could Beck secretly hate her just for being human?

She stabbed the tip of the wooden sword into the dirt floor of the training arena, grinding it downward and trying to forget the idea.

She had no logical reason, but she was confident she could find a way to help in the war. She was human and young and inexperienced, but she was eager, she wanted to learn, and she wanted to fight. If she was given a chance, she felt sure she could prove people like the elf from the Dining Hall wrong.

She let out a long sigh. She needed to talk to someone she knew didn't hate her.

It was with this in mind that she opened the door of room number fourteen ten minutes later.

"Code word?"

Tobin grinned, looking up from his table where he'd been sorting his playing cards into piles. "Pumpernickel."

"What's in the envelope?" she asked, walking over and sitting down next to him on the cot.

He frowned, shaking his head. "What envelope?"

"It means what's going on with you?"

"Oh, I didn't know that one."

"That's weird," said Scarlet, propping her feet up on the table and resisting the urge to smile at her own onside joke.

"I'm doing good," he replied. "Check this out, we've made music."

He stood up.

"Music?"

"Just hold on," he walked to the wall and rapped his knuckles against it: once–twice–three times–again and again to form a steady beat. Then suddenly from the other side came a series of quick-paced knocks. With a little imagination it did sound a bit like music.

"Dungeon wall," said Scarlet. "My favorite musical genre." She tried for a smile.

Tobin frowned. "What's going on?"

She wondered how he could read her so easily. "Nothing."

"Come on, you seem... off." The drummer on the other side of the wall ceased as Tobin's beat ended.

"I'm just–," she stopped.

As she looked at him, curls framing his earnest, concerned face, she could remember him telling her that she might be the bravest person he'd ever met. He actually thought she was up to the job the Fate Stones had chosen her for. If she told him she was being bullied, would that change?

"I don't want to talk about it."

Tobin held her gaze for a moment, then nodded. "That's alright. But if you ever need someone to talk to–well, I'm a good listener."

"Thanks," she said. Already the crushing feeling Enyalios had put in her chest was lessening. She looked for a way to change the conversation, eyes landing on the sheets of paper she'd left for Tobin during her last visit. She leaned over and picked them up off the table. They were blank. "You didn't write anything?"

"Yeah, um," he scratched his nose. "I've been busy."

Scarlet bit her lip, but it was no use. She laughed out loud. "With what? Wall music?"

"Well we've made two different melodies," he said quickly, taking the sheets of paper out of her hand and setting them back on the table. "Actually, the second one is really something, would you like to hear it?" He started to stand up.

"Hold on," said Scarlet, "you're trying to change the subject. What's the real reason?"

Tobin sat back down and picked at the edge of the blanket on the cot. He shrugged.

"Is it that you don't want me to read them? It's okay if you don't want me to." She tried to ignore the hurt she felt that he might not trust her to read what he'd written. "But I still think you should write them down. The ones you told me in the dungeon were really good."

"I can't," said Tobin, studying his hands.

"Sure you can, I swear I won't look unless you give me permission–"

"No, it's not that," he said. "I can't–I can't read or write." He didn't look at her as he said the words, almost like he was admitting to a terrible crime.

"Oh." The thought that he might not be able to write had never crossed her mind. Everyone in her village had learned to read and write in school. Her dad had taught her even sooner. "I didn't think about that."

"I never went to school," he confessed. "I was too busy working the farm. My family needed me at home."

She didn't reply, unsure of what to say.

"It's not that I didn't want to," he said quickly. "And I think I could've learned it. I'm not stupid or anything."

"I know you're not stupid," said Scarlet quickly, looking at him even though he wasn't looking at her. "Tobin, you don't need to convince me you're smart, I know you are. And you could've told me that you couldn't read or write. I wouldn't–I don't think any less of you for it. If you want, I could teach you." Scarlet said the last thought as it came to her.

Tobin looked at her for the first time since the conversation had started. "Wait–really?"

"Yeah, if you'd like that."

"I would," said Tobin, a wide smile breaking across his face that made Scarlet tingle inside. "When can we start?"

Scarlet grabbed the sheets of paper from the table and seized the pencil. "Right now."

The Hinterland

Chapter 17

Tasha woke up quickly, her breaths coming far too fast. *Around her there was screaming–screaming everywhere.* But her room was silent. *The world was red, she was watching the life she knew burn.* But she was in darkness. *This was her fault, she was the one who had done this.* She was sitting alone against the wall.

As the nightmare faded from her, the room–her room–came into focus. It was new, given to her, despite her protests, after she'd been chosen.

It was in the West Tower, across from Scarlet's, and was far bigger than the one Beck had taken her to when she'd first come to the fortress. The bed was bigger, too. It looked softer, but Tasha still preferred the floor.

The only light in the room was coming from a small lantern on the bedside table. She pushed herself forward onto her knees. In the light of the lantern she could see the floor where she'd been lying was scorched. Not just where her hands had been, but anywhere bare skin had made contact.

It was getting worse, and while she was asleep, there was nothing she could do to control it.

At least in this fortress the walls were stone, not wood. Not like– she shook her head. No. Not now, not today. If she could have it her way, she would never relive the memory again.

But it was like she could see the memory through a little window in her mind. The window was growing bigger, and bigger, and bigger–

And she was twelve again.

And she'd tried so hard to do it all right, but how much could you really do when your feelings were flammable?

Tasha jumped to her feet. In a smooth, vicious motion she pulled her dagger from its sheath at her hip and slashed through the mattress of the bed in front of her. Feathers flew around her like white, fluffy rain.

The feeling of the dagger in her hand, and the motion of ripping into the bed, pulled her back to herself. The window got smaller, shrinking to the corner of her mind where it stayed. Where it resided always like a ghost haunting her.

The room felt suddenly stifling. She turned, flung open the door, and stepped into the hallway beyond.

Wandering out into the hallway she made her way to the only other place in the fortress she ever spent time in: the Main Courtyard. She needed to train, to focus, to push her emotions out the only way she could—when she used her daggers.

It was early morning, and the sun was just starting to come up. The sky was still dark, but streaked with purples and pinks like strokes from a paintbrush. As soon as Tasha stepped into the courtyard, she realized that she was not alone. Someone else was already there.

She stood in silence for a moment, watching Beck as he trained.

She'd assumed he wasn't bad. The easy confidence about him suggested it—but now she had a feeling every bit of that confidence was deserved. He trained like a warrior. His movements were quick and precise, each strike built up in the muscles of his arms and shoulders, released with a timing that made the blows land like bolts of lightning.

He stopped, wiping an arm across his brow. "Hey Tasha."

She started. "How did you know I was here?"

"Heard you," he said, turning around. He pointed a finger to his ears. "Elven hearing is gold."

"How did you know it was me?"

"Anyone else would have said hi." There was sweat gleaming on his brow. "But you seem very determined not to make friends."

"Well, aren't you quite the detective."

"Is that a hint of sarcasm I'm detecting?" asked Beck, raising his eyebrows. "So, she does have a sense of humor after all." He sheathed his sword.

Tasha almost smiled. She stopped herself, knowing the reaction would only encourage him, but his grin made her feel like he knew.

"So, that duel?" he asked.

"Not right now."

He nodded. "Why not? I noticed you've got some sort of no-touching thing. Is it that? It's okay if it's that. I get it."

"It's–" it wasn't exactly the no-touching thing. Her powers were never a problem when she was fighting. The problem was that a dueling partner could easily turn into a friend. And friends... friends were too risky. "I don't think it's a good idea."

"Okay, I'll stop asking," he said putting his hands up as though in surrender. "But, if you ever change your mind, I'm here every morning. You've always got an invitation to join me."

"What are you doing here this early?" Tasha asked. "Don't you already train with a unit?"

He shrugged. "Yeah, I have training later. But that's for the war, and the unit, and other pixie dust. This is for me."

She considered him. It was as though an understanding was passing between them. A sense of connection which, Tasha realized with jolting unease, felt good.

She didn't think before stepping back. "I've got to go."

He watched her for a moment, and for a second Tasha wondered if he was going to call her on her lie. She had nowhere to be and he must know it. But he nodded. "No problem." He turned back to the training dummy and unsheathed his sword.

Tasha turned and made a beeline for the Dining Hall. The need to train had disappeared, replaced with the need to get away from a new danger.

"Scarlet, you'd better not eat that meat."

Yet again, Scarlet found herself in the Dining Hall having breakfast with Beck. She was glad to have someone to talk to, but she couldn't help but wish Tobin was across the table from her instead of the green-eyed High Elf. Especially with her new paranoia that his friendly demeanor might be nothing more than an act.

"Why not?"

"Because I know just about everything about this fortress, and I still have no idea where it comes from."

Scarlet wrinkled her nose at the strips of red meat on her tray. On second thought, maybe she would just eat the eggs. She began to dig into the yellow fluff.

"By the way," added Beck, "I think your magic test is tomorrow."

Scarlet's eyes widened. He said it so calmly as though it wasn't the most exciting thing that would ever happen to her. "What?"

Beck opened his mouth to answer–and then stopped, eyes seizing on someone behind her. He stood up, fast enough that his chair flew back. Scarlet looked to see who it was, half-expecting to see Tasha, but a new figure was entering the Dining Hall.

"Cerulean!" called Beck.

The newcomer was a boy–an elven boy based on his pointy ears. He looked around Scarlet's age, skinny and taller than she, with an explosion of messy white hair at the top of his head. His face was pale and well defined, but as he turned to Beck, Scarlet saw that his attractiveness was somewhat marred by a sharp scowl.

But then he registered who had called his name and his scowl lessened, not disappearing completely, but becoming more of a light frown as he walked toward them.

"I haven't seen you since I got back," said Beck, walking to meet him in front of the table. "I know how much you roam, but I was getting worried. What have you been up to since I've been gone?"

The elf–Cerulean–shrugged, shoving his hands into his pockets. "The usual." His voice was hard. Scarlet wondered if he was another High Elf she would have to watch out for.

"The usual?" asked Beck, eyes narrowing. "Meaning..?"

It seemed that, perhaps, the younger elf's "usual" wasn't a good thing.

"You would know if you'd stayed," answered Cerulean, scowl returning full force.

"C'mon, don't be like that," said Beck. "I had to go. My father volunteered me, he said it would look good when I run for the Elven Court."

"You told me you didn't care about the court."

Beck's eyes widened and he glanced around as though worried someone had overheard. "I also told you not to repeat that." His voice had gone low.

"Oops," said Cerulean, not sounding especially apologetic. He sat down across from Scarlet and propped his feet up on the table.

"You didn't get into trouble again, did you?" asked Beck, sitting down and watching Cerulean with a wary expression.

"I don't think I ever get out of trouble to begin with." The words themselves could have been a joke, except Cerulean might be playing poker for the emotion he showed.

"What happened?"

"I got a little apartment, you should have seen it," answered Cerulean. "It was real nice. Had a bed and a locked door and everything. It's fine though, I'll have you over next time."

"What do you–" Beck stopped. "They locked you up?"

Cerulean shrugged. He leaned onto the back two legs of his chair, letting the front two rise into the air. "They said I had one strike too many. Something about not knowing what else to do with me."

Beck clenched his jaw. Scarlet wondered if he was going to get mad. She had never seen him angry before. In fact, she had never seen him not in a great mood. Not even when she'd found him and Elowen tied up in the monster camp and had accidentally cut him with the knife.

But then Beck let out a long breath. "What started it this time?" he asked, leaning back in his chair.

Cerulean opened his mouth, then closed it. He glanced at Scarlet then back to Beck. "Can you just pretend to be my mother some other time?"

Beck looked like he wanted to argue, but he took another breath, exhaling slowly through his nose. "Fine." He made his voice high-pitched. "But we're not done here, young man."

Scarlet couldn't stop herself from giggling.

Cerulean rolled his eyes. He looked to Scarlet. "Who are you?" He sounded bored, though his gaze held a spark of interest.

"Scarlet Mount," she said, extending a hand.

He eyed her with a lazy expression, then shook. His grip was firm, his expression uninterested. "As you've probably gathered, I'm Cerulean."

"Are you a High Elf?"

He nodded. "Are you a human?"

She nodded. She watched his face carefully, looking for any reaction to her answer, but he didn't seem to care.

Instead he stretched, extending his arms in front of himself and interlocking his fingers. The motion pulled the edge of his long sleeves back and Scarlet caught sight of two marks on his left forearm—like tattoos—before he noticed her looking and pulled his sleeve back up.

She decided not to ask about them.

"Avenbeck," a new voice met Scarlet's ear, this one familiar. Elowen had appeared out of nowhere. It seemed their table was very popular this morning.

"Uh-huh?" Beck asked, shoveling a steaming forkful of eggs into his mouth. Scarlet had never seen anyone eat with as much vigor as he did.

"Your father needs to talk to you."

Beck looked up quickly. "Did he say why?"

"No, but he's been trying to find you for a half hour."

Beck stood up, grabbing his tray. "Shi—"

"Avenbeck," said Elowen sharply.

"You're still getting mad at him for cussing?" asked Cerulean, squinting at her. "He's eighteen."

"While he's in uniform," said Elowen, gesturing to Beck, who was fitted in his set of armor as usual. "He represents The Alliance as a whole. So yes, no cussing when it can be helped."

Cerulean's eyes rolled. "No one minds but you."

Elowen pursed her lips but didn't reply. Beck shoveled down one last bite of eggs. "See you guys later."

He and Elowen turned and left.

"She doesn't let anyone in her unit swear," said Cerulean. "Makes them run laps if they do. She takes pride in it. I think she just does it to show them all who's boss."

"I didn't think Beck was in her unit?" asked Scarlet.

"He's not, but she'd still tell him to run laps," he snorted. "And Beck would do it."

"Cerulean!" Suddenly they were joined by yet another newcomer.

"Mera!" said Scarlet, grinning.

Mera ignored Scarlet and stalked up to Cerulean. She was holding a book in her hand. "Are you okay? They wouldn't let me go see you."

Cerulean nodded, "I'm just dandy," he replied, straight-faced. "Just gre–"

"In that case–" Mera smacked the top of his head with the book. "You. Complete. Gnome."

The chair started to fall backward, and he had to grab the edge of the table to stop himself from falling.

"Holy sprites Mera, a 'good to see you' would do," Cerulean rubbed the top of his head, scowling.

"What's wrong with you?" asked Mera. "Three on one? Did you honestly think that was going to work out in your favor?"

"I may have been overly optimistic."

As she watched him, Scarlet marveled silently at just how impassive his face remained.

"Twice this month," said Mera, setting the book on the table and putting her hands on her hips. "Do you like getting beat up?"

"It's a main hobby of mine, actually."

Mera scowled, picking up the book and smacking him in the head again.

Cerulean swore. "Are you really going to get mad at me for getting beat up by beating me up?"

"You have to stop doing this," said Mera, pulling up a chair and sitting down. She frowned at him.

He fisted his hand on the table. "It's not my fault."

"Who started it?" asked Mera.

"They did," answered Cerulean without hesitation.

"Let me rephrase. Who threw the first punch?"

He scowled, running his tongue over his teeth before answering, "I did."

She let out a frustrated groan.

"Alright, I'm sorry," he said. He said it sarcastically, but Scarlet thought she heard a hint of realness underneath. She couldn't be sure.

Mera didn't reply for a moment, then her expression softened slightly and she let out a long sigh. "Fine." She relaxed in her chair. "I see you've met Scarlet?"

"We were just acquainted," said Cerulean.

"How long have you two known each other?" asked Scarlet, looking between Cerulean and Mera.

"About a month and a half," said Mera. "I met him when I got here. Cerulean, did you know that Scarlet is one of the Chosen?"

Cerulean raised a single eyebrow. He did it so smoothly Scarlet felt like he must have practiced. "Interesting."

Scarlet's stomach flip-flopped under his intense gaze. He'd been looking at her before, but now he really looked at her. Like she was a line of writing that he was trying to memorize. If she was a line of writing, she wondered what she would say. Would it be something that would impress him, or something that would make him think less of her?

"I just got here a couple days ago," she said.

He nodded, finally looking away.

Scarlet looked past him into the courtyard behind the Dining Hall. She could see Enyalios entering for their second training session. "I've got to go."

She stood up.

"See you later," said Mera with a smile.

Cerulean did nothing to acknowledge her goodbye.

Maybe, Scarlet thought as she started toward the courtyard, Enyalios' mood yesterday had been the result of a bad day. Maybe this next session would be different.

But no level of optimism could drown the creeping feeling of dread in her stomach.

Chapter 18

"I'm on time," said Scarlet, entering the arena where Enyalios was already waiting.

He scowled. "If you truly cared about your learning you would not settle for just barely being on time. As the High Elves say: early is on time, on time is late, late," he gave her a pointed glare, "is unacceptable."

Scarlet considered the quote. "But then wouldn't everyone always be late?"

Enyalios' scowl deepened. "What?"

"If I come early, then that makes me on time," said Scarlet. "But if I'm on time that makes me late. So, it's impossible not to be late."

"That's not how it works."

Scarlet shrugged. "If you say so."

His lip curled, but instead of arguing he asked, "I trust you have practiced on your own since our last session?"

Scarlet's stomach plummeted. Had he told her to practice? She didn't think so. "You mean our session yesterday?"

He raised his eyebrows in a way that suggested she and the word stupid were a synonym in his book.

"No," said Scarlet. "There wasn't time between sessions for me to practice."

He scoffed. "No time? Tell me what you did yesterday."

"I–uh–" she hesitated. She'd spent most of her night chatting with Tobin, working on teaching him to read. She had a feeling Enyalios would deem the activity a waste of time.

"Just as I thought," said Enyalios. "If you want to get better, you have to practice. There is no such thing as natural talent. You couldn't name a single skilled sword fighter with natural talent."

"What about Beck?" asked Scarlet. The High Elf seemed to be naturally good at everything he did.

"Avenbeck? Son of Deimos?" asked Enyalios, laughing. The laugh had no humor in it. "You think he has natural talent? No. His father put a sword in his hand as soon as he could hold one. He's trained in the halls of the High Elves with various experts; he's learned dozens of fighting techniques. What you are seeing is no natural talent, it is learned talent. If you want talent like that you have to sweat for it. Do not expect me to teach you the art of sword fighting if you cannot even take the time from your day to train on your own."

"I didn't know I was supposed to," said Scarlet.

"Now you do." He picked up the wooden swords from where he'd set them on the ground and tossed one to Scarlet. This time she caught it by the handle.

"Let's begin," and instantly Enyalios swiped at her. She jumped back, away from his sword's arc. He stepped closer; she stepped farther. He swiped again, this time clipping the edge of her sword and throwing her off balance. Then the flat of his blade hit her back and sent her sprawling to the dirt floor of the arena.

She stood up and brushed herself off. Dirt dusted her knees.

"How'd you do that?" she asked. The movement of the sword had been too quick for her to even register.

"It helps to be a High Elf," answered Enyalios. "We are built faster, quicker, and stronger."

"Aren't all elves born with extra speed and agility?" asked Scarlet. "Not just High Elves?"

"All elves are born with physical characteristics that trump those of humans, but High Elves are superior in mind."

"Would all elves agree with that?" asked Scarlet.

"If not, it's because they are ignorant."

Scarlet took that answer as a no. In fact, she had a feeling Elowen, as a Crescent Elf, would be very angry if she heard Enyalios now.

"Let's go again," he said.

Scarlet seized her blade.

He swung at her and she batted blindly. By pure luck her swing managed to glance off of his blade, stopping his strike.

Scarlet grinned, joy filling her insides the way sweet chocolate fills your mouth when it melts on your tongue. Enyalios looked furious.

For the rest of the training session Scarlet didn't land a single hit on Enyalios or his blade. Instead, her sword flew out of her grasp over and over again. Every time Enyalios hit her blade, his sword smacked against her knuckles until Scarlet was certain it was on purpose.

By the time Enyalios announced the session complete, her knuckles were red and raw. But still, she could feel the fluttering feeling resting in her stomach that the successful swing had given her. It was enough to leave her with a smile.

She retired to her room, planning on changing into a new, non-sweaty pair of clothes and then revisiting the library Mera had shown her.

She had just finished changing when she heard a knock at the door. She walked across the room and opened it.

"Code word?"

Scarlet's mouth fell open.

Tobin leaned against the door frame, curls bouncing around his ears and his smile the biggest Scarlet had ever seen it.

"Tobin?"

He laughed at her expression. "It's me. Though I still don't know if it's you. You haven't answered my question. You could be a monster." He wiggled his eyebrows at her.

"Pumpernickel," she said, rushing to get the word out so she could ask what she wanted. "They let you leave?"

"Yeah, they talked with Elowen and Beck, and asked me some questions, then they let me go. Good thing too, I was getting bored. My wall buddy was gone today."

"This is great!" said Scarlet. "I was just going down to the Alleyway, you should come with me. Holy sprites, you haven't seen anything yet–there's so much you have to see. You haven't seen the Main Courtyard, or the Ranged Courtyard, or the Market, or the–"

"Slow down," said Tobin with a grin. "You're forgetting to breathe."

"Just come with me," said Scarlet.

Ecstatic, she stepped past him into the hallway. "Is that your room?" he asked. Peering through the doorway.

She nodded.

Tobin shook his head slowly, eyes wide. "My family's entire house could fit into here three times."

"I know, it's huge," said Scarlet, closing the door as they started down the hallway. "Where are you living?"

"Well, they got me a room right near the infirmary. I told them that I've always wanted to be a healer and they're short-handed, so they're only too happy to apprentice me."

"You want to be a healer?"

"Yeah," he nodded. "I've always liked the idea. I just never thought I'd be able to. But now, if you're still willing to teach me how to read and I apprentice in the fortress infirmary, I might–I mean, maybe I could learn how." He looked at the floor, a small hopeful smile on his face.

"You would be an amazing healer!" said Scarlet. "And of course, I'm still going to teach you how to read. In fact, we can have a lesson in the library now." They wound through the fortress until they reached the Alleyway.

"You ready?" Scarlet asked, finding the correct door.

He nodded, and they stepped inside.

Instantly, his jaw dropped.

The library was even grander than Scarlet had remembered it and the room was filled with the dusty, enticing smell of old books. It was a smell Scarlet loved–a smell that reminded her of her happy place: inside the pages of a fairytale, lost in lines and words that formed worlds around her. A smell that reminded her of home and long nights reading with her father.

Tobin ran his hands through his hair. He seemed unable to form the words to describe what he thought. Instead, he stared up at the chandelier, and the balconies, and the rows and rows of books on their shelves. He was far too distracted to notice the way Scarlet's jaw had tightened.

"Scarlet!"

Scarlet looked for the owner of the voice, the memory of home momentarily swept away.

"Up here!"

Mera was waving to her from the second balcony. Scarlet waved back. "Cerulean, Scarlet's here!" shouted Mera.

Cerulean's head appeared over the railing of the third balcony. He nodded to her.

"Come down here, you two," said Scarlet. "There's someone you need to meet."

Mera clambered down the ladders, reaching the floor before Scarlet had time to cross the room. Cerulean took his time, slowly making his way down before finally stepping onto the floor and approaching the others. He looked just as bored as he had in the Dining Hall, throwing himself into one of the fat, cushioned chairs.

"This is Tobin," said Scarlet. "He came with me from the Wraith's fortress."

"I heard that you brought your guard, but I didn't think it was true," said Mera, looking at Tobin like he was a strange creature she was seeing for the first time.

Tobin cleared his throat and glanced at Scarlet.

Cerulean said nothing for a moment, only studied Tobin with narrowed gray eyes. "You worked for her? The Wraith?"

Tobin shifted and stuck his hands in his pockets. "I–yeah. I did."

"He didn't want to, though," said Scarlet quickly, stepping over to stand next to him. "And he helped me in the dungeon. I would have gone crazy without him."

Cerulean didn't say anything. He continued to consider Tobin with eyes so suspicious they bordered on angry.

"Nice to meet you, I'm Mera," said Mera, stepping forward and holding out her hand.

Tobin shook it. "Nice to meet you too."

Scarlet sat down in a chair and Tobin sat down in the one next to her. Mera followed suit, and soon they were all seated around a low table.

"You ever kill anybody?" asked Cerulean eying Tobin. "While you were working for her?" He crossed his arms and leaned back in his chair.

"No," said Tobin, shaking his head hard. "Never."

"You sure?" Cerulean looked relaxed, but his tone was the opposite.

"Cerulean," said Mera sharply.

"What?" asked Cerulean, voice also sharp. "I'm trying to find out what he's capable of."

"Tobin's training to become a healer," said Scarlet. She looked at Cerulean pointedly. "He wants to help people."

Cerulean said nothing.

Tobin looked at the floor and began to quietly rap his knuckles against the wooden arm of his chair. He didn't seem to realize he was doing it. Scarlet recognized it as the beat he'd played on the wall of his former jail cell.

Suddenly, Cerulean straightened, eyes sparking. He began to knock on the arm of his own chair.

Tobin heard it and looked up, eyes widening.

The sounds turned into a rythm Scarlet had heard only once before.

"No way," said Tobin. "You're my wall buddy?"

"Well, surely we can find a better name for it than that," said Cerulean, ceasing his rapping. "Room fourteen?"

Tobin nodded. "Room thirteen?"

Cerulean nodded.

Tobin smiled and Cerulean smirked. Scarlet though it was the first time she had seen the moody elf look anything but annoyed. The tension in the room died.

"No way!" said Tobin again, this time with more joy than disbelief. "I was worried you were going to be some old lady or crime-committing dwarf or something."

"Nope," said Cerulean. "Just a crime-committing elf."

"What were you there for?" asked Tobin.

"Fight."

Scarlet noticed that he didn't say he had started the fight, despite the fact that he'd admitted earlier in the Dining Hall to throwing the first punch.

"They threw you in a cell for that?" Tobin asked, brow creasing.

Cerulean gave a shrug. "One too many I guess. And you were there for having been one of the Wraith's guards?"

Now it was Tobin's turn to shrug.

"I was just showing Tobin around the fortress when we found you two," cut in Scarlet.

"Did you get to the dragons yet?" asked Mera.

"What?" asked Tobin, doing a double-take.

"Clearly not," commented Cerulean.

"Let's show him!" said Mera, jumping up.

Scarlet and Tobin got to their feet, and Cerulean pulled himself up from his chair.

They started to the library door and opened it, stepping into the Alleyway. As they did, someone passed by. Someone with bright red hair.

"Hey, Tasha," said Scarlet, waving.

Tasha nodded to her, rounding the corner and disappearing.

"She scares me," whispered Mera. "She's always got those daggers with her and she never talks to anyone. Plus, there's the thing that happened in the monster camp. I've heard she killed dozens of them at once."

"Sounds like a freak," said Cerulean, shaking his head.

"Hey, don't call Tasha a freak," said Scarlet, rounding on him. She balled her fists. "She isn't like that; she's a hero. She saved me and Tobin in the Hinterland, which was the only reason we made it here. Elowen and Beck would have died too, if not for her."

"Alright, alright," said Cerulean, putting his hands in the air. Scarlet thought she saw a hint of amusement coloring his gray eyes. "Sorry."

"Thank you," said Scarlet, giving him one last glare and turning away from him. "Now, let's go look at some dragons."

"Alright, alright. Sorry." From around the corner Tasha listened to the conversation play out.

"Thank you," said Scarlet, sounding more fierce than Tasha would have expected her capable of. "Now, let's go look at some dragons."

There was the sound of a door opening, then closing, and in a moment the hallway was silent.

After a second Tasha pushed away from the wall and slipped down the hallway. She hadn't been planning on eavesdropping–except she'd heard her name–heard it from Scarlet's mouth as the girl defended her.

Why would Scarlet do that? She'd done nothing but try to push Scarlet away. Nothing she seemed to do worked. Maybe nothing would. Maybe Scarlet was too determined to become Tasha's friend. Her and Beck both.

And befriending Tasha was just about as dangerous as befriending a Hinterland Wolf.

This made up her mind: she had to leave. Surely by now the orcs would no longer be in the area.

She'd give herself until tomorrow night to prepare and decide on the best way out, then, under the cover of darkness, she would leave before anyone would know to stop her.

Chapter 19

Scarlet woke to a knock on her door.

Groggily she clambered out of her blanket, wincing as the cold air hit her bare arms. The corners of her eyes felt sticky, and she rubbed at them as she stumbled to the door.

Beck was waiting for her.

"Hey there Scar," he said, smiling. "What's in the envelope?" Scarlet yawned. She couldn't understand how anyone could be so energetic in the morning, but Beck was perky as ever, armor on and hair immaculate as always.

"What time is it?" she asked, squinting at him.

"It's six in the morning."

"Six in the morning?" Scarlet shook her head at him in disbelief. "When did you get up?"

He considered, mouth moving as he silently worked backward through his day. "Four."

"In the morning?"

He nodded.

"But–" Scarlet couldn't think of any reason a sane person would get up that early. "Why in the world would you wake up at four?"

"Well, I trained in the Main courtyard for a half hour," answered Beck. "Then I went to take inventory in the armory. After that I went to run a handful of errands for my father, then to check in on a few people in the infirmary. I also told a friend I'd get her stand ready in the market since she's been ill. After that I ran down to Elowen's room because there was some conflict over which elite unit was supposed to have the Main Courtyard in the afternoon on Tuesday, which needed to be cleared up, and finally I was sent here to tell you that the Council is ready for your magic test."

"My magic test?" Scarlet immediately forgot everything else he'd said. Were Beck not there she might have jumped up and down. As it was, she forced herself to stand normally.

Somehow, though, it seemed he knew what she was feeling. "You excited?" he asked, grinning at her.

"Of course, I'm excited." She suddenly didn't feel tired anymore. "Let's go!"

"Wait," said Beck, putting up his hands. "You might want to change out of your pajamas first, Scar."

Scarlet glanced down at her silky nightgown.

"Oh, yeah."

"I mean, up to you," said Beck. "I'm not trying to dump your potion here, but personally, I never wear my nightgowns when I go to see the Council."

Scarlet snorted. "Give me five minutes."

She closed the door.

Five minutes later she stepped out of her room dressed in a light purple tunic and tan trousers. She'd pulled her hair back and tied it tight. "I'm ready."

Beck led her through the fortress, the whole time talking non-stop. She stifled yawns as she made conversation with him.

As they walked she tried to memorize their path, but they took too many twists, turns, stairways, and narrow corridors. It was at least ten minutes before they stopped. "We're about to enter the North Tower," said Beck, gesturing to the door in front of them.

Scarlet nodded, head bobbing up and down, "Let's go."

"Sprites," he laughed. "Impatient much?" But he reached forward and pulled the door open.

They entered a large circular room. The ceiling was high, and the walls were made mostly of tall glass windows. The space made her think of the library, and she found herself wondering if it was in a tower too.

Scarlet looked out the windows and found a breathtaking view of the Hinterland. For something so deadly, it was beautiful. She could see the distant green forest where she'd been kidnapped and the luscious, rolling plains where she'd been held captive. Although... looking over it, she wondered if it was supposed to seem that still. It appeared eerily stagnant, like even wind didn't dare to enter.

She pulled her attention away from the view and to the room itself. It was cozy with a fireplace, soft, red carpet covering the floor, and matching chairs set around a table at the center of the room.

At the table sat Deimos and Eldritch. They stood as Scarlet and Beck entered.

"Scarlet, welcome," said Eldritch. "Thank you for coming."

Beck turned to leave.

"Avenbeck, you may stay," said Deimos.

Beck hesitated before turning around. Scarlet assumed he had plenty of other things he needed to do, but he stepped to the table and took a seat. Scarlet followed his example and soon all four of them were seated. Beck sat to her left and the eldest elves sat across from her.

"I'm sure Avenbeck has told you why you're here," said Deimos, looking to Beck who was ruffling his own hair with one hand. He quickly re-smoothed it.

"We are ready to test your magic," continued Deimos, turning his gaze back to Scarlet. "The rest of the Council Members are preoccupied, so only Eldritch and I will be conducting the test today."

"I've never done anything that seemed like magic before," said Scarlet. The confession came out in a rush like a word avalanche, but she felt a need to begin the process with complete honesty.

"That's alright," said Eldritch kindly. "Even some elves aren't able to harness their wicks and use magic until they're your age. Luckily, we have many methods to see if you have magical capabilities without you having shown them yet."

He gestured to the tabletop.

For the first time Scarlet got a good look at the array of items scattered on it. There were a few stones, a staff, an assortment of bottles filled with curious, unidentifiable objects, and a long thin needle that made Scarlet's mouth go dry.

"Our first test is unreliable, but it's also very simple," said Eldritch. "So, we think it's worth a try. We need you to pick up that staff." He pointed to the staff on the table. It was long and gold with a large red jewel at the top. "The jewel atop the Staff of Gundra is supposed to glow when held by a person with magical capabilities."

Scarlet admired the staff. Carefully, she reached toward it. Around the table Beck, Scarlet, and Eldritch held their breaths. Deimos crossed his arms, looking unconcerned with the proceedings.

Then the staff was in her fist.

Collectively, the group exhaled.

"That's alright," said Eldritch, eyes on the dull rock at the staff's tip.

Scarlet's shoulders slumped.

"As I said, it's unreliable," repeated Eldritch. "Let's move to the next one."

"Eldritch, I've already told you none of these are dependable," said Deimos, with a sigh. "My idea would be much quicker and more accurate."

Eldritch gave Deimos an exasperated look. "We already decided your way is too risky." He looked to Scarlet and ignored Deimos, who from the looks of him, had not decided on anything. "Let's just have you attempt to use magic." Eldritch said. "Perhaps you have been unable to use your wick because you have not had the proper instruction."

"How?"

"Close your eyes."

She did as he instructed.

"Now focus on the energy you feel."

Scarlet focused on the nervous energy that was scribbling in her chest.

"Try to get a grasp on it."

Scarlet scrunched her face, unsure of how to do what Eldritch was instructing, but determined to try.

"Now hold out your hands."

Scarlet did so, her palms facing up toward the ceiling.

"Try to force the energy through them."

Scarlet scrunched her face even harder than before, clenching her teeth. She focused on her energy as she tried to harness it, to rein it in like a wild horse and then release it through her warm hands. And as she did so, she felt... nothing. Nothing at all.

She opened her eyes, heat creeping up her cheeks. "I don't feel anything."

"Again, that's alright. It's an unreliable test," said Eldritch. "I think it's best that we move on to –"

"Eldritch, that's enough. Your methods are not working. My method will." Deimos was watching them as though they were children playing with toys.

Eldritch scowled. "We talked about this; it is out of the question."

"You decided it was out of the question, I decided no such thing," said Deimos. Eldritch's eyebrows sank as he scowled. "If we want an absolute result, there is only one option."

Scarlet looked to Beck to see if he understood the conversation any better than she did. He looked confused, but after a moment his expression began to morph into one you might wear if you see a storm closing in. "You can't–" he started, but Deimos interrupted him, still looking to Eldritch.

"If I attempt to drain her, we would discover whether she has magic or not. It's the only way to be certain."

"It's too risky," said Eldritch, standing up. Even standing he seemed smaller than Deimos. "She's human. Yes, if she has magic it would show when it transferred to you, but if she has none, you will begin to directly drain her life energy, running the risk of killing her."

"You do not have to explain it to me, Eldritch, I know how my own powers work," snapped Deimos. "But I am experienced. I will not use it to excess." He stood up to face the Crescent Elf. He was taller than Scarlet remembered. She shrunk back in her chair.

Now Beck stood up to face his father. "Even if you don't kill her, it hurts–you'll hurt her."

Deimos' eyes were like sharp chips of green glass. "It is crucial to The Alliance that we know her capabilities. I am sure Scarlet will understand."

"Father–"

Deimos rounded on Beck, his tone becoming low and sharp. "Silence, this is not a matter in which you have say." Deimos looked back to Eldritch.

"This is unwise," said Eldritch.

"Then let us ask Scarlet what she thinks," said Deimos. "Perhaps she will understand the necessity of such action."

All three standing elves turned to look at Scarlet. Eldritch had his lips pressed tightly together. Beck gave a slight shake of his head. Deimos had his eyebrows raised, waiting.

Scarlet bit her lip. She couldn't help but be afraid of the pain, but she was desperate to know whether she had powers. It was her curiosity versus her fear.

Curiosity killed the cat. She pressed her lips together as her mother's voice sounded inside her head. *That's what the good Lord gave the cat nine lives for.* And there was her father's.

But she didn't have nine lives. She had one. One chance to make a difference in the world, and if this test would help her do that...

Her hands clenched in her lap. "I'll do it."

Beck and Eldritch's eyes widened simultaneously. It seemed they hadn't thought she'd agree to Deimos' plan.

"You heard her," said Deimos. "At least someone here understands priorities." He stepped away from the table. "Scarlet, come this way."

He pushed up his sleeves.

Scarlet stepped out from behind the table and stood a few feet from Deimos.

Beck ruffled his hair again and this time didn't bother fixing it.

"I'll try to be gentle," said Deimos. Somehow the words did nothing to reassure Scarlet. Deimos' eyes were still hard, but there was a spark in them, and he ran his tongue over his lips. He seemed almost eager to begin. It was just about enough to make Scarlet back out, but she steeled herself. This would all be worth it if Deimos discovered a single drop of magic inside her.

The High Elf held his hand out toward her, palm down.

Scarlet took a deep breath.

Then suddenly she was in pain. A piercing burn was in her chest.

Scarlet gasped.

The pain did not throb, or fade in and out. It was constant, simply there, unending. It attacked her and she was powerless to stop it. It had become a part of her. Or maybe she had become a part of it. She was more pain than person.

Scarlet doubled over. She clutched at her chest. She didn't realize she was dropping to her knees until she had.

"Stop!" She heard Beck's voice.

She saw Deimos' green eyes. His flexed fingers.

And then her vision cracked like broken glass.

She could see nothing but a figure in front of her.

Feel nothing but pain lancing through her body.

Then suddenly the figure before her was pushed aside by a second figure, and the pain in her chest vanished all at once. She slumped onto the red carpet. Her world was blurry, her arms weak. Somewhere very far away people were yelling.

"You were going to kill her!"

"I was being thorough. Clearly, I overestimated your ability to handle yourself when I allowed you to stay."

Slowly the world was beginning to repair itself, sliding back into place and shifting to a point of clarity.

Beck and Deimos were standing above her. Beck's back was to her, so all she could see were his tense shoulders, blocking his father from view. Scarlet didn't mind. She didn't especially want to see what expression went with the voice she'd just heard Deimos use.

"Scarlet, are you alright?" Eldritch knelt beside her.

"I'm fine," she said, sitting up. Oddly enough, she felt completely normal now that the draining itself was over.

"I apologize, Scarlet," said Eldritch, placing his hand on her shoulder. "I should never have allowed that to happen. You are too young for such things."

But now that the pain was gone there was only one thing Scarlet cared about. "Am I magic?"

Eldritch shook his head. "If you were magical Deimos would have been able to pull excess magic from you, which he could not do. So no, you are not magical."

The crushing disappointment was almost as painful as the draining she had just experienced. She'd been so sure she would have magic. She'd been clinging to the hope like a drowning man to a raft. Without magic, why was she here? Could she really make a difference in this fortress, in this war, without special powers?

"We should send you to the infirmary," Eldritch said, forehead creased.

"I feel fine," said Scarlet truthfully, but Eldritch had turned his attention to the other two in the room.

Deimos was talking to Beck in a low voice. Scarlet still couldn't see Beck's face, but his hands were clenched at his sides.

"I'm taking Scarlet to the infirmary," said Eldritch, loud this time.

"No, I will," said Beck quickly, spinning around to face them. He knelt to Scarlet. "Can you walk?"

She nodded, and he helped her to her feet.

Without a backward glance he led her out of the room.

Chapter 20

"Scarlet, you're not going to training after what just happened. Beck said that–"

"I told you, I'm fine," Scarlet sat on the edge of the infirmary bed, feet dangling off the side. "This is ridiculous. I've been fine ever since the draining ended. It doesn't hurt at all anymore, and I can't skip training. It's in ten minutes." She could already imagine what Enyalios would say if she didn't show. Probably that a High Elf would never skip training.

Tobin shook his head. "Absolutely not. You're not going." He had been in the infirmary when she had gotten there. His apprenticeship had already started.

Scarlet slid out of bed. "You know the last letter I was teaching you?"

"S?" he asked, nose crinkling. "Like in star?"

"You know what also starts with an S?"

"What does this have to do with–"

"See you!" said Scarlet, sliding off the bed, stepping quickly across the room, yanking open the door, and whipping out of the infirmary.

She dashed down the hallway and toward the Main Courtyard. It was true that she no longer felt any pain or discomfort from the draining. In fact, she was suffering no side effects at all. Had she possessed magic like an elf, she knew the draining would have affected her magic using abilities, depleting them temporarily. But because she was completely, frustratingly, non-magically human, she felt fine.

"I'm here," she said, reaching the arena red-faced and winded. "I'm early."

"By a minute," replied Enyalios scathingly.

Scarlet frowned. "I was coming from the infirmary."

He seemed unconcerned. "We are going to start with physical fitness."

"Pushups and stuff?"

"Pushups?" said Enyalios, brow creasing as he scowled.

"You know–" said Scarlet. She realized she was unsure of how to describe it, so she scrambled to the ground and did a quick one for example.

Enyalios scoffed. "Of course, you humans would name them such a thing. Those are Globe Straddles."

Scarlet laughed and Enyalios' eyes sharpened as though he was personally offended. "We will not be doing Globe Straddles, we will be running."

"Where?"

"Throughout the fortress."

"Wouldn't it be better if–"

But he was off, running toward the Main Courtyard's exit with the unnatural speed of an elf. Scarlet took a deep breath, then sprinted after him.

It seemed he was only jogging, but she had to run as fast as she could to catch up before he rounded the corner. His gait was smooth and agile compared to hers, and he seemed to be gliding instead of running. Meanwhile, each of her clunky steps thumped loudly against the stone, and under the hot sun sweat was already beginning to form on her scalp. She wondered how much of the distance between them was because she was human and he an elf, and how much was due to her lack of athleticism.

"This way," said Enyalios, turning a corridor. Scarlet followed, her breaths becoming painful. She had to force out every exhale and fight for every inhale. They ran upstairs and downstairs, through the market where Mera waved from her family's stand, and up another set of stairs.

If she weren't so out of shape, Scarlet would have enjoyed the run. It was interesting to observe the fortress in action. Crowds of people traveled the hallways, and Scarlet caught many of them looking at her curiously, or even pointing at her.

Not only were the people interesting, the fortress itself was begging for her attention. They passed through courtyards open to the sky, into covered hallways, onto open balconies jutting straight out of the mountainside to face the Hinterland, and then back into the torch-lit depths of the mountain. As they ran Scarlet realized that the fortress was even bigger than she'd realized. From one of the balconies she counted over a dozen turrets spiking out of the mountain. A few of them were large, but many of them were small with flat tops. If she squinted she could make out glinting, armored figures standing on them. Maybe they were lookouts?

She supposed it only made sense that the fortress was guarded.

They burst into what looked like a miniature courtyard with grass for a floor instead of stone.

"We can stop here," said Enyalios.

Scarlet hunched over, putting her hands on her knees as her words came out in gasps. "Where are we?"

The courtyard was empty except for a gaggle of elves in the corner. An older elf stood at the center of the group.

"This is where the young elves train," said Enyalios.

The old elf in the corner shouted something and immediately the young elves fanned out into pairs. Scarlet realized that they were each holding small wooden swords.

"How old are they?"

The Hinterland

"Them?" asked Enyalios, looking them over. "I believe they are ages eight through ten."

"They're fighting in the war?" asked Scarlet, jaw dropping.

"Of course not," said Enyalios. "But swordplay is part of every young elf's education. And even though they are too young now, they may be fighting by the time this war ends."

Scarlet watched them. Could the war really last that long? The pairs started to duel. They were clumsy, but their strokes had intent, and they were focused. The more coordinated elves side-stepped blows and returned them.

They were good. Better than good, considering they were so young. Definitely better than her. Scarlet felt her stomach drop as she watched them. She couldn't do half the things these eight-year-olds were doing. She looked at Enyalios. His eyes weren't on the young sword fighters. Instead, he'd been watching her face with a smirk twisting the corner of his mouth. Scarlet had a sudden feeling that he had wanted her to see this—to see how she compared to these juvenile elves.

She felt a blaze of anger rush through her as she rounded on Enyalios. "Why do you hate me so much?"

"You seem moody today," he replied, raising an eyebrow. "Is it, perhaps, your failed magic test that is causing this aggression?"

Her eyes widened. How did he know about that already? "It wasn't a failed test," said Scarlet, "Not having magic isn't the same as failing."

"You think not?"

Scarlet shook her head, midnight-black hair whipping around her face. "I don't need to be magic. Maybe I'm meant to be a great sword fighter."

"You think so?" he asked, his eyebrows hitching upward ever so slightly. Enough to show that he didn't believe her.

"I think I could be if you would actually teach me instead of trying to prove to me that High Elves are better than humans!"

Already she felt an ocean of emotion from the day's activities. Every word from Enyalios' mouth was sending waves across its surface.

Enyalios' eyes narrowed. "I have been doing my best to teach you, but a teacher can only do so much. For real progress the student must put in effort."

"I've been doing nothing but putting in effort," said Scarlet. "You just don't like that I'm human. But that doesn't change the fact that I'm the one the prophecy chose. It didn't choose one of your High Elves. It chose *me*."

"A prophecy made by a Crescent Elf," said Enyalios, smirk turning to sneer.

Scarlet hadn't known who the prophecy was made by, but she didn't much care. "So, you're saying you don't believe the prophecy because it wasn't made by a High Elf? Everyone else believes it."

He leaned toward her, lowering his voice. "You would be surprised how many doubt. Especially when we were told the hero we had been waiting for was you."

Scarlet stamped her foot against the ground, angry tears rising in her throat. She swallowed them down. "Maybe I could be a hero—just do what you're supposed to do! Teach me."

"It's a waste of time," said Enyalios, looking away. "A human can never do the job of a High Elf."

He turned his gaze to the small elven sword fighters, still dueling in the grass.

"You're wrong about me," said Scarlet, voice going low with anger and dragged down by the effort she was putting into holding back tears. He didn't look at her to acknowledge that she'd spoken, or even when Scarlet turned and left the miniature courtyard.

She rushed down a set of steps, looking for an empty room to hide in before the angry tears weighing on the backs of her eyes grew too heavy and spilled out.

She found an open door and rushed in. The room was empty, and to her view, blurry. It seemed to be some sort of armory with blades of all sorts laid out on tables around her. She closed the door and retreated to the back of the room, not really taking in her surroundings much before sitting down against the wall.

She clenched her hands into fists as tears began to spill down her face.

Enyalios was wrong. The Fate Stone had chosen her. She wasn't an elf, she wasn't experienced, she wasn't physically impressive, but she was smart, she was clever, and most of all, she was determined. And if her father's fairy tales had taught her nothing else, it was that you could do anything if you wanted it enough.

She wished her father were here to tell her that himself. He'd know exactly what she should do.

She swiped at her face, annoyed at herself, but the tears weren't stopping–in fact, at the thought of her father, they were only coming harder.

Her eyes were simply leaks that an ocean was seeping through, and her frustration with Enyalios was only a small part of what made up the waters.

A small grunt of anger escaped Scarlet as the tears continued. If Enyalios were to see her like this, it would only confirm everything he'd said about her. She pulled herself to her feet.

Her eyes fell on a small knife on a nearby table, and in a rush of reckless hot-headedness she picked it up and rammed it against the wall, throwing all her anger into the blow. It skittered against the stone. The scraping, paired with a grunt of frustration from deep in Scarlet's chest, was loud throughout the cramped armory–so loud she didn't hear the door open. But as she drew her arm back she suddenly realized she was no longer alone.

Scarlet froze as she stared at Tasha who was watching her from the doorway.

Her eyes widened as she searched her mind for a reasonable explanation to give Tasha for what she'd just seen, but no words came to mind.

"You're holding it wrong."

"What?" Scarlet's mouth came open a bit.

Tasha crossed her arms and replied with a voice that was stiff, as though she was unaccustomed to using it. "The knife. Your grip is wrong."

"Oh–yeah..." said Scarlet, rubbing her foot against the floor. She hoped Tasha couldn't see she'd been crying, though she figured it would be hard to miss. She couldn't see herself, but she could feel the wet paths down her face and taste the salt on her lips. "I was just–I was just in here practicing."

"You're a terrible liar," said Tasha, face impassive. She could have been wearing a mask for the emotion she showed.

Scarlet set the knife on the table and let out a frustrated sigh. "Fine. I was crying."

Tasha's face didn't change at all, yet Scarlet still felt as though she was being judged. Perhaps it was just the way Tasha held herself–like she was a wolf and everyone else prey. It was unnerving to be around, and at the same time, Scarlet wished she could copy it.

"You would, too," she snapped.

"I don't cry," answered Tasha. She didn't say it like she was bragging, but instead like she was speaking cold fact. The way she spoke was blunt and clipped, with each word sounding as strong and straight as a soldier.

"Then maybe you've never had anyone say you're a waste of time because you're human," Scarlet replied with a scowl. She suddenly wished she were still holding the knife-not to use, but because she felt like having a weapon in hand would somehow make her feel stronger. As it was, Tasha's piercing gaze made her feel small and transparent.

Tasha's eyes narrowed. For a moment a flash of something other than cold disregard flickered in her eyes. Her gaze shifted toward the exit, as though she was considering leaving, then back to Scarlet. "Who?" It was the first time she'd suggested any interest in their conversation.

"Doesn't matter," said Scarlet, heat creeping up her neck as she realized she'd said more than she'd planned to.

"Clearly it does to you," said Tasha, face still straight. It reminded Scarlet a bit of Cerulean, although his blank expression always came off more bored than menacing.

Scarlet cleared her throat. She looked away from Tasha's stare, which was so strong it felt like she was being physically held in place.

As Scarlet's gaze strayed downward she noticed that Tasha's left hand had gone down to her dagger hilt. Her thumb was massaging the wood in a circular pattern–around and around and around–it was hypnotizing.

Scarlet's eyes narrowed slightly as she focused on the movement and Tasha's hand jerked away from the handle.

Quickly Scarlet looked up, and the sudden desire to move on from whatever had just happened forced the truth from her. "My–uh–my trainer."

Tasha's eyes narrowed. "The elf from the Dining Hall?"

"One of his friends," admitted Scarlet, flushing and rubbing her nose.

Tasha nodded. The nod was sharp, just like everything was with her.

"I'm going to–" Scarlet paused, looking at the floor. She was unsure of what to say to get out of this conversation, but she was ready to go somewhere more private. Like her room. Her room with her books that held other worlds she could escape to until she didn't feel so bad about her own. She opened her mouth to finish the excuse and looked up—but Tasha was gone. It seemed she, too, had grown tired of talking.

Tasha walked across the courtyard, hands far warmer than she liked. She pulled her daggers from their sheaths and flipped one into the air, catching it smoothly by the handle. As she turned her attention to the maneuver, her focus shifted from her emotions, and her hands began to cool.

She forced herself not to look back toward the armory door.

Don't get involved, she thought to herself. *Scarlet isn't your responsibility. You don't care what happens to her.*

But for someone who didn't care, her hands were still a little too hot.

She grunted in frustration and flipped the dagger again. Still, the distraction wasn't enough to make her forget. *Don't get involved*, she repeated in her head. *Stay out of it. Tonight I'm gone into the Hinterland and everything can go back to normal. I can return to facing the normal dangers.* The predictable dangers—the ones with talons and claws and teeth. She never had to wonder what they were going to do. They were going to try to kill her, and she was going to try to kill them, and one of them would succeed, and one of them would be forgotten.

It was harsh, but it was the life she was accustomed to. But people? They were harder.

Remember the plan, she reminded herself. *Don't get involved and leave tonight.* But since she was leaving... would it matter if she got involved, just slightly, if she disappeared directly afterward?

Tasha gritted her teeth and spun a dagger. The blade rose, cartwheeled in the air, caught the sun, and fell to her hand, fitting into her palm like it had been made to be there: smooth wood against rough callused skin. She'd made up her mind before she caught it.

She scanned the area and almost instantly found a familiar face.

Elowen had strolled into the Main Courtyard through a side arch.

Tasha sighed, then approached the elf, who paused as Tasha stopped in front of her.

"Do you know where Scarlet's trainer is?" It was all she needed, then she'd deal with the rest on her own.

"What do you need Scarlet's trainer for?" asked Elowen, eyes narrowing.

Tasha scowled. "Nothing."

Elowen raised her eyebrows. "You asked me where he is, so clearly there's something."

Tasha gritted her teeth. "It doesn't matter. Just tell me where I can find him and I'll go deal with the problem myself."

Elowen shook her head. "If you have an issue with Scarlet's trainer you can bring it up with the Council–they're the ones who assigned him."

"I don't need a council to do my business," said Tasha, voice tight. She didn't need a bunch of old, pompous people to take care of the problem. If she wanted it done well, she'd do it herself.

Elowen lowered her voice. "Listen Tasha, I get that you're used to a... harsher setting. You're accustomed to dealing with things by yourself. But we're not in the wilds of the Hinterland, and you're not on your own anymore."

Tasha almost rolled her eyes. Of course, she was on her own. She wasn't alone, but she was still on her own.

Maybe Elowen could tell what Tasha was thinking, because she added, "I'm sorry, but whether you like it or not, any problems with Scarlet's trainer go to the Council."

Tasha didn't reply for a moment. She didn't trust the Council to get the job done like she could, but passing the problem on to them would also make it easier for her to leave without being roped into anything.

"Fine. Take me to the Council."

"You know, you could just tell me the problem," said Elowen. "I'm a Right Hand, it would be easy for me to–"

"Take me to the Council," Tasha interrupted. Her voice was firm, but her hands were cool. Her mission had cleared her mind, focus rising over feelings.

"Follow me."

In ten minutes they were in front of the Council Room doors. The guards on either side of the entrance stepped out of the way the moment they recognized Elowen.

Tasha and the elf walked in.

Behind the doors, the Council members were clustered around a wide table in the middle of the room. There were a few people with them Tasha didn't recognize from her earlier meeting with the Council and could only assume were Right Hands, like Elowen.

At the sound of the doors opening, everyone in the room had turned to look at her. The dwarf quickly folded something on the table, though Tasha couldn't see what it was over his broad shoulders.

"Tasha," said Deimos. "What a lovely surprise. Have you perhaps considered our offer further?" She looked to her left and realized that Elowen had vanished. She'd gone to join the other Right Hands.

Tasha turned her attention back to Deimos. "I don't have an answer for you yet," she said, lying through her teeth. She had an answer, but he wouldn't like it. And he would know what it was tomorrow morning. "I've come for another reason."

Deimos frowned. The other Council members all looked at her with interest. Thayla especially looked curious.

"Yes?" asked Thayla.

"Scarlet needs a new trainer."

Most of the Council Members looked taken aback by this proclamation. Deimos only considered her with lazy, uninterested eyes. "No."

The reply and its tone gave Tasha the sense that he was holding a grudge from her refusal to agree to stay. Then again, she had a feeling he held a grudge against anyone who didn't grovel at his feet.

"Why would you request that Enyalios be replaced?" asked Thayla, frowning.

"He's unfit for the position," said Tasha. She had decided on the walk to the Council Room that she wouldn't tell anyone she'd caught Scarlet crying in the armory. It would only make the girl seem vulnerable.

"Enyalios is perfectly capable," said Deimos. "There is no one more fit for the position, I assure you."

"I'm sure one of the Crescent Elves could–" started Eldritch. His voice died as Deimos glared at him.

"No one is more fit for the position," repeated the High Elf.

Tasha scowled at Deimos, stroking the hilt of her dagger with the tip of her pointer finger, not even realizing she was doing it until she'd repeated the motion multiple times.

"We cannot spare any of our soldiers for the training of a child," the High Elf continued.

"It seems to me that somewhere in this fortress you'd be able to find someone to train her who'd care more about teaching her than her race," said Tasha. Her hands had begun to heat up like they'd been under the sun for hours.

Some of the Council members murmured, but Deimos only looked angrier. "He is teaching her. If he goes hard on her, it is only to prepare her. We will not replace him. As I said, there is no one better."

And as her hands continued to warm from the inside, from her blood and through her veins, she heard herself speak before her mind even knew what she was about to say.

"I am." Her words came out calm, which was a miracle because inside her head her own voice was screaming at her. What was she getting herself into?

Deimos looked at her for a moment, then he threw his head back and laughed. "You? You think you could replace Enyalios? You believe you would be a better trainer than him?"

"Yes." Her voice was strong. It filled the whole room.

The Council watched her with widened eyes, except for Deimos, whose eyes had narrowed so much Tasha was surprised he could still see.

"You can't replace Enyalios," said Deimos, voice hardening as he realized Tasha was serious.

"Why?" she asked, words going low. "Because I'm human, and a human could never replace a High Elf?" The truth was that she was not human, but he didn't know that—nor would he ever.

There was an intake of breath from around the room as Council Members and Right Hands recognized the accusation.

Deimos didn't reply, just glared at her. Finally, he turned and appealed to the rest of the Council. "Tasha cannot train Scarlet, she has yet to even take the evaluation test to be placed in the army."

Tasha's thumb massaged at the hilt of her dagger with increased speed. "The test is usually a duel, yes?" She was sure Beck had said so at some point.

Eldritch nodded.

"Then I'll duel Enyalios for the right to train Scarlet. It takes care of both problems at once." She held her head high, speaking the words like a command instead of a suggestion.

Deimos shook his head immediately, but Tasha turned to Thayla. She seemed to be the only Council member with the confidence to speak against Deimos, and so far she'd appeared reasonable.

The nymph frowned as she thought.

"Absolutely not," said Deimos. "It is not how things are done. You are new here, but we have a process for doing things—"

"Hold on, Deimos, this isn't a bad idea."

Deimos turned to Thayla. "Yes, it is—"

"Tasha, will you step away for a moment please?" asked Thayla, undisguised exasperation playing across her face.

Tasha gave a nod and stepped to the side of the room. The Council members clustered around the table. They spoke in low voices, but not as low as they could have been. She realized that they were underestimating her ability to hear them. After all, were she the human they thought, it would have been impossible for her to make out the conversation. As it was, Tasha could hear every word.

"This is ridiculous; she is unqualified," started Deimos.

"No," interrupted Thayla. "This is in our favor. If she trains Scarlet, she will have to stay. Otherwise, she'll want to leave."

There was agreement from the other members.

Tasha hands heated considerably as she considered the ramifications of her actions fully for the first time. She cursed internally. All her plans were falling apart due to one stupid, anger-induced, move. If not for the way Deimos was looking at her–like she was a peasant who wasn't worthy to lick dirt off his shoes–she might have backed out.

Instead, she stared him down and didn't look away until he did.

"Fine," growled Deimos, speaking again to the other Council members. "But, she must best Enyalios. If she doesn't win, she doesn't train Scarlet."

The Council members turned back to Tasha.

"Tasha, we agree to your proposition," said Thayla.

"When do I duel?" Tasha asked, pushing red hair out of her face.

"We'll give you time to prepare, but we need it to happen before the end of the week," said Thayla. "Other than that, you may choose the day and time."

"Now."

Some of the Council members looked shocked. Thayla just smiled. "I thought you might say that. Let's go find Enyalios."

The Council Members escorted Tasha down to the Main Courtyard, where they gathered around one of the training arenas.

Tasha took a moment to study it. It was round, at least twelve feet in diameter, and with short, wooden walls around the circumference that reached up to her knees. The floor was dirt, softer than the stone floor the rest of the courtyard was paved with.

Enyalios had already been summoned to the Main Courtyard, and he was warming up on the other side of the arena. Watching him, Tasha felt a rare glint of amusement. He was prancing around, swinging his sword left and right and throwing in a random lunge every now and then. Tasha crossed her arms and watched. After a few moments he noticed her spectating and scowled, straightening up mid-lunge and puffing his chest.

"Are you ready–" started Thayla, but Tasha was stepping into the arena before the nymph could fully get the words out.

Was she ready? Of course, she was ready. She was never not ready.

Enyalios stepped over the wall, holding his sword in his fist.

Already Tasha was sizing him up, watching his stance, inspecting his grip.

"The rules are simple," announced Deimos from where he stood outside the arena. "The duel ends when someone gives up or first blood is drawn. You may concede at any time. Enyalios will be using his sword. Tasha, I assume you are using your daggers?"

Tasha nodded, whipping them out of their sheaths.

"First, bow to your opponent," said Deimos.

Tasha and Enyalios glared at each other. Neither inclined their heads the slightest bit. It was clear Enyalios was not going to bow to a human.

Tasha bowed to no one.

Deimos smirked. He did not force the bow. "On my go," he announced. There was a moment of silence as the Council members watched. Out of the corner of her eye, Tasha could see others in the Main Courtyard taking interest, beginning to walk toward the arena.

"Go!"

Enyalios lunged forward and instantly Tasha's mind shifted into a new gear. It was like diving into freezing water. She was suddenly awake, alert, alive. She was without emotion, without feeling, without thought–she just *was*.

And the focus made her fireproof. Made her free.

She side-stepped Enyalios' blow. He struck again and she noticed a flaw in his posture, his grip, a hesitancy to his swing. She moved out of the way.

He swiped. She ducked beneath the blow. He was leaving his left side vulnerable.

He snarled, bringing his blade toward her harder than before. She darted to the left, knocking the blade off course with one dagger and jabbing the other toward him. His eyes widened as the dagger neared the skin of his arm, mere centimeters away. Then she pulled back, stepping away from him.

His face paled.

She could have ended it there, and he knew it. Just as she wanted him to know it. But it wasn't just purely to intimidate him that she'd withdrawn her strike–she wasn't ready for the relief of the duel to be over yet.

He attacked, and this time she blocked with her blade instead of dancing away. He answered the parry, and she answered the strike. The noise of metal on metal filled the courtyard. It sounded like someone had kicked a helmet down a set of stairs and it was hitting every step on the way down.

He whirled, spun, darted, trying to get past her defense, but her daggers kept him at bay.

Finally, he slowed, stepping away from her and watching her warily, planning for his next attack.

But it was her turn.

Tasha lunged. Enyalios jumped backward, caught by surprise from her sudden switch of defense to offense. She jabbed at him, and he threw up a parry, stumbling back as he did so. The back of his legs hit the arena wall. The impact of the wood caught him off guard. He glanced back to look at it and Tasha took her opportunity. She flicked his blade from his hand with a quick smack to the hilt.

He made a choking sound as the blade flew from his grasp.

Tasha dropped her left dagger and grabbed the front of his robe with her free hand, holding him in place against the wall. With her right she brought her second dagger up where he could see it.

"Do you concede?"

He glanced at the dagger, visibly swallowing, but when his eyes returned to her face they were filled with more hatred than fear. His jaw worked. "To a human? Never." And he spat at her.

Her fingers twitched around the handle of her blade, grip on Enyalios' robe tightening. He winced, she held his gaze, the blade of the dagger quivered–then Tasha let her right arm fall to her side, dropping the weapon to the dirt below. It landed with a thud and a cloud of dust.

Enyalios' eyebrows went up, relief playing across his face. The fear in his eyes evaporated.

Tasha balled her fist and rammed it into his nose with the strength of a hammer.

There was a crack and blood splattered across the dirt next to her dagger. Wet red on dry brown. Enyalios howled, hands going to his face.

Tasha released his robe and stepped away, retrieving her dagger from the ground and wiping it on a fistful of her shirt to remove every speck of dirt. As she sheathed it, she was suddenly aware of the crowd around them. The sides of the arena were surrounded by an audience. For an audience so large, the courtyard should have been full of chattering, but instead they watched with deadly silence as Enyalios moaned and cupped his bleeding nose in his hands.

"That's first blood," said Thayla. Tasha looked at her. The nymph queen's face was blank, but there was a glimmer in her eye... was it amusement? Admiration? Tasha wasn't sure.

Deimos was watching Enyalios with a deep scowl. He looked at Tasha, and when their eyes met, it was like a clashing of knives.

Tasha held his gaze for a moment, then she turned away and stepped out of the arena. The crowd parted to let her through.

"Tasha, wait," said someone behind her. Out of the corner of her eye she saw someone reach out for her arm. Instantly, she pulled away, whipping around to face–Thayla.

"Don't touch me." Tasha didn't try to disguise the sharpness in her voice.

Around them, the crowd was starting to leave the arena, going back to their business. Still, the courtyard was void of its usual conversations. Now it was full of whispers.

"You'll need to start training Scarlet as soon as possible," said the nymph.

Tasha gritted her teeth. In the rush of the duel she had forgotten about that. "Give her tomorrow off, I'll need a little time to... prepare." *How were you supposed to go about training a fourteen-year-old?*

"Also," continued Thayla, brushing her black, blue-tipped hair over her shoulder. "As you know this duel doubled as an evaluation to decide where you would fit into our movement. I would like to offer you a spot in an elite unit. It's clear you have the skill for it."

A unit? Tasha turned the thought over in her mind. "I like to work alone."

"Maybe a Lone Wolf, then?" asked Thayla.

Tasha didn't know what a Lone Wolf was, but based on the name, it already seemed like a better fit.

"A solo warrior," said Thayla, perhaps realizing Tasha didn't know what the term meant. "Sent on individual missions, usually on your own, possibly with a partner, depending on the mission."

That sounded more Tasha's style. But she wasn't quite ready to agree to fight for The Alliance.

Tasha crossed her arms. "I have questions."

Thayla raised her eyebrows. "And those are?"

"I want to know the details of this war."

"The Council already told–"

"Told me basics," interrupted Tasha. "I need to know all of it."

Thayla considered. She scanned Tasha's face as though looking for something. Tasha didn't know what that something might be, but Thayla must have found it, because she said, "Follow me," before turning and beginning to walk quickly across the courtyard.

Tasha followed after, passing through archways, winding halls, and finally, the Council Room doors. It was empty now except for the two of them. Their every footstep echoed around the room.

Thayla led Tasha to the table the Council had been gathered around earlier. On top of it was a scroll, which Thayla unrolled and laid flat.

The scroll was a large, detailed map. Tasha could see blue oceans, green plains, mountains penned in black ink, and labels like: Devil's Crib, The Crimson Peaks, and Orc Highlands, along with other names that were too small to make out without bending closer. In the middle of it she could see a large black splotch. The Hinterland. She was somewhere in there, she thought, looking at the ink stain.

"The Wraith exposed herself as a threat a few months ago," said Thayla. "We don't know much about her, only that she came into power in a small territory here–" she pointed to a spot on the map. "We realized she was a threat when she began to attack elven villages along here–" Thayla's finger traced a path down the paper, and with every inch it traveled Tasha pictured burning villages and armored soldiers. "We got word back that she recruited only a few of the elves she captured. Most of them she bled dry." She paused. "You're human, so you may not know, but that's the term we use for when a leech drains you until you die."

Tasha didn't know much about draining, but she knew that it would be a horrible way to be killed. She frowned at the map.

"Meanwhile, she began attacking the human territories around her own," said Thayla. "She began to quickly build up an army, recruiting those she captured."

"What exactly is she trying to do?" asked Tasha. "Just gain power?"

Thayla looked at her, face completely serious. "More than that. She doesn't simply want to have power. She wants to have all of it. She wants to be the power."

"What are you saying?"

"She wants to kill us all," said Thayla, eyes locked on Tasha's. "Every elf, nymph, dwarf–you get it. Anyone capable of magic, or benefiting from supernatural abilities."

That, Tasha thought, *would include people who can catch on fire.*

She ran her thumb along the hilt of her blade. "Is that even possible?" Thayla was talking about wiping out entire races–races that had existed for as long as anyone could remember.

"Not everyone thinks so. The dwarven king refused to join us, along with many elven villages. But there's never been a leech as powerful as the Wraith. It might seem ludicrous but look at what she's done in just a few months." Thayla retraced the trail of conquered villages.

"And what's The Alliance doing to stop her?" asked Tasha, frowning.

"For a while there were too few of us to intervene, and all we could do was visit the elven or human villages she'd gone through, looking for survivors, or recruiting from areas she hadn't reached yet. But we've grown in numbers, and we're ready to make a bigger difference. We sent out resistance just a few days before you arrived," said Thayla. "To these points." She pointed to two spots on the map. "Their missions are to stop the Wraith's soldiers from taking out anymore villages. However–" she hesitated. "We haven't heard back from either group for a couple of days. Other than that, we are preparing for a full-on battle. We have to be ready to face the Wraith's army when she comes for us."

"And exactly how big is the Wraith's army?" asked Tasha, eyes narrowing. Only a sizable force would be capable of threatening a fortress full of magic-users.

"We don't know exactly," said Thayla.

"Why?" asked Tasha. "Don't we have spies?"

"It's not that," answered Thayla, smoothing a wrinkle in her robe. "There are too many to count."

Tasha just stared at her.

"She's continuing to take out new villages every week," said Thayla. "Our spies say new recruits come in everyday–many of them there by force, trying to keep the Wraith from killing them or their families."

Tasha nodded, processing the information.

"All in all," said Thayla, "This is going to be a hard fight."

Chapter 21

The sky was dark when Tasha stepped into the torch-lit courtyard. Today she walked lightly, determined not to be heard until she wanted to be. The only sounds in the courtyard were from Beck as he trained: quick breaths and the thumps of his sword against the stuffed training dummy.

Tasha had tried to resist the urge to come, but her fight with Enyalios the day before had reminded her how freeing it was to be stripped of her powers, if only for a few minutes. The desire to duel again had been overwhelming, and she never caught fire while she fought, so really, it was risk-free. At least, that's what she told herself.

She paused in place, watching Beck finish his sequence. After a few moments, he stopped to wipe the sweat off his brow with the back of his arm.

"Duel?" Tasha asked.

"Mother of mushrooms!" yelped Beck, jumping and whirling around. "I didn't hear you—" he recognized her. "Tasha?"

She nodded. "Is the invite still open?"

"Not going to break my nose, are you?" asked Beck. He grinned at her.

She pursed her lips. "You heard about that?"

He laughed. "Who didn't?"

Tasha nodded. "I see word spreads fast around here."

"Well, you dueled, and beat, a High Elf from the Romane Line. So yeah, you're the fuss of the fortress right now."

Tasha had no reply to that.

"And you didn't just beat him," added Beck. "You humiliated him. Multiple people have told me that you were just toying with him. Not to mention, you broke his nose."

"He got what he deserved," said Tasha, tone clipped. She crossed her arms.

"I don't doubt it," said Beck, putting his empty hand up in an "I come in peace" gesture. "But I think you should be... careful. You definitely made enemies with that duel."

"I'm not afraid of Enyalios," answered Tasha.

"I wasn't talking about Enyalios," answered Beck.

"The High Elves?" she said, raising her eyebrows.

He shifted his sword from one hand to the other and nodded.

"You're a High Elf," pointed out Tasha. "And aren't you from an important family line?"

"Yeah," he said, scratching his nose.

Tasha nodded. "And you still want to duel, even with all the High Elves mad at me? It seems like you would want to keep your distance if you were smart."

"Whoever said I was smart?" said Beck, laughing. "Besides, someone has to give you a challenge."

"Spoken with the confidence of a true High Elf," said Tasha.

Beck shook his head. "That's not the same. I've earned my confidence."

Tasha nodded, realizing that anyone who got up every day to practice before the sun was up, had earned the right to be confident in their abilities.

"Anyway, if we're going to do this, we should get started," said Beck. "I have a pocketful of things to do in half an hour."

The Hinterland

"What are the rules of our duel?" Tasha asked, pulling out her daggers.

Beck paused, thinking. "Until one of us gives up, or the sun rises."

"Perfect," they stepped into one of the training arenas—the same one Tasha had dueled Enyalios inside of. Beck raised his sword and Tasha her daggers. She could see Beck already studying her stance and grip. She did the same to him but spotted no obvious errors.

"Go," he said.

And Tasha was in her zone. From the look in Beck's eyes, she thought that maybe his mind had also shifted into gear. Maybe this was some sort of escape for him, same as it was for her.

He took a swing and Tasha side-stepped. His strike was faster than Enyalios' had been. He quickly sent another blow her way, and she blocked it with one of her daggers, jabbing with the other one. He dodged, batting the blow aside.

He was excellent, his technique flawless.

They clashed again.

And again.

And again.

Metal on metal.

Blade on blade.

She spotted an opening and prepared to attack it, before realizing it was too easy. She narrowed her eyes. A trap.

She feigned a jab as though falling for the bait, then as soon as his stance shifted, she spun, attacking his other side. He darted back just in time. After she had gotten too close to Enyalios he had sharpened, becoming angry. Beck, on the other hand, laughed. It was the strangest response she had ever seen from someone who'd just about been stabbed.

It seemed they were perfectly matched.

Their strikes became so hard and fast it evolved into a masterpiece. They were like painters on a canvas, detailed and in-color. Tasha fought in red and out of the lines. Beck painted with a green that matched his eyes: calm, eloquent, and with a kind of joy rather than a pure desire to win.

Sweat prickled on Tasha's brow.

Beck's hair was becoming wilder with each move.

Again, they came together, and flew apart, and threw themselves at each other again like a band of elastic connected them.

For ten minutes they were torch-lit silhouettes, shadows dancing on the courtyard walls, then, as Beck's sword came down and Tasha blocked it just in time, light flooded over the courtyard walls as the sun rose.

Tasha and Beck sagged, instantly dropping their weapons. They panted, out of breath. It had been a while since Tasha had fought that hard without winning. Maybe the thought should upset her, but instead it filled her with an exhilarating feeling that surely would have caught her hands on fire had she not been so tired.

Beck sat down against the wooden arena wall. "Holy sprites. You're amazing."

"You're not bad either," replied Tasha, sitting down a few feet from him.

Beck grinned. "So, same time tomorrow?"

Tasha pressed her lips together. Dueling with Beck challenged her. It would push her to be better, and she found that she wanted to say yes. But that realization was like a warning bell in her mind–saying yes would be dangerous. It would be risky. It would be stupid.

And she hadn't survived on her own for so long by making stupid decisions.

She opened her mouth to say no. "I'll be there."

"Great," he stood up and offered her his hand. She could see him better now that the sun was rising. He was wearing a short-sleeved white tunic and black pants. With his arm outstretched, Tasha could see a mark on his wrist–like a tattoo–but it was still too dark to quite see what it was.

She shook her head and got to her feet without his help. "Right, I forgot," he tucked his hand in his pocket. "No touching." He stretched, then stepped out of the arena. "I'll see you tomorrow."

Quickly, before he could walk away, she spoke, feeling the need to keep the situation under control before things got out of hand. "This doesn't make us friends. Just dueling partners."

"Pixie dust," said Beck, waving his hand dismissively. "We can be both."

"No," said Tasha sharply, eyes narrowing. "Just dueling partners."

"Sprites, you're really not a people person, are you?" asked Beck, shaking his head.

"No, I'm not," said Tasha, then she shelved her daggers at her hips, stepped over the arena's low wooden wall, and walked out of the courtyard.

Scarlet woke to birds singing outside of her room. She slid out of bed, stepped to the balcony doors, and flung them wide, walking into the dusty, golden morning beyond.

She breathed in the clean, morning air. Today was a new day. A new opportunity. A new chance to prove Enyalios wrong.

The view of the Hinterland was incredible. The plains were rolling and misted over slightly. It was almost enough to make her forget how dangerous it was—well, until she looked into the green and saw a huge hulking shape silhouetted by the rising sun. She squinted at it, and as she watched, it moved. She gasped and rushed back into her room, slamming the doors behind her. Even though the thing was miles away she still felt like something was pinging around in her chest.

There was a knock on the door and she jumped. Taking a deep breath, she glanced through the window and took one last look at the shape before crossing her room.

Kicking the chair aside and relieving it from its guard duty, she pulled the door open to reveal Elowen standing in the hallway.

"Elowen, what are you doing here?" she asked.

"I have news," said Elowen, "may I come in?"

"Alright," said Scarlet, opening the door all the way to give the elf room to step inside. "I'm glad you're here, there's something you should see." She led Elowen to the window and pointed to the dark mass on the plains. "There's something out there."

Elowen nodded. "I know. The monsters in the area have been increasing."

"Why?"

Elowen grimaced. "They're coming to where the blood is."

Scarlet shivered and decided to change the subject. "What was your news?"

"I wonder if you already know what happened yesterday afternoon?" asked Elowen.

Scarlet shook her head. She'd retired to her room early after her experience with Enyalios. She'd stayed there for the rest of the night, reading the books on the shelves against the wall. "No, I don't."

"Enyalios is no longer your trainer."

Scarlet's eyes widened. She should have seen this coming–should have known Enyalios would only train a human like herself for so long before he walked away. "He quit?" she asked.

"Not exactly," said Elowen slowly.

"Did he... did he leave?" asked Scarlet, brow creasing.

"He's currently recovering from an injury."

Scarlet gaped. "What? He's hurt?"

"His nose is broken."

"What broke it?"

"Tasha's fist."

Scarlet's eyes went even wider. "What happened?"

"She dueled Enyalios for the right to train you. She won."

Again, Scarlet's eyes got wider. Now they were so big it was like they took up most of her face. She fell backward onto her bed. "Holy sprites."

Elowen gave a small laugh. "I see Avenbeck's rubbing off on you."

"Tasha's my new trainer?" asked Scarlet.

"That she is."

Scarlet didn't know what to feel. Her emotions were in a knot: she couldn't find their beginning, or their end to make sense of them. She was glad Enyalios was no longer her trainer, but Tasha—well, frankly, Tasha made her feel shaky inside. There was something about the way she walked, talked, acted: like she was at all times ready to drive her daggers into you.

"Do I have training with her today?" asked Scarlet.

"She's given you the day off," said Elowen. "You'll have your first session tomorrow."

"Alright." Scarlet stared at the ceiling above her, lost in thought. Tasha couldn't be as bad as Enyalios, right? She was human, so at least she wouldn't make Scarlet feel guilty for her lack of magic. That was a relief. The reminder of her magic test was like a jab to the stomach.

Elowen moved for the door.

"Elowen?" said Scarlet, not looking away from the ceiling.

"Yes?"

"Do you think I can still help the war even though I don't have magic?" she assumed Elowen would know about the magic test by now.

There was a moment of silence, then Scarlet felt the bed shift as Elowen leaned against one of the bed posts.

"Why would you need magic to help win the war?" asked Elowen.

Scarlet shrugged, face going red. She stared at the ceiling, determined not to look at Elowen as she spoke. "Everyone in the Council expected me to have magic. They thought I would sort of cancel out the Wraith's powers, but I can't. I can't be what they want me to be."

"And you shouldn't try to," said Elowen.

Scarlet's eyebrows scrunched, and she sat up to look at the elf. Elowen was still leaning against the bed post, eyes fixed on the morning sky through the window. When she spoke again, it was in a clear, firm voice. "Don't try to be what anyone else wants you to be, or the best you can hope to do is meet their expectations." She looked at Scarlet. "Do you understand what I'm saying?"

Scarlet nodded. She felt as though the words had struck a chord deep in her, like they were strumming an instrument in her chest. She tucked them away in her mind to remember. "Thanks, Elowen."

Elowen nodded, pushing off the bed post. "I've got to go. I'll see you later, Scarlet."

Scarlet watched as she left. It was only after the elf was gone that Scarlet remembered Elowen couldn't use magic, either.

After getting dressed Scarlet hurried out of her room and, after remembering that Tobin was apprenticing at the infirmary, started in that direction.

Scarlet ran through the infirmary door and spotted Tobin right away, talking to a patient lying in one of the infirmary beds.

He looked up and spotted her.

She opened her mouth, but before she could even get out the words, he said, "Pumpernickel." Then added, "Give me just a minute Scarlet, I have to grab something from the back for Lina here."

He nodded toward the patient on the bed. Scarlet smiled at the little girl sitting on top of the sheets. She was elven with her brown ears turned up in perfect points. There were blue beads in her dark braids.

"I'll be right back," said Tobin, before turning and walking through a door.

"Hi," said Scarlet to Lina. The elf could be no more than nine. "What are you here for?"

The Hinterland

"I broke my arm," said Lina. "But Tobin said he's going to make it all better."

"That's good," said Scarlet. "Are you..." she squinted, unsure. "A High Elf?"

"I'm a Forest Elf," said Lina, shaking her head.

"Oh, sorry, I don't know how to tell."

"There's not really a good way to tell if you haven't been around us much," said Lina. "But High Elves talk different than us Forest Elves. My parents call it 'fancy talk'. And Forest Elves never get tattoos, so if you see an elf with tattoos, it won't be a Forest Elf."

Scarlet blinked. It seemed there were many things she still had to learn about elven culture.

"What–"

"Alright, let's get that arm fixed," said Tobin, walking back in and holding the supplies he needed. He set the bandages on the bed.

Lina straightened and Tobin began to work on her arm. He was quick, and his hands were sure and steady. Watching him, Scarlet didn't think she'd ever seen him so confident in anything.

"All done," he said, stepping back five minutes later.

Lina slid off the bed, her arm newly equipped with a splint and sling. "Thanks!"

"You'll need to come back in three weeks."

She nodded and ran out of the room.

"I'll have to make sure we contact her parents," said Tobin. "They're both soldiers. They're busy training right now, but we'll need to let them know what happened."

"Seems like you're doing a lot in here for just starting your apprenticeship," said Scarlet.

"Well, the infirmary is short-handed at the moment," explained Tobin. "The nurses need the help. They're in the back right now helping someone with a more serious wound."

"How did someone get wounded?" asked Scarlet, imagining a duel gone out of hand.

"They were part of a group getting supplies out in the Hinterland," said Tobin. "It's dangerous out there."

Scarlet swallowed. With everything going on, she sometimes forgot that they were in the Hinterland, the most dangerous place in the known world–or maybe the unknown world, considering how little of it was mapped.

"When do you get off?"

"I can go now," said Tobin, "my shift is over. Where are we going?"

"I think we should find Mera and Cerulean."

"And then what?"

Scarlet shrugged. "Then we go look for trouble or make some."

"Um," said Tobin, "what sort of–"

"Not seriously," said Scarlet, the spark in her eyes dimming a bit, "it's just something the kids would say in my village." It was a phrase she hadn't heard in... weeks. In all the commotion she rarely had time to dwell on what she had lost, but the whisper of home ached in the back of her mind like a constant headache. It seemed ages ago that she had walked to school with her friends, snuck into the woods to climb trees, or stayed up late reading a book in her cot, her parents' gentle snores sounding above her. But it hadn't been long ago. It hadn't even been two weeks ago.

"You alright?" asked Tobin.

Scarlet snapped back into focus. Tobin was standing in front of her, forehead scrunched with concern.

"Yeah, yeah I'm fine," said Scarlet. "I was just thinking about–" she shook her head. "You ready to go?"

"Yup." They walked through the infirmary door and into the hallway.

"Oops," said Tobin as they walked. "I meant to be mad at you for running out of the infirmary yesterday. But I forgot."

Scarlet snorted. "Would you like to be mad now?" she asked, grinning at him.

"Nah," he replied with a shrug. "I'm not very good at it."

She laughed. "Hey," she said, switching topics. "Did you hear that Tasha's going to be my new trainer?"

"Yeah, I know," said Tobin. "She broke Enyalios' nose. He was in the infirmary yesterday. He wasn't very happy. Neither were the other High Elves that were there."

"Other High Elves?" Scarlet asked.

Tobin nodded. "There had to be about a dozen of them that showed up. The nurses had to force them out so they could even fit in the room to fix the nose. They were loud, you could hear them from down the hallway."

Scarlet felt a chill going up her spine. She had a feeling an angry High Elf could be trouble, but angry High Elves plural? She licked her lips, which had gone dry.

"Where are we going to find the others?" asked Tobin. They'd walked to the Dining Hall.

"Mera's family runs a stand in the market," said Scarlet. "I bet she's there. Hopefully she knows where Cerulean's family lives."

They walked into the Main Courtyard where they had to dodge between training warriors, then up a set of stairs, through the second courtyard, up more stairs, and into the market.

Scarlet walked down the row and stopped in front of Mera's stand. There was no one there. She frowned, turning to Tobin and opening her mouth to say something, when there was a bang. A muffled voice came from behind, or maybe under, the table.

Scarlet stepped to the counter. "Mera?"

Almost instantly a head popped up. "How may I help–oh, it's you." Mera grinned at Scarlet. Her hair was uncontrollable as always, and she had a live frog in her fist. "One moment." She ducked behind the table again, and when she reappeared, the frog was gone.

"Can you take a break?" Scarlet asked. "I have a day off."

"Sure," said Mera. "But let's wait until Cerulean gets here."

"Cerulean's coming?"

Mera shrugged. "He always turns up eventually. He doesn't really hang out with any other people."

"Isn't he friends with any of the High Elves?"

Mera shook her head. "Nope. Not with–" she stopped, eyes latching onto something behind Scarlet. "Told you."

Scarlet followed Mera's gaze and saw Cerulean moving through the crowd. He wore a plain white tunic that matched his hair, his hands in his pockets.

He stopped when he reached them and gave them all a greeting nod.

"You showed up just in time," said Mera. "We were just about to leave."

"To where?" he asked.

"I was thinking the library," said Scarlet.

"We were just at the library the other day," said Cerulean.

"But I was thinking," said Scarlet, voicing an idea she'd been turning over in her head. "That we could search all the books in the library and see what they say about the Hinterland. Maybe we can find out about different parts of the Hinterland and piece them together. We could be the first to map it."

Mera nodded, looking excited. Tobin's eyes were sparked with curiosity. Cerulean shook his head. "Right, because no one's ever thought of that before."

Scarlet frowned. "Were the books here when you arrived at the fortress, or did the elves and humans and others bring them?"

"We brought some," said Mera, "But I think most were already here. That's why we have to be really careful with them, some of them are really old."

Scarlet wondered who could possibly leave so many books behind. Maybe, she thought with a drop of worry tinging her thoughts, someone in a hurry to leave.

"Then these books might have information in them that other people didn't have," she said to Cerulean.

Cerulean raised an eyebrow and shrugged as if to say "whatever".

"Let's go," said Mera, and they started down the market.

It was Tobin's first time in the market, Scarlet realized. He kept pausing to look at the things on the stands. He stopped to stare at the caged monkeys one vendor was selling, and again to gaze at a cart loaded with jars and small bags full of bright candies.

"Those look amazing," said Scarlet, stopping to look.

"Do you want some?" asked Cerulean.

"Really?" Tobin asked. Scarlet wondered when, if ever, he'd had candy. Even in her village it was a rare treat, surely his family wouldn't have been able to afford it.

"Sure," said Cerulean.

"Don't," said Mera, shaking her head at the elf.

He ignored her. "Be right back."

"Cerulean, don't–" Mera started again, but he slipped away from them and toward the candy booth. Instead of walking up to the counter he sidled up to the side of the table.

Tobin and Scarlet watched with their brows creased. The instant the man selling the candy looked away, Cerulean gave a quick glance around the stand, and swiped a vibrant bag off the counter.

Scarlet and Tobin gasped as they realized what he was doing. Mera groaned.

He tucked the bag under his tunic and walked across the path back to them, only pulling it out once he'd reached them. "Here you go," he said, brandishing it.

"That's alright," said Tobin, biting his lip. "I don't want them."

"You did just a minute ago," said Cerulean, shaking the bag. The red candies rattled inside.

Tobin shook his head. "I'm good."

Cerulean scowled. "That's fine. More for me."

Together they walked down to the library. When they reached it, they found it mostly empty except for an old nymph, reading in the corner. He took one look at them as they clamored in, snapped his book shut, and left.

"Should we just start reading the books?" asked Scarlet.

"That is what you tend to do in a library," said Cerulean. He was so straight-faced she couldn't tell if he was joking, making fun of her, or doing both at the same time.

"I meant for learning more about the Hinterland," Scarlet replied.

"Let's start by reading titles and making a pile of the books that might have some information," said Mera.

"Perfect," said Scarlet.

"There are four levels to the library," said Mera, looking up at the three balconies above them, "so each of us can search one."

Scarlet nodded, then noticed Tobin shifting uncomfortably beside her. "Actually," she piped up, "each level is so big, maybe we should pair up. Tobin and I can search the bottom one, you two can search the second level."

Mera shrugged. "Alright."

The Hinterland

Cerulean gave no indication that he agreed or disagreed with the plan, looking slightly bored and tossing a few pieces of candy into his mouth.

Tobin gave Scarlet a grateful smile as the other two started up the ladder to the first balcony, and she smiled back. Together they crossed to the shelves against the wall and began to pick at the books.

The library was warm and quiet, and Scarlet felt the minutes begin to blur.

As she investigated, she used the time to fit in a quick reading lesson with Tobin.

"You got it," she said, nodding as he succeeded in reading yet another book title.

"What's that one called?" asked Tobin, pointing to a glossy, gold decorated book higher on the bookcase.

Scarlet propelled herself onto her tiptoes and pulled it down. "A guide to Elven Culture." She considered it for a moment, then placed it on the book pile nearest her. She had two, one considerably taller than the other.

"Another one for your personal pile?" asked Tobin.

"There's a lot to learn about the people here," said Scarlet, trying to defend her teetering tower of books. "Lina in the infirmary this morning was telling me some stuff about the different types of elves, and it just showed me how much I don't know yet."

She turned back to the shelves and ran her fingers over the spines of the books. She stopped on another one, pulling it out and reading the cover aloud. "A Monster Encyclopedia." She turned it over and read off the back. "All you need to know about trolls, goblins, orcs, and more."

Tobin glanced at the cover and said, "Maybe avoid them?"

Scarlet laughed, even as she placed the book on top of her "personal pile." "Do you think they've found anything?" she asked, gesturing to the balcony above their head.

"Hopefully, we've been here for an hour," said Tobin.

"We have?" said Scarlet, doing a double-take.

He nodded.

Scarlet backed away from the wall of shelves, craning her neck to see up to the first balcony. Mera was on her knees, looking at the bottom shelf. Cerulean was leaning against the balcony. The two of them seemed to be bickering, though Scarlet couldn't hear what they were saying. "Hey," she called. "You guys find anything?"

"*I*," said Mera, looking at Cerulean pointedly, "found a couple of things, but not much. This one talks about the Fringe some," she held up a book with a vivid blue cover. "But we already know a little bit about that. It's the middle of the Hinterland we need to learn about." She stuck it under her arm and started down the ladder. Cerulean followed after.

They amassed their findings on the short table. There were four books in total for their Hinterland research. After setting her Hinterland books on the table, Scarlet returned to her second pile. She put her arms around it and heaved upward. The books came up over her head.

"You found all those?" asked Mera.

"They're for me," said Scarlet.

"Some light reading?" laughed Mera.

"They looked interesting," panted Scarlet as she tried to carry her pile to the table–and failed, because at that moment the book at the top of the pile slipped, tumbling toward her face. She shrieked and fell to the floor, books toppling around her.

Mera gasped, Tobin rushed over to help her up, and Cerulean snorted. Tobin and Mera began to help pick up the books, and after sticking his candy bag in his pocket, even Cerulean walked over and picked one up from the floor. "A History of Prophecies?" he read.

Scarlet nodded. "I'm hoping it'll have something about the prophecy I'm in. The Council didn't tell me what the prophecy said exactly, and I forgot to ask. I'm hoping it's in there."

"Doubt it," said Cerulean, tossing the book onto the table. It landed halfway open. Scarlet glared at him and went to close it properly. "Only a few people were present when the prophecy was spoken," said Cerulean. "And they've kept the details private. It is strange though that they didn't tell you anything, considering you're in it."

"Maybe they forgot?" said Scarlet.

"Or they're hiding something," said Cerulean, throwing himself into one of the chairs and propping his feet up on the table.

Scarlet hadn't thought of that. Would they hide something from her? After her experience with Deimos, she wasn't sure she would put anything past him. Not after that flash of excitement she'd seen in his eyes right before he caused her the worst pain she'd ever felt in her life. But what about the rest of the Council? Would they lie to her?

"They probably just forgot," she said. "I'll just ask them next time I see them."

"Sure," said Cerulean, "but if they don't give you answers, there's one more thing we could try."

"What?" asked Scarlet, curiosity piqued.

"They'll definitely have it written down somewhere. They'd have to make sure they don't forget any details. We could go find the paper copy."

"Wouldn't that be restricted if they're keeping the details hidden from the public?" said Scarlet.

"Yup," he replied, pulling his bag of candy back out of his pocket.

"So you're basically saying we should break the rules and sneak into wherever the prophecy is kept?"

"Yup."

"Nope," said Mera.

"Nope," said Tobin.

Nope, thought Scarlet, but she bit her lip and said nothing.

"Just a suggestion," shrugged Cerulean.

"Let's look at these books," said Scarlet, changing the subject.

They spent the next hour combing the books for any information about the Hinterland. But other than learning that its edge was mostly wooded, except for one part that was sea (unmapped sea of course) they didn't discover much.

Finally, they stopped, returning their books on the Hinterland to the shelves. Tobin and Mera both took a few of Scarlet's books so she wouldn't have to carry them all on her own. Cerulean shook his bag of candy and insisted that his hands were full.

They left the library, walking out of the Alleyway and into the Main Courtyard.

"I've got to go." said Cerulean. "I've got training."

Mera raised her eyebrows. "You hardly ever go to training, what's different today?"

Cerulean shrugged, "Just feel like it."

"Beck asked you to go?" asked Mera.

Cerulean shrugged again.

"How do you know Beck so well?" asked Scarlet.

"We're roommates," said Cerulean.

"How does that work?" asked Scarlet, nose scrunching.

"We share a room," said Cerulean, straight-faced as always. "Hence the name roommates."

Scarlet made a face at him. "You know what I mean. He's years older than you."

"He's eighteen, that's only a three year difference," said Cerulean. "And it'll only be a two-year difference soon when I turn sixteen."

"I guess I just didn't realize there were roommates here," said Scarlet. "I have my own room." Immediately she wished she'd kept quiet, realizing she may be more privileged than she'd realized.

"That's normal," said Mera, nodding her head and assuaging Scarlet's concern. "Every family gets their own room. But sometimes the people serving in the army choose to live in the soldier barracks, and then they get a roommate."

"So Beck doesn't live with his family?" asked Scarlet, frowning. She knew that he at least had one family member in the fortress.

"No," said Mera. "And Cerulean–" she stopped, cheeks reddening and eyes darting to him.

"And I don't have a family," finished Cerulean, so blunt that Scarlet blinked.

Unsure of what to say to that, she opted to saying nothing. The others followed suit, and it was in complete and awkward silence that they crossed the Main Courtyard. After a few seconds Cerulean broke off in the opposite direction.

Once he was gone Scarlet turned to Mera.

"How come he lives in the soldier barracks? Why doesn't he just live on his own like me?"

Mere hesitated. "He did live on his own for a while. It didn't go so well. He technically shouldn't be allowed to live in the soldier barracks, because he's too young to be a soldier. But Beck pulled a few strings for him."

Scarlet nodded. It seemed like something Beck would do.

"Want to come with me to the market?" asked Mera, changing the subject. "I've got to feed the frogs for my mom–if she's found them, that is."

Scarlet bit her lip, tempted. "No, I want to get some practice in before tomorrow's training." She said her goodbyes to Mera and Tobin, who set her books against the courtyard wall. Once they left, she spent the rest of the afternoon in the Main Courtyard, using a sword she found in the armory, and trying to imitate the moves of the warriors practicing in the courtyard.

When the sky darkened, she hurried to grab some dinner from the Dining Hall, before going up to her room, enlisting the help of a friendly dwarf to carry her books.

Right before she fell into bed she looked out the window to find that the monster she'd seen out in the Hinterland was gone. That should be a good thing, but a shiver went up Scarlet's spine as she dragged her chair in front of the bedroom door.

She liked her monsters where she could see them.

Chapter 22

"So, are you feeling ready to train Scarlet?" asked Beck, bringing his sword down in a long arc.

With a grunt Tasha parried the blow with both daggers and made a move of her own. "Do you usually have conversations while you duel?"

"Would you willingly have a conversation with me if we weren't–" he ducked "–dueling?"

She considered, deflecting a strike and trying to decide how to reply. She chose honestly. "No."

They were dueling in the Main Courtyard again. The sun had not yet risen, and as far as Tasha could tell they'd already been fighting for at least ten minutes.

"Then I have to ask now if I want an answer," said Beck.

Tasha gritted her teeth. Talking required thinking, and she didn't duel to think, she dueled to *not* think.

"I'll make you a deal," she whirled her blade "–you let us fight in silence–" she jabbed it at him "–and I'll let you ask me one question when we're done."

He blocked her attack and returned it. His swipe was shallow without as much power as his strikes from the day before. Surely, he wasn't losing endurance already?

"Any question?"

"Yup." She parried and lashed at him.

"And you'll answer truthfully?" he asked as he side-stepped–almost too late. He was definitely moving a bit slower than yesterday. Still, his technique was excellent.

"Probably not."

He laughed, sounding a little out of breath. "Well thanks for your honesty about not being honest."

She didn't reply.

"Fine, fine," he struck at her and she dodged. "And to trade diamond for diamond, I'll let you ask me one question too."

"I didn't ask for a question." She swiped at him.

He managed to shrug and parry at the same time–something Tasha hadn't thought possible before.

They battled for another ten minutes, and then the sun came up, painting the courtyard light gold. Instantly they both stepped out of the arena and collapsed against the courtyard wall, gasping for breath.

"Alright," panted Beck. "One question."

"You can't let us catch our breath first?" asked Tasha.

"Is that your question?"

She scowled at him.

"I don't have time to wait," explained Beck, sliding down to sit against the wall. "I've got errands to run for the Council–" He yawned before finishing "–I have to go in about five minutes."

"Why are you so tired today?" asked Tasha, sitting down too.

"I'm fine," he said, straightening against the wall as though trying to prove it.

She crossed her arms. "I didn't ask if you were fine. I asked why you're tired."

He hesitated, then gave in. "There was an impromptu Council meeting really late last night."

Tasha nodded. "So what, they can call a Council meeting whenever and wake you up if you're asleep?" If someone tried to wake her up in the middle of the night just to talk, they would regret it.

Beck nodded. "Yup, pretty much. But I was already up, so it worked out anyway."

"Partying with Lug?" she asked. Her voice was almost teasing, except she wasn't the type of person who teased, and instead the comment came out sarcastic–even condescending in tone.

But Beck seemed to translate what she meant, because he smirked at her before shaking his head and saying, "Nah, my roommate gets nightmares–wakes me up sometimes. Anyway, the Council meeting went for a couple hours."

"What was the meeting about?" asked Tasha, eyes narrowing. Anything that was worth a midnight Council meeting was something she wanted to know.

Beck rubbed at his jaw and hesitated. "I'm not really supposed to talk about it." He paused. "But honestly, everyone's going to know by the end of the day." He looked at her. "Stuff around here is about to get hot as hellfire."

Tasha waited for him to elaborate.

"The resistance groups we sent out got killed," he said, grimacing. "Everyone–I mean none of them survived. We just got news back from one of our spies. We'll have to tell their families today, and if you thought news of your duel with Enyalios spread fast, just wait. People aren't going to be happy."

Tasha crossed her arms and looked away from him, raking her eyes across the courtyard as she processed this news.

The Wraith and her forces were not to be underestimated.

Beside her Beck shifted against the wall and said, "Alright, my turn to ask a question. Same as before: do you feel ready to train Scarlet?"

A funny question to ask someone who spent most of her time trying not to feel anything, thought Tasha, but she didn't answer with that. "Yup."

He side-eyed her. "Is this one of your honest answers, or...?"

"That's two questions."

He put his hands up. "You're right. White flag."

Tasha almost rolled her eyes. She didn't understand half of what he said most of the time.

He started to get to his feet.

"She's fourteen," said Tasha, standing up. "How hard can it be?"

Beck nodded. "Well how did you learn? Just teach her like that."

Tasha raised her eyebrows. "I learned by walking into the Hinterland and getting attacked by monsters."

Beck paused. "Sprites—I take it back." He squinted at her. "Is that really how—"

"I thought you had things to go do," she reminded, voice sharpening.

"Right. You're right," he said with a nod, and if her sudden shut down of the conversation had phased him, he didn't show it. "One thing first, though. I noticed your daggers are getting blunt. I can sharpen them if you want."

"I can sharpen my own daggers," said Tasha, scowling. Could he not tell by now that she could take care of herself?

"Yeah, but I can do it magically," said Beck. "It's much faster, and usually works better."

Tasha paused. She could easily sharpen the daggers on her own, but she couldn't resist a sudden nudge of curiosity. Deciding that there was no harm in it, she handed him the daggers. She noticed that as she passed them over, he was careful not to touch her hands, placing his fingers as far from hers as possible so that he actually held the daggers by the blades.

Once he had them in his hands, he flipped them to hold them by the handles, and shifted both of them to his left hand, holding them so that their blades pointed skyward. He extended his other arm, hand up. A single, pin-prick sized spot at the center of his palm began to glow like the sun was under his skin. The light, pale as ivory, began to spread until his entire hand was illuminated. The strange light began to curl from his fingers like shimmery, white smoke. He gave his hand a single, sharp shake, and the smoke flattened out, becoming a flat blade of light around his hand.

Beck set the blade of light against the first dagger. Tasha expected the dagger to go through it, but instead the light was solid. He ran the edge of the light across the dagger and with a couple short scrapes the blade was sharper than Tasha could ever remember it being. He repeated the process with the second.

"Here you go," he said, as he passed them to her. "Now in our next duel you can stab me better."

Tasha snorted. She felt the unfamiliar urge to laugh. It had been a long time since she'd felt the way she was feeling now. And of course, with the feeling came heat in her palms.

As the danger of her own hands returned, like a weight pushing her down, whatever she'd been feeling vanished.

"I have to go." She turned and began to walk away in the direction of the Dining Hall.

"Again tomorrow?" Beck called after her.

She was nodding before she could stop herself.

Scarlet straightened, puffing up her chest and trying to look as confident as she wanted to feel. She tried to walk tall. Like Beck always did, or Elowen.

She'd eaten a hearty breakfast, spent some time roaming the marketplace with Mera, and now it was time for her session with Tasha. Just the thought made her feel a little weak at the knees.

Sure, she thought, trying to reassure herself. *Tasha was a little terrifying, but she couldn't be worse than Enyalios, right?*

Scarlet fake-strutted into the Main Courtyard and found Tasha almost immediately. She was leaning against the wall, lazily flipping her dagger into the air and catching it as it came back down. Scarlet stopped and watched the maneuver a couple of times before forcing her feet forward.

"Hi Tasha," Scarlet gave a small wave.

Tasha nodded to her. Without another word, she pushed off the wall and gestured for Scarlet to follow. She led Scarlet to an unoccupied corner of the courtyard.

"What are we going to learn?" asked Scarlet. "Are you going to teach me how to break noses?" She fake-punched the air and grinned at Tasha.

"First, that's not how you punch," said Tasha, not returning the grin. "Second, no. We'll get to that later. Today we're doing physical conditioning."

"Working out?" asked Scarlet. Now it was her turn to look unamused.

"Knowing the correct way to stab a person, and having the physical strength to do it, are two very different things," said Tasha.

Scarlet nodded, though she felt apprehensive. She had never been one for working out, and her experience with Enyalios hadn't made her any more fond of it.

"What's first?" asked Scarlet.

"We'll start off with a basic exercise," said Tasha. "Push-ups."

"Otherwise known as Globe Straddles," commented Scarlet.

Tasha frowned. "What?"

"It's an elven thing," said Scarlet, shrugging. She hoped Tasha's workout wouldn't be as intense as Enyalios' had been.

"How many?" asked Scarlet, dropping to the ground. To her surprise, Tasha dropped down next to her.

"Until you can't do anymore," said Tasha.

Scarlet didn't like the sound of that. She grimaced at the stone floor.

"Go," said Tasha.

Scarlet and Tasha went upward together. *I'll just keep pace with her*, thought Scarlet. But almost instantly she realized that wasn't going to work. Tasha pumped out push-ups like a machine, arms folding smoothly at her sides. Meanwhile Scarlet's arms stuck out awkwardly with her elbows wide and wobbly, hair flopping in her face as she went up and down. She wasn't even at ten yet, and already her arms were burning. She glanced at Tasha and found that she was still going at a steady pace.

Scarlet glared at the stone floor and kept going. Her elbows folded and unfolded, her back bobbed up and down. For half a minute there was no sound except for Scarlet's heavy breathing and the clashing of metal from other parts of the courtyard.

"I can't do anymore," gasped Scarlet, rising up and holding herself there. She looked at Tasha whose pace had not slowed.

"This is what I call a Live-or-Die-Moment," said Tasha. She barely sounded winded. "It's like the moment in a fight when you want to give up. You can taste the blood in your mouth. It would be easy to drop your weapon. But in a real battle that's the same as accepting death. So, do you push onward, or do you let go–do you live or die? It's a choice." The challenge in her voice was clear.

Fine. Challenge accepted.

Scarlet let out a breath and went down, and up. Her arms were shaking. Down and up. Sweat dripped down her nose. She pictured

Enyalios watching. Down and up. She plummeted downward. She inched upward and held herself there, catching her breath.

Tasha was still going, though perhaps she had slowed slightly. She glanced up. "Time to choose, Scarlet. Live or die?"

"Live," Scarlet grunted, and she did another. And then her arms gave out, and she collapsed to the ground.

"How many?" asked Tasha, standing up.

"I think that was seventeen," said Scarlet, cheeks flushing as she wondered how many Tasha had gotten.

Tasha nodded. "Seventeen is your number to beat. Seventeen is where you reach your Live-or-Die-Moment."

Scarlet only had a minute of rest before they continued. By the end of the session Scarlet knew her Live-or-Die-Moments for various exercises, and she suspected they were going to be a regular part of her sessions with Tasha. They finished off the training by running, where Scarlet discovered that her Live-or-Die Moment was just short of a mile, at which point she'd tripped over her own feet and fallen into a wall.

She was sweating profusely, and dead-tired by the time Tasha told her they could sit down and stretch.

"And I thought Enyalios' session was hard," gasped Scarlet. "I thought this would be better." She moaned as she reached to touch her toes.

Tasha side-eyed her. "It is better. You've just confused better with easier."

Scarlet was too winded to reply.

"Be here, same time tomorrow," said Tasha, then she got up and left the Main Courtyard.

Scarlet sat against the wall for a second, catching her breath. She was about to head to the Dining Hall when Deimos entered the courtyard.

Without pausing to think, Scarlet rushed to her feet and headed toward him. "Hey, Deimos!" she called.

He spun to face her, and she instantly felt like turning around and walking away. Before the magic test, seeing Deimos had always reminded her of Beck because of their matching features, but that was no longer the case. Looking at him now, all Scarlet could think of was the pain of the draining: the feeling of her bones weakening, blood slowing, nerves withering under skin that was becoming little more than paper–easily torn.

"Um–" for a moment she forgot what she was saying. She swallowed, looking at the ground and away from him to regain some focus. "I was wondering about the prophecy." She fidgeted with the hem of her tunic. "Could I hear it?"

Deimos looked Scarlet over as though he was evaluating every piece of her. When he spoke it was slow and strong, "I'm afraid not."

Scarlet gathered her courage. "Why?"

"It's not open to the public."

Curiosity killed the cat, her mother's voice said in her head.

That's what the good Lord gave the cat nine lives for, replied her father.

"I know," said Scarlet, swallowing again and looking Deimos in his sharp green eyes. "But I'm not like the rest of the public. It's about me, after all. Shouldn't I be able to see it?"

Deimos' eyes darkened. "I'm afraid these things are too complicated for you to understand."

Before Scarlet could open her mouth to argue, he turned and swept away.

Scarlet glared at the ground. She hated being treated like a naïve child. She was young, but she wasn't stupid, and she had already seen things most fourteen-year-olds hadn't, and never would. Or maybe he had been referring to her being human–which wasn't any better. Or maybe… maybe the Council really was hiding something.

"Interesting, don't you think?"

Scarlet jumped as someone spoke from behind her.

During her conversation with Deimos Scarlet hadn't seen Cerulean enter the courtyard, but it seemed he had heard everything.

Cerulean cocked an eyebrow and glanced in the direction Deimos had gone. "I'm slightly suspicious."

Scarlet frowned, following his gaze. "Yeah, me too."

"So, you want to find that prophecy?"

Scarlet bit her lip. She wasn't sure she trusted Cerulean, but she realized that she trusted Deimos less.

Curiosity killed –

Scarlet pushed away her mother's voice. "Let's do it."

Chapter 23

Scarlet raced down the passage and rounded a corner. She skidded to a stop outside the infirmary door and was reaching for the handle when the door slid open and the very person she was looking for stepped out.

"Tobin!"

He jumped. "Hey, I was just going to drop these off at the infirmary storage room near the Main Courtyard." he waved a couple empty bottles.

She nodded. "I'll come with you. Cerulean and I made a plan, and he's telling Mera, but I have to tell you so–"

Tobin cut her off with a groan. "Hold on–you made a plan with Cerulean? Why do I have a bad feeling about this?"

Scarlet just started down the hallway in the direction of the Main Courtyard and gestured for him to follow. "Just listen."

It took Scarlet less than a minute to brief Tobin on the plan, as, thus far, there wasn't much of one.

"So, just to make sure I've got this right," said Tobin frowning as they turned a corner and started up a flight of stairs. "You want to sneak into the Council Room in the middle of the night to see if the prophecy is in there, so you can make sure the Council isn't hiding anything from you?"

Scarlet nodded, "I want to know what that prophecy says. And Cerulean–"

"See, I just don't know if we should be listening to Cerulean," said Tobin, eyes forward as they stepped onto the landing and started down a passageway.

Scarlet looked at him. "I thought you two were wall buddies."

"He just..." Tobin hesitated. "It doesn't seem like he always makes the best decisions."

"Alright," said Scarlet, "maybe he doesn't always make the best decisions, but–"

"And now he's convinced you to sneak into the Council Room to steal a prophecy," said Tobin, "which is most likely going to end badly. He seems like a bad influence."

Scarlet laughed. Tobin sounded like her mom. "Maybe we can be a good influence."

Tobin stopped. "You really aren't worried about being around him?"

Scarlet shook her head. "I don't think he's dangerous, if that's what you mean."

"I didn't exactly mean that he's dangerous," said Tobin, glancing around as though expecting the elf in question to be hiding somewhere nearby. "I just think you're too trusting."

"Maybe," said Scarlet. "But I also trusted an enemy guard in the Wraith's Fortress, and that turned out pretty well." She grinned at him.

He blinked and looked down. It seemed he had no response to that. Scarlet just grinned wider and continued walking. Tobin followed, and they continued in silence down the hallway, getting closer to the Main Courtyard.

"You don't have to help," said Scarlet after a moment. "Three of us will be enough." Although, internally she drooped a little at the idea of doing it without him.

Tobin moistened his lips, silent for a long moment. Then finally he said, "I'll help."

Scarlet raised her eyebrows in surprise, "Really? You sure? You don't have to."

He nodded, "I know. But if you really want to know what this prophecy says, then I'll help you get it. You deserve to know."

Scarlet smiled, "Thanks Tobin. That's really sweet."

He shrugged, "Well, I figure you're probably going to need someone with some experience in one of the fortress' jail cells, because that's probably where we're all going to end up."

Scarlet grinned. "That's what I'm bringing Cerulean along for, actually."

"Forgot about that," replied Tobin with a snort of amusement. "Guess Cerulean got to my job first."

Scarlet shook her head, "But there's no one I'd rather pull a heist with than you."

Tobin's eyebrows scrunched as he considered the comment, "That... is the weirdest compliment I've ever received. And by far my favorite."

Scarlet grinned at him, and opened her mouth to reply, when suddenly she paused. "Do you hear that?"

Tobin stopped and listened too. "Who's yelling?"

They looked at each other, then ran down the hallway toward the direction of the shouts: the Main Courtyard.

They entered through an archway and instantly found themselves part of a large, hollering crowd, every person faced toward the center of the courtyard. They couldn't see exactly what was causing the commotion, so they pressed onward through the surging sea of people. Finally, they squeezed into a gap and the entire scene came into view.

In the middle of the courtyard, two elves were fighting in a circle of space, not with weapons, just with their fists. One's hair was long and white, the other's was short and black. Besides that Scarlet couldn't see any other details, they were moving so fast.

As she watched, the black-haired elf landed a blow and the crowd's yelling heightened, some calling for the elves to stop, others encouraging them.

"What are they fighting about?" asked Scarlet to no one in particular, eyes widening as she watched them.

"They're High Elves from rival houses," answered the nymph to Scarlet's right, and she jumped, not having expected the voice. "One of them had a brother in one of the failed resistance missions," continued the nymph. "Big blow on the line's honor, failed missions are."

"High Elves are wild about honor," added a dwarf behind them who had apparently been listening in.

"Second guy brought it up," finished the nymph. "And this happened."

"That's awful," said Scarlet, mouth falling open. "Why would anyone do that?"

The nymph shrugged. "Why do the High Elves do anything? Probably still mad about some past wrong."

"Or holding a grudge over something that happened in the High Elf war," added the dwarf.

The nymph nodded, "Could be–civil war wasn't too long ago."

Scarlet opened her mouth to ask another question, when suddenly a new person entered the circle of space the two elves were fighting in.

"Alright you two, break it up," Beck was wearing his armor as always. He held himself in a way that made him seem older than the two fighting elves, even though they were both clearly his senior by many years.

They ignored him, continuing their brawl.

They flew apart momentarily, and Beck stepped forward, quickly inserting himself between them. "Enough–"

The black-haired elf launched forward and swung at the second, but Beck leapt into action, catching his arm and throwing it back.

He looked between the two elves and shook his head, "C'mon guys, I'm getting tired of breaking up fights today. If you're going to beat each other up, at least do it in private, alright?"

The white-haired elf growled something, voice too low for Scarlet to hear, but she thought she picked up on the words: "I'm gunna–"

"While I admire the creativity," replied Beck, "we're actually trying to keep gut-twisting to a minimum if at all possible. Pretty sure we have a policy about that–plus the infirmary's already full."

There were some snickers from the crowd, causing the two elves to glance around. From their expressions, it seemed they hadn't realized they had such a large audience.

Beck began to speak to the two elves again, this time quieter so that not everyone could hear.

Tobin glanced at Scarlet. "Show's over I think."

She nodded and the two of them slipped out of the crowd, skirting around the edge of the courtyard and into the north-facing hallway. "Is the infirmary really full?" asked Scarlet, glancing at Tobin.

Tobin nodded. "There have been lots of fights today. The news about the resistance groups hasn't gone over well. People are upset."

Scarlet frowned and the rest of their walk to the storage room was in silence. Once they reached it, they split ways. Tobin had to return for another shift in the infirmary, and, after promising Tobin she'd keep him updated with any news of the plan, Scarlet started up to her room to read some of the books she'd gotten from the library.

Once she'd reached her room, she retired to her bed, book in hand.

She'd just opened the first page when there was a creak and the bookshelf against the wall swung open. Scarlet gasped and jumped backward, falling off the bed and onto the floor.

Someone snorted and Scarlet stood up to see that the bookshelf had opened like a door, revealing a familiar figure– "Cerulean?"

"The one and only," answered Cerulean, crossing his arms and leaning against the side of the new doorway that had just appeared in her bedroom.

"What just–what?" Scarlet stared at him, mouth hanging open.

"Passageway," he said, gesturing to the dark tunnel behind the bookshelf. "They're all over the fortress. Most people just don't know it."

Scarlet spluttered for a moment, unsure what to say before blurting out, "You can't just barge into my room like that! I could have been changing."

To her surprise Cerulean actually reddened slightly. He brushed a strand of messy, white hair out of his face and muttered, "Didn't think about that."

"That's why my room has a door," she said, gesturing to it. "That you can knock on. Why not just use that?"

"Why would I use a door when I could use a secret passage?" Scarlet opened her mouth to snap back–then hesitated as she realized he had a point. "How did you even know where to find my room anyway?" she asked, changing the subject.

He shrugged. "Everyone knows this tower has been set aside for the Chosen to stay in, I just had to figure out which room was yours."

She squinted at him. "You're lucky you found mine first then."

"I guessed wrong the first time," he admitted. "But the room was empty, so it didn't matter."

Scarlet shook her head. "If you'd walked into Tasha's room, she would have killed you."

"Probably," agreed Cerulean, pushing off the doorway and taking a step into the room. "So, in other words, I risked my life to come see you. You're welcome."

Scarlet rolled her eyes, "What do you want, Cerulean?"

"Did Tobin agree to help?"

Scarlet nodded.

"Good," said Cerulean. "So did Mera. We have to figure some stuff out though before we can actually go for it. You need to investigate around the Council Room and look for entrances other than the main one. I'm going to see if Beck knows how long the Council members stay there every day, and if the doors are guarded even after they're gone."

Scarlet nodded. "And why am I doing the investigating around the Council Room?"

"Because you're Chosen, so you won't get in trouble if they catch you looking," he replied. "If they catch me poking around, I'll probably end up in a holding cell again."

Scarlet nodded. "Alright, I'll do it." She bent over, picked up her book that had flown onto the floor when she'd fallen, and set it on the bed before sitting back down herself.

She saw Cerulean's eyes rake over the cover. The words, *A Guide to Elven Culture*, were written in bold letters across the front.

"Anything else?" she asked.

"Nope," he shook his head. "That's all. And I have to go, so I'll see you later."

"Where are you in a hurry to?" she asked, raising her eyebrows.

"Beck's got a free night," said Cerulean. "So we're going to see if we can teach the little dragons in The Alleyway how to do tricks." He smirked, which as far as Scarlet could tell, was the closest he ever got to smiling.

She nodded, grinning. "Sounds fun. You'll have to tell me how it goes."

Cerulean nodded. He turned away to leave, then paused and glanced back, looking at the book on the bed. "And if you want to learn about elven culture, don't read about it," he shook his head as though the mere idea was the stupidest he'd ever heard. "I'm an actual elf. Ask me."

And with that he walked into the darkness of the passage and closed the shelf behind him.

Scarlet rolled her eyes before getting out of bed to drag the chair over against the bookshelf. She didn't need any more surprise visitors. Surely, next time he could use the door like a normal person, even if she did see the appeal of using the secret passages. Were it not so late she would have gone to explore them herself, but she yawned as she glanced out the window. She needed sleep.

She set her book on the floor, pulled her bedside table in front of the bedroom door to replace the already occupied chair, climbed into bed, and extinguished her candle.

She took one more glance out the window before falling asleep: no monsters in sight. But that didn't mean they weren't there.

There was smoke in her lungs.
Thick.
Like cotton in her chest.
She couldn't breathe. She couldn't breathe–she couldn't–and the ceiling began to collapse.

Tasha wrenched her eyes open, flying up into a sitting position. The nightmare had caused her hands to burn, but it wasn't just her hands– it was racing up her arms, she could feel the tingle up the back of her neck, pressing behind her eyes. It was boiling her blood. And though she was pulling in air through short, abrupt inhales, she still felt as though was suffocating.

She scrambled to her feet, forcing herself to take long, deep breaths, closing her eyes as she tried to quench the feelings the dream had awoken inside her.

Her powers, though she wanted to deny it–were getting worse. Just as they had when she was a child. At least now she was in control when she was awake, but only barely. Only by swallowing down her emotions. And what happened when she couldn't? What happened when she got too angry? Too sad? Too happy?

That last one had never been one she'd had to worry about before, but now–her duels with Beck had been leaving her with new feelings. Like earlier, when she'd been tempted to laugh for the first time in years. It was only her exhaustion after the duels that was saving her from exposing herself.

But soon she would build up endurance and the duels wouldn't be so taxing on her energy. Soon she would be dangerous again.

She looked out the window. Usually, she would have headed down for her duel five minutes ago.

Sweat dripped down her forehead as she crouched down to pick up her daggers, resting on the floor next to where she'd been sleeping. She rubbed the wooden handles with her thumbs, then flipped one and caught it. Usually that helped to refocus her, but the dream was still too vivid in her mind, her palms still too hot. She could still feel the smoke. Smell it. Taste it almost.

She felt pressure rising in her chest. She needed to release it–she needed to explode.

She needed to duel.

But that no longer felt like an option. It was too risky.

She felt as though her thoughts were fraying, emotions splintering even as she tried to rein them in. The air around her fingertips was becoming sweltering–and Tasha rammed her dagger into the nearby dresser. She slashed at it, first with the left dagger, then the right, cutting into the soft wood.

It wasn't the same as dueling, but as her full attention turned to the feeling of the blades hacking into wood instead of the war in her own mind, she could finally feel herself regaining a hint of control. She pulled back, breathing hard as she slid her daggers into her belt.

The side of the dresser was now marred with scars. Behind her was her bed, mattress mutilated from a few nights before. Below her was the floor where she'd been sleeping, stone blackened from heat.

Could she be around anything without destroying it?

Tasha flinched as someone knocked on her door.

She hesitated before opening it a crack, positioning herself to conceal the interior of her room.

Beck stood behind the door, armor on and shining, hair neat like usual, green eyes full of life, and, despite the time, looking more awake than Tasha thought she'd ever looked in her entire life.

His crooked grin appeared the moment she opened the door. "What's in the envelope? I thought I should come check on you. You didn't come down at your usual time, and you don't seem the type to sleep in."

"I'm fine," said Tasha, willing him to leave. "I'm not going to duel today."

He squinted at her, and she saw him taking in her damp hair, sweaty face, ruffled jacket, which she'd fallen asleep in, and her heavy breathing. "You sure you're fine, Tash?"

His voice was sincere, and Tasha knew other girls would have melted at having a boy like Beck at their door, but all she could think was: *how easy would it be for me to destroy you too?* A person like him, who was too friendly for his own good and made her feel emotions she didn't have experience controlling. *Too easy.*

"I said I was fine," she snapped, voice rising and becoming as sharp as the daggers at her sides. "Go away Beck."

A flash of hurt registered on his face just before she slammed the door.

The moment the door was closed she locked it tight and set her back against it–not that she expected him to try to enter. He would leave, and after this he would hate her. And she didn't care. It was what she wanted. She wanted him to hate her, because then he would leave her alone. And she wanted to be left alone.

The words weren't as convincing as they had once been.

Tasha closed her eyes as she leaned against the door. She set the back of her head against it, letting cool air chill the sweat on her neck. She was certain, as she stood there, that never had anyone wanted more badly, to be powerless.

Chapter 24

Scarlet stepped into the training center and scanned for Tasha. The courtyard was just the same as always, gray cobblestone, gray walls, gray archways, but with the midday sun above everything was edged with gold: the beards of dwarves, the glinting blades of swords, and the shining, fiery hair that Scarlet was looking for.

Tasha was against the wall on the far side of the courtyard. Her hair was pulled back, but a few strands had escaped and were blowing free in the wind, framing her face in deep red. She was flipping her dagger–a maneuver that had become familiar to Scarlet by now. Today though it was irregular: quicker than Scarlet had ever seen it, and constant. Usually, Tasha finished after one or two flips, today she continued over and over, so that the blade was in perpetual orbit above her hand. It scissored through the air so fast it was a blur.

Watching it sent a spiral of anxiety through Scarlet's stomach, as though the blade itself was whirring through her insides.

She shook off the feeling and crossed the courtyard to reach Tasha. As soon as she arrived Tasha sheathed her dagger, pushing off the wall and shoving the reckless strands of hair out of her face. The strands tucked into place behind her ears, falling in natural tangles that were perfectly imperfect. Looking at Tasha, Scarlet couldn't help but wish for her hair, red as the devil's tongue, and her smooth, flawless skin, tanned by the sun to the color of warmth and sand, all of it contrasting the harshness in her stance and expression.

"Let's get started," said Tasha, pulling Scarlet from her thoughts. She reached for the ground and picked up a sword. She held it out to Scarlet, hilt first, and Scarlet accepted it from her, wrapping her fingers around the hilt slowly as though half-expecting the weapon to attack her of its own accord.

It wasn't a wooden practice sword like the ones Enyalios had trained her with. The blade was very real and very sharp. Scarlet's arm sagged under its weight, even though the sword itself was small compared to most.

"Are we–are we dueling?" asked Scarlet, voice a little squeakier than she would have liked. But dueling Tasha? That sent more than a spiral of anxiety through her–something more like a spike of nerves right into her chest. Seeing her own expression in the blade Scarlet quickly tried to rearrange her face and mask some of her fear, straightening her shoulders so that she was unnaturally stiff.

Tasha raised an eyebrow and snorted. "You? Dueling me? We haven't even begun to go over the basics. I could kill you in a second. Or at least separate several important limbs from your body."

Scarlet's shoulders sagged in relief. In fact, she was too relieved to feel offended or dispirited by Tasha's comment. With renewed enthusiasm she shifted to hold up the blade, angling it a bit so that the sun lit up the side in an explosion of sparkles. "What are we doing then?"

"First, show me how you hold it," said Tasha.

Scarlet looked down at how she was already gripping the hilt: two-handed with fingers crisscrossed. She looked at her hands for a moment, back to Tasha, back to her hands, then swallowed before saying, "This is how I hold it."

She braced herself for laughter or a scathing comment, but Tasha just examined Scarlet's hold and said, "Your grip's wrong."

Scarlet felt a rush of heat across her face as she reddened. The feeling was also accompanied by a sudden blaze of anger toward Enyalios. Her grip had been wrong during all those training sessions? And he hadn't told her? She gritted her teeth and gripped the handle so tight her knuckles turned white. She imagined how it would feel to plunge the blade right into Enyalios' stomach.

"Hold it like this," instructed Tasha, pulling out her dagger and holding the handle with two hands as though it was a sword.

Scarlet studied the grip for a moment, then mimicked it, right hand clenching the handle and left hand going just below the hilt.

"Now fix your stance," said Tasha, demonstrating even as she said it.

Scarlet copied her.

"Feet a little farther apart. Right below your shoulders."

She nodded as Scarlet listened.

"Bend your knees a little. You're too stiff. And that foot needs to face sideways slightly."

Scarlet shifted her stance yet again.

"Now we work on your swing," said Tasha, seemingly satisfied. "I want you starting in the fool's position, like this–"

"Why's it called–"

"*Don't* interrupt me."

Scarlet swallowed under Tasha's glare, suddenly remembering that she had once watched Tasha massacre an entire encampment of monsters without help. Scarlet proceeded to shut up.

"The Fool's Position," continued Tasha, "is a good starting position. It makes you look vulnerable when really you have great maneuverability."

"So, it's a trick?"

Tasha smirked. "It's a trap." She demonstrated the hold again, and once Scarlet was able to copy it, Tasha continued. "When starting in this position its most likely that your opponent will attack first—you want them to. So, I want you starting here then going into a parry. Like this."

Tasha wheeled the dagger through the air, almost too fast for Scarlet to follow. As it ended its arc, Scarlet could perfectly imagine the sound it would make as it clashed against an enemy's blade—practically feel how the crash would reverberate through one's body.

Scarlet hefted her sword and attempted to copy the move, but her swing was slow and sluggish compared to Tasha's swift, brutal strike.

"Go again," said Tasha. "This time don't shift your feet so much."

Scarlet did it again.

And again.

And again.

With each swing it seemed like Tasha found a new flaw in her stance, her posture, her movement of the sword.

By the time she swung for what must be the hundredth time, Scarlet felt a ball of frustration growing in her chest like a knot.

"Good."

Scarlet blinked, straightening in her surprise. "What?"

Tasha had her arms crossed over her chest: the same stance she'd been holding for the last twenty minutes as she'd watched Scarlet. "That one wasn't horrible. I want you to keep practicing this—" she paused, eyes stuttering, then locking, on something behind Scarlet.

Scarlet let her arms go limp, sword swinging to her side as she turned to look.

Beck and Elowen had run into the Main Courtyard from a side arch. Elowen's brown braid was thumping against her back as she ran, and Beck was flying beside her with long, even strides. Together they sprinted into the Dining Hall and between tables, going toward the exit on the other side.

Scarlet realized they were headed in the direction of the Council Room.

It seemed Tasha realized it, too. Her eyes narrowed. "Lesson over," she said, and instantly stepped over the edge of the arena, the heels of her hunting boots slapping against the cobblestone.

Scarlet understood her sudden change in attention. Two elves running to the Council Room? Something was happening. She stepped over the edge of the arena too.

Scarlet looked to Tasha, and they exchanged a quick glance before simultaneously, as though they'd come to a silent agreement, breaking into a run in the direction Beck and Elowen had gone.

Tasha's strides were long, and though they'd started running at the same time, Scarlet was over half a hallway behind her when Tasha reached the Council Room.

They weren't the only ones heading in. A few elves, nymphs, and a human were also entering as they reached it. Scarlet recognized many of them as Right Hands. Most were sun elves, which made sense. During her short stay in the fortress she'd already run across fifteen Sun Elf Right Hands in the Dining Hall, or when walking the corridors. Many of them had introduced themselves to her.

The guards who always stood to the left and right of the Council Room doors were struggling to talk to everyone walking in, and Scarlet and Tasha slipped in with the rest, sidling against the shadowed wall once they entered so that no one noticed their arrival.

The Council Room was in uproar. At least thirty people were jammed into the space, each trying to talk louder than the next. The Council Members had abandoned their seats at the front of the room and were in the crowd, Right Hands clustered around them.

From where she stood, Scarlet could see, between the shifting people, a table at the center of the room. A map lay across its surface. She could make out swathes of green and blue, along with several black squiggles that she assumed were labels.

The Hinterland

In front of the map stood Deimos. Today he was wearing a long robe, gray as cold morning mist. He scanned the map, then looked up, surveying the room with a clinical expression on his face. He seemed completely at peace with the chaos around him.

Behind him stood Beck, armor on as always. Scarlet couldn't help but wonder if he ever took it off. Despite having been sprinting only minutes before, he didn't seem winded at all. As usual, his hair was neat, like he'd just combed it. His expression was serious as he looked at the map. He glanced up, as though sensing he was being watched, and his gaze snagged on Scarlet and Tasha. Usually, Scarlet would have expected one of his crooked grins, but today the elf quickly looked away from the two of them.

Frowning, Scarlet glanced at Tasha to see if she had noticed, but the other girl was looking determinedly at the side of the room opposite of Beck.

Scarlet didn't have time to think about it before Deimos' booming voice filled the room. "Silence! Everyone, come to order!"

The conversations throughout the room shuddered to a complete stop, all except for a few dwarves in the back who were talking too loudly to hear the High Elf. Deimos cleared his throat and instantly their conversation died and they straightened, muttering apologies as they turned to face him.

Deimos' eyes flickered with clear, unmistakable annoyance, but he turned to address the crowd at large. "As many of you know, another Fate Stone has ignited."

Scarlet's eyes widened and a feeling like bubbles erupted in her chest, bouncing left to right fast enough to make her nauseous while also filling her with energy. She looked quickly at Tasha, but Tasha showed no signs of surprise or shock. Instead, she looked as she usually did: intimidating and slightly irritated.

Scarlet looked back to the center of the room as Deimos began speaking again. "Luckily, it's one of ours, meaning the Wraith doesn't yet know about it, giving us the chance to reach the next Chosen before she does."

Some murmuring broke out around the room.

"In addition, the Fate Stone is already glowing strong," continued Deimos. "Not enough for the next Chosen to be inside the fortress, but based on the intensity, we think we have an idea of where to look. The nearest village to us is located here, right outside the cusp. It's a Forest Elf village, and that's where we expect to find the next Chosen. If they're not located there, they would have to be roaming the Hinterland on their own—which is obviously very rare. Almost unheard of."

Scarlet couldn't help but glance at Tasha out of the corner of her eye. Tasha looked indifferent.

"Here's where the village is located." Deimos placed one long, pale finger over a spot on the map. He tapped the pad of his finger against it so that it made a light thump sound. As he talked he continued to press his finger against the spot, crushing the village beneath it. "We need to act quickly before any of the Wraith's spies have a chance to alert her."

Scarlet blinked. The Wraith's spies? She blinked again. Of course, the Wraith had spies—of course she did. Scarlet had just never considered it. Never considered that anyone in this fortress could be waiting for the perfect opportunity to drag her back to the Wraith.

Anyone in this room.

Unable to help herself, she glanced around the crowd with new suspicion. She wasn't the only one. Around the room narrowed eyes were flicking back and forth between faces.

Scarlet shook her head and forced herself to refocus on Deimos who was saying "–we need to decide who will go collect the next Chosen."

The room broke into tumultuous discussion again.

Scarlet's head snapped from left to right as she tried to take in everything that was going on. Her eyes darted from conversation to conversation.

Beside her Tasha studied the map carefully, arms crossed as she squinted toward the table. Scarlet squinted at it too, but she couldn't see more than splotches of color, so she turned her attention away and back to the others in the room.

The dwarves had huddled into a circle, so close Scarlet could have braided their beards together (if she knew how to braid, which she did not. Her mother had always braided her hair for her).

At the thought something sunk in her stomach like an anchor. It had been a while since she'd felt her mother's soft hands in her hair, gently tugging Scarlet's wild black locks into something tidy. Her mother was always able to do that: take a mess and fix it. Scarlet could use that now. Shaking her head, she attempted to push the thought away, trying to convince her heart that she didn't have time for such emotions at a time like this, but it seemed the anchor could not be removed from where it had dug itself into the pit of her stomach, at the bottom of a sea of emotions.

There was movement out of the corner of her eye, and she realized that Tasha was looking her way, eyes perhaps drawn to Scarlet's sudden head shake. The intensity of Tasha's gaze was enough to make Scarlet momentarily forget what she'd been thinking about as she quickly broke eye contact and scoured the room for anything else to focus on.

Across the room from her, Elowen was in deep conversation with Eldritch, both of them gesturing energetically, and in front of the table Deimos was speaking to Beck, who was shaking his head.

She wished she could hear what they were saying, but the room was too loud. It was like putting your ear next to a hive and expecting to make out the buzz of one specific bee.

Scarlet resisted the urge to put her hands over her ears as the noise reached a crescendo.

And then there was a flash of light from the center of the room, and instantly every head turned to look, voices dying all at once in an abrupt massacre of sound. Thayla stood in front of the table. She had one arm raised, and an orb floated on her palm. It was similar to the one Beck had made to help guide them through the swamp in the Hinterland. Thayla closed her hand, and the orb was eaten by her fist. "If I can have your attention, please."

And the attention was all hers. She smiled and began to speak in a voice so calm and clear Scarlet would still have stopped to listen if the room was on fire. "This is a Forest Elf village we're sending our soldiers to, so it's Forest Elves we should send."

Deimos immediately opened his mouth, but before he could cut in Thayla held up her hand and added, "Not just Forest Elves, other groups may send a couple of their own, but it should be mostly Forest Elves. In addition–"

"I'll go."

Scarlet cracked her neck in her hurry to look at Tasha, mouth falling open. Some of the others in the room had similar reactions, clearly just noticing the presence of the two Chosen. Scarlet reddened as everyone's eyes turned in her direction and she immediately began rethinking the tunic she had chosen to wear that day. She wondered how Tasha could stand so tall with everyone looking at her like that.

Thayla hesitated, exchanging glances with a few of the other Council members before saying, "I'm not sure that would be wise."

Tasha scowled, lips thinning. "Why not?"

"It could be dangerous," replied Thayla, wetting her own lips with her tongue.

Tasha shook her head. "We should reach the next Chosen before the Wraith even hears about this Fate Stone and sends soldiers. Besides, even if something does go wrong, I think I've proven I can fight. Just ask the last person who dueled me."

She was, Scarlet knew—and so did everyone else in the room—talking about the duel in which she'd broken a High Elf's nose with her fist.

Scarlet resisted the urge to laugh out loud. Across the room she caught Beck and Elowen exchanging glances as they fought similar urges. Beck swiped a hand over his mouth in the pretense of rubbing his nose, but Scarlet suspected he was grinning under his hand. Deimos, however, looked less than pleased. His expression made Scarlet feel as though she should be telling Tasha to run.

Whispers broke out among the room and spread, contagious as a fever. Scarlet heard the word "nose" from five different directions at once.

Thayla paused for a moment, letting the noise die down before saying, "You're young, perhaps someone with more experience should be sent."

The comment caught Scarlet by surprise. She'd almost forgotten Tasha was only eighteen.

"Experience?" asked Tasha. Her eyebrows lowered. "Has anyone else here lived in the Hinterland for years? I have experience."

Thayla opened her mouth... and closed it.

Scarlet wondered why she wasn't just saying what was clearly her reason for wanting Tasha to stay at the fortress: she was Chosen and needed to be kept safe at all costs.

Within a second of the thought, Scarlet was hit with the answer. She'd known that Tasha being Chosen was being kept quiet, but maybe she'd underestimated just how quiet. She looked around the room with new eyes. How many people here knew that they stood in the same room with not one, but two Chosen?

"We don't want you to get hurt," said Thayla, clearly choosing her words carefully.

"Would you prefer someone else to get hurt?" asked Tasha, and suddenly Scarlet felt certain that Tasha too had realized Thayla's dilemma—

and knew just how to use it. "Why should my safety be more important than anyone else's?"

There were some grumbles around the room–grumbles that Thayla clearly heard as her eyes traveled over the faces in the crowd. She looked back at Tasha but didn't say anything. There was, Scarlet realized, nothing she could say.

Tasha raised her eyebrows. The battle had been invisible to most, but she had won it.

"It will be your first mission with us," interjected Eldritch, and Scarlet looked at him, wondering how he planned to rectify the situation. "And most of the soldiers we send will have fought in one of our missions before. We should send you with a partner to stay with you at all times and make sure you understand how we do things."

Partner. Understand how we do things. He could say whatever he wanted, but his real intention was clear: a bodyguard.

Tasha must have understood too, because her brown eyes narrowed, glinting almost purple in the light from the chandelier above. "I'm a Lone Wolf. I don't do partners."

"This time you do," said Thayla, seizing on Eldritch's idea.

"I don't–"

"It's non-negotiable."

Tasha scowled, eyebrows slanting over her eyes. Her jaw tightened and Scarlet noticed that one of her fingers reached down to stroke the hilt of the dagger at her hip, before she let out a long breath through her nose and growled, "Fine."

"Perfect," said Thayla. "Now we must decide who your partner will be–"

"My son will do."

Scarlet didn't have to look to know it was Deimos who had spoken.

If Beck was surprised at being volunteered, he didn't show it. He glanced sideways at Tasha. Their eyes met for a moment before both pairs flitted away.

"Avenbeck can also act as a representative of my people," spoke Deimos, and then, as though anyone could forget: "the High Elves."

"This mission is not about representation," said Thayla, nostrils flaring.

Deimos smiled coldly at her. "Of course not. His job will be to accompany Tasha."

Thayla frowned at the High Elf before looking away. She impatiently threw a blue-tipped lock of hair out of her face before glancing between Beck and Tasha, "Fine. You two, go get ready."

Tasha gave a sharp nod and left Scarlet's side, walking toward the Council room doors without looking at her new partner even once. She walked out of the Council Room and Beck strode out after her, doors slamming shut behind them with a final thrum that seemed to reverberate throughout the whole room for several seconds after.

"Alright, we have less than half an hour to decide who else is going," said Thayla. "If you're not a Council Member or a Forest Elf, get out. And remember, tell no one what you've heard here. You alone have been trusted with this information."

Thayla finished speaking and turned to the other Council Members, noise breaking out in the room as people began to leave.

Scarlet quickly darted out of the doors, bouncing between people as she did so.

Once she had left the room behind, she walked slowly down the hall, replaying everything that had just happened. A third Fate Stone had lit up.

A third Fate Stone had lit up.

At the thought, Scarlet broke into a run down the hallway, whipping around the first corner, and going even faster when she ran around the second, her destination set and Thayla's sending words lost on her.

She turned another corner and– "Scarlet?"

She slowed for a moment. Cerulean was striding down the hallway toward her, hair a disaster (though at this point Scarlet had come to expect that), and eyebrows raised. "What're you running for?"

Scarlet panted, "Something happened. I only want to explain it once. Just follow me."

He opened his mouth to answer, but before he could get the words out she bolted down the hallway.

She heard him groan behind her, some muttered words, then the sound of footsteps. It was only a couple seconds before he'd caught up to her, elven speed easily matching hers so that they were running side by side. She turned yet another corner, dashed a little ways down the corridor, wrenched open the infirmary door, and practically flew through it.

"Tobin–"

She skidded to a stop.

Someone in the infirmary was yelling.

The someone in question was a High Elf woman seated on the far bed, legs crossed daintily in front of her. The woman had pale, fair skin and long blonde lashes that glittered like they were two nets catching light. Her eyes were large and luminous, and deep blue like two cool lagoons. She would have been extraordinarily beautiful, but her features were somewhat marred by the furious expression she was wearing on her face. Her pretty pink lips were ripped open into a snarl, and her clean white teeth glinted like snake fangs.

Cerulean sprinted in behind Scarlet just in time to hear the woman bellow, "–away from me!"

Her yell was directed at the very person Scarlet was looking for. Tobin stood at the end of the bed, hands in the air as though in surrender.

"What's going on?" asked Scarlet, taking an automatic step toward him.

"I–" he started to speak but didn't get far.

"I'll tell you what's going on," answered the woman. "They expect me–an esteemed member of the Hawthorne Line–to sit back and allow this human to bandage me." She spat out the word human as though it was foul, like a clump of dirt in her mouth, and as she did so she waved her arm so they could also see a shallow cut, only as long as Scarlet's middle finger, on her skinny forearm. "I would never let the likes of him touch me," she finished, ending her sentiment with a sniff and a scowl.

Heat rushed to Scarlet's chest like boiling water. She reddened with it, opening her mouth to snap back, when someone else beat her to it.

"You're absolutely right."

Scarlet spun to look at Cerulean, mouth falling open. Sure, she had realized that at times Cerulean could be less than nice–but this? This was a step beyond condescending sarcasm.

"He shouldn't touch you," Cerulean plowed on. "You don't deserve his help."

It took the woman a moment to realize that he wasn't actually agreeing with her, but when she did, a sneer appeared on her face that made something in Scarlet's gut shrivel. "He's a human!" she said loudly, casting Tobin a nasty look.

"And you're a bi–"

"I'm a member of the Hawthorne Line!" The woman cut him off before he could finish. "How dare you speak to me–"

"I don't care what tree your family is named after!"

Both their voices had risen, crashing through the infirmary like wild animals set free, starved for the fight.

The woman stood up, making a show of clutching her cut with the hand of her other arm. "I will never let a human touch me, I would rather die!"

Cerulean's nostrils flared. "I hope you do!"

Tobin's eyes widened–Scarlet felt a sudden surge of amused panic–and suddenly Cerulean and the elven woman were both bellowing at each other, voices too loud to hear what they were really saying.

"Cerulean!" yelled Scarlet. "Cerulean!" But he couldn't hear her. He was completely lost to his anger.

Suddenly, a door at the end of the infirmary burst open and a healer, dwarven with a white apron, came hurtling through it. She shouted something that was lost to the clamor, and when she realized her voice was going to make no impact, she gestured violently to the door.

Quickly, Tobin and Scarlet converged on Cerulean, each of them pushing him toward the exit. He resisted for a moment, before giving in and allowing them to lead him out of the infirmary, though he didn't stop yelling throughout, and managed to direct an obscene hand gesture at the elf near the bed before they could shove him through the door and slam it closed.

They stood in the hallway for a moment, Scarlet and Tobin breathing heavily from physically tugging Cerulean through the doorway, Cerulean panting from yelling and, of course, being physically tugged.

The elf leaned against the wall, shaggy hair falling over his eyes as he recovered his breath. He frowned and his teeth flashed as white as his locks as he growled, "I hate High Elves."

"Me too, they're the worst," agreed Tobin, voice adamant before realizing who he was talking to and adding quickly, "no offence."

"None taken." Cerulean crossed his arms and swung his gaze to Scarlet. His breathing had leveled out, and he pushed off the wall so that he was standing straight. "So, do you have anything interesting to tell us, or are you just wasting our time?" His expression had gone from intense anger to intense boredom in less than a second. It was like he had a mental switch so that he was always caring too much, or not at all. Scarlet couldn't help but be a little scared of how fast and unpredictable the change was.

The Hinterland

But she shook off the feeling, looked between the two boys, lowered her voice, and said, "A Fate Stone lit up."

Tobin did a double-take and even Cerulean couldn't hide a moment of shock, but after a second he said, "One of ours, or one of theirs?"

"Ours." Scarlet answered. "And they're leaving tonight to get to the next Chosen before the Wraith does. Tasha is going, and Beck, and a bunch of Forest Elves."

"Why wood el–" started Tobin, but he was interrupted by Cerulean, whose arms had come uncrossed as he stared at Scarlet. "Beck's going?"

Scarlet nodded.

Cerulean's jaw tightened and in his eyes Scarlet saw it–the exact second the switch happened in the elf: the absence of feeling, to the overpowering presence of it.

"But he told me he wouldn't have to leave on another mission for a while," argued Cerulean, voice darkening as though he was accusing her of lying.

"Well he's going to make sure Tasha doesn't get hurt," answered Scarlet. She opened her mouth to continue, but Cerulean didn't seem to care what she had to say, because he muttered something under his breath, said in a slightly louder voice, "I'll see you guys later", and stormed away down the corridor. Scarlet could only assume he was going to find Beck, and in that moment, she felt very happy not to be the green-eyed elf.

Tobin and Scarlet watched him disappear around a corner before Tobin said, "Why Forest Elves?"

Scarlet took a moment to explain everything to him: what had happened, who was going, and where they were headed. She finished and panted, having largely explained everything in one breath.

Tobin blinked like he'd been hit over the head with a hammer made of information. "That's a lot."

Scarlet nodded. "I just wish I could go like Tasha is."

"I don't," said Tobin, shaking his head. "I prefer you here where it's safe."

Scarlet dug her foot into the ground. "I just feel useless, staying here and waiting."

He shook his head again, brown eyes narrowing in concern, which was ridiculous, because he shouldn't be worried about her when there were others about to risk their lives journeying through the Hinterland to save the next Chosen.

"You're not useless," he said gently. "It's just not your turn yet. But it'll come, I know it will."

Scarlet nodded. She just hoped it came soon.

Tasha launched into the hallway, determined to get some separation between herself and her new partner, whom she vividly remembered yelling at that morning.

She'd been hoping to avoid Beck completely for today, and for the rest of her time in the fortress. In fact, it had been part of her reason for volunteering for this mission, not to mention the growing sense of confinement the fortress was giving her. At least this would let her feel some freedom again. But as for avoiding Beck? It seemed luck was not on her side. Now she would have to deal with an angry High Elf, and in all honesty, she was getting tired of angry High Elves.

Tasha could hear Beck's footsteps behind her, and she made a firm decision not to look back to see exactly where he was. But after another moment it became clear that he wasn't going to be behind her for much longer.

The footsteps quickened and– "Holy sprites, you're a fast walker." Beck jogged to her side.

He didn't sound mad... but he had to be. It had been just hours ago that she'd slammed a door in his face and shouted at him. Tasha looked straight forward down the hallway. "Maybe you're slow."

Out of the corner of her eye she thought she saw him grin, before pausing his pace and saying, "Do you even know where you're going?"

No. "Of course I know."

Beck continued to stand behind her. "You sure? Because you just walked past the armory door."

Tasha stopped, ran her tongue over her teeth, then turned to face him. He stood beside a wooden door with his hand sitting on the handle, and his eyes holding a twinkle that was, in that moment, infinitely annoying.

"You could've just said you didn't know," he said, doing an extremely bad job at hiding a smile.

"I did know," she replied. "You distracted me."

He shook his head. "White flag then, that's my bad." But he was grinning in a way that told her he didn't believe her excuse.

He held open the door for her, and she walked through, watching him out of the corner of her eye the whole time. She was still waiting for the anger that had to be coming.

Beck stepped in after and gestured around the room. There were suits of armor hanging from hooks on the walls, helmets lining shelves, and a bucket full of stained cleaning rags in the corner. The entire room smelled like sweat and metal. "Alright, we have metal armor, and leather-"

"I want leather," said Tasha instantly. She needed something that would be flexible and allow her to move freely.

"That's fine, it'll give you more maneuverability," said Beck. "The only problem is it can be penetrated easier than metal, even by a good string-snapper."

Tasha shook her head, "A what?"

"A good shot from a bow," explained Beck.

"Well good thing I don't plan on getting shot," answered Tasha.

"Don't jinx it now," he said with a light laugh, stepping forward to pull a set of leather armor from a shelf on the wall. He handed it to her, his fingers dancing away from hers almost instinctively. "You can change in there," he added, pointing to a door on one side of the armory. "I'll wait here while you suit up."

Tasha nodded stiffly, turning away with the bundle of leather weighing down her arms. Surely, he hadn't forgotten about this morning already? Maybe he was waiting to say something? Maybe he was planning to get back at her later and this was just a cover up? She scowled. If that was his plan, it wasn't going to work.

Tasha rounded on the elf, fingers already feeling warm as though they had been under the sun for several hours. "If you're trying to trick me, it's not going to work." She resisted the urge to draw her dagger, even though her fingers were itching to flip it, to calm this heat pulsing in the pads of her fingers. Instead, she rubbed her thumb into the pad of her pointer finger.

Beck's eyebrows sank. "Trick you? Tash, trick you about what?"

And now Tasha's hand did find the hilt of her dagger as she ground her thumb into the familiar wood, holding her bundle of leather with one arm.

"You're really going to tell me you're not mad at me after what happened this morning?" She studied his face, waiting for fury to awaken in the green of his eyes. None did. "I slammed a door in your face, yelled at you, and you expect me to believe you're not angry?"

He shrugged and waved his hand in a dismissive gesture. "Well, not everyone's a morning person." And now his eyes did light up, not with anger, but with the brightness that often came into his eyes when he teased her.

She wouldn't fall for it. No one was like this: so easily forgiving–so happy to move on. Not anyone she'd ever met. She crossed her arms and met his half-grin with a scowl.

He scanned her face, realized she wasn't satisfied with his answer, and sighed. "Honestly Tash, anger never works out for me. It's too easy for people to use it against you. Besides, I figured that what happened this morning was my fault. I shouldn't have bothered you. You've made it pretty clear that you want us to be dueling partners, not friends."

Tasha blinked. She *had* said that. She could remember saying that. So wasn't it a good thing that he'd listened?

Why didn't it feel like a good thing?

Quickly, before she could continue that train of thought, she tightened her hold on the bundle of armor in her arms and said, "I'm going to change."

He just nodded, and she turned around to walk through the door he'd pointed to earlier.

Closing the door behind her she took off her jacket, setting it to the side. She always wore it, even dueled with it on, always preferring to show as little bare, flammable skin as possible, but in case of battle, she would leave it off today. She changed into the leather armor quickly and tied her hair back. As she stepped to the door to walk back into the armory, she caught sight of herself in a mirror propped against the wall.

The armor was molded to her perfectly, supple and soft with straps on the legs and waist to tighten if needed. The gentle brown of the material contrasted the red wine hue of her hair. At her hips the suit had two loops that her daggers easily slid into, and her arms were bare and unrestrained, cool air stinging against them.

She nodded, and the girl in the mirror nodded back, chin tilted upward defiantly and eyes sharp. And though Tasha could feel the slightest pinging of heat in her palms, the girl in the mirror didn't show it.

A moment later she stepped into the armory. Beck sat on the bench against the wall, head bowed and black hair hanging over his face as he used a thumb to wipe at a smudge on his metal chest plate.

Having heard the door close he addressed her without looking up. "Alright," he eradicated the smudge and straightened. "They'll be expecting us in the–"

He looked at her and his voice stumbled, eyes widening just a fraction.

"What?" she frowned at him, chin indenting slightly. His eyes were looking at her with–was it surprise? Shock? She couldn't tell.

He hastily looked away, refocusing on the spot where the smudge had stained his chest plate and beginning to scrub at it with his finger again. "Sorry–I just–I've never seen…" his voice trailed off.

And she realized what he was struggling to say.

He'd never seen her without her jacket. Which meant he'd never seen what those years in the Hinterland had done to her–the years when she had been young, and undisciplined, and her inadequacy with her daggers had left her arms vulnerable and in close proximity of the talons and claws of the monsters she'd encountered.

Without a teacher it had taken her years to master her weapons, years of lessons that she had learned the hard way. And now the lessons of the Hinterland striped her arms.

"My scars." Tasha finished for Beck.

He nodded, and now he did look at them, as though her acknowledgement of their existence made them real. His lips parted slightly, the solemn expression on his face not one she recognized.

His eyes traced the scars, raking over the ones that were nothing more than little white marks, the ones that were long and red, the ones that were distant memories, and the ones that still stung even after all these years.

He sucked in a breath. "How did–" and then he swallowed his words. "Sorry–I shouldn't–" he shook his head as though reprimanding himself.

He was, Tasha realized, trying to avoid a situation like the one that morning. It had made him cautious. He was attempting to do what she wanted–what she'd said she wanted–be a dueling partner, not a friend.

Tasha moistened her lips, then cleared her throat. "Remember after our duel yesterday, the one question deal?"

He looked back up at her, eyebrows rising, before nodding.

She nodded back, giving him silent permission.

"How did you get those?" he asked, voice going a little quieter than usual as though the two of them were sharing a secret.

"I lived alone in the Hinterland for years," said Tasha, shrugging. "That comes at a price."

Beck swallowed, eyes still tracing every trench in her skin. When he spoke again it was slowly, as though he was worried about pushing too far. "Was it hard?"

She chose to ignore the fact that he had already surpassed his asking rights. "Aren't these enough to answer that question?" She gestured to her own arms. She realized that her tone was more clipped than she meant it to be, but this–this type of conversation–felt unnatural.

"I meant the being alone," he said softly, not looking her in the eyes and instead turning his focus to tightening a strap on the leg of his armor.

"It was necessary," she replied, speaking without thinking.

He looked up, lips curving downward at the corners as he considered what she'd said. "What do you mean it was–"

"I think it's my turn to ask something," she broke in, voice cutting his question in half before he could ask it. It was as though the pieces of the unfinished question had fallen to the floor, causing an echo that rang around them.

But Beck ignored her abrupt, rather obvious change of topic, simply turning his attention to tightening the straps on his armor again and saying, "The reins are yours."

"What's that?"

He paused, looking where she was pointing. His sleeve had hitched up, and she could see the same mark she'd noticed once in the courtyard. Something like a small tattoo on his wrist.

"Oh–that," he shook back his sleeve and turned his arm toward her so that she could see the mark better. He paused and Tasha couldn't tell if he was deciding how to explain it or whether he wanted to explain it. "It's an angel scar."

For the first time Tasha could make it out clearly. It didn't look like a scar, it really did seem to be a small tattoo about the size of a large coin. It was stenciled in black, and she finally realized what shape it was. A hummingbird: small and delicate looking. The hummingbird's head crested Beck's tan wrist, its long, slender beak extended, wings wide behind its back, one visible eye seeming to look directly at her even though she knew it wasn't real. It was intricate and detailed, fragile and majestic, and even Tasha, who was not one for sentiment, recognized that it was beautiful.

"Oh," said Tasha. She nodded, as though she knew exactly what an angel scar was.

He must have guessed that she was only acting, because he cleared his throat and said, "It's an elven thing. You get an angel scar when someone you're bonded to dies. The shape the mark takes usually represents the person in some way. Elves are automatically bonded to all their immediate family members the moment they're born–and sometimes they use the binding spell to bond with other people they're close to. But it's not something people do all the time. It's kind of a sacred thing. Sort of..." he paused as he looked for the right word, "intimate I guess."

Tasha nodded and Beck went silent, going back to tightening his armor.

She glanced one last time at the angel scar on his forearm. Now that she knew *what* it was, she couldn't help but wondering *who* it was, but she bit back her curiosity and, after another moment, she ripped her eyes away from the bird entirely as she began to tighten her own armor, tugging harshly at every buckle and strap.

She had just reached one of the last buckles when the armory door slammed open and a figure stormed in. It was a young elf, white hair unruly and expression fierce. His eyes found Beck and narrowed.

Beck straightened, having been wiping a smudge off his helmet. "Hey, what's in the envelope Cerulean–"

But the younger elf cut him off. "You said you wouldn't be going on another mission. You said not for a long time." The accusation in his voice was unmistakable.

Tasha quickly looked away, tightening a strap she'd already tightened. But Cerulean didn't seem to even notice she was in the room.

"I didn't think I would be," said Beck, setting the helmet down. "I got volunteered. It was kind of out of my control."

Cerulean's expression didn't change. If anything, it just hardened.

"It should be a fast one," added Beck quickly. "I promise I'll come back before long."

"You're not really in the position to make promises," said Cerulean, voice descending to a snarl. "You're breaking the last one you made right now. You almost died on the last mission!" He gestured to nothing. "You're really stupid enough to go on another?"

"I'm sorry," said Beck. He sounded sincere. "I'd stay if I could."

Cerulean didn't seem to care. He shook his head, grey eyes sparking. "You know what, don't be in any hurry to get back. It'll give me time to find a new roommate who isn't a liar." Then he turned on his heel and stormed out of the room, door slamming behind him so hard Tasha was slightly impressed. He hadn't looked strong enough for it.

She looked at Beck who let out a long breath, "I... think I'll deal with that when I get back."

Tasha nodded, deciding not to comment. She went back to adjusting her armor.

They were quiet for a few moments that ticked by like years, but Beck seemed unable to stay silent for too long, because after a second he glanced at her and asked, "So is your hair naturally that red, or do you dye it or something?"

Tasha snorted and shook her head. "You really think I've been spending my time in the Hinterland dying my hair?"

He shrugged. "I don't know how you spend your time other than occasionally breaking noses. And everyone has a weird hobby."

Tasha raised her eyebrows, smirk playing across her face. "Oh really? And what's yours?"

He laughed and finished tightening his last strap, standing up and flashing her a crooked grin before heading toward the door. "Wouldn't you like to know?"

She shook her head, one side of her mouth turning up into a smile. He was annoying, and overly friendly, and extremely nosy, but Tasha didn't know if anyone else she'd ever known would have seen her scars and cared like he did. The realization came with a strange feeling in her chest that she internally stomped on before even allowing herself to identify it. Fast, before she could continue thinking, she followed him out of the armory.

Chapter 25

Well dear reader, I'm sure you were getting very comfortable out there in the Hinterland, tucked away as you have been in the folds of the unmapped, guarded by stone walls and shadowed by turrets. So I apologize for what I am about to do, but it is now that you must take a step back in time. Because hours before the third Fate Stone lit up, right about the time Tasha was slamming her bedroom door in Beck's face, someone was waking up.

Amber opened her eyes to birds singing.

She closed them again and rolled over with a small groan. The bed felt so soft this early in the morning, and the air was biting compared to the heavy blankets. Maybe, concluded her fuzzy mind, if she closed her eyes tight enough, she could fall back to sleep? She clenched her eyelids, but it was of no use. Now that she was awake her sensitive, pointed ears would not let her ignore the melodies coming from outside her window. They quivered, picking out individual notes with the ease of experience.

That long, lilting cry? A Blue-Beak, also called a Fairy's Friend by the elven younglings in the village.

That harsh, heartbroken tune? A Corkscrew Sparrow.

And lastly–Amber's brown, lightly freckled nose crinkled as she smiled–that sweeping melody that spoke of midnight rain and barefoot frolics? None other than a Tip-Tailed Amber Jay. Amber couldn't be sure, but she liked to imagine that the bird was her namesake.

She opened her eyes and heaved up into a sitting position, wiggling her toes as she tried to wake them. She blinked rapidly, adjusting to the sunlight coming in through the glassless window, and when her eyes focused, she was able to see the bird sitting on the sill. It was the size of her fist, its white wings detailed with black design so intricate it was like the feathers were tattooed. The tip of its tail was amber colored like it had been dipped in gold. It glinted in the sunlight, which was sifting through the forest canopy above Amber's home.

Amber forced herself to look away from the jay as she slid off the bed, bare feet settling onto the uneven wooden slats of the floor. The morning cold stung her skin as she crouched down and pulled a pouch from its spot beneath the bed. She opened the small pouch, grabbed a handful of its contents before dropping it, and straightened to shuffle to the window. She yawned as she reached it, mouth so wide she felt like her face was splitting in half. With one hand she rubbed at her glazed eyes, while her other hand dropped its contents–bird seeds–onto the sill.

The bird hopped back and waited patiently as the tear-shaped seeds fell in front of it. Breakfast delivered right to its feet.

It was a spoiled little thing, thought Amber as the last seeds fell from her palm and it hopped forward to peck at its meal. She pampered it far too often–but even on the coldest mornings the small bird made her feel warm inside, so it was a fair enough trade.

Amber yawned again and gazed out the window. The forest around her home left her small house mostly in shadow, but there were some spots where the morning light shone through the leaves. The mossy woodland floor was painted with bright splotches as though a giant had taken his paintbrush to it. It was so light out–too light out... *way* too light out.

Amber whipped around and rushed toward her bed. She ducked to her knees and reached down, her hands feeling for the clothing she'd set for herself the day before.

She was running late for work.

She found the cloth, yanked the outfit into the light, and proceeded to strip from her nightgown so quickly it was as though she was racing. She was done before the bird on the sill had nibbled its last bit of food, and when she was finished, she stood in a light green dress that went down to her knees. It was made of heavy cloth and tied around the waist with a belt. She yanked her brown cloak off the peg on the wall and wrapped it around her shoulders, then shoved a pair of thin, cotton slippers over her feet.

She glanced out the window, trying to gauge just how far she was running behind, but could tell nothing except that the jay was almost done eating.

She stepped to the mirror, hung on the wall with a nail and some worn string, and gave herself a quick scan: skin smooth and cinnamon-stick brown, hair in tight, frenzied, chestnut-colored curls that puffed out around her face and descended only as far as her shoulders, freckles like pixie dust across her nose, and full, pink lips parted as she looked at herself with her own bright blue eyes.

She gave herself one last look, turned around, grabbed a slice of bread from the kitchen table as she passed, and swept out the door into the cool morning beyond. Her feet stepped over the threshold to find damp, dew-dressed moss, soft and cushiony under her toes. It was everywhere, like the skin of the forest: coating the ground, licking up tree trunks, layering branches, and giving the village its name: Moss Meadows. At least that was what the villagers called it, although the village was so small, so far from other civilization, and so out of touch with the outside world, that hardly anyone knew Moss Meadows was there at all. It existed in its own tiny pocket of the universe. A corner in the corner of the world. Amber liked that it was separate. Sometimes she liked to look up though the canopy and imagine the blue above as her own small sliver of sky.

But now was not the time. She was already behind schedule–as if the day wasn't going to be stressful enough already. Amber's gut twisted with nerves like her stomach was just a pit containing a mass of writhing serpents, all flailing around and biting each other.

But she shook her head and took a bite of the bread fisted in her hand, hoping the pumpkin spice would appease the snakes.

Amber hurried down the path, chewing on the thick bread as she went.

She swallowed her bite and yawned, the path widening out before her and splitting into a three-way intersection. The path she stood on obviously led back home. The path to the right would lead into the village. The path on the left would lead out.

No one ever took the path on the left. Well, almost no one. No one except her parents. But now was not the time to dwell on the past.

Her return to the present was punctuated with a swift gust of wind that yanked at the skirt of Amber's dress as she started to the right. The path led, like a main artery, straight into the heart of the village. After she'd walked for a few minutes, she passed the first village house. It was wooden, with moss riding up its sides and its roof sagging. It looked time eaten, as though the long years had nibbled away at its boards and chewed at its foundation.

Most of the village houses were in similar states, but this one was especially worn, just like its owner: Widow Windrow. The old elf had lived there as long as Amber could remember, spending her days making teas out of forest plants and threatening to kill the rabbits that got into her garden. The threats were, of course, impossible. With a shiver of anticipation, Amber remembered that soon it would be impossible for her, too. The snakes in her stomach thrashed.

Amber swallowed, suddenly realizing that she'd clenched her fists and smashed her slice of bread into a pulp.

She unclenched her fingers and kept walking.

As she went, the houses beside the path began to multiply: two across from each other, then three in a row, then four, then the path broadened and disappeared as Amber stepped into the Center Circle, or The Village Eye, depending on who you asked. The eye was the center of the village, from which every path stemmed.

The Eye was large, round, and paved with stone. The structures lining its sides were not homes, but shops and restaurants. Some of them were already open with elves flitting around them watering the flowers in the window gardens and straightening the signs on the doors.

She made a beeline for the shop farthest across the circle, breaking into a jog as she neared it. She glanced left and right, hoping the others in The Eye hadn't noticed her present state of disarray. But no one was paying her any mind as she whipped through the door of Annalie's Home of Healing–except letters had fallen off the door sign, so now it read: Ann ie's Home of Healing. Beneath it was a second sign that read: *open to small critters and creatures*. And then below that yet another sign: *faerie dragons not allowed*–that one was a more recent addition.

As the door shut behind her, Amber closed her eyes and inhaled deeply. There was the smell she loved: a perfect blend of smoke, syrup, and the color red.

"What are you doing, Fairwing? Meditating? Open your eyes and get over here. I don't pay you to stand around and sniff the air."

Amber's eyes snapped open, and she reddened. She always took a moment to breathe in the fire-sugar scent, she'd just never been caught at it. But now Annalie herself watched Amber from across the room, hands on her hips.

"Sorry Ma'am," said Amber, willing her cheeks to un-redden. They refused her request.

"Get to work," replied the elf, classic scowl on her face.

Amber had been working at the healing home for seven years, since she was twelve, and she had still never heard Annalie laugh. She'd only seen the elf smile when she got paid.

Amber walked across the room to where a table was pushed against the wall. She set down her squished bread and turned back to Annalie, who was standing across the room at a table of her own. On the surface before her was a fluffy, horned Buffalo Bunny.

Annalie held a small shiny tool in her hand and was using it to blunt the animal's horns by sawing it quickly back and forth over the sharp points. The creature had a long green stalk between its teeth. It didn't seem to care that someone was shaving down the weapons atop its head, perhaps, because it couldn't feel it, or maybe by instinct knew the points would return in just a few weeks.

Amber pitied anyone who kept a Buffalo Bunny as a pet. The upkeep was ridiculous.

As though sensing Amber's gaze, Annalie said, "There's a bird waiting for you in the back."

Amber shoved another quick morsel of cinnamon dusted bread into her mouth as she stepped sideways to open the door to the back room. She walked through and instantly the space filled with squawks, hisses, growls, and roars. Here the walls were lined with wooden cages containing creatures of all shapes, sizes, and varying levels of magic.

Amber hated to see them all caged. Seeing anything trapped in a place it found uncomfortable gave her a heavy feeling in her chest–a feeling only borne from understanding. But despite her feelings, it was necessary that they be confined like this. Otherwise they would run away, tear each other apart, or damage property–all things Annalie could not afford.

The cage closest to Amber contained a large resplendent bird. The Fire Wing Hawk had bright red feathers and two long wings. One was tucked neatly to its side, the other was partially extended, its tip hanging limp at an odd angle. Years of experience told Amber it was broken.

She opened the cage with a small click and extended an arm for the hawk to mount, which it did with little hesitation. It had clearly been trained well, she thought, as she exited the back room with the bird perched on her arm.

Returning to her table, she set the bird on the wooden surface and began a careful examination of the wing. It took her all of two seconds to locate the break.

Now it was time to do the thing—the one thing—she did well. She brushed a tight spiral of hair out of her face, extended her arms over the bird, and opened her hands directly over the break. The magic rose up in her like warm liquid in her chest. It was right below her surface, waiting to be called upon. An ocean in her, and she was just dipping into it, wetting the pad of her finger as her palms flared with light.

She concentrated the magic, letting it tangle itself around the broken bone, twisting, wrapping, warping—snapping it whole.

The hawk gave a sharp cry of pain. It shook itself as though throwing off the feeling, then it loosed its wings outward and they extended—both of them full and majestic. The break was healed completely.

Amber looked up, a small smile on her face as the bird flapped its wings up and down in cautious testing. The smile dropped as she realized that Annalie was watching from across the room.

Their eyes met and Annalie looked away, going back to filing the horns of the Buffalo Bunny.

After all these years Amber still caught Annalie watching her magic every now and then. It was just a testament to how unusual Amber's ability was—most elves wouldn't have been able to fully heal the bone she just had, yet Amber could still feel her magic pulsing to be used again.

She could only assume that it had something to do with the identities of her parents. Their wicks must have been impressive for hers to be this vast.

Her proficiency in magic was the only thing her parents had ever given her, and Amber would happily give it away if she could just be like everyone else. The theories around her unknown parentage already set her apart in the village. It was the reason she kept the true depth of her abilities to herself, only using them here or on her own. She'd never even tried to test their extent. No reason to separate herself from the others any further.

There was laughter from outside the shop and Amber peered out the window to see a group of elves approaching the door. She recognized them all, but that was no surprise in a village as pocket-sized as Moss Meadows.

"Must be here for the bird," said Annalie, who'd also looked out through the window. "You handle it."

"Actually," started Amber, "maybe I should–" Annalie shot Amber an eyebrows raised, lips pursed, you-were-already-late-do-you-really-want-to-test-me look, and Amber closed her mouth just as the door swung open and the elves entered.

The female leading the party stepped forward. She was tall and brown-haired with cheekbones so sharp they looked hazardous. Her name was Sylvina, and Amber knew that she lived in Corner West. She nodded to Amber. "I'm here for my bird."

"I–I that's her," said Amber, gesturing to the hawk on the table and already internally smacking herself for the stutter.

"I can see that," replied Sylvina smoothly, the side of her mouth quirking upward. The two behind her snickered.

Amber gave a small smile, shifting her feet and allowing the bird to hop onto her arm. "Her wing was broken, but it's fine now. She's a really pretty bird, I almost wanted to steal her." She tried for a friendly laugh. It came out thin and breathy.

None of the others so much as acknowledged the weak attempt at a joke. Amber's laugh died, and she gave a small cough.

"How much do I owe?" asked Sylvina.

"Um, four," started Amber, "sorry–five coppers."

Sylvina nodded and began digging through a pouch on her hip. As she rummaged, Amber realized the two behind her were talking.

"I'm wearing green," the elf on the left–Fayne–was saying. "To complement my eyes." Her eyes, which were deep brown, probably would go well with a green Amber figured.

The one on the right, Brentley, glanced at Amber. "Are you taking the oath tonight?"

For any other nineteen-year-old elf, it wouldn't have even been a question. After all, it was village tradition, part of the coming-of-age ceremony. But it was a Forest Elf tradition, and with no parents around, and only rumors about who they might have been, well... she had no way of proving she was an actual Forest Elf.

"Yeah," she said eagerly, heart rate picking up as she entered the conversation, and mind racing as she tried to consider what she could say to keep herself in it. "I'll be there–"

"I can't wait," cut in Fayne, and the rest of Amber's comment died in her throat, shriveling and falling down, down, down, to rest like a rock in the pit of her stomach.

"My dress is going to be decorated," Brentley was now saying. "It's beaded."

Amber took the opportunity to squeak, "Mine too."

Sylvina's eyebrows went up slightly. "Really? You seem like a plain dress kind of girl."

Brentley and Fayne giggled.

Amber bit the inside of her mouth. Was that an insult? What did it mean to be a "plain dress kind of girl"? Was it bad?

The elves continued their conversation, and this time Amber didn't bother trying to join.

It was always like this when she tried to talk to the other village elves. She'd lived here her whole life, and still she'd never been one of them. It was as if they spoke a different language. No matter what she did, Amber couldn't understand them. And they never even tried to understand her.

Sylvina handed Amber the five coppers, took ahold of the empty cage, and clicked her tongue. Her bird perked up at the sound, opening its wings, and flapping after the elves out the door.

Amber turned back to her table, bracing her hands against it so that her palms ground into the rough wood. She breathed in deeply, trying to calm her heart, which always quickened in conversations like the one she'd just had.

Annalie, who must have heard everything, did her the kindness of continuing to work in silence.

Amber allowed herself a few more breaths before retrieving another injured animal from the back room—this one some kind of mole looking creature with a fat blue body—and beginning to assess its injury.

"So, you're taking the oath tonight, then," said Annalie, finally acknowledging that she had indeed been listening.

Amber nodded, realized that Annalie couldn't see it, and said, "Yes." Then with a spark of annoyance, "I am nineteen, after all, and it's the coming-of-age ceremony."

"A Forest Elf ceremony," Annalie answered, blunt as always. "A Forest Elf oath. We are inclined to protect the wild. You may not be a true Forest Elf."

Amber gritted her teeth. "I've grown up here my whole life. My inclinations are as much Forest Elf as the inclinations of anyone here."

"No need to be offended," replied Annalie, not turning away from her work as she filed the horns back and forth, back and forth. "I only think that you should consider the consequences."

"I have no reason to ever break the rules of the oath," said Amber, turning to Annalie. "I've never been one for hunting, so I see no consequences."

Annalie simply finished her work, set the file down, and hoisted the Buffalo Bunny into her arms. She started toward the door to the back room, opening it with one hand. "Don't be a fool, Amber. It's magic, and where magic is involved, there are always consequences."

The door swung shut behind her, and Amber had a few moments alone to think about what Annalie had said. But really... there were no consequences. Only benefits–only the possibility that maybe this was what she needed to truly become part of this community. To learn the language of the other elves around her, so to speak. This was what it might take to be one of them completely. It was a wild hope, but most hopes are.

Then Annalie burst back into the room with a clipped: "Get back to work," and Amber was thrown back to business.

Amber left Annalie's healing home with a feeling in her chest like her heart was being repeatedly zapped by bolts of lightning, causing it to tremble and spasm. She'd had all day to contemplate her taking of the oath, and with every hour her knees felt weaker. Taking the oath didn't concern her nearly as much as where she would be taking it–in The Village Eye, with everyone watching.

She would be displayed for every elf in the village to look at and dissect with their gaze. Not to mention, it was a blood oath. She shook her head, trying to force herself away from all thoughts of the ceremony, even as her heart seized with another bolt of lightning.

She reached home as the sun was beginning to set, casting her small house in shadow. Her skin was peppered with icy pin pricks up her arms and the nape of her neck as she stepped into her dark house. Quickly, before it was too dark to see at all, she lit a fire in the fireplace.

She rotated her hands in front of the fire's hot maw, trying to shake off the icy pin pricks, before pivoting to where her dress hung on the wall. It was blue, and beaded, just like she'd told the elves earlier.

Amber peeled off her work clothes and brought the dress up over her head. It slid down her like water, material flowing–practically slithering into place against her curves. It fell down to her ankles where it grazed the tops of her bare feet when she moved. The beads circled her waist before sprawling upward like roots and lining the neckline.

She bit her lip, staring at her own reflection in the mirror. Was it too much? Was it too little? Would it be too different, or too boring, or – she groaned aloud, running her fingers over the rounded beads that edged her waist, and accidentally setting the dress askew. She worked quickly to readjust it. She was running late for the second time that day.

She smoothed the dress, guiding the material until it settled on her hips just the way she liked it.

By the time she was finished, she had all of five minutes to get back to The Village Eye, and it was with sweaty palms and a quickly beating heart that she swept out of the door.

She was in such a hurry she didn't even get a good look at the quaint, cozy home she'd lived in for nineteen years, before she turned at the crossroads and left it behind.

The Village Eye was lit with torches by the time she arrived, their light replacing that of the waning sun.

It seemed, she thought, as she entered the crowded paved circle, that everyone had shown up. Amber could barely walk without getting bumped by another villager.

The shops, which were usually closed around this time, were all open and lit from the inside. They beckoned to passersby with promises of food or trinkets. Amber could already see at least a dozen people eating Butter Buns and younglings trading pieces of candy. The villagers took every excuse to have a good time.

The ceremony had not yet started, thank the above, and Amber pivoted, trying to figure out where to go. Finally, by standing on her tiptoes she spotted the tall, gorgeous elf who'd come to pick up her bird from Annalie's Healing Home only hours before. Sylvina was standing at the center of The Village Eye. Amber dropped from her toes and began to wind her way through the crowd. She found all the nineteen-year-old elves standing in a clump at its center, and no one seemed to notice as she darted in behind them.

She toyed with the sleeve of her dress, grinding the material between the pads of her fingers as the voices around her merged into one like the rush of a waterfall.

Crack!

Amber wasn't the only one who jumped as the sound filled The Village Eye. Every face turned to look at the edge of the circle where an old elf stood, fingers flared with magic. As though the first magically magnified sound hadn't been enough, he clapped his hands together once more, ensuring he had everyone's attention. Amber rubbed her nose, hoping no one had noticed that she'd jumped on the second clap, too.

"Thank you all for coming." The elf was the oldest member of the village. He was hunched and weak, and he only hauled himself out of his home once a year for the sole purpose of conducting this ceremony. Each time it seemed his wrinkles had multiplied.

He stepped toward Amber and the others standing at the center of the paved circle. The crowd parted as he walked, fanning out to the sides of The Eye.

The old elf was extremely slow, shuffling across the stone with less pace than a snail. Every face stayed turned to him as he made his journey. Finally, he reached the center.

"Today," he said, voice creaky as old floorboards, "we gather for the coming-of-age ceremony and the taking of the oath."

Heads nodded around the circle. Amber swallowed. There were far too many eyes on her, and suddenly she wished this dress didn't fit her so well. It would be better if it were big, and baggy, and hid her like a bug under a leaf. Instead, she was cold, and vulnerable, and in the open for all to see.

"Today," continued the elf, "we accept these younglings into adulthood, fully members of our village and representatives of our culture."

His gaze swung to the far side of the circle. "Today, they become pillars of strength. Pillars that will stand tall like the trees of our beloved forest, displaying proudly the values that we, the people and protectors of the wild, do uphold."

And now his gaze turned to them. She could have sworn he was looking right at her.

"Today, they take the blood oath."

Amber rubbed her sweaty palms against her dress as the elf turned, yet again, to the watching crowd. His arms lifted, and his words came out long and drawn out like he was speaking in cursive. "Bring forth the blade."

An elf detached himself from the watching crowd. He cradled a wooden box in his arms.

Amber felt the inside of her mouth go dry as he crossed the circle and opened the box in front of the old elf, who removed a long, thin blade from its cushioned interior. "The blade of Dynmari," he muttered, holding it up carefully with one hand gripping the handle and its tip displayed in the palm of his other. "This blade has dwelled in our village since the day it was founded. The first blood oaths taken here were taken with this blade, and the same will be said for the last."

He turned his steel-gray, cold as mist, no-going-back gaze on the small group behind him. But again, Amber could have sworn he was staring at her. The rest of the village, the other elves, the world, fell away, and it was as though it was just the two of them and the knife standing in darkness. Then he asked, "Who first?"

"I'll go." Sylvina strode forward. She flipped a strand of chocolate-brown hair out of her face and held out her hand, fingers splayed and palm open. She smiled at the old elf.

"Repeat after me," he said, not smiling back. He began to recite the words of the oath. The words blurred in Amber's ears as she watched the blade.

Sylvina repeated every sentence he gave her, voice clean and calm.

The elder lifted the blade. There was a flash and a line of blood appeared on Sylvina's palm. A small wince was the only indication that she had felt any pain.

The elder closed Sylvina's fingers over the red stripe, his hand covering her fist. "For the rest of your time, for every moment you breathe and your heart beats, by the blood in your veins and on the metal of my blade, and by the honor of your soul, you are bound."

His hand flared with power, then fell dark just as fast as it had ignited.

Sylvina gave a small shudder, and the elder removed his hand. Slowly, she uncurled her fingers. The mark had already scarred over, a small slash on the center of her palm, about as long as a fingerprint.

It would stay on Sylvina's skin forever, left by the same branch of magic Angel Scars were born of.

Sylvina stepped away and a new elf stepped forward. A sort of line had formed and Amber, distracted by the ceremony, was last. No surprises there.

As Amber waited for the elves to take their oaths one-by-one, she wondered again if her dress was too tight, because it certainly felt like she was suffocating. The line was moving fast–too fast–and suddenly her feet propelled her forward and she was standing in front of the elder.

She held his gaze for a moment before he prompted, "You have to hold out your hand."

She nodded, thrusting it toward him before she could change her mind. Please, please, could it stop shaking? But she seemed to have no control over it.

"Repeat after me," he said, voice weather-worn and crackly. "I solemnly vow that I...."

"I solemnly vow that I..."

He widened his eyes at her and she quickly added, "that I, Amber Fairwing."

He nodded. "Shall, in respect to the wild and the value of life–"

She repeated.

"Never take the life of another."

Again, she repeated.

The blade lifted in preparation of the final line. "Or my heart shall be stilled too."

Harsh rules, but that was the way of blood oaths. They were vicious vows. Promises borne of pain.

Amber gritted her teeth. "Or my heart shall be stilled too."

The blade came down and Amber let out a sharp breath as the metal seared across her skin.

She barely had time to look at the cut before the elder had fisted her hand and wrapped his own around it. "For the rest of your time, for every moment you breathe and your heart beats–" *what was that sound?* "–By the blood in your veins and on the metal of my blade, and by the honor of your soul–" *was that a screech from above?* Amber looked up. Throughout The Village Eye others were doing the same. But the elder with his battered old ears was oblivious. "–you are bound."

And then there was a shout from above. Multiple shouts from above. Now even the elder heard. Everyone in the village looked up just in time to see dark masses appear in the sky directly above them. They were like moving pieces of night.

Then, with an echoing screech, two collided. One of the dark masses tumbled from the sky, down, down, down—and straight toward Annalie's Healing Home.

There were screams from the villagers, and just before the mass hit the building's wooden roof, something leapt from its back: a figure who hit the ground and rolled before jumping to his feet. He pivoted, wincing as a griffin crashed into the healing home. "Sprites, this is not going according to plan." Then, green eyes flashing, he twisted to face the villagers. "Everyone needs to get to shelter—now!"

And then griffins rained from the sky and the world as Amber knew it, ended.

Chapter 26

Scarlet couldn't sleep.

She paced in her room, occasionally stepping onto the balcony to check the night sky for returning griffins. There were none. Each time she walked back into her bedroom, she had to remind herself that there shouldn't be. Not yet. They'd only been gone a couple hours.

She took a book off one of her bookshelves and flipped through a few pages, not comprehending any of the words. After a minute she put it back, flopped onto her bed, and put a pillow over her face. Her feet itched for action, so she jumped up and walked out onto the balcony again.

Still nothing.

Of course, nothing.

There should be nothing.

Unable to wrestle with her restlessness anymore, Scarlet walked back through the balcony entrance, across her bedroom, and straight to the door. She swept out of it into the hallway beyond. As she walked she ran her fingers over the carvings on the passageway walls. She traced the pad of her pointer finger over the tail of a dragon. It sat atop a mountain overlooking a trail of smaller peaks. The carving had a small inscription: The Spire. The words jogged something in Scarlet's mind, but she couldn't quite place it. So she kept going.

The Hinterland

She wandered through hallways, not really caring where she was going as long as she was going somewhere. Her feet led her down stairs, up stairs, down hallways, up hallways, until finally she walked into one she recognized: The Alleyway. She moseyed down it, almost like she was in a dream.

It had just occurred to her that the library was in this hallway, and maybe she should go there, when the calm was broken with a bang as a door flew open and a figure flew out. "And stay away!" came a gruff voice from inside, then the door slammed. The figure stumbled for a moment then leaned against the wall.

Scarlet groaned. She recognized that figure. And the room he'd come out of.

"Cerulean," she said, coming up behind him. "That's the pub. You're not supposed to be in there. You're underage."

Cerulean looked at her. He squinted as though trying to bring her into focus. "Scarlet–" he set his back against the wall and put a palm against the stone like he was steadying himself. "What are–where'd you come from?" His words were coming out in chunks and blurs. His hair was even messier than usual as though someone had ruffled it over and over again. Something had stained the front of his tunic. Something with a sharp, potent smell.

Scarlet looked him up and down. "Are you... drunk?"

He gave a very un-Cerulean like laugh. "Don't tell Beck." And then as he said the words his expression fell, all evidence of the laugh instantly washed away by a tide of something new. "Is Beck back yet?"

"No, they haven't been gone long," answered Scarlet, scowling at him.

"I wanted him to stay," said Cerulean. "But he left." He shook his head, a sorrowful expression on his face. "Everyone always leaves." He pushed himself off the wall and took a few uneven steps toward the door he'd just been thrown out of a minute before. "I'm going back in."

"Nope," said Scarlet, grabbing his arm. "You're coming with me."

"Where are we going?" he mumbled, allowing himself to be led down the hallway.

Scarlet wasn't sure how to answer that question. She wasn't sure where his room was, and even if she found it, she wasn't sure whether he should be left alone. She'd never been stuck with a drunk teenage elf before. She felt a gentle tug on her hair and swatted Cerulean's hand away. He'd pulled on a strand of her black locks.

"No touching," she scolded, like he was a small child that needed reprimanded. She was going to kill him. Later. Right now she had to make sure he didn't accidentally kill himself.

"I like it," he replied. "It's dark–" he struggled for the right words "–like ink." He paused. "Like dark ink." Then he gave another laugh that wasn't quite his own. Not that she had much to compare it to. She rarely, if ever, heard sober Cerulean laugh.

They entered the Main Courtyard.

"Uh oh," muttered Cerulean.

"What?" asked Scarlet.

But Cerulean pulled away from her, stumbled into the Dining Hall, and proceeded to throw up violently into a trash bin.

Scarlet stood by as he wretched, trying to figure out a plan. Maybe he could tell her where his room was?

He straightened, a hand on either side of the bin's rim.

"You done?" asked Scarlet, crossing her arms. Her voice came out harsher than she'd meant it to, but she was upset with him for putting her in this position. Half of her wanted to abandon him. Whatever happened to him was his own fault. But they were friends. Sort of friends. More friends than not. Plus, he was Beck's roommate, and she was definitely friends with Beck.

The Hinterland

"I feel better now," said Cerulean, stepping away from the trash bin. His words were still tripping over each other and he swayed slightly where he stood.

Scarlet bit her lip. Now would be the time to ask him where his room was. But watching him stumble to one of the Dining Hall's many columns and lean against it, she wondered again whether he should be left alone. The fortress had plenty of sharp weapons, balconies, and other dangers for someone likely to do something stupid.

She frowned, remembering that this was Cerulean, who was likely to do something stupid even when he was sober.

"C'mon." She grabbed his hand. It was clammy. "We're going."

"Back to the pub?"

"No," she scowled, before putting a hand on his arm to steady him and leading him out of the Dining Hall.

She guided him down the following hallway. He tripped over his feet and she had to haul him upright. "I think my feet are bigger," he stared down at his shoes. "Are my feet bigger?"

"Definitely," said Scarlet, tugging him left out of the passage and up a flight of stairs.

"Should make swimming easier," he slurred, and even though he was looking straight down at his feet, he still managed to trip at the top of the steps, causing Scarlet to push him upright so that he didn't topple back down them.

"How much did you have to drink?" she asked him. In the back of her mind, the part that couldn't help but ask unnecessary questions, she wondered whether elves had higher alcohol tolerance than humans.

"Uh–like..." he considered, "...like half."

Scarlet rolled her eyes and gave up on getting a helpful answer from him. The journey up to her room felt excruciatingly long.

Finally, they reached it. Scarlet shut her bedroom door, and let go of Cerulean, who was looking around as though trying to figure out where they were, even though he'd been here before. He wavered a little on his own but stayed upright.

Scarlet walked to the bed and pulled a basket of blankets from under it. She pulled out a thick one and laid it on the floor.

Crash!

Scarlet jumped as something shattered onto the stone. She looked up to see Cerulean standing next to the dresser, the remains of a vase of flowers on the floor around him.

"Oops." The elf looked at the destruction with eyebrows slightly raised. He gestured to it. "It broke."

"Cerulean!" She didn't particularly care about the vase, it had been there when she'd arrived, but she certainly wasn't looking forward to cleaning up every shard. "Don't mess with anything!"

He looked at her like a puppy caught digging up holes in the yard. "That's my bad," he slurred.

She shook her head and grabbed a spare pillow from her bed.

To her left doors whined open as a gust of chilly air swept into the room. Cerulean was wandering onto the balcony.

Scarlet set the pillow on top of the first blanket, reached toward the basket for a second–then remembered that Cerulean was drunk.

She straightened and rushed for the balcony. Cerulean was leaning over the rail, stretching dangerously far as he looked over the Hinterland. She ran to him, heart beating as fast as her footsteps against the floor, and yanked the right arm of his tunic, propelling him back. The sleeve pulled up so that in the light of the moon she could see two tattoo-like marks on his forearm. She remembered noticing them once before in the Dining Hall. But that time he'd covered them as soon as he'd seen her looking. This time he didn't even notice.

"Let's go back in," said Scarlet, looking away from them and eager to get him as far from the balcony rail as possible. "We should sleep. It's getting late."

"I don't want to sleep." He was looking at the stars above them. Her hand still held a fistful of his sleeve.

"I think you need it."

He shook his head. "I don't like sleep; I always see them die." His eyes were like mirrors, reflecting the stars. Until he looked at her. Then they were just dark pools, gray and infinite. He lowered his voice, tone changing like he was telling her a secret as he leaned forward. She could smell the drink on him. On his shirt. On his breath. "I don't want to see them die."

Scarlet didn't break his gaze. She had the urge to ask him more and shoved it away. It was rare that she did not let her curiosity win out, but this once she would refrain. Because what Drunk Cerulean had just told her was not something Sober Cerulean would have said. Not in a million years.

She let go of his tunic and took his hand. Gently this time, like he was breakable.

"C'mon Cerulean," she said softly. "Just come in, please?"

He allowed her to guide him off the balcony and into the room. Despite his earlier protests, he lay down on the blanketed floor, head sinking into the pillow.

"Just try closing your eyes," she said, pulling out the basket to find a second blanket to cover him. She rummaged through, choosing the darkest one in case he threw up again.

When she turned back to him, his eyes were shut. "Cerulean?"

He didn't reply. The elf was already asleep.

Carefully, she spread the blanket over him, making sure it covered his entire body.

Yawning, she decided she'd do the irresponsible thing and clean up the vase tomorrow. She climbed into bed and pulled the blanket up to her chin.

Her last thought, as she drifted off to sleep, was that she hoped the mission was going as planned.

Chapter 27

Everything was going so well. Until it wasn't. Which, dear reader, I'm sure you can agree, is how most things tend to go.

One moment Tasha had been riding a griffin, airborne next to Beck. Behind them had soared all ten of the other mission members, all of them Forest Elves. They wore varying amounts of armor, some in leather, some in metal, some with their arms and legs bare, others with every inch of their skin concealed. But each of them wore a red armband on their right arm, directly below their shoulders, marking them as members of The Alliance. On the center of each band was a spiral with a single, diagonal slash through it: the symbol the Fate Stones were marked with.

Tasha wore one, too. It had been handed to her by a solemn-faced nymph right before departure. It was strange, to be marked as belonging to a group, the band constricting but warm around her bare arm.

The journey was easy. With so many riders, they hadn't needed to worry about attacks from the small dragons that roamed the sky, which were too clever to target such a large party. So Tasha spent the trip riding next to Beck, speaking little, but content to listen. And Beck gave her plenty to listen to.

He'd just been telling her an amusing story about a brawl he'd once witnessed in Lotus Manor, Deimos' estate where he'd lived before the war, when he'd stopped and pointed at a spot in the not-too-far-off distance. "There. I think that's the village."

As they'd gotten closer, it became clear that it was indeed the village. Soon, they'd been able to see that there seemed to be some kind of illuminated circle. They could just barely make out movement in it. As the tiles of the roofs below came into clarity, they positioned themselves directly above it.

Beck had stopped his griffin and the rest of The Alliance members reined theirs in to surround him. He may have been sent to shadow Tasha, but he also held, clenched in his fist, the Fate Stone, and not a single rider present was questioning it. Considering how much younger he was than the others, this recognition of leadership might have seemed ludicrous, if not for the way he sat on his griffin and held himself upright like a king. He saw their trust and shouldered it with all the confidence in the world.

He displayed the Fate Stone. It was glowing as green as his eyes. "The next Chosen is definitely here."

And that was the moment that it all went wrong. A screech ripped the silence to shreds, and a griffin came barreling from the night sky.

Tasha just had time to realize that the rider was wearing all black with no red armband in sight, before the griffin dove toward Beck's.

Beck swore, swerving and barely avoiding the rogue rider, who hurtled past him into the night. But there were more screeches, this time from all directions. Beck shoved the Fate Stone into a nook of his armor. "Ambush! Get to the ground!"

They surged downward, and as they did so, a wave of griffins, all mounted by riders in black, broke free from hidden pockets of the night sky and tore after. There were screams from below–and then yells from members of The Alliance as a feathered mass rammed into the side of Beck's griffin.

Beck spun out of control, griffin free falling toward the village. The animal got in a few flaps, just enough to slow its fall, before crashing into a building below.

With the wind ripping at her eyes, her own griffin plummeting downward, Tasha couldn't see what happened to Beck–just the griffin amid the broken bones of the building. Then, with a scratching of talons, her griffin touched down on stone.

More of the beasts landed left and right, arriving with such force it shook the ground. Riders were dismounting. The Alliance members were pulling out weapons. Villagers were screaming.

Tasha heard the first clash of metal. Then another. Then many at once. Then one from her own blade, singing as it defended her from an attack she had barely noticed in time. Her body shook as she held off the blow, but she threw back the arm of the attacking human soldier and stabbed. Something warm hit her cheek. She didn't have to check to know it was blood.

"Tasha!"

She whirled to face the voice that had sounded in her ear. There was Beck, sword drawn and shoulders tense. The crash had left him without a scratch–seeing him intact loosened something in her chest she hadn't realized had tightened.

"You need to hide! The Wraith's soldiers weren't supposed to be here, and The Alliance needs you to survive this."

She shook her head, "I'm part of this mission. I'll fight like the rest."

There was a sound at her side and she whipped around, daggers raised–when the black-clad soldier crumpled, the blunt of a sword having been rammed into his head.

Tasha rounded on Beck. "I had that."

"I had it first," he answered. "Now hide, Tasha. I'm serious."

He spun as a yell split the air, sword in hand and arm coiling back for a strike.

Tasha turned in the other direction and ducked beneath the arm of an enemy soldier, reemerging in the thick of battle.

The black soldiers were everywhere, like mold, growing and invading on all sides. And Tasha was ready for it.

She darted–ducked–dodged. A blur came from her left and she was locked in battle. Her blades sparked as they collided into the soldier's sword. She stabbed. He blocked. He swiped. She side-stepped. He struck again, and she danced away, licking the sweat from her upper lip. Again, they engaged and flew apart. Tasha's thumb massaged the handle of her dagger and she prepared for another clash. Then, out of the mob, Beck's body slammed into the enemy soldier, tackling him to the ground.

The man gave a cry of surprise, before his head hit the stone and he lay still.

Beck jumped to his feet to face Tasha. "I told you to hide!"

"I have a mission!" she repeated.

"So do I," he answered. "To keep you safe! And mother of mushrooms, you're making it difficult."

And then the conversation ended as three of the Wraith's soldiers bore down on them.

Tasha quickly dispatched one and spun to where the others had stood, just as the last one fell to the ground, a shard of light in his chest.

The magic glow dimmed from Beck's hand as he reached into his armor and pulled out the Fate Stone. It was glowing green, all of its cracks illuminated with emerald fire. "Tasha, The Alliance can't lose you or this. Run down that path and take shelter in the first house you see." He pointed. "I'll find you when it's safe to come out."

"I don't–" but it was too late, because without a pinch of hesitation he tossed the Fate Stone to her.

Quickly, she flipped one of her daggers airborne, snatching the stone before the handle landed back in her palm.

She opened her mouth to speak again, but he cut her off. "Go! And do not, I repeat, *do not* die."

"Well there goes my plan for the evening," she answered, the sarcasm automatic.

The side of Beck's mouth quirked upward like he couldn't help it, then he raised his sword and turned back to the battle.

Tasha hesitated, scowled, then turned and ran. Each step felt wrong. She shouldn't be searching for cover like some child. But this–this stone in her hand? This could decide the fate of a war. And Beck had given it to her without a hint of doubt in his eyes. So she sprinted like she never had before.

The Village Eye was a thicket of bodies. She slid under an extended arm, leapt over a low kick, and launched herself toward the path Beck had indicated–when she realized something had changed. The Fate stone had flared. It was clenched in her hand, and still the glow was so intense the light forced itself out between her fingers.

She froze, standing on the rim of the paved circle, which was currently the edge of the battlefield. Slowly, she opened her hand.

She looked at the Fate Stone, ignited and begging for her attention, then up at the house where she was supposed to hide. She made up her mind in less than a second.

Tasha turned and scanned the battlefield. The center circle was in disarray. The Wraith's soldiers were like ink staining the village. They tripled The Alliance's forces, and it was only with flashes and bangs of magic that the elves were surviving. There were griffins still rampaging around the fighters, shrieking and flapping their wings, throwing down elves and humans alike.

Tasha's gaze roved over the screaming, writhing, battling masses. And there, closer than an arrow's shot away, was a figure that caught

Tasha's attention. The figure was on her knees, hands above her head as six of the Wraith's soldiers bore down on her. Tasha didn't recognize her, so she must be one of the villagers: the only one close enough to be making the stone react like it was.

The realization kicked Tasha into action. In an instant, she was running. Her feet slapped against the ground and she flew across the stone. But not fast enough. Not before one of the Wraith's soldiers slammed the flat of his blade into the elf's head and she crumpled.

The soldiers were distracted, standing around the felled elf, and Tasha gripped her daggers as she crept up behind the group. One of them was barking orders, voice blunt. "Drag her to the center with the others and—" Tasha blurred out his words as she focused, positioning herself at a soldier's back. She pulled back her blade and stabbed. It sunk home, burying itself deep into the softness between the man's ribs. She yanked it out, and the soldier fell to the ground, like a curtain pulled back to reveal her. Five helmeted faces turned in her direction. Ten eyes looking at her through metal slits.

Tasha wiped the dagger across the front of her leather armor, returning it from red to silver. "Who's next?"

"Attack her!" The command came from the largest in the group, and it was obeyed instantly.

Four soldiers started toward her, all but the commander.

One of them lunged, and the switch flipped in Tasha's mind.

She slid to the left, swiping her leg under him and slamming her knife into his stomach. She felt no remorse as he crumpled. She felt no triumph. She was only cold, raw focus. The rest would come later.

She whirled away from a jab, landing a well-placed elbow into a soldier's nose and, a moment later, a kick into another's stomach. A slash of pain striped her arm as she took her first blow of the night. Snarling, she spun, clashing blades with the attacker. She flicked his dagger away and kicked him as he stumbled. He fell with a clatter of armor.

The last soldier, a female, stepped toward Tasha. Tasha darted to the left. The soldier's head snapped to follow her movement, long braid whipping out from under her helmet. Tasha rebounded, grabbing the braid and yanking, pulling the soldier's head to the side and felling her with a well-timed strike.

She turned to the commander, his dead and unconscious soldiers at her feet.

He hefted his sword. From the way he gripped it, she could tell he was better than the others. His arms were bare and his muscles rippled, ready for the fight.

Tasha burst forward. She struck with both daggers, but he deflected them. He thrust at her, she darted away. Again, he thrust, and again she darted. She lunged forward, and he snapped his sword up, the blow wrenching her right dagger from her hand.

The dagger clattered to the stone, but Tasha ignored it, stabbing with her other knife. He dodged, dropping his sword and managing to grab her extended arm. She recoiled, but too late. He tugged her forward, whipping her around and pulling her in so that her back slammed against his chest. One of his arms circled to pin hers. The other arm went around her throat. And tightened there.

Tasha bucked, gripping the dagger in her left hand as she fought for breath. She tried to shove it into him, but her arm was locked to her side. His clench around both arms and neck constricted.

She threw her head back, beginning to feel lightheaded.

If ever there was a time to catch fire, it would be now. But she'd never willed it before. Never wanted to before. Her mind told her hands to light, but even now, drowning out of water, something else, something ingrained inside of her–something deep and terrified–begged of them the opposite. The battle surged around her and in her, and both began to blur. Her mind was spinning. Around and around and around and around. *Live or die, Tasha?* She could hear her own voice in her mind. Her own words.

*I choose to liv*e, thought Tasha. And she bucked.

I choose to live. She thrust upward.

I refuse to die. And she sunk her teeth into the arm around her neck.

The man swore in her ear and his arm loosened.

Tasha wrenched her left arm away, and without hesitation she slammed the blade straight into the man's stomach. He gurgled and fell to the ground.

Tasha doubled over, gasping for breath. She wretched, spluttering and blinking as she drank in air.

"Hey–you alright?" Tasha looked up and found that one of the Forest Elves from The Alliance had appeared in front of her. He still had his griffin at his shoulder, which was just shy of a miracle, because most had already flown away or were rampaging around the center circle.

She brought in another deep breath and didn't bother answering his question. "Take this elf and get back to the fortress." As she talked, she found the dagger the man had knocked from her hand, scooping it from the ground.

"What?" The Forest Elf's eyebrows went up. "But I have to stay and help find the–" He stopped as Tasha pulled out the Fate Stone, waving it in front of his face. His eyes locked on the green glow.

"She's the Chosen," panted Tasha, slipping the stone under her leathers. "Get her back to the fortress."

The Forest Elf gave a single nod, then he crouched and picked up the unconscious female, brown curls bobbing around her lolling head as he lifted her. There was a knife on the ground beside her. Tasha hadn't noticed it before, but now the elf crouched and picked it up before walking to the griffin.

Tasha didn't wait to watch them mount. She turned away, determined to throw herself back into the fight. But during her live-or-die moment, the battle had turned one-sided. The circle was flooded with black uniforms and were she not right on the edge of the battle she would have been spotted by now.

Before she could decide what to do, a familiar voice whisper-yelled, "Tasha, with me!" Beck darted toward her, coming from somewhere just outside the battlefield. He charged down a path, beckoning for her to follow.

She gave the invaded circle one last look before sprinting after. They dashed down the path until they'd passed a couple houses, then Beck veered to the left. The windows of the next house had no glass, and he dove through one. Tasha followed suit, vaulting through the window after.

She rolled, barely avoiding crashing into a wooden table leg and scratching her bare arms on the rough floor. Her hair, which she'd tied back during their flight had come undone, and she pushed the tangles out of her face, rising to her feet.

"We're outnumbered," said Beck, leaning against the wall and breathing hard. "They've captured almost all the villagers. They're gathered in the middle of the village. Alive, but only until the Shadows figure out which one is the Chosen–"

"The Shadows?" asked Tasha.

"The Wraith's soldiers," he answered.

"Since when?"

"Since I made it up two minutes ago." He shook his head and waved his hand dismissively. "We'll work on it. But it's not priority right now. They've eliminated most of The Alliance members. I thought they'd gotten you, too," he side-eyed her. "I tried to find you at that house. You didn't stay where I told you to."

"Don't take it personally," answered Tasha, wiping her daggers on the tablecloth of the kitchen table next to her. Red smeared over yellow embroidered flowers. "I never do what anyone tells me to." She sheathed her blades, grabbed a handful of the cloth, and used it to wipe off the shallow cut on her arm.

"That," he replied, "I believe." There was a yell from somewhere down the path. Beck glanced out the window, then he sunk to the floor so that he was sitting against the wall. Tasha peered out and saw that a couple of soldiers were standing at the start of the path as though considering whether to walk down it or not. Tasha crouched so that she was on the same level as Beck.

For a moment neither of them spoke, both of them listening. The one-room house was calm, and the air smelled like the pages of an old book. With every exhale, motes of dust were sent flying through the air, spinning and whirring through space.

"They must have finished fighting," said Beck, voice low. There were no sounds from the soldiers outside. "They've probably got the village surrounded. Soon they'll have to start checking the houses for us. They need to find the Fate Stone to figure out which of the villagers is Chosen."

"None of them."

"What?" Beck's eyebrows shot upward.

"None of them here," said Tasha. "I found her. Sent her back to the fortress with one of The Alliance members." She pulled out the Fate Stone. Its light was dim—barely there. "See. She's not here anymore."

Beck looked frozen for a moment, then he broke into a broad smile. His shoulders sagged against the wall and he gave a quiet laugh. "You're the top dragon, Tash, you know that?" He shook his head. "Thank the above—now we just have to get you out safely."

There were voices outside and Tasha realized that the soldiers had decided to start exploring the path.

"Listen," hissed Beck, "there are griffins still running all over this village. We need to find one and you can ride back to the fortress."

Something about the way he said it made Tasha frown. "What about you?"

He waved his hand dismissively. "I'm gunna stay. I have to try to help those villagers. Once the soldiers figure out the Chosen isn't here, they'll kill them all." He grimaced. "Or worse, take them to the Wraith for her to drain to death."

Tasha stared at him for a moment. Finally, she sat against a table leg and crossed her arms. "Beck, you know how I survived for so long in The Hinterland?"

"No, but I'd like to," he said, green eyes instantly colored with curiosity.

"Not making stupid decisions."

"Alright," Beck rested his head against the wall, stretching both his legs out. "I see where this is going. But this wouldn't be a stupid–"

"Yes," interrupted Tasha. "One of your stupidest, actually. This isn't the time for heroics. There are dozens of the Wraith's soldiers out there," she gestured toward the window. "It's too much of a risk."

Beck ran his tongue over his teeth. "Maybe it's a risk worth taking. Those elves need help. They don't deserve this. They don't deserve what's going to happen to them."

There were clatters from outside and Tasha could only assume that the soldiers were searching the first house on the path. She ignored the sounds and glared at Beck. "No, they don't, but you won't be able to save them. Not against so many."

"I have to try." There were flecks of blood on Beck's clenched jaw. His hair was matted and his armor was stained with dirt and more crimson, which somehow made his green eyes seem even brighter in the dim kitchen. More determined.

She tried one more time. "Beck, remember that kid in the armory? The one mad at you for leaving?"

Beck blinked. "Cerulean?"

Tasha nodded. "In case you couldn't tell, that wasn't anger, it was fear. He's afraid you're not coming back. When I ride to the fortress and I have to tell him that you're dead, do you really want this to be the reason I give him? That you abandoned any chance of returning by running headlong into a pit of enemy soldiers on a suicide mission?"

The determination in Beck's eyes wavered. Tasha leaned closer to him, forcing him to look at her before saying in a quiet, firm tone, "You told him you'd come back."

Beck blinked again. His eyes focused on the ground, refusing to look at Tasha for a moment. But his tense shoulders and the way his nails were digging into the wood floor told her that something she'd said had struck a chord. Finally, he looked up, dragging a hand through his hair before almost instinctively re-smoothing it. "You're right."

"I know I'm right," she said, pushing herself away from him and tying her hair back again with a spare length of string she'd had tucked in her armor. "Now we need to find a couple of griffins." There was no way she was going to share one with him. Not if there were any other options. Not while her blood was pumped with adrenaline and her fingers were ready to spark any minute.

He nodded and opened his mouth to speak when there was a crash from nearby and he stopped. The soldiers must be in the house next door.

Tasha's head snapped left then right as she looked for an escape. Her gaze seized on the window at the back of the house. It was the only exit that wouldn't be in perfect view of the other house's side window. She gestured at it and instantly Beck was on his feet. Tasha stood, ran to the window on her toes, and shoved herself through it without hesitation. It was smaller than the one they'd jumped through before, but she quickly landed with a soft thump on the damp moss outside.

Beck's face appeared in the window and Tasha said, voice nothing more than a hiss, "It's small–I'm not sure you'll fit."

Both of their heads snapped to the left as there was another bang from the other house.

"I'm not sure there's any other option," Beck whispered back, and he pushed his head through the frame.

As Beck began to force himself through the window, Tasha crept to the side of the house, peeking toward the direction of the soldiers in the other building. Through the side window she could see them stepping toward the door. Soon they would move on.

Tasha shrunk back into the safety of the back wall. She looked up at Beck, who was almost halfway through. "They're about to get to this house."

"Alright," he answered. "But... I may or may not be stuck."

Tasha cursed. "Of course, this couldn't be easy."

"Trust me, this isn't what I wanted, either," he whispered back. His head and shoulders were mostly out of the window, but one arm was out and the other was wedged between the sill and his chest. "I can't get out or go back in. You'll have to pull me." He extended his free hand.

Tasha froze, looking at it. She glanced left and right searching for other options. The door of the other house slammed.

"Um, Tash, maybe sometime in the next thirty seconds, please," Beck had twisted his head at the sound as though he would be able to see the soldiers. Which, of course, he couldn't.

But Tasha's eyes had locked on something under the window. It was cloth of some sort–a dress left on a log to dry. She grabbed it and thrust a side at him. "You hold this side. I'll pull on the other."

"Are you sure you can't just–"

"No."

He wasted no more time in arguing and held on tight to his side. Tasha tugged. She could hear the soldiers walking down the street.

"Are you moving at all?"

"No, still stuck." He shook his head, grip on the dress unfaltering. "Curse my massive muscles!"

Tasha couldn't decide whether Beck's tendency to joke in high-pressure situations was bravery or stupidity. She gave the dress a wrench. If he didn't come free in the next couple seconds, she'd have to abandon the dress and use—

"Wait, I'm moving!" All at once Beck tumbled through the window.

He jumped to his feet, dusting off his armor. "If you could not mention this to anyone at the fortress, that would be great—"

They heard the door of the house open. Instantly, the pair of them dropped to their knees, pressing against the wall. Tasha glanced at the woods stretched out in front of them, then up at the window directly above their heads. Maybe if they snuck along the wall and then ran, they wouldn't be seen?

They both stiffened as the soldiers began talking.

"Check under the table," said a gruff voice.

Someone sighed. "There's not going to be anyone under the table," this voice was extremely high-pitched and female.

"Check anyway," growled the first voice. "Whichever one has the Fate Stone is still out there. And one of the Chosen."

Tasha's eyes narrowed. They must be talking about the Chosen she'd sent back. Although, why wouldn't they assume she was one of the elves rounded up in the center of the village?

"If she was here, you'd think she'd be easy to spot," answered the female. "If her hair is as red as we were told."

Tasha stilled. She exchanged looks with Beck. Both of them pressed farther against the wall like they were trying to melt into it.

"If she's here, we'd better find her," said the man. "Otherwise, the Empress won't be happy."

"Well, she's not under this table," replied the female, and there was a clatter from within the house as though something had been knocked over.

"Alright, let's move on," the male gave in.

Beck and Tasha stayed still for a few more seconds. Then with a slam, the door opened and closed.

Instantly, they ran for the woods. Tasha's legs burned with exhaustion, screaming at her to stop, but they carried her all the same, and in a few seconds she and Beck had been swallowed in pitch black forest.

Beck slowed, his voice still a whisper even though there were no soldiers in earshot. "Lots of the griffins ran into the woods. Let's just search the trees skirting the village."

Tasha gave a nod that Beck could only see in the darkness because of his elven eyesight. Luckily, Tasha, not the human she pretended to be, had heightened vision too. Around her everything seemed painted in shades of blue instead of black.

They tiptoed through the darkness, silent for a few minutes.

Then Beck breathed, "Tash, I think that's one."

She peered to where he was pointing. A shape was shifting in the darkness. Even with her improved vision, Tasha couldn't quite make out what it was for sure.

They crept closer.

"That's a griffin," said Beck, relief breaking through his voice. He jogged toward it, Tasha coming after him. It turned and saw them. Beck reached a hand out to it before a screech, ear-splitting and terrible, erupted from its beak.

Beck jumped back. "Not one of ours!"

Tasha whipped around as a crashing came from somewhere in the forest.

Someone was yelling. Many someones were yelling. The shouts were coming from multiple directions and getting louder. Even if they ran, they would be chased, and without a griffin there was no way they could escape. Instantly, Tasha palmed her daggers.

"Tasha, hide!" It seemed to be Beck's favorite thing to say tonight, thought Tasha as she ignored him.

Light was starting to come through trees, flickering like torchlight.

"Tasha!" Beck was in front of her. "Just this once, listen! Go find a griffin and get out of here. I'll deal with this and try to find you, but don't wait for me, alright?"

Everything in Tasha was telling her to fight. The instinct was soaked into her skin, it sat in her chest and surged in her fingertips. But fighting would do them no good without a griffin. She sheathed her daggers.

Beck turned toward the yells and pulled out his sword.

Tasha clenched her hands into fists, then she turned and hurtled into the forest.

She would find a griffin, just as he'd said. But she would not leave him. Even if she should. Even though there was a voice in her mind screaming at her: *don't you remember how we survived in the Hinterland?*

The first clang of metal filled the forest.

Tasha barreled through the trees, abandoning all thoughts of stealth. The soldiers were well occupied.

She scanned as she ran, searching, searching, search–something moved. She stopped. The something was partially shielded by a tree, but Tasha could still see the tip of a wing. She'd found another griffin.

She slowed as she approached it, gritting her teeth as the sounds of metal on metal continued to echo throughout the forest. Though, she realized as she reached it, it would mean far worse if the sounds of the fight were to cease.

She took a final step toward the beast and snatched its dangling reins. It looked at her with large, gentle eyes, completely benevolent.

This griffin belonged to The Alliance.

She paused, listening. Beck was still at it. And so was the voice in her head telling her to leave him. To save herself and survive as she always had. But it seemed the voice had no control over her feet, because they were moving, leading the griffin toward the violence. It resisted the pull on its reins but gave in after a few sharp tugs.

The sounds of the fighting were growing more distant. Almost like Beck was leading the soldiers away. He probably was. Fool.

She dragged the griffin through the trees, yanking its reins every time it hesitated. Finally, she saw torchlight up ahead. The light was coming from the edge of the forest where the trees met up with the backs of houses.

Tasha snuck to the edge of the woods and watched. The griffin stood behind her, chewing on a clump of moss. She held onto its reins, unsure of whether she could risk dropping them to help Beck.

Four soldiers had backed Beck up against the wall of a house. But surrounded and cornered though he was, Beck showed no fear as he leveled his sword at them.

Beck fought like he was unleashing a monster from within himself. Tasha recognized many of his moves from morning duels. But the soldiers were not as agile as she, and each maneuver hit its mark.

He was right, he was left, he was everywhere at once. He knocked two soldiers out with the flat of his blade and sent another sprawling with a hard kick to the stomach. He turned to the last one, and they began a fierce duel.

Something moved in the shadowed tree line. Something only a stone's throw away from Tasha. A black-clad soldier stepped into the light, bow drawn and aimed at Beck. Beck didn't see the new soldier, his focus completely on the man he was dueling.

"Behind you!" Tasha yelled, stepping forward and dropping the reins without realizing it. But Beck didn't seem to register her yell as his sword slammed into his opponent's.

The arrow released. It spiraled through the air, spinning toward the green-eyed elf and the spot at the back of his neck that his armor didn't quite cover.

And Tasha made a stupid decision.

Or maybe it wasn't a decision at all. Maybe she didn't fully realize what she was going to do until she was doing it–didn't expect to lunge forward, diving through space and time and distance until the arrow was piercing her skin.

Tasha hit the ground hard. She gave a scream of pain, a burning filling her body at the spot where the metal had penetrated flesh.

Behind her, Beck finally bested his opponent, smashing the hilt of his sword into the man's forehead. He whirled, eyes searching for Tasha, sharp ears alerted by her cry. His eyes seized first on her, then on the man standing on the forest's fringe, and he connected the pieces. With a yell, he thrust his hand forward and a missile of light flung itself toward the bowman. It hit the man with such force he stumbled backward, head colliding with the thick trunk of a tree before he crumpled.

Beck dropped to his knees beside Tasha. "Tash, what happened? I heard you yell, but I didn't–" his words stopped. He hadn't seen her get shot, she realized. He didn't know what she'd done. But now he did see the arrow.

Beck cursed. The arrowhead had sunk into the side of her stomach. Just how deep, Tasha couldn't tell as the pain became overwhelming. Blood was staining the grass. Spots of black were crawling over her vision like flies.

Beck looked up and saw the griffin, still on the tree line. His green eyes hardened. "Hold on Tash–hold on. I'm going to get you out of here."

She could see the world beginning to blur, smearing along the edges. But she was determined not to lose consciousness. Because who knew what might happen then? Would her powers sleep with her, or would they stay awake and completely out of her control? But despite the danger, her eyelids shuddered.

"No," said Beck. There was a hint of panic in his voice that she'd never heard before. "Hold on, Tasha–" His hands were lighting up with magic... or was that just her seeing things? And was she imagining yelling in the distance?

Her world was turning sideways. She tried to focus on him. Found his green eyes. Seized on them just long enough to choke out three words that at the moment felt more important than anything else. *"Don't touch me."*

Then her vision cartwheeled and she fell into deep, deep darkness.

Dear Reader, this book closes with two griffins. One is landing in a courtyard, jostling the unconscious figure on its back as it touches down beneath the shadow of the tower in which a sleeping child dreams of prophecies. The second griffin is in flight and still terribly far away from home. It carries a bleeding girl and an elf, whose hands are pressed to her skin, doing their best to staunch the crimson as he guides his mount to the last place one would expect anyone to go for help: over the boundary of the Hinterland. But some lines are meant to be crossed.

The trouble is, it's hard to know which ones until you've already crossed them.

The Hinterland

The End
(except it's really just begun)

Acknowledgements

Show's over folks. At least until book two. But a few final words of gratitude before I close the curtains.

Thanks be to God! All things are possible through him. Some things are *only* possible through him. This book was one of those things.

Mbili Mbili, thank you for hearing out my rambling plot ideas during all those late-night walks, teaching me your writing tips, and making all those edits. Most of all, thank you for sharing your love of writing with me. This book is published proof that I really am my mother's daughter.

Dad, thank you for supporting my writing from day one. I can still remember you reading my little penny-apiece picture books, reacting to each page with an Oscar-worthy performance. I've taken your motto to heart: dream big, so that if you fail, at least you fail epically. Thank you for teaching me to be fearless with my dreams and for loving this book as much as I do.

Nate, Jack, Ethan, and Cooper, thanks for being an inspiration. There's never a boring day with you around. You give me a reason to be curious about what every tomorrow will bring. Nate, you're a terrible editor (but thanks for trying and being the first to ship my characters). I'd fight dragons for you guys.

Tate, thanks for answering all my publishing questions and being one of my biggest fans. I'm so grateful to have you as a friend. Who else would consistently reply to my 3am text messages (sleep schedules are for cowards)? Also–tag–you're it again.

Maya, thank you for being the smart and steady to my crazy. I always know I can count on you, and I'm so glad we met. Plus, Balderdash would be a whole lot less fun without you.

James, thank you for always getting me. You always know how to make me laugh (and for good reason, not just because I shouldn't). I don't know what our little gang would do without you. Also, I'll consider letting you read book two. No promises though.

To the C's, Elana, Oliver (no you can't have a free copy), Sydney, Andrew, Becca, Ice, Gentry, Annica, Emma W., Cas, Mari, Dani, Rylee C., Christian S., and Riley B. (I think the murderboarding worked), when I started high school my dad told me not to worry about trying to be popular, because when it comes to friends, you really only need a handful of really good ones. Thanks for being in my handful.

Also, Sydney, I know they forgot your senior quote in the yearbook. Unfortunately, I can't fix that. However, now that I have a book of my own... without further ado–Sydney Beecham's senior quote: "My biggest advice: 'never get involved in a land war in Asia', but only slightly less well known is this: 'Never go in against a Sicilian when death is on the line!'"

Mamaw and Papaw, thank you for all your support! I wrote half this book while downing sweet tea from you guys.

Grammy, here–do you think you can figure out how to work this copy? I'm kidding, thanks for supporting me and my writing. I love you to the moon and back.

Thank you to Aunt Ashley and Stacy, Uncle Bryan and Joe, and my cousins, you've never failed to support all my crazy dreams.

Christian W., (I mention you with the editors too, but check it, you get a whole sentence for being my OG) thanks for being my editor through every draft of this book to ever exist, and my co-founder of the little writing club in the woods.

Emma S., thanks for reading through this book back when it was 488 pages long. You were always willing to hop on the phone or text me paragraphs of feedback. I'll be forever grateful for it!

Boo and Beth, I'm so thankful for your constant support. You have always been there for me, encouraging my writing, being soccer cheerleaders from afar, and giving me an example of what it looks like to walk in faith. Plus, that pro-writing subscription caught over 200 incorrect dashes... so thanks for that, too. You guys are the best.

To all my cheerleaders in the DAR (special mentions to Darlene Lewis, Linda Teany, Rhonda Beck, and Diane Day), thank you for supporting that little girl who found your essay contest brochure all those years ago. She's a bit older now, but she still hasn't forgotten the confidence you gave her to pursue her writing, or the way your contest showed to her the importance of sharing a story. I'm forever grateful to you all! And also, (I may be a bit biased, but I'm also right) Wa-Pa-Ke-Way is the best chapter!

Thank you to every staff member of The Hendricks County Icon and The Republican who took a chance on a high school intern and encouraged me in my writing. I'm so thankful for everything I learned during my time with you.

And while I'm talking about newspaper people–shoutout to Mr. Caulton: the ringleader of the incredible, chaotic circus that was my home away from home at AHS: the newsroom. Thank you for growing my love of writing and my confidence to do something with it.

Thank you, Marianne Skarvan. You inspired me to continue writing, no matter the challenges.

Thank you, Coach Josh George, for hyping this book up like you wrote it. The discipline and persistence that you and your program taught me helped make this book possible. Go Bulldogs!

Thank you to Dr. Julie Walters who answered my disturbing questions on arrow injuries. Bet that wasn't what you were expecting during our appointment.

Special mentions to some amazing and greatly appreciated editors: Zubia, Isaac, Indie, Luke, Emma S., and Christian W. This book would not be what it is without you all.

Lastly, thank *you*: the one reading this book. No, I may not know your name, but if you read through every page of duels, kidnappings, and prison breaks in this novel, then I know a little bit about you after all. On the flip side, I am woven all throughout these pages, and by now you know me more than you likely realize. It's been a pleasure to meet you.

Thank you again, everybody, love you all.

Yours truly,
Audrey Faletic
Isaiah 43:1-2

About the Author

Audrey Faletic never considered the possibility of not writing. As soon as she could hold a pencil, and long before she could hold it right, she was creating stories. However, it took her eighteen years before she finally finished something she was ready to show the world: the book in your hands. She plans to send plenty more your way.

When not writing, Audrey can be found spending time with her four younger brothers, playing spoon-related pranks, out on the soccer field, highlighting way too much in her bible, skateboarding, side-questing in her small red car, or getting hot chocolate with her friends.

For an accurate and unbiased description of herself, she felt it would be best to allow some close friends of hers to summarize who she really is. Here are their untampered with reviews:

"She's... eccentric."
"She was the spooner."
"She thinks salad is rabbit food."
"She has no filter."
"She hates and loves sparkling water at the same time."
"She is creative and a daredevil, so if you hang out with her you might be doing something crazy, or hear something out of the box, like zombie apocalypse survival plans."

The Hinterland

kdp.amazon.com
Copyright @ 2025 Audrey Faletic
All rights reserved.
9798286073351

Made in the USA
Coppell, TX
04 January 2026

68095982R00204